CONALL II

THE RAVEN'S FLIGHT

EITILT AN FHIAIGH DHUIBH

TITLES BY DAVID H. MILLAR

Conall: The Place of Blood - Rinn-Iru
Conall II: The Raven's Flight - Eitilt an Fhiaigh Dhuibh

CONALL II

THE RAVEN'S FLIGHT

EITILT AN FHIAIGH DHUIBH

DAVID H. MILLAR

vi

Conall: The Raven's Flight - Eitilt an Fhiaigh Dhuibh
Copyright © 2015 by David H. Millar

A Wee Publishing Company
Houston, TX, USA
http://www.aweepublishingco.com

Paperback ISBN 978-0-9916640-2-3
eBook ISBN 978-0-9916640-3-0
ISBN-10: 991664027
ISBN-13: 9780991664023
Library of Congress Control Number 2015904846
A Wee Publishing Company, LLC, Houston, TX

Conall: The Raven's Flight - Eitilt an Fhiaigh Dhuibh is a work of historical fiction. Apart from obviously historical figures and places, all names, characters and incidents are either the product of the author's imagination or are used fictitiously, and any resemblance to actual persons, living or dead, establishments, events or locales is entirely coincidental.

To Lauren

ACKNOWLEDGMENTS

"Team Conall" continues to grow. First and foremost, thanks to Lauren, my longsuffering editor who has to put up with my grumping at the red ink on my precious manuscript. Next is Pam, my longtime friend, who fills a multitude of vital roles - first chapters' feedback, beta-reader and my encourager who is always asking, "Have you written the next one?" A big thank-you goes to Brendan, Drew, Judith, Nick and Susan who valiantly read the draft manuscript and made extremely perceptive comments.

Acknowledgments go to Eddie Kelleher at the University of St. Thomas, Houston, Texas for continuing to advise on the Irish Gaelic, and also to Catriona Parsons from the Office of Gaelic Affairs, Nova Scotia, Canada for her help with the Scots Gaelic pronunciations. Apologies to Catriona and Eddie if my interpretation of their fine Gaelic is a wee bit off the mark.

Thanks go to Ida at Amygdala Design for the great cover artwork. Finally, thanks to Aidana at WillowRaven Illustration & Design Plus for the map illustration and interior formatting.

Contents

Pronunciations

Conall II: The Raven's Flight - Eitilt an Fhiaigh Dhuibh is a yarn set in ancient times. It revolves around the Celts and in this case, Irish and Scottish Celts. As far as possible, I have attempted to use "authentic" Irish and Scots Gaelic words and phrases for personal and place names, and for a few phrases. A summary of the Gaelic used throughout the story is listed below together with suggested pronunciations. In some cases the translation of the particular phrase or word is also provided.

I am very open to better suggestions for what should be the best pronunciation of the Gaelic or a better choice of word. So please do contact me. My contact details are given at the end of the book.

That said, it is the tale that counts. Feel free to pronounce the Gaelic in any way that gives you the most enjoyment.

IRISH GAELIC PERSONAL AND PLACE NAMES

Ailill Mac Máta	AHL-il mak MAWta
Áine	AW-nya
Albu (Britain)	AL-boo
Brighid	BREED
Brion ó Cathasaigh	BREE-un o-KAS-akh
Brocc	BRUK
Cassán	KAS-awn
Cathán ó Bric	KA-hawn oh BRIK
Cian Craobhach	KEE-in CRAY-v-akh
Conall Mac Gabhann	KON-ul ma GAWN
Craiftine ó Cuileannáin	KRAFT-in o QUILL-an-awn
Cúscraid Mac Conchobar	KOO-skri MAK KRUH-who'r
Danu	DAH-noo
Deaglán ó Neill	DEG-lawn o NEE-ul
Deda Mac Sin	DAY-da MAK SHEEN
Eirnín	ER-neen
Eochaidh Ruad	OHY ROO-uh
Ériu	AY-roo (Ireland)

Fearghal Ruad	FER-ul ROO-uh
Fionnbharr	FYUN-var
Íar Mac Dedad	EER MAK DAY-da
Labhraidh	LA-ra
Macha Mong Ruad	MAHA MUNN ROO-uh
Mag Mell (Warrior's Heaven)	MAW MELL
Medb	MAY-ve
Mongfhionn	MUNN-yung
Mórrígan ni Cathasaigh	Moe-rig-gAHn nee-KAS-akh
Ráth na Lairig Éadain (Lurigethan)	RAW nuh LAR-ig AY-dan
Sárán	SAWR-awn
Tadhg	TYG
Taobh Builleach (Tievebulliagh)	TAV BWEEL-ah
Tir inna n-Óc (Land of Youth)	CHIR nah nog
Tir Tairngire (Land of Promise)	CHIR TARG-ne
Toirneach	TOR-nah
Torcán ó Dubhghaill	TURK-awn o DOO-l
Tuathal	TOO-al
Urard	UR-urd

OTHER IRISH GAELIC PHRASES AND TERMINOLOGY

Aes Sidhe (Demi-goddess)	ASH shee
An Fiagaí Dorcha (Dark Huntress)	un FEAR-gi DUR-uh-ha
Ard-Righan (High Queen)	AWRD-ree-an
Bean-sidhe (Foreteller of death)	BAN-shee
Bealtaine (May Festival)	BYAHL-tih-nuh
Bodhrán (Irish drum)	BAR-awn
Brat (Hoodless cloak)	BRAT
Bróga (Shoes)	BRO-gah
Caomhnóirí (Personal guard)	KWAYV-nor-ee
Ceannairí céad (Leader of 100)	KAN-ari KAYD
Ceannairí na míle (Leader of 1000)	KAN-ari nuh MEE-le
Céili (Dance)	KAY-lee
Chomhairle (Council)	an HOR-ya
Cinn Péinteáilte (Painted Ones)	KEEN PENT-or-tah
Connachta (Mid-west Ireland tribe)	KAWN-ah-ta
Craic (Fun)	KRACK
Cret (Carriage/box of chariot)	KRET
Dún do bheal (Shut your mouth)	DOON duh VAY'l
Fénechas (The Law)	FAY-ne-kas

xvi

Fidchell (Early Irish chess/checkers) FEY-hil
Geis (Curse and/or Gift)   GEH-sh
Go raibh maith agat (Thank you)   GUH RAW MA AG-ut
Imbolg (February Festival)   IMBOL-ugh
Ionsaí (Attack)   UN-see
Léine (Children's garment)   LAY-na
Lugnasad (August Festival)   LOON-a-sad
Mná-Sidhe (plural of bean-sidhe)   M-naw SHEE
Póg ma thoin (Kiss my arse)   POHG muh HOE-in
Ruiri (King)   ROO-ree
Samhain (November Festival)   SOW-wen
Sidhe (Demi-goddess)   SHEE
Slántu (Cheers/Good Health)   SLAWN-tu
Striapach (Whore)   STREE-ah-pah

SCOTS GAELIC PERSONAL AND PLACE NAMES

A' Chrìon Làraich (Crianlarich)   Ah KRAY-un LARR-ich
Ailde   AL-ja
A' Mhòinteach Mhór (Moine Mhòr bogs) Ah VON-chuk VO-de
Aos na h-Àirde (People of the Heights) IS nah HAR-je
Aos a' Chùirn (People of the Stone)   IS ah-HOE-nuh
Aos an Eich (Horse People)   IS an-YICK
Aos an Fhithich (Raven People)   IS an- ICHE
An Linne Sheileach (Loch Linnhe)   an LAY-nuh-ya HILL-och
Aos na Coille (People of the Forest) IS nah CULL-ya
Aos nan Caorach (Sheep People)   IS nan-COOR-awk
Aos nan Cat (Cat People)   IS nan-KAT
Aos nan Con-Seilge (Hound People)   IS nan kon-SHIL-uh-guh
An t-Aos-Sìthiche (People of the Sidhe) An TIS SHE-kuh
Artair   ASH-ter
Bearach   BAY-ruch
Beinn an Laoigh (Ben Lui)   BANE an- LOY-yuh
Beinn Nèamh-bhathais (Ben Nevis)   BANE NYEAH-var-ish
Caol   KOOL
Carmag Mac an t-Sionnaich   KAR-ah-mak mak an-CHUN-ich
Ceana   KEMA
Ceallach   KELL-awch
Ceann an Locha (Head of the Loch)   KOWN an-LAW-kuh
Cinn Tìre (Kintyre)   KIN CHEER-uh
Cùil Daothail (Culduthel)   KOOL DOOL

Diadhaidh	JE-ah-ee
Drostan Ruadh	DROST-an ROO-ag
Dùn Athad (Dunadd)	DOON AT
Dùn Na Mèadaidh (Dumyat)	DOON nah-VEIGHT
Dùnsgéitheig (Dun Skeig)	DOON-SKAY-kuh
Eachdonn Breac	ISH-down BREK
Failbhe	FAL-uh-vuh
Finnean Mac Sèitheach	FIN-yan mak SHAY-ke
Gràinne	GRAN-yuh
Loch Nis (Loch Ness)	LAW-kuh NISH
Loch Obha (Loch Awe)	LAW-kuh OWA
Maol Chinn Tìre (Mull of Kintyre)	MOOL KIN CHEER-uh
Na Mèadaidh (The Maeatae)	na-MAY-er-dee
Mòrag	MOR-ak
Morna	MOR-nah
Na Daoine Smeurta (The Smeared)	nah DANE-yuh SMUR-tah
Na Daoine Tùrsach (The People Who Chant)	nah DANE-yu TUR-sak
Ròidh Mac Eachdonn	ROY mak ISH-down
Ualraig	OO-ul-rik

OTHER SCOTS GAELIC PHRASES AND TERMINOLOGY

A ghlaoic (Fool)	uh GLOY-ick
Brògan (Shoes)	BRAW-ken
Broch (Tall stone tower, usually circular)	BRUK
Cam-ghob (A forest bird, like a parrot)	KAM-gope
Comhairle-Chatha (High Council)	KOOR-luh KAH-ha
Fàilte (Welcome)	FALL-tcha
Sùlaire (A diving seabird)	SUE-lar-ah
Tànaiste (Second-in-command)	TAN-ish-the
Tuireadh (Death chant)	TOUR-egg

Albu
N
W
E
S
Dùn Na Daoine Smeurta
Càrn Liath
Drochaid A' Bhanna
Na Daoine
Tùrsach Crannog
Cùil Daothail
Loch Nis
Beinn Neamh-bhathais
An Linne Sheileach
Morna's Home
Beinn an Laoigh
Cuscraid's Fort
A' Chrion Làraich
Dùn Athad
Dùn Na Mèadaidh
Loch Obha
Dùnsgeitheig
Maol
Chinn
Tire
Ceann an Locha

CHAPTER 1

Cassius Fabius Scaeva, Patrician and citizen of Rome, was an arrogant, dissolute bastard. It was thus an affront to his dignity and considerable ego that he was a slave. According to his master, he was a bloody poor one, too. Adding further insult to injury, the cause of his downfall was a barbarian - the High Queen of Ériu, Macha Mong Ruad.

The gaunt Roman aristocrat scratched at recent flea bites and drew a lice-infested cloak around his unwashed body. In those brief moments before his master commenced prodding him through daily chores with beatings and arbitrary abuse, Cassius again railed against his lot in life. As the cold, pre-dawn sky began to blush red, the Roman shivered against the wooden wall of the stall he shared with the livestock and measured his options.

A year had passed since Macha had arranged his kidnapping and transport to the farthermost part of Albu — a land he knew better as the Tin Islands. At the periphery of the known world, the wedge of moorland and marshes was bounded on two sides by a bitterly cold sea and to the west by towering snow-capped mountains swaddled in dense forests and wildwoods. There, wolves, bears and lynxes prowled the land. Pairs of golden eagles soared high above, scanning for young sheep and red deer.

The local tribes lived in semi-permanent, scattered settlements consisting of small clusters of utilitarian dwellings built of stone, wood and thatch. There was little need for forts. Chieftains often moved their people from place to place. The land was too meager for farming so a nomadic lifestyle was as inevitable as it was practical. As far as Cassius could see, the only assets worth protecting were the vermin-riddled herds of cattle and sheep.

A few circular, stone towers – brochs, stood here and there. They had been built more for vanity than defense and were not favored by Cassius' captors. Their only real fort was on a coastal promontory at the edge of the tribe's territory. A second fort stood on an island off the northern coast. At the thought, Cassius snorted derisively through his twice-broken, aquiline nose. What idiot puts a fort on an island at the edge of the world? Who did the noble think was going to attack him? The fish?

Cassius had counted five minor tribes in this north-eastern region. Their borders were marked by huge standing stones carved with intricate curling, tribal designs. The people belonged to the Cinn Péinteáilte – the Painted Ones. Their bodies were covered in variations of the same designs either painted or etched permanently onto their skin using metal and bone needles. The designs were their armor and so they fought fiercely and naked.

The Roman's owners were known as the Na Daoine Smeurta – The Smeared. The tribe's name was derived from a tradition of coating their bodies with a mix of animal blood and fat. In times of war, the blood of human enemies was preferred. To the sensibilities of an aristocrat such as Cassius, the stench of rancid fat was especially rank in the warmer months, although it did not seem to bother the tribe members. In winter, however, the layer of fat gave the Na Daoine Smeurta some protection from the harsh cold. It could also prevent an enemy from getting a good grip in a closely fought battle.

Three tribes took their names and characteristics from wild animals or fowl: the Aos an Fhithich or Raven People to the south, the Aos nan Cat or Cat People to the north and the Aos nan Caorach or Sheep People to the west. Beyond the Aos an Fhithich lay the territory of the Na Daoine Tùrsach, a fanatical religious community of priest-warriors whose tuireadh - death chants, struck fear even into the hearts of Cassius' captors. From snippets of conversation, the Roman had gleaned that much larger tribes inhabited the great highland forests and lowlands further to the south.

Apart from occasional cattle-raids, the Na Daoine Smeurta had little contact with neighboring tribes. Cassius fervently wished that he too had no contact with them. The language of the tribe was gruff and heavily accented. It was strikingly different from the softer, more melodic tones of the inhabitants of Ériu.

Cassius' neck muscles knotted as his thoughts were drawn to Conall Mac Gabhann. The vivid, bitter memories of his nemesis produced a dull throb in his temples. The young barbarian had shocked the Roman with his revenge-driven tenacity and resourcefulness. Grimly, though only to himself, Cassius conceded that it was he who, having arranged the slaughter of Conall's family, had spurred Conall along the path from lowly apprentice blacksmith to warrior king.

In an absurdity of fate, Cassius' most likely escape from his current predicament lay in Conall's relentless quest to find him. The Roman was also aware that this path would probably lead to an excruciatingly painful death - unless he had something with which to bargain. Some piece of information that would at the least cause Conall and his witch-queen Mórrígan to pause.

The Roman smiled in small comfort before his ribs bore the dull thud of his master's calloused bare foot.

CHAPTER 2

A day's walk inland from the northeastern coast of Ériu, Ráth na Lairig Éadain sat upon a towering black nipple of rock that rose up from the gleann floor. Fishermen and traders from the small coastal villages in the shadow of the fortress had been happy to provide information on Cinn Tìre and the inhabitants of the long narrow peninsula across the sea. The Aos an Eich – The Horse People, according to lore, were thought to be descendants of the Ulaid – the people of northern Ériu.

Conall Mac Gabhann sat on the grassy verge of the cliff and gazed east toward Albu. As he listened to the squeals of laughter from his daughters, Danu and Brighid, playing tag behind him, Conall reflected that not so long ago he was an apprentice blacksmith helping his father. Now, he was a warrior king bent on avenging his parents and sisters' murder and had the responsibility for a growing army and their followers. The scars on his hands were from blades, not errant cinders or hammers.

He intended to avoid a costly skirmish when his army and people made landfall on Cinn Tire and from what he had heard, horses were the key. Íar Mac Dedad, his friend and the commander of his fledgling cavalry, had a passion for life and for horses that knew few limits. Hence Conall had chosen him to lead the delegation. As a gift for the Aos an Eich's king, Íar had selected some fine horse-stock from his personal herds. Accompanied by Deaglán ó Neill, Cian Craobhach and a small group from Conall's caomhnóirí – his personal guard, Íar set off to negotiate passage through Eachdonn Breac's lands. It was the first step in the quest to find Cassius.

Eachdonn Breac, king of the Aos an Eich watched the group approach from his vantage point on the thick, stone-faced ramparts of Dùnsgéitheig. The wall, five paces thick at its base and clad with stone on both its inner and outer surfaces, protected the king's residence. There was only one entrance. It looked eastward and was imposingly lined with cut stone and finished with solid oak gates. The gates were secured with a heavy beam that mated with slots cut into the stone.

The outer wall rose to one and a half times the height of a warrior. Broad stone steps had been cut on each side of the entrance, allowing access to the inner parapet. Fifty of Eachdonn's spearmen lined the rampart. A similar number of horsemen waited out of sight behind the fort.

Local fishermen had alerted Eachdonn to the galley anchored in the cove at Ceann an Locha on the narrow peninsula of Cinn Tire. Of itself, the presence of the ship was not unusual. Traders and merchants from the tribes in the far south, as well as Greeks and Phoenicians, were fairly frequent visitors. The hardy breed of horses his people raised was highly valued for work and war. Since the early days of the tribe, horses had provided a constant resource that was used for trade and barter.

Astride their horses, the three men at the front of the small group rode with the posture of seasoned warriors — relaxed, but alert for trouble. Ornately decorated helmets glinted in the sun. Rust-colored leather inlaid with iron scales protected their torsos and legs. Each carried a small, circular shield painted red and embellished with a black raven. A set of three javelins in a leather sheath was strapped to each horse's flank. Even from a distance, Eachdonn could make out that the riders and their guards were supplied with a range of swords and axes.

The strangers were accompanied by a ten-man guard that kept pace with the riders and held to a disciplined formation as they tramped along the rutted trail. Their helmets were less ornate, but they too wore armor of leather and iron over a short tunic of soft leather. Most wore brightly colored pants that ended in boots or bróga - shoes. Each carried a tall shield spanning from chin to knee and with the same insignia - a black raven on a red sky.

Eachdonn absentmindedly brushed his hand over long, auburn hair that hung like a horse's mane over his broad shoulders. Tugging at random clumps of knots, he thought he might need a haircut. "Their weapons and armor are certainly uncommon," he mused. A small patch of bristles on his recently scraped chin annoyed him. But the king's attention and deep, fern-green eyes were inevitably drawn to the horses. With a note of admiration and envy he sighed. Eachdonn loved his tribe's ponies with a fierce passion, but the ones approaching were sleek and powerful beasts, at least a hand taller than his shaggy breed. Possibilities swept through his mind. "Let's hope they have honor as well as great taste in horses."

Due to the tides, it had been late-afternoon when the group arrived at Maol Chinn Tìre — the headland of the peninsula. The landing on the shingle beach was uneventful - save for the numerous oaths and curses shouted as men splashed their way through bone-chilling waters. A second round, populated liberally with more swearing and threats of roasted horsemeat, broke out when Íar, Deaglán and Cian's horses shook themselves dry. The men's few remaining dry clothes were soon soaked.

"Quit your complaining!" Íar said. The tenor of his voice was disturbingly similar to that of his horse. "We'll make camp here for the night and journey on at dawn. Build a good fire with the driftwood. We'll eat, sleep and get an early start." To Deaglán, who had just removed his helmet and was tying his long, fire-red hair back from his face with a leather thong, he said, "Take two men and make a quick survey before the light fades. Find a path off this beach. See if there are any threats we should be aware of." Deaglán moved off.

At first light the band strapped on armor and weapons. The season had turned from winter to spring, yet the weather remained bitterly cold. The men made good use of their brightly colored, heavy woolen brats as well as leg wraps and multiple layers of tunics and socks.

Steep cliffs worn smooth by the blasts of stormy seas and by gathered winds that flayed the land with sand and rock rose up from the shoreline. Deaglán led the party to a well-trodden pathway which would allow passage for man and horses.

Immediately adjacent to the coastline the land was mostly flat and tended by many small homesteads. Beyond the fertile coastal plain, the land became hilly moorland, sparsely populated with oak, ash, aspen, birch, rowan, holly, willow and alder. The rugged countryside was still covered in a thick layer of packed snow, broken only by splashes of bright orange and yellow from prolific gorse bushes. Indigo tinted crags and snow-capped peaks swaddled in silver-gray clouds towered in the distance.

Their journey was well-observed, but did not appear to cause undue alarm. The only attack they faced came from children who, hiding behind dry stone walls, launched volleys of snowballs. Squeals of delight followed when a few of those walking returned fire - although with restrained strength. As the small band rounded a bend of the meandering coastline, a large fortified roundhouse came into view.

The dwelling made good use of the crag upon which it sat. To the front there was a thick, stone-faced rampart and ditch while behind, a sheer cliff face plunged to the waters below. As Íar's group approached, men armed with spears and shields positioned themselves in front of the building. The leader pointed ahead with his spear and in a rolling growl of a brogue said, "Continue along this path. Ye'r expected. If ye pick up your pace, ye'll make Dùnsgéitheig before dark."

As Dùnsgéitheig came into view, Deaglán was incredulous, "By the Hag, Íar. Another fort! We've travelled less than a day from the cove and this is the second that we've seen. The Cinn Péinteáilte must like building forts. Or they do a lot of fighting."

The much older, shaven-headed Cian laughed at his red-haired nephew, "Aye, although that last one was more of a fortified home.

Trees appear to be scarce so it's understandable why they use stone and dirt." Nodding towards Dùnsgéitheig he added, "But that is much better built. More like a fort."

Deaglán sighed, "Cúscraid is going to have to do some thinking if we need to crack any of these open."

As they drew alongside him, Íar Mac Dedad roared with laughter at the craic shared between the two men. His laughter was infectious and soon the guard had joined in, with the raucous sound carrying to the bemused warriors on the walls of Dùnsgéitheig.

"It would seem our visitors are in good spirits," Eachdonn remarked as he watched the group's leader walk his mount slowly forward.

When within hailing distance of the fort, Íar stopped and removed his helmet. As he shook long, braided hair the color of deep amber with streaks of sandstone, he looked up at the men on the wall. Their spear tips were plainly visible glinting in the afternoon sun. In a booming voice he called out, "I am Íar Mac Dedad, son of ruiri Deda Mac Sin of Curraghatoor on the land of Ériu and loyal servant of ruiri Conall Mac Gabhann." He held up the reins of two magnificent horses, "We come as friends, and bring greetings and gifts." Following Íar's lead, Deaglán and Cian removed their helmets and cantered forward to stand alongside.

"He certainly has a voice to match his girth," Eachdonn remarked to the warrior closest to him. The man simply nodded his head in agreement. The king leaned forward, placing his hands firmly on the smooth, gray stone of the ramparts, "Enter as friends and eat with us." To himself he added, "Let us hope that you also leave as friends."

At the center of the roundhouse, a blazing wood and peat fire provided light as well as warmth. As the evening passed, the light from the flames and rushlights grew obscured through a dense haze of aromatic smoke. The dim light did nothing to disguise increasingly flushed cheeks caused by the heat and abundantly flowing beer. Indeed it transpired that Íar and Eachdonn shared both a love of horses and beer. It was not long they were intent on seeing who could drink the most.

In the early hours of the morning, the sound of reveling and belching was gradually replaced by grunting, snoring and farting as sleep gradually overcame the revelers. Finally admitting defeat, Eachdonn stood, nodded to Íar and staggered to a nearby bed. Pausing briefly to fart, Íar slowly broke off a final slab of bread, wiped the fat from a haunch of boar and sank his teeth into the roasted, pink flesh. He washed the food down with more beer before slumping across the wooden table.

A short time later as morning arrived, Deaglán awoke to a fragile stomach and pounding headache. With a moan of, "Shite," he tossed several furs aside and stumbled outside. Muttered curses near the doorway and sounds of retching followed. In contrast, Eachdonn, Íar and Cian looking none the worse for wear were already deep in conversation. They chuckled at the young man's distress. "Young ones!" remarked the king. "They just can't keep up."

"You can tell he was well brought up. He had the good manners to puke outside," said Cian. The others laughed.

Eachdonn sliced a wedge of cheese with his dagger and refilled his jug with milk. "I'll be frank, Íar. With the size of Conall's army and the people that accompany it, you're already bigger than some of the tribes in the far north. The larger tribes to the east and south will either see you as a threat or want to hire your warriors as mercenaries. You may not even get a chance to approach the ones to the north-east. They don't speak the same language as us and are eager to fight."

"And what of you, My Lord?" asked Íar. "Do you see us as a threat?"

Íar and Cian waited as Eachdonn considered his answer. The king shook his head. "You and I share a love of horses," he said. "Your king's gift was well chosen - much better than trying to bribe me with gold." Glancing at Cian and amused at Deaglán's wobbly gait he said, "And I have kinship with my brothers from the Ulaid. Conall Mac Gabhann is young, but discerning. Tell him from Eachdonn Breac, king of Aos an Eich, that he and his people are welcome to travel through our lands. I shall look forward to greeting him and his queen at Dùn Athad."

A few weeks later, Íar returned to Ráth na Lairig Éadain bearing gifts for Conall and his queen, Mórrígan. Of more importance, he brought a hand of friendship and permission to land at Ceann an Locha on the eastern shore of the narrow peninsula. At Eachdonn's suggestion they would use the fort at Dùnsgéitheig as a base of operations. With the main army settled, Conall and his Chomhairle – his council of advisers, would travel north to Eachdonn's main residence, the fortress of Dùn Athad.

CHAPTER 3

Pytheas stood on the deck of the galley and took a deep breath. His nostrils filled with the sweet scent of cedar wood. The calming slap of wavelets against the hull lifted his spirits even higher. The small, swarthy and somewhat overweight Greek merchant chuckled as he observed his cargo embark. His sharp eyes took in the nervous glances of his passengers, many of whom had never been on a small boat, let alone a galley. He noted that many sported handsome gold and silver torcs, bracelets and clasps, intricately designed belts and scabbards and finely embroidered and fringed brats.

On this rare, cloud-free day, Maol Chinn Tìre was clearly visible from the limestone cliffs that guarded the northeastern shores of Ériu. Only a narrow strip of cold water separated Ulaid lands from the headland of Cinn Tìre. The journey would be short, although the strong currents and frequent sea mists that plagued Maol Chinn Tìre were not to be underestimated. A light breeze under the powder-blue sky fluffed Pytheas' black hair. "The seas would be calm for a sailor," he thought, "but maybe a little less pleasant for Conall's people."

The merchant-sailor was well-known to the people of northern Ériu – the Ulaid, for his trade in goods. This contract, however, was unusual. His instructions from Ériu's flame-haired and quick-tempered High Queen, Macha Mong Ruad were clear-cut: "Get the bastards off my territory and do it with all speed." He could understand why. The High Queen had been resoundingly defeated and humbled before her army and nobles by Conall at the battle of Ráth na Lairig Éadain. Although handed over gracelessly, the gold payment for the job would compensate more than adequately for the monotony of fulfilling the contract.

Pytheas easily recruited enough ships to do the job. Galley captains happily took the gold as an extra piece of business. Most traded with the southern tin mines. After their final group of passengers disembarked they would sail south to pick up a load of ore and journey to the warmer climates of the Great Sea and their home ports.

The Greek was impressed by Conall's tribe. No longer were they a loose gathering of itinerants. They were united, a purposeful people protected by an army whose battles against greater odds were already being lauded – even in Rome. Leader and ruiri, Conall Mac Gabhann, a hard-muscled, intense young man of barely twenty-four summers, bore the scars of battle on exposed hands, arms and thighs, and in the torment reflected in his gray-blue eyes.

It was testament to his ability that Conall had brought together and commanded the respect of, a diverse group of men and women as advisers. This group of rogues, mystics and warriors, known to Conall's people as the Chomhairle – the Council, projected an aura of strength, cunning and dread. As well, there were Conall's fiercely loyal caomhnóirí, one hundred elite warriors who seldom strayed far from their leader. They had fought side-by-side with the king in the worst of circumstances, and were devoted to ensuring his safety.

In the planning of the journey, Pytheas spent many long evenings with Conall and his haunted, yet beautiful, emerald-eyed queen, Mórrígan. Pytheas felt his brain shrink as Conall drew knowledge from him with probing questions about the lands of Cinn Tire and the Cinn Péinteáilte, as well as the southern territories of Albu and the tribes that surrounded Rome and the Great Sea. Often their conversations were brought to a close by the frequent headaches that plagued the intense young leader.

As for Mórrígan, her presence made Pytheas uneasy. The intricate paintings and designs permanently etched into her pale skin projected a constant, heady aura of seduction and darkness. He was more than happy that their conversations together were limited.

While satisfied with Íar's report concerning Eachdonn, Conall was not about to take risks with the well-being of his people. The plan was to land the army at Ceann an Locha and secure the area. Then the people would disembark and journey to the agreed camp site at Dùnsgéitheig. Conall was more than grateful for the wise heads of his quartermaster, Cian, and that of the civil leader, Seanán, for managing the logistics of the exodus.

The snorting of uneasy horses as they were led up the boarding ramp broke Pytheas' contemplations and he glanced up. Smiling broadly and bowing with a grand flourish, he regarded Conall, Mórrígan, their daughters, Danu and Brighid and their new son, Tuathal.

"Welcome to my kingdom. Please come aboard."

Conall smiled wanly at the Greek. Pytheas' assurances that with a calm sea the voyage would take at most from dawn to mid-day did little to quell Conall's rising anxiety. He was not looking forward to the journey, but was doing his best to put on a brave face. Unlike his commanders, whose strategy for coping with the short voyage was to get blind drunk, Conall had decided that as king he should set a better example. He uttered a slightly annoyed and envious sigh as slurred cheers and shouts of, "Move along up there!" came from Fearghal, his battle commander, Cúscraid, his master of defense, and Brion, the brother of Mórrígan. With a curt nod to the ship's captain, Conall and his family took their designated places at the prow.

The flat-bottomed bireme lurched as forty pairs of oars dropped into the waters and propelled the ship from the crystal clear shallows into the deeper, green-blue waters. On the land, a flock of ravens took flight and accompanied the galley. Conall gripped the wooden rail, grimly assuring himself that he was just maintaining his balance. Since the men were wearing armor, and few could swim, they would have little chance of surviving should any ship sink during the crossing.

Even with a fleet of thirty galleys, it took a full cycle of the moon to transport the army, its followers and animals across the narrow neck of water. At each sunrise and until the sun set, Conall stood on the cliffs at Ceann an Locha watching each galley disgorge its cargo. The army took precedence, but ere long they too appeared along the cliff top waiting anxiously for their loved ones to arrive and disembark. By all accounts the flight was successful with only two ships lost. Íar, however, was particularly distraught as one contained horses.

The Chomhairle and half of the caomhnóirí took up residence in the cluster of roundhouses within the walls of Dùnsgéitheig. A substantial camp was erected against the fort's ramparts for the people and the rest of the army.

In the weeks following the landing at Ceann an Locha, faces wore a brave façade, but eyes betrayed wistful memories of Ériu - a land that would always be home. The geis laid upon their king by the aes sidhe meant it was a land to which they were unlikely to return. Matching the melancholy was a resolute determination to thrive. Around the camp fires in the evenings, tears flowed as ballads and tales of Ériu were sung accompanied by wailing pipes, harps and the insistent beat of the bodhráns. Inevitably, as time passed, fonder and more pleasant reminiscences supplanted darker memories.

Glistening wet in the fine rainfall, the stone fortress of Dùn Athad perched atop a teardrop shaped, moss-covered escarpment. The view from the fort was breathtaking with clear sightlines far into the distance. Few could launch an attack on Dùn Athad and remain unseen or avoid being sucked into the marshland of A' Mhòinteach Mhór that surrounded the crag. A wide river curved and coursed westward through the valley toward the sea.

A shimmering rainbow arced across the silver sky as Cúscraid and Conall climbed towards the fortress. The entrance was through a natural gully on the south-eastern side, followed by a climb up a terraced hillside. Cúscraid pointed to the ongoing construction of two lines of perimeter defenses that made use of stone and wood ramparts and deep, wide ditches. "Eachdonn Breac must have really pissed someone off to prepare fortifications such as these."

Conall, panting with the steep climb, silently regretted volunteering to take his daughter Danu, now five summers old, on his shoulders. Catching his breath he nodded, "Unfriendly neighbors and active warbands. We'll make the best of the king's hospitality, but remain vigilant." A sharp slap on his head reminded him of his daughter's competitive nature.

"Da! Brighid is catching up. I want to be first to the ráth."

As Conall rolled his eyes at a grinning Cúscraid, he added, "It may be a while before we meet or make other friends or allies."

Conall glanced around at a rare sight. The tall, granite sculpted Fearghal Ruad, his battle commander and mentor, for once without his favored longsword, was being whipped and urged on by Conall's other daughter, Brighid. Fearghal's mock cries of pain and anguish were greeted by giggles from Danu's dark-haired twin. His jaw set, Conall lengthened his stride.

"Like father, like daughter," Cúscraid murmured with a shake of his head. He soon found himself abreast of Brion and Áine, who had adopted a much more leisurely pace with their son, Cassán. The boy's mass of bronze-red curls fought against the cap his mother insisted that he wear.

As they passed through the entrance of Dùn Athad, Cúscraid admired the solid walls that stretched back for ten paces before giving way to the open yard and dwellings. He was eager to learn of their construction. Mongfhionn, the statuesque Sidhe, paused briefly to touch and draw strength from the solid oak gates.

Eachdonn Breac, accompanied by his queen, Ceana, stood before a towering broch at the center of the fort. They were flanked by his trusted chieftains. Ceana was a tall woman with high cheekbones brushed pink by the chill wind. Porcelain skin and waist-long tresses of fair hair contrasted with the king's ruddy, wind-burned complexion and auburn mane. Ceana's expression was friendly, but watchful and alert.

Íar strode forward and bowing gracefully for a man of his bulk said, "Perhaps I should make the introductions?" Eachdonn smiled his assent. "My Lord, it pleases me to present my king, Conall Mac Gabhann and his queen Mórrígan ni Cathasaigh." Conall stretched forth his hand in friendship. His steady gaze held Eachdonn's as he received a firm grip in response.

A startled gasp escaped from Ceana as Mórrígan slipped her hood back and was followed by a hastened apology, "Please excuse my rudeness. Your paintings are intricate and beautiful. Often such would be associated with the Cinn Péinteáilte to the east and north and we have not found our neighbors to be overly friendly."

"Overly friendly!" snorted Eachdonn, "There's understatement. At the slightest sign of weakness that bastard Drostan Ruadh of Aos na Coille – The People of the Woods, would slaughter us and add this territory to his." The king slapped the rock of the broch, "Only solid rock, thick walls and sharp spears preserve the peace in these lands." A flicker from Ceana's hazel eyes interrupted the king's diatribe. "But enough of this talk, let's eat, drink, sing ballads and tell outrageous tales. We can speak of more serious matters over the next few days."

Glancing over Conall's shoulder, Eachdonn caught sight of the smaller figure of Pytheas. "Glad you could take up my invitation." The merchant smiled and bowed. Eachdonn took note of the tall, dark-skinned Spartan, Nikandros and said, "Traders such as our friend, Pytheas, are not unknown to us. This dark warrior intrigues me." He then bowed to the Sidhe, who stood beside Fearghal. "As do others in yer party."

The skin around Eachdonn's glinting green eyes then crinkled in amusement as he addressed Nikandros, "The winters in Ériu are nothing compared to here. In this land ye'll freeze yer balls off in that short tunic. Never worry, I've excellent wolf pelts that ye can choose from."

Nikandros bowed deeply and laughed politely at Eachdonn's words. Quietly to Fearghal he said, "Should I learn some new swear words for this land?"

"Nah, Eachdonn and his people will understand 'Póg ma thoin' and the others you have acquired. Mind you, from what I've heard, I doubt we'll get close enough to the Cinn Péinteáilte for language to matter! Give me back my sword. Let's go fill our bellies with the king's hospitality. I'm starving and thirsty after that climb and Íar tells me that they brew good beers here."

The following sunrise, dry mouths and sore heads were managed with a simpler repast of oatmeal, bread, hard cheese, honeyed milk and cool spring water. Plain talking was the order of the day. Eachdonn opened up the conversation as he broke the crust of a loaf of freshly baked bread, savoring its aroma before taking a bite. "Between the wagon trails and trading ships, we're not isolated and are well informed of news from all around this island as well as Ériu. I know who ye seek. My information is that the Roman is a slave with the Na Daoine Smeurta. The last news that reached us was before the winter. If yer quarry is still alive it speaks well of his ability to survive."

Conall made to speak, but the king held a friendly hand up, "Let me continue a wee bit longer." Ceana rolled her eyes. Eachdonn loved to talk. "The Na Daoine Smeurta inhabit the furthest reaches of this land, across great valleys, dense wildwoods and forests, tall mountains permanently covered in ice and snow, and bottomless lochs. The weather is unpredictable. Only the Aos nan Cat, who take their name from the lynxes that inhabit the mountains, live further north.

"The tribes of the north are fierce and deserve respect. Their sigils are etched into their skin with bone or iron. The bastards believe their painting is their armor. They fight naked or almost naked - even in the coldest weather. The land they live on shows them no mercy and they show none to strangers. They have few forts or brochs, using the mountains and forests as their defenses."

Eachdonn gnawed another mouthful of bread. "Before ye reach the Na Daoine Smeurta, ye'll likely battle yer way through the Na Daoine Tùrsach — seriously disturbed people ruled by a fanatical queen." Rubbing his chin he paused and thought briefly about the raven symbols that emblazoned the army's shields and banners as well as Conall and Mórrígan's helmets. "Possibly the Aos an Fhithich, although that could be an interesting encounter."

"What size of armies can they field?" asked Brion before biting appreciatively into a slab of sharp-tasting yellow cheese.

"Not huge. Their warbands number anything from fifty to five hundred men. If they had to, each of the smaller tribes could probably field five, maybe ten thousand warriors aged from fourteen to forty summers. But ye miss my point. They rarely fight in open battle. They strike hard and quickly and then disappear into the land. It will be a toilsome journey across the mountains to reach the Na Daoine Smeurta. Truthfully, it would be easier to liberate yer prize from the Otherworld.

Eachdonn regarded Conall with concern, "Yer army will find the task challenging," he said, sweeping his hand in a wide arc. "Ye certainly cannot take yer people. There is no warmth in the air and even in early autumn the weather can turn nasty. They would perish in the mountains." Swallowing a mouthful of milk, Eachdonn added one more comment. "The tribes are a superstitious lot. If the Lady Sidhe or yer queen would travel with ye then that might be an edge that would prove useful."

Fearghal nudged Nikandros at the far end of the table, "They certainly scare the shite out of me." Mongfhionn and Mórrígan's heads swiveled towards him. The bluff warrior instantly became the focus of two piercing stares.

Until that moment, Pytheas had listened quietly, but with increasing interest in the discussion. He now said, "You may not need to traverse the mountains." Then smiling with some amusement at Conall and his party he continued, "But you will need to develop a love for sailing!"

Curious, Conall and Eachdonn ignored the moans and groans of the others and signaled the Greek to continue. "A few days' sailing north along the western coastline, there is a body of water known as An Linne Sheileach. This leads north-east along rivers and lakes to Cùil Daothail, a major trading and iron-working settlement protected by the Aos na Coille, but which also borders Na Daoine Tùrsach territory. From there it is a manageable march through pinewood forests, moors and coastal plains to the domain of the Aos an Fhithich and then to the Na Daoine Smeurta.

I've often pondered whether my smaller galleys could make the trip. If it were possible it would avoid having to sail around the northern coasts with their treacherous currents and squalls. My offer is to transport a small raiding party to Cùil Daothail. After that I will sail south to trade on the eastern coast and then on to the Great Sea. You, unfortunately, will have to make your own way back."

"Well that's a possibility," said Conall. "What of the rest of the army and people? We need to consider how we'll feed almost five thousand and find shelter for the winter." Looking to Eachdonn, he said, "I'm sure our friendship with Aos an Eich would be somewhat strained with such a large group on their lands. Our gold, while not meager, will not last forever and we'd have to turn to raiding just to survive."

"Ye could take and hold Dùn Na Mèadaidh."

Eachdonn's stark statement was met by murmurs of "Impossible!" from the king's chieftains. Ceana shifted uncomfortably.

"I knew it. We're back to fighting crap odds, aren't we?" Cúscraid said.

"What did you expect?" Fearghal ran a distracted hand across his stubbly cheek and chin. "Few of us will die old men."

Cúscraid laughed at his friend, "So you still consider yourself young?"

"Bastard!" Fearghal said and glanced at Mongfhionn. "Oh, I can still keep my end up."

"Dùn Na Mèadaidh is several weeks journey east," Eachdonn said. "As its name suggests, it's the fortress of the Na Mèadaidh. The fort sits on a hill at the western end of a long, narrow mountain range and is surrounded by a valley of woods and bogs. If ye can take it, it can be defended and the land around is rich in sheep and cattle. There are a good number of mines too. It is on the major route south and should not be difficult for your raiding party to locate — assuming they survive the Na Daoine Smeurta." Eachdonn waited for some reaction to this information from Conall and the Chomhairle.

After a long pause, Conall said, "We'll meet to plan further, tomorrow. In the meantime, let's enjoy the king's generous hospitality."

Before long, Eachdonn was left with only Ceana at his side as he mulled over the day. "Have you taken leave of your senses?" she said, interrupting his thoughts. "You know who rules at Dùn Na Mèadaidh."

Eachdonn sighed with a resigned air, "I know, but it is the only logical choice. If Conall's people remain on our lands it's certain we'll fight. Tell me, where else could Conall settle his people?"

Ceana looked at him sternly, "And there's no other reason?"

Exasperated, Eachdonn growled as he refilled his beer, "Ye know as well as me. Finnean Mac Sèitheach's warbands cause us constant trouble and disrupt trade. Of more concern are the rumors that the white-haired bastard has forged an alliance between the Aos na Coille, the An t-Aos-Sìthiche – the Sidhe's Hounds, and the Aos nan Con-Seilge – the Hunter's Hounds. I, no, *we* cannot allow the Cinn Péinteáilte to band together and drive us into the sea." Eachdonn took Ceana's hand and gazed into the ever changing green and gold of her eyes, "There is no love between ye and your brother. He cut yer father's throat and likely would have done the same - or worse, to ye had I not rescued ye."

Ceana snorted derisively, "Rescued me! You stole me when I was only ten summers old during a cattle raid, then used me as a fidchell piece to forestall my father from slaughtering you and your people."

Eachdonn's arms encircled Ceana almost squeezing the life from her, "Mere details, my queen. With the gods' blessing it has worked out well - for both of us." As he held her, Eachdonn felt his manhood stir against her warm body. Hoarsely he changed the subject, "Since ye'r no longer a child and it would appear I haven't drunk so much that I can't satisfy yer wild passions, I think we should retire."

A swift and stinging slap of Ceana's hand left a red welt on Eachdonn's cheek. She turned and padded on bare feet across the slate floor towards the stone steps leading to their private quarters. In that short distance she had disrobed, presenting the king with a full view of her round white arse as she disappeared from view.

Eachdonn laid his beer mug on the floor and followed. By the time he reached the upper room, he had somewhat inelegantly stripped and was plainly looking forward to taking his queen.

Later, as Ceana lay flushed on her bed, her finger traced the tiny beads of now-cold sweat between her breasts and circled the dark areola that surrounded still hard nipples. She smiled. She had never been with another man and had never regretted it. Eachdonn's style of rutting was forceful, but he managed to combine this with a satisfying longevity. Even should his hardness flag, her mouth was more than willing to ensure that was but a temporary delay.

As she listened to Eachdonn's loud, contented snoring, Ceana recalled the evening's discussion. She warmed to the thought of her brother, Finnean's departure from Dùn Na Mèadaidh – even better if he were dead. But Dùn Na Mèadaidh rightfully belonged to her, not some newly titled king from Ériu. The steel in Conall's eyes told Ceana that once installed in Dùn Na Mèadaidh, he would be hard to dislodge. She needed a piece in this game loyal only to her.

"You're the ruiri, Conall. You should stay with the main army," Íar said. "A few hundred against thousands is not good odds. Let others bring the Roman to you."

Mongfhionn nodded her agreement with Íar, "The risk is too great."

Conall sighed in exasperation. His Chomhairle had spent most of the morning trying to persuade him to remain with the army. With jaw set he said, "Enough. I will lead the raid north with Fearghal, Torcán, Deaglán and Mórrígan - and, if she agrees, the Lady Mongfhionn. The warband will be two hundred and fifty strong plus half of Mórrígan's archers. We'll also bring Fearghal and my hounds." He was relieved to see, at last, resigned acceptance on the faces of his council.

"To reach Dùn Na Mèadaidh, the army will first traverse the

forests of the Aos na Coille. Assuming we succeed, Brion, Íar, and Nikandros will lead the assault. Once the ráth has been taken then command of the defenses will be Cúscraid's responsibility and we'll send for the people. I'll ask Eachdonn to provide an escort." There was a general murmur of approval for the plan.

"If the Goddess wills it, we'll march on the sixth sunrise."

Conall's rise from the table was stopped short by a cough from Pytheas. The merchant had been permitted to observe the Chomhairle's deliberations. A broad smile spread from the Greek's mouth reaching eyes that sparkled like dark opals.

"I suppose four or five days should cover the basics."

Warily, Conall asked, "Basics?"

"Well, your men will be replacing mine as rowers. How else did you expect to transport three hundred warriors along with weapons, armor and supplies? Even with your men rowing, we'll need eight galleys."

A greenish pallor tinged Conall's face as he recalled his first journey on the sea. Disconcerted looks from Fearghal, Torcán and Deaglán told him that his trepidation was shared. Enjoying his new friends' discomfort, Pytheas continued, "My men will instruct yours. One of my best men will be assigned to each ship to supervise and keep the stroke beat as we travel." Allowing his words to be absorbed for a moment, he concluded, "We'll start the training at first light tomorrow."

Resigned to his fate, Conall stood up and said, "You have a disconcerting sense of humor, friend." He walked outside with Mórrígan to get some air.

CHAPTER 4

Grunts of red-faced men kept time with the slap and swish of oar blades. They pulled on wooden grips darkened with sweat and smoothed through use. The blades straightened to near parallel with the sea before rotating to strike the waves like a sùlaire diving into the water. Sweat poured from semi-naked bodies as taut arm and bulging thigh muscles propelled the vessels forward. Pytheas smiled approvingly as he watched Conall's men stroke in time with the beat of the drum. In five days they had progressed from snagging oars and going around in circles to travelling in the correct direction and at a reasonable speed. The men had also learned to furl and unfurl the square sails, to drop the masts and to beach and carry the light galleys.

Eachdonn and Ceana observed Conall's warband of two hundred and fifty men, twenty-five archers plus supplies and two pairs of wolfhounds, assemble at the river mouth west of Dùn Athad, on the sixth sunrise. The dogs were in a happy frenzy, the men more reserved. Once joined by a handful of Eachdonn's hunters, who would act as guides, the party would be complete.

The galleys rocked on the gentle swell as they were boarded. Shields were lashed to the side of the galleys, while weapons were stowed within reach. As gifts of gold and armor were lowered into the waters, Mongfhionn and Mórrígan each stood in the prows of a vessel and chanted, asking the Goddess for journey mercies.

On the shoreline, Conall drew Íar, Nikandros, Brion and Cúscraid aside, "I value Eachdonn's counsel," he said, "yet it will be challenging to take Dùn Na Mèadaidh before winter sets in. Eachdonn may be open to persuasion to provide additional men for the assault – if only to ensure we leave his lands." In a low tone so as not to be overheard, he added, "As a precaution, evaluate defensible positions between Dùn Athad and Dùn Na Mèadaidh – even if they lie in Eachdonn's lands." The four nodded in agreement. "Cúscraid, I leave my children and my people in your care," Conall said and turned to splash through the cold surf to his waiting galley.

As they rowed away from the beach, the early morning sea mist drifting on the gentle breeze was replaced by light rainfall. With distance, the wind off the saltwater gathered strength making the waters choppy, but also filling the vessels' solitary, black sails.

The persistent cold mizzle soaked into garments. It was uncomfortable and annoying, but only temporarily. Within a short period of exertion, the oarsmen had shed most of their clothes.

"A pleasant distraction and unexpected bonus!" opined Mongfhionn.

The sight of the near-naked, sweating men, muscles straining and grunting with each stroke brought a smile to the Sidhe's countenance. Fearghal could do little more than smirk like a little boy at the look on Mongfhionn's ageless and unblemished face.

The fleet swept in a wide arc northwards. Avoiding submerged rocks and treacherous currents, they hugged the coastlines of islands, large and small. Most were no more than moss-covered rocks scoured by the wind and sea and populated by neither man, beast nor tree.

By mid-day the sea breeze had strengthened into a strong headwind and rain lashed the boats. Sails were gradually reduced and eventually furled. As he observed the darkening skies, Pytheas shook his head and prayed to Poseidon. The galleys were still holding their course, but were plainly struggling to maintain a good speed. The fleet was also starting to lose its chevron shape and he feared that those at the rear might drift away, especially if they were still on the water at dusk.

Pytheas made his way to Conall's bench, stepping in harmony with the rolling motion of the waves. "We're not making as much progress as I had hoped. If they can't rest, the men will become exhausted. According to my charts if we continue north between these islands and then veer northeast, we should come to a peninsula. We can search for a good stretch of shore to beach the ships and rest for the night." Breathing hard, his shoulder-length dark hair plastered to his head, Conall nodded and focused once more on keeping his stroke in harmony with the others.

Evening was rapidly drawing in. Overcast skies lent a slate-blue hue to the rugged landscape. Standing in the bow, Mórrígan heaved a sigh of nervous relief as the steep cliffs of the peninsula broke to reveal the refuge of a shale beach. She turned and gestured to Pytheas who, in turn, signaled the other ships. The Greek sailor was relieved to hear the breaking of waves against cedar wood replaced with the crunch of pebbles as eight galleys rode the surf onto the beach. The men quickly stowed oars and jumped into the cold waters to drag the flat-bottomed ships ashore.

The beach itself was narrow, forming the sea-facing edge of a small tidal lagoon. Ignoring the grumbling of the men, Pytheas had them drag and carry the vessels to the safety of the pond. The last thing he needed at the start of their journey was the boats drifting away during the darkness.

Conall and Fearghal quickly surveyed their location. There was little cover on the beach and the wind and rain was picking up. Fortunately, a hundred paces back from the pool a stand of pine and silver birch had stubbornly resisted the harsh conditions. "Move the men to the trees before we freeze to death," said Conall, "We're wearing even less than Nikandros!" Fearghal shivered and nodded in agreement while rubbing goose-pimpled arms vigorously. He shouted orders to Deaglán and Torcán to get their men moving.

A thick carpet of pine needles provided a welcome bed for the men as they gathered around campfires built from drift- and greenwood branches. Flames crackled, flaring skyward as pine branches and cones caught alight. The fragrance of pine filled the night air. Conall sat across the fires from Mórrígan and watched her intensely. She glowed as the firelight caught and accentuated the painted designs on her face, arms and legs.

His queen had been distant since the battle at Ráth na Lairig Éadain. Although they had been rescued, the kidnapping of their twin daughters, by Macha Mong Ruad, preyed constantly on Mórrígan's mind. She had become yet more withdrawn and morose after the birth of Tuathal. The latter Conall attributed to a difficult and exhausting childbirth. Lately he had found it hard to understand or know what his queen was thinking. He was perturbed at the glances shared between Mongfhionn, Fearghal and Nikandros whenever Mórrígan was near. It was as if they were uncertain of her and protecting him from something... but what? Shaking his head in frustration, he stood, grabbed his brat and lay down beside his queen. Soon he drifted off to sleep.

Mórrígan looked deep into the heart of the fire, felt its warmth and yet shivered. Though the heat of the fire flushed her cheeks red, she only felt cold. The death of the degenerate king and murderer of her parents, Eochaidh Ruad, should have given her peace-of-mind and soothed her tortured soul, but this had not come to pass. She loved Conall and their children fiercely, yet her mind was divided. Disturbing voices in her head sought to make her tread a darker path.

She tried to resist, but sometimes their insistent murmurings overruled all other thoughts. In this land of the Cinn Péinteáilte, Mórrígan could sense a tantalizing, ancient power calling to her and she was drawn to it. In her more lucid moments, she prayed to the Goddess that Conall could rescue her from her torment before it was too late. Now, she was thankful for the strong arm that had lay across her breasts.

The Sidhe observed Mórrígan and sighed. Seeds of darkness had found a fertile ground in the young woman's bitter soul. Mongfhionn had sensed the change and confirmed it when a sad Nikandros had shared his observations of Mórrígan's delight when with slow deliberation she had cut a helpless enemy's throat. A part of Mongfhionn blamed herself for starting Mórrígan along a path to understand her potential powers. It was not, however, her responsibility to command Mórrígan to act or behave in a certain way. That was Mórrígan's choice.

Like Mórrígan, the Sidhe had felt the call of strange and sinister voices within a short time of her setting foot on Cinn Tire. As they travelled north, the whisperings were getting stronger and more insistent. She breathed deeply as she rested against and drew strength from the single, ancient oak tree in the copse. She prayed to the Ancient Ones for wisdom.

It was Mongfhionn's duty to ensure that Conall fulfilled his geis and she would do this without hesitation and without compassion or mercy. She was grateful for Fearghal. The Sidhe sighed once more. A brave, loyal and uncomplicated man, Fearghal could also be frustratingly naïve. Resting his head on her ample cleavage, she let the rhythm of his breathing guide her to sleep.

CHAPTER 5

"So Eachdonn Breac is setting his dogs on me?"

Finnean Mac Sèitheach queried the plainly nervous man before him. Ceallach bobbed his head several times glancing uneasily at the white-haired king and the tall warrior who stood in his shadow. He quickly bowed his head to avoid Finnean's intense red-violet eyes.

"That he considers me such a threat could be the best compliment the bastard has ever paid me."

The tall, pallid-skinned king of the Na Mèadaidh was a striking figure. Reputedly a master at diplomacy and subterfuge, he was also known for his abrupt changes of mood, a trait leaving him with few battle victories of which to boast. As well, his envoys and spies were never quite sure how their news would be received.

Finnean had forged strong alliances with his neighbors and in doing so the Na Mèadaidh, a relatively minor, though prosperous tribe, had extended its influence. The king preferred to use his considerable powers of persuasion, a network of informants and well-placed bribes to safeguard his borders. Given that his neighbors' normal way of life was to constantly war among each other, this was a laudable achievement.

The king knew that the fortress of Dun Na Mèadaidh was well located, but was not unassailable. Thus, he relied on the Aos na Coille in their dense forests to the north and the An t-Aos-Sìthiche and Aos nan Con-Seilge to the east to guard his flanks. His plots and schemes had one goal - a grand alliance that would sweep the other tribes into the sea and would, of course, choose Finnean as its ruler.

A cruel, arrogant smile crept over Finnean's face, his attention briefly diverted by his reveries. He shook his head and rubbed his smooth, high forehead as if distracted. Ceallach still stood before him, waiting, rocking almost imperceptibly from foot to foot. Finnean waited to speak until the poor man was barely able to stop pissing himself.

"I have other work for you." The spy resisted a great sigh of relief as the king continued, "Ride to the broch at the northeastern end of Loch Obha. Give Drostan Ruadh of the Aos na Coille my best wishes. Inform him that an army from the west will shortly enter his forests."

Ceallach nodded and as quickly as he could reasonably excuse himself retreated from his Master's presence. Finnean turned to his battle commander, "He has been an excellent spy and loyal, but he knows too much. See to it he has a quick and merciful death when his mission is accomplished." The commander smiled through crooked yellowing teeth and bowed his head in acknowledgment.

Íar led the army northeast along the cattle and hunter trails that ran by Loch Obha. The loch teemed with pink-fleshed fish and eels which provided a ready supply of fresh food for the army.

It was a crisp, late summer morning following the celebration of the feast of Lugnasad. Early mists hovered over the still waters of the lake. Its glass-like surface was disturbed only by fish surfacing or droplets of dew falling from the overhanging trees.

The force of over two thousand men, cavalry, chariots, archers and hounds together with blacksmiths, fletchers and supply wagons were augmented by two hundred and fifty of Eachdonn's riders and a similar number of spearmen. At first the king had remonstrated, quite strenuously, at Íar's request for men. While he had no hesitation in promoting an assault on Dùn Na Mèadaidh, Eachdonn appeared hesitant about trespassing Aos na Coille lands.

In the end, and raising Íar's suspicions, the king's men were set under the command of one of Eachdonn's younger captains. Many of Eachdonn's closest chieftains and captains were also his kin. Ròidh, an enthusiastic, red-haired warrior of seventeen summers was no exception. Indeed, it transpired that Ròidh Mac Eachdonn was the firstborn of Eachdonn and Ceana. Íar was consoled by the fact that, if needed, the lad would make a fine hostage.

The loch was skirted by a dense ribbon of wildwood and stretched a good four days' march in length. Stands of silver birch, ash, alder and oak fought against the domination of the pines. Thankfully, the thick tree canopy held back the persistent rain, but the dense brush of fallen branches, mosses and ferns made progress slow. Clumps of thorn bushes and nettles, and swathes of waist-high spear-thistles with their pink-purple flowers combined to also make it painful.

A few hundred paces back from the shore the land became increasingly forlorn. A sparse vista of rocks, moors and marshes supported a few farms and a scattering of sheep and cattle. Deep purple ribbons of heather and clusters of orange and yellow-flowering gorse thrived conferring upon the land a deceptive beauty and softness.

On the fourth sunrise, the moors and rock-strewn landscape gave way to a vast tract of pine forest. Instead of the tranquil splashes of fish in the loch, the evening air was filled with the sounds of predators – lynxes, bears and wolves on the hunt. Only one thing remained constant - the accompanying flock of ever watchful ravens.

It was midday when the army broke cover at the far reaches of the loch. Across from them, on a spur of land that jutted out into the waters, a tall round broch watched over the pathways that led into the lands of the Aos na Coille.

Ceallach delivered his message to Drostan Ruadh and was anxious to be on his way. The envoy had no intention of returning to Dùn Na Mèadaidh. He prided himself on his skills as a hunter and an observer of men. Ceallach found reading a person's intentions was often easier than following an animal's trail and his instinct for survival told him Finnean Mac Sèitheach was not to be trusted.

"That fox presumes too much." The king of the Aos na Coille scowled as he stood before the broch. With his one eye, the left having been removed by a bear when he was fourteen and foolish enough to believe he could hunt alone, Drostan could clearly see the camp of the invaders and the trails of blue-gray smoke from their cooking fires. He could even smell the mouth-watering aroma of grilled fish. Yet the subject of his ire was not the foreigners on his territory, rather it was Finnean Mac Sèitheach. Ceallach waited patiently and was rewarded with a curt, "Go. There's no reply."

The envoy bowed as he backed away from the king, reclaimed his ponies and rode north – away from Dùn Na Mèadaidh.

Ceallach was especially vigilant on this journey and was rewarded when he discovered his shadow. Not expecting to become the hunted, the man was taken unawares as he was making camp. He was knocked unconscious with the aid of a large club and stripped of his clothes and anything of value. With a few painful and deep cuts, Ceallach severed the muscles and tendons at the back of the assassin's thigh, rendering him unable to walk.

Indifferent to the hapless killer, Ceallach packed and took up the reins of his newly acquired spare pony. "It is already dusk," he thought. "A crippled man will not wait long until the wolves find him." Naked, apart from his tribal markings, and bleeding massively, the would-be murderer begged for mercy. He was shown none. "Amateur!" Ceallach spat, glancing back at the crippled body as he walked away.

Although he had several brochs, Drostan rarely used them. He was disdainful of other tribes who looked to their stone forts and dwellings for safety. The forest was his love, his mistress and his fortress. Finnean could rot in the Otherworld for all Drostan cared, but this was his forest and no-one was allowed passage unless he granted it.

The king stretched well-muscled arms over his head and breathed deeply as he enjoyed the early morning rain on his bare torso. He called to his guard, "Fetch my axe and shield. Let's go meet our troublemakers."

Fionnbharr's sharp eyes spotted the logboat as it made a steady path across the narrow stretch of water, "Guests for breakfast," he said. "Four or five chieftains and a guard of ten - all half-naked. Maybe they're friends of yours, Nikandros!"

"Póg ma thoin, you young whelp." Nikandros tried hard to seem severe, but failed miserably as a huge grin spread across his face.

"How long have you been with us, Nikandros? Five... six summers? Surely you should have mastered a wider range of insults by now." Cúscraid's own widening smile was interrupted when a few pieces of grilled fish caught in his throat making him cough and splutter.

Nikandros laughed and handed his friend a leather pouch filled with cool spring water. "Serves you right, arsehole," he said.

They were joined by Brion and Íar in watching the approaching boat. "Have the ceannairí céad rouse the camp," said Íar. "Let's look professional and plant a few seeds of doubt in their minds. This could be a trap so I want as much warning as possible. Send Áine and her archers into cover, tell Cian to move the wagons, and Brion, get your chariots out of sight, but come back to help us greet our guests." As Brion nodded and loped off, Íar turned to face the waters and added, "Spread the pickets out wider, use young Ròidh's riders, but tell the lad to get over here. We may need someone who speaks their language."

The logboat, watched by the quiver of archers concealed in the trees, skirted the protruding, tangled roots of a clump of oaks. Its keel scraped against the gravel bottom at the water's edge and Drostan and his men scrambled over the side, splashing the remaining steps to dry land.

This group was comprised of tall men with shocks of thick

copper-red hair. Some clearly had not shaved for a long time. They were neither lean nor overweight, but brawny and coiled to spring into action. Their battle scars and watchful eyes told that they were not to be underestimated. All wore patterned pants of vibrant reds, greens, yellows and oranges together with leather brògan laced with thongs. All sported impressively tattooed upper-bodies and faces imprinted with swirling blue designs covering just about every piece of exposed flesh.

The one-eyed Drostan was a head taller than his men. A scar stretched in a single, ragged line from his left forehead to his chin, and then continued down his chest in a series of parallel lines where the bear's claw had ripped his flesh. The scars rippled through his paint, heightening the ferocity of his bearing. His one good eye was amber like an eagle's and his sight was just as sharp. The king held a large battle axe effortlessly in his right hand. A small round shield rested on his left arm. A wide torc of gold rested on his thick neck and numerous bands of gold and silver strained to hold back arm muscles marbled with blue-purple veins. Drostan strode without hesitation into the camp.

"Who speaks for ye?" he barked, scowling at those assembled before him. Looking at the puzzled faces and hearing a few words spoken, the king rolled his eye taking on a pained expression. He spat out his next words in a thick brogue that was barely understandable to his audience. "From the Island, bastard Westerners. Who's yer leader?"

Grasping what had been said, Íar nodded to Ròidh, and they both took a step towards the king. Drostan glowered at the huge warrior who stood as tall as he and looked as if he were built from the stones of the king's broch. The massive chest and square shoulders of Íar together with his shoulder-length, plaited, ginger hair and great beard were impressive by any standards. A long cavalry sword hung from his belt, but his favorite weapon, a long-handled axe, was balanced in calloused hands. A discerning glance at the bearing of the men standing behind Íar told Drostan that they too were well acquainted with war.

Íar held Drostan's gaze without blinking. "And who might you be?" he said. There was an audible groan from Ròidh at the insult that had just been delivered.

The silence was agonizingly long before a great, twisted smile broke across Drostan's scarred face. "I am Drostan Ruadh, king of the Aos na Coille and ye are trespassing," he said and nodded to his men. "Let's eat breakfast and talk. I'll have some of my fish that ye'r cooking." Three of his men joined the king while the others held back, remaining alert. Pointing to the clump of trees Drostan added, "Ye'll not need those bowmen perched in yon trees. This is a time for talking. Ye'll know well when it's fighting time."

Suitably fed, the adversaries continued to size each other up across the smoky cooking fire as they washed the last bites of food down with beer. It was a contemplative tableau. The morning silence was broken only by the gentle lapping of water on the shoreline, the cluck and bubble of a nearby spring and the yowling in the distant trees of a lynx calling to its mate.

"We mean no harm. We're just passing through," Íar volunteered.

"I'm well aware of your intentions and while I've no great liking for that wraith, Finnean, I've an agreement to aid him if he is attacked."

"He hasn't been attacked – yet," Brion said. As he smiled, the long ridge of white scar tissue on his left cheek gave his visage a strangely cracked look. Áine found his visage pleasing – or so she said.

The Aos na Coille king guffawed, "Good scar. Ye I like!" Drostan's countenance then shifted. "Ye'r on my lands, without my permission and if I'm any judge of men ye've little intention of leaving. If I let ye pass, every warband in the land will be snapping at my heels." He sighed and shook his head, "My armies outnumber ye greatly and we know the woods. Go back, find another way. Save yer strength for Finnean."

"We can't do that," said Cúscraid looking around at his comrades who grimly nodded in agreement.

"Aye," replied Drostan with a tinge of sadness. "A pity. We'll show no quarter – and we'll expect none." With that, the king of the Aos na Coille stood and made his way back to the logboat.

"Any ideas?" asked Íar.

Brion was the first to speak. "It will be tough to get the chariots and supply wagons through the forest perimeter. The trees and undergrowth are just too dense. We'll have to cut our way through and that'll take time." Then he added, "Although, from what the scouts say, once we're beyond the first hundred paces, it's old forest. The trees will be more widely spaced."

"Our shield wall will not be of much use in the forest," added Nikandros. "Still, the men are well-trained to fight in free-for-alls. The archers and Íar's cavalry along with Eachdonn's men and riders will prove very useful."

Cian scratched at the sprinkling of gray bristles on his shaven head. "No matter what way you examine this, we're heavily outnumbered by an enemy who knows this land like the veins on his whore's tits. We need an edge or Drostan will exhaust us with constant ambushes."

"He can't be everywhere," Cúscraid said hopefully. "From what Eachdonn told us, this forest and Drostan's territory stretch to the coasts on the east and west."

Ròidh stood nearby with Fionnbharr and Brion's brother, Brocc. He coughed discreetly. "Spit it out son," Íar said. "If you've something to say, speak up."

The young man blushed heavily, but spoke clearly, "The Aos na Coille don't have many forts or brochs – or even settlements. Drostan has always seen the forest as his fortress, but I remember my father speaking about a trading settlement called A' Chrìon Làraich in one of the low valleys. It lies at the junction of several hunters' paths east of here. It would not be a long journey, though our supply wagons would likely make it slow."

Brion said, "What advantage does this get us over Drostan?"

A fleeting petulance crossed Ròidh's face. Like his father, he loved to talk. "Information from my father's informants points to several of Drostan's younger sons and daughters living in A' Chrìon Làraich."

"Hostages!" said Cian.

Nikandros grinned like a cat that had just snagged a mouse. "This could be the edge we need."

"Any idea how many warriors will be guarding the settlement or its defenses?" Cúscraid asked.

"No, but it's in the heart of Aos na Coille lands, protected by forests and high mountain ranges. Drostan likely wouldn't expect anyone to attack so deep into his territory. It may be only lightly defended," said Ròidh.

"On the other hand," said Brion, "it could be the most heavily defended part of Drostan's domain. I wouldn't expect Drostan to leave his children without protection."

"We need a strategy to get to A' Chrìon Làraich," said Íar and absentmindedly picked crumbs of food from his beard while everyone considered the idea. "In the meantime, Ròidh, take a squad of your riders and scout east. Find a path that will take the wagons and chariots. Mark out the areas that would be good ambush locations." The young warrior, eager to prove his worth, nodded and trotted off to select his men.

The leaders were deep in thought after assessing Ròidh's report. To the east, a small tributary flowed into the main river before it swept northward. At this point the land was rich and fertile. Its black soil supported a lush profusion of shrubs and trees making travel almost impassable. Cleared, it would make fine land for planting crops or grazing cattle.

There was a hunter's path and according to Ròidh if they continued eastwards they would eventually break through the forest and arrive at a great mountain range. Beinn an Laoigh, the highest permanently snow-covered peak, would be impossible for the army to traverse, but on its northern side was a small valley that by-passed the steepest tiers of the high mountains. The valley merged with a greater one that led east from the mountains and into the lowland forests surrounding A' Chrìon Làraich.

"The pathway through the wildwood will need widened for the wagons and chariots. Once we're through the worst there'll be more room in the older forest. It's our only real option," Cúscraid said. He waited for a response.

Nikandros' braided, blue-black tresses fell forward as he shook his head. "The moment we break camp here, Drostan will attack and harry us. It's certain that while we've been scouting and planning he's been gathering his warriors. It would take us at least a cycle of the moon to reach A' Chrìon Làraich – if we had a clear path, if we weren't being attacked, and if the weather stays reasonable."

"What if there was a way to get our bargaining pieces earlier?" All eyes turned to Cian. Having got their attention he continued, "Nikandros is right, but as well as that, A' Chrìon Làraich is nearly mid-way to Dùn Na Mèadaidh. We'd be half-way to our destination before we could use the hostages. And that's if we survive Drostan's ambushes and are in any state to fight a battle."

Momentarily, Íar looked puzzled, as did the others, but then he laughed, "You're suggesting a raid."

Cian nodded, "Indeed. We need the hostages sooner. So we go get them."

Nikandros slapped Cian on the back, "Not bad for an old man! A lifetime of beer and striapacha haven't addled your brain - yet!"

"Bloody, half-naked barbarian!"

Ignoring Cian's response, the Spartan spoke soberly, "For speed and surprise, it has to be a cavalry raid. Given that we don't know Drostan's strength at A' Chrìon Làraich, all the riders - ours and Eachdonn's will be needed. Íar, it has to be either you or me to lead."

"It would be better if you remained," said Íar scratching at his great, red beard. "Your battle experience together with Cúscraid, Brion and Cian will be needed to ensure there's an army to come back to. As always, we'll be in Cúscraid' hands for the defenses."

As expected, each day Drostan launched minor skirmishes to test their strength and delay them. The clashes resulted in few serious injuries to either side. Thus, the army reached the river tributary in good time and without much opposition.

To the west and north, thickly forested mountains swept down to the river's edge, while to the south and east, a seemingly endless, wooded valley guarded the army's rear.

As he surveyed the landscape with Nikandros and Brion, Cúscraid pointed to the languid river, "We'll build our camp from where the tributary flows into the main river and about two hundred paces west along the river bank. The main river is roughly fifty paces wide and the stream is around twenty. That gives a reasonable barrier on two sides. Plus, if we build where I'm proposing, we'll block the best ford.

"The next crossing is about three hundred paces downstream at a large sand bank. We'll seed the sand bank with caltrops and stakes. That should slow Drostan's attack and they'll be within reach of our arrows and javelins."

"How long will it take?" asked Brion.

"A man-high, double-walled stockade can be erected between two sunsets if we use all the men. I'm figuring on the camp being about two hundred paces each side. That way we can man the perimeter with half our men. The remainder will stand by as reserves.

"We'll dig a ditch on the western wall as I reckon that's where Drostan will attack. A single entrance will be on the forest side. Íar's men will protect everyone while they cut timber and erect the stockade, but once the camp walls are up then he and Ròidh can ride for A' Chrìon Làraich." Cúscraid paused then added soberly, "We might need to hold this camp for a while."

Íar looked at his friend quizzically. "That's a fair-sized encampment, Cúscraid. Are you sure it can be done?"

"Do we have a choice? Even at that size it will be a tight fit for men, wagons, chariots and any horses you don't take with you. But the men can suffer that for the short time we'll be here."

Íar stared at Cúscraid momentarily, and then grinned broadly, "Well, it's no drinking and an early to bed for you. It's a good job that you don't have your woman with you. She'd use up all your strength!"

Dawn broke with the *kraa kraa* of flocks of startled ravens. They took to the skies, disturbed by an army slashing and hacking at the dense undergrowth. The steady rhythm of axes against wood was followed by the groan and shriek of trees as they crashed to the forest floor. The men soon had little need for their layers of autumn clothing and discarded them, resulting in a continual round of strident cursing as brambles, thorns and thistles tore at exposed flesh.

The volunteers for digging the foundation ditches for the stockade posts and the two-man wide ditch on the southern and western sides sent furious oaths into the air as well while they fought with thistles, thorn stickers and the roots of the trees. In a short time, they were covered in a thick layer of mud that ran sliding and flowing, refilling their excavations as water from the river seeped into the ditches.

By mid-morning, the trees and undergrowth had been cleared as well as a wide area deep into the woods. The sounds of axe blades on trees continued as posts were cut and sharpened. Men coated in sweat and dirt grunted explosively and strained muscles as they dropped heavy wooden stakes into their allotted holes. A third of the length of each stake was buried while the remainder of its length, sharpened tip pointing skyward, remained visible. The finished stockade was shoulder height allowing for flexibility of weapons while holding a solid footing.

At dusk, flares of teal, yellow and red flickered from blazing camp fires - testament to the many varieties of wood used in the construction of the camp. The twilight air was pleasantly refreshing. Scents of wood smoke, pine, birch and peat mingled, overwhelming the pungent odors of sweat and dirt. Exhausted, satisfied warriors with bloodied and blistered hands were thankful for the salves provided by Fionnbharr and his small band of healers. The abundant supply of beer and other special brews also helped.

Íar's broad smile mirrored the depth of respect with which he held Cúscraid. Even to the casual observer, it was plain to see that Cúscraid had not allowed trees to be chopped down randomly. The southern and western walls were not only protected by deep ditches filled with sharpened stakes and thorn bushes, but also before them lay open spaces — killing grounds - that stretched out for several hundred paces beyond the ditches. The dirt from the excavations had been piled up on the outer edges of the ditches along with any unused tree limbs and branches.

Cúscraid and Íar praised the gangs of men as they walked the perimeter. Most had collapsed where they had worked, asking for food and drink to be brought to them. Íar's admiration of the double wall of stakes tied together with ropes and supported by banks of dirt was obvious. He was amazed at the efficiency with which Cúscraid and Cian had marshaled their labor. Noticing the revision that Cúscraid had made to his original plan, the massive warrior smiled. The camp now had two entrances. One faced south towards the ancient forest and the mountains, the other faced west, allowing the army to fight on the cleared ground if needed.

As he observed his work, Cúscraid allowed himself a smile of satisfaction. "Maybe we can introduce Drostan to the shield wall after all."

The day had not been without its challenges - or casualties. Aos na Coille warriors sent by Drostan to disrupt the work at the camp attempted to wade across the shallow ford. The first few warbands were surprised and turned back by a hail of iron from Áine's archers. Naked bodies were no match for the black-shafted barbs. Before long, the clear, cold waters of the meandering river were tinted with swirls of blood. Lifeless bodies floated downstream and became stranded on the river's many sand bars. More and more warbands were pushed into the battle by Drostan's chieftains. Eventually their sheer numbers and use of throwing axes forced Áine's band of archers to seek cover.

As he watched Áine being forced backwards and the river crowded with Drostan's men, Íar decided it was time to enter the fray. Five hundred horses galloping along the narrow strip of dirt between the river and the stockade turned it into a quagmire. Javelins were drawn and hurled. Drostan's warriors screamed as the swirling designs and blue paint of their spiritual armor yielded to the arms-length, iron spikes. Men and women entered Mag Mell in a welter of blood and gore.

Their javelins exhausted, the riders turned their mounts crashing into the river. Swords and axes were quickly drawn from leather-covered sheaths. In the bloody, muddied waters horses and men thrashed around seeking space and advantage. Blades slashed downwards cracking skulls, carving shoulders and opening up backs. Exposed bones glistened white in the morning sun. Relentlessly, the Aos na Coille warriors were forced back to the northern side of river.

The slaughter in the river abated when both sides, having gained the measure of each other, withdrew to their own ground. The rustle of feathers and the *kraa kraa* of ravens filled the air as the flocks took wing. Scavengers roused from hiding eagerly feasted on the unexpected bounty.

Harsh, guttural commands were relayed across the forest slopes to warbands further along the river. Howls of fury accompanied the next wave of attackers. Iron nails and sharpened wood spiked bare feet as the warriors tread across the downstream sandbar. Shrieks of pain pierced the air. The unfortunate who tripped or were pushed aside by their comrades were impaled multiple times. The coarse white sand was soaked garnet-red and the blood of the brave leached into the slow moving waters. Those who managed to negotiate the field of spikes fell to the spears of Ròidh's horsemen.

"In the name of the gods, what are the bastards up to?" Drostan stood next to his tànaiste – his second-in-command, Bearach, as the sun set and gestured at the fort that had risen from the woods. He was annoyed, although this had more to do with being caught wrong-footed than at the loss of several hundred men. Drostan's plans to use the forest to harry the invaders had been rendered obsolete. "Call the Comhairle-Chatha – the High Council. New plans need to be discussed."

In the camp, Íar made sure his men tended to their mounts. Each was brushed, fed and watered, and checked for minor cuts and bruises that could deteriorate on the journey. It was his intention to ride out before sunrise on the next day. Íar glanced over at Ròidh and smiled approvingly at the young warrior. He too was ensuring his men had their ponies ready.

Íar observed that Ròidh more than once took measure of the powerful and taller horses of Íar's warriors. There was a fleeting tinge of sadness and envy in Ròidh Mac Eachdonn's eyes as he weighed the two breeds. Like his father, he loved their ponies, but these great beasts were in another class. The young man sighed, and with an affectionate slap on his pony's flank, turned his focus back to ensuring the beast was in top condition.

Ròidh was startled at Íar's booming voice directly behind him. "We gave the king, your father, a gift of horses. It seems only right that his son who fights alongside us should also receive a similar gift." Ròidh turned to see Cúscraid, Brion and Cian standing with broad smiles on their faces. Nikandros led forward a beautiful chestnut stallion, sixteen hands high and offered the reins to Ròidh. Íar stated the obvious, "He's a good horse, take care of him – or answer to me."

The horse snickered as Ròidh stroked his long forehead and then snorted, tossing his head up and down. "Oh you'd better give him a few parsnips," Íar added. "That one has always had a bit of an attitude. He's likely to pee or shite on you if you annoy him!" With a laugh the men left an astonished but happy Ròidh to get to know his new mount.

CHAPTER 6

At the lagoon, the day was greeted with long sighs of relief as men emptied overnight bladders into the pond, and a broadside of farting as each man tried to outdo his neighbor. Arching an eyebrow at Mórrígan, Mongfhionn said, "Well, I am not bathing in *that* water this morning."

Mórrígan smiled. She could not understand the Sidhe's need to bathe every day, especially since Mongfhionn's milk-white body was totally free of hair - apart from her head. Mórrígan's habit was to bathe at the beginning of each quarter of the moon. She considered this to be more than enough and she had a lush red bush between her legs. As she yawned and stretched, the musky underarm fragrance of stale sweat wafted upwards and her nose crinkled. "Perhaps I missed a quarter," she murmured.

Cooking fires were stoked and crackled happily in concert with the dawn chorus. In anticipation of another hard day of rowing, the men ate heartily of rabbit stew, oatmeal and cheese, washed down with honeyed beer or spring water.

Under Pytheas' watchful direction, the galleys were carried to the beach and launched. This morning, the vessels were escorted along the narrow strip of water by a pod of curious black-headed seals. Rowers bending to their work watched enviously as the sleek bodies moved effortlessly through the water.

The morning wind was light and the square black sails flapped in accompaniment with the strike of oars. By and by the rhythm of the slap and swish of oars absorbed the minds of all as they sailed northeast along a great rocky landmass. Spirits were buoyant. The early morning sun had little strength, but was a welcome change from the rain. Faces were flushed red from the exercise and high-lighted with lines and circles of salt from the spray. Most, including Conall, had lost their sickly green-gray pallor, and few felt the need to throw up at the slightest wavelet. In fact, Conall was starting to enjoy the solitude of rowing.

By mid-morning they entered the narrows. At high tide, the is-land they passed was little more than a rock and was dwarfed by the breathtaking dark beauty of the mainland. The fleet left the narrows and struck out northwest into open waters that led to a long, narrow island and the start of the sea loch of An Linne Sheileach.

At first Conall thought it spray from the sea that splattered on his thighs, but the droplets dried without leaving the usual trace of salt. The skies glowered. As the galleys skirted the island, heavy clouds of ash-gray and purple were backlit with the occasional flash of lighting thrown by the gods, their mocking voices heard in the rolling thunder. Conall gazed in awe and felt the wind increase. He watched, mesmerized, as a solid curtain of rain rushed towards the ships.

"Furl the sails," Pytheas shouted, suddenly aware of the dan-ger. "Drop the masts. Row into the waves. Keep the bow facing into the wind." Twenty pairs of oars propelled each galley into the jaws of the squall. The storm's leading edge pockmarked the rising swell. Sheets of rain and hail swept from bow to stern as the boats struggled to keep moving forward. Those not manning oars grabbed anything that would hold water and frantically bailed out the mix of saltwater, ice and rain.

Battered by the wind, the fleet's speed dropped dramatically. To Conall, it seemed they were buffeted by the tempest for a long time, but the storm proved fast moving, eager to test its strength farther afield. It lashed the fleet with a final flourish of lightning and thun-der and moved on. The ships wallowed, drifting and bobbing on the swell. Exhausted rowers lay over their oars and retched in the aftermath of the intense battle with nature. The storm had passed, but the creeping blast of coldness had not. In a short time the naked men were shivering violently and teeth chattered. Hands and feet became numb, movement sluggish and clumsy.

"Get them moving, Conall," Pytheas glanced with alarm around the galleys. Near panic, he shouted louder, "Get them moving or we'll perish on the seas." He stumbled to the stern, grabbed the drum and with clumsy, wax-white hands began to thump out a beat. "Row you bastards. Row or die!"

The oarsmen in each ship sensed rather than heard the deep, insistent beat of the pace drum. At the bows, Mongfhionn and Mórrígan stood - arms wide, as they chanted, urging the men back from their torpor and prevailing upon the Goddess for mercy. Conall snapped himself alert. "Fight!" he roared in anger, taking hold of his oar. "Fight as though you were on the battlefield." Soon the clumsy movements of the nearly dead became a fluid rhythm as muscles warmed and brains were freed of the numbing fog of cold.

Mongfhionn paced up the center of her craft cajoling Fearghal and his men into action. The tall warrior glared at her, "Some help with the weather you are!" he said, referring to the Sidhe's powers to command earth, water and skies. His reward was a stinging smack across his scarred, bristle-covered face.

"If the Goddess had wanted us dead, we would be dead. Get these men rowing. Follow Conall and alert the other galleys. We are not safe yet."

Fearghal ruefully rubbed his reddening cheek, "You can sure deliver a slap, but so can I on that fine arse of yours," he said, with a glint in his eye. Pretending she had not heard, but inwardly chuckling, Mongfhionn made her way to the bow as Fearghal thundered out, "Pick up your oars. Row!"

The world became a lighter shade of gray as dark clouds scurried from the skies. Late afternoon, eight galleys crunched onto the pebbles of a narrow beach near the far end of the island. The land beyond was hilly and spartan. Sandy slopes were held in place with hardy dune grasses, brightly colored wildflowers and bushes ran almost to the water's edge.

"Pull the boats in and secure them," Conall called out hoarsely, "then unload." He pointed inland, "We'll make camp over the lip of that dune. Light the fires. Pytheas, we'll examine the galleys for damages in the morning."

Hauling with the rest, Conall chuckled. "We should put some clothes on to save the women's blushes," he said, provoking a cheer from the men. "Although, seeing what the cold has done to our cocks maybe we should be embarrassed!"

Blazing fires with their smoky bouquet warmed spirits and bodies. A defensive circle of thorn bushes and sharpened spikes enclosed the weary travelers. Sizzling food accompanied by beer heated by red-hot daggers encouraged everyone to relax and the craic to flow.

"I hope you're not considering galleys being a permanent part of the army, Fearghal Ruad," said one of the veteran warriors looking sternly at Fearghal before his face broke into a wide smirk. "Too much bloody work!"

Laughter rippled around the campfires and dozens of conversations tumbled around as each warrior related increasingly exaggerated stories of giant hail, of selkies and sea monsters that only they saw and of the huge fish that they almost teased from the waves. Shattered from the day's activities, the men wrapped their brats around them and fell into a well-deserved sleep.

Conall drew Torcán and Deaglán aside the next morning. "Finish your meal, then take a few men and scout south and north." The two friends nodded and loped off to find their men.

After inspecting the men and their armor and weapons, Fearghal and Conall tramped to the shoreline with Pytheas to inspect the galleys. "I'm not sure what's worse," Fearghal grumbled, "being stuck on this rock or crossing these waters."

The Greek was pleasantly surprised that, although his ships had taken a beating in the storm, they remained in good order. Several masts needed strengthened, tears in the square sails required stitching and cables tightened. The galleys remained watertight mainly because of the in-built tension between the cables and the hull – an advantage of their design. "Two sunsets, maybe three, should repair any damage from the storm and we can resume our journey," he said. "Thankfully, we are now in An Linne Sheileach and the waters should be much easier to navigate."

Mid-morning, Deaglán returned reporting that the northern part of the island appeared to be unpopulated apart from a few scattered crofts. It was mid-day when Torcán arrived back. He described a large broch only a morning's march south from the camp. Situated on a rocky crag that overlooked the east coast, the gray-stone broch was about thirty paces wide and twice as tall. There were steep slopes on the northwest and southeast sides, but easy approaches on the northeast and the southwest. To no-one's surprise, the latter were guarded by stone walls.

Blue-gray smoke from peat fires had been filtering out of the thick thatched roof. By Torcán's account it appeared that the broch was home to the extended family of the island's chieftain. Likely the compound only had fifteen or twenty warriors together with their women and children.

"The broch's no threat," Conall thought as he helped manhandle a splintered mast from one of the galleys onto the beach, but he gave Torcán another set of instructions. "Keep a watch on the broch. If they don't disturb us, we'll not bother them."

Torcán acknowledged this and was about to walk away when Fearghal's voice boomed out, "You didn't mention the ages of the women in that broch." Amid hoots of laughter from the men he added, "Keep your cock in your pants, Torcán ó Dubhghaill!" Torcán was twenty-one summers. While steadfast and the bravest of warriors, Torcán was rarely burdened by common sense. This, in addition to his muscular body, rakish good looks and impressive manhood meant that he was every father's nightmare.

Torcán rolled his eyes and grinned, "I won't do anything you wouldn't do, Fearghal."

"And we all know where that has lead," said Mongfhionn.

CHAPTER 7

Night was fast drawing in and the little girl knew she had strayed well beyond the limits set by her mother. Morna looked around, not overly concerned. The only animals she was likely to meet were some stray cattle or sheep from her father's herds and she well knew the path back to her home. Morna was ten summers old. She smiled through as yet unspoiled teeth and pushed flowing red tresses back from her pale face. Her berry-stained hand left reddish-purple streaks of juice on lightly freckled cheeks. If anything, the added coloring made the child prettier.

The stranger offered a hand and she took it with innocent trust. They strolled across the moors through the fields of purple heather that Morna loved until they came to a great stone atop a raised mound of dirt and rock. She knew the stone well and had often played in its shadow. Carved with intricate designs it seemed to resonate with a strange power. Many years ago, during a violent storm, the stone had tumbled over and now lay prone on the ground. With the stranger's help, the little girl happily jumped up onto the flat, gray slab. She smiled once more at the shadowed face of the hooded and black-cloaked stranger.

The Blood Moon rested on the horizon, watching, bathing the land in cerise-red. Dark clouds scurried across its face. Ravens crossed the orb before seeking refuge in the sparse clusters of trees that bordered the still waters. There was an instant of calm silence before the shriek of the bean-sidhe shattered the night.

Gray cloak flaring, the Sidhe stormed about the camp, pacing restlessly, her agitation increasing with each step. Her eyes burned the color of the moon. Men shrank back from her fierce countenance as they sought the safety of the fires. She chanted strange words over and over as if trying to call on ancient powers to repel primal demons. In response, sheets of lightning sporadically lit up the night.

On the other side of the camp, Mórrígan ignored the thorn barrier that tore at her naked body and stumbled across the boundary. Her designs shimmered in the light of the fires taking on the color of the hunter's moon. She mumbled incantations that had no meaning – even to the Sidhe.

Mongfhionn stared at Mórrígan as she approached and breathed out a one word accusation. "Why?"

Mórrígan's dark, vacant eyes took on a wild, yet pleading aspect. "Others," she rasped. Tadhg, who had been standing nearby caught his queen as she collapsed. The young man was startled when a flash of lightning revealed teeth and lips stained with blood. Fragments of what appeared to be skin and fur hung from her fingernails.

Around the campfires, men with stunned and nervous expressions looked to Conall and Fearghal. "On your feet," Conall called out. "Full armor and weapons. Man the perimeter. Pytheas, once we've had a roll call take enough men to protect the galleys." Everyone stood rooted to the spot, "Now!" he roared.

Fearghal looked sourly at Mongfhionn, "Explain. That was the bean-sidhe's call. Yet you stand before us. Why?"

Mongfhionn inclined her head and having collected her thoughts snapped, "I am not the only sidhe in the world. It was one of my lesser half-sisters most likely." While outwardly calm, Mongfhionn was agitated that she had not felt the close presence of another sidhe.

"Someone has died."

It was a statement rather than a question and Mongfhionn bent her head in confirmation. "My sister will not depart without knowing that the ribbon connecting a soul with its body has been severed."

In some disquiet, Conall joined them, "I've settled Mórrígan. Tadhg and Urard will keep a watch over her. She's in shock and has been badly cut by the thorn bushes." Absentmindedly he rubbed his throbbing forehead in an attempt to make sense of the evening's course. Then he said, "Torcán is missing."

"Shite! Let's hope he's between some girl's legs rather than in the arms of the Goddess," said Fearghal. "There's not much can be accomplished before daylight. I'll organize the men into watches."

Conall agreed. Still unbalanced by Mórrígan's actions and appearance he walked, shoulders slumped, to the campfire. The ever faithful Urard towered over his charge. Plainly confused and distressed, the giant said, "The queen. I never saw her leave." Curtly waving the huge warrior aside, Conall lay down beside his queen and took her in his arms until she rested in a fitful sleep.

With his usual sense of decorum, a bleary-eyed Torcán staggered into the camp at sunrise and shouted, "What's to eat? I'm starved!" Fearghal strode over and smacked him in the jaw. It would be some days before Torcán could eat solid food again. As he struggled to rise, an oak staff thumped his chest and then rested its gnarled head on his throat, the pressure just enough to let him breathe.

"Where have you been?" a grim-faced Mongfhionn hissed through gleaming white teeth. To a confused Torcán, they looked very much like sharp fangs. He saw that swords were drawn and several of his comrades were fingering their axes. Mystified at what his crime could be he sensed that honesty would be his best defense and smiled weakly.

"One of the girls from the broch was very pretty," he muttered.

Fearghal raised his fist again and Torcán flinched, "By the Hag, boy. You were supposed to be watching. That cock will get you killed. Did you not hear the bean-sidhe?" He turned and stomped away in frustration.

Mongfhionn, her staff still resting on Torcán's throat, bent over,

"Hear me well, Torcán ó Dubhghaill. You may rut and ride all the pretty girls that spread their thighs for you, but if you don't keep your wits someone will cut your balls off." With that the Sidhe twisted the staff enough to leave a reddening bruise on Torcán's throat, then turned and strode to join Conall and Fearghal. Only on his deathbed would the reddish-purple bruise fade from Torcán's throat.

"My caomhnóirí and the archers will search in the direction of the broch." Conall said. "The rest will remain and guard the camp and galleys. I'll take Torcán - if only because at least he knows the path — and is familiar with one of the locals."

Mongfhionn nodded, "I'm coming with you."

"So am I." The group turned as one to see Mórrígan, her eyes bloodshot and with shadows under them from a lack of sleep. She wore her armor and was accompanied by Urard and Tadhg. Conall sighed and signaled his consent.

The great rock lay mid-way between the camp and the broch. On this day it was marked by a circlet of ravens. They soared high above, their feathers glistening blue-black against silver-gray skies. The fowls' usual raucous *kraa kraa* had taken on a mournful resonance. An overcast morning and the muted rumble of distant thunder matched the somber mood of the group as they approached.

As the band got closer, a small bundle of what appeared to be rags was lifted by the wind from the motionless object atop the stone and flapped onto the path. Conall picked it up and grimaced before passing it on to Mongfhionn. It was a small child's léine — not unlike those his daughters wore. The light-colored cloth was stained red and torn. A single tear coursed down the Sidhe's cheek. The archers formed a skirmish line and with a leaden heart Conall led his men forward.

A piteous sight met the group and one that seared the minds of each present. It would haunt the dreams of many for the remainder of their days. The fathers among them wept openly, the younger men tried in vain to forestall their tears. A corpse, for the spirit of the little girl was long gone, was stretched naked over the rock. The once vibrant green eyes were open, frozen in time – a reflection of the shock of her last memories.

Once garish and rose-pink, the slash across her throat had dulled to purple-blue. The child's blood stained the granite rock, damming it for eternity, and lay congealed in black pools on the dirt and mosses. Even the battle-hardened warriors blanched at the gaping wound in the child's chest. Her heart had been ripped out.

Ashen-faced, Conall turned to Mongfhionn and Mórrígan, "By the Hag, someone will pay for the blood of this innocent. I don't care who it is. I swear, their heart will be torn from their body, but they will suffer much more and longer before that." The firmly clenched jaw and the direction of his steel-gray eyes left Mongfhionn and Mórrígan in little doubt as to where his suspicions fell.

Shaking off her shock at the broken child, Mongfhionn reached upwards to unclasp her cloak. Her hand briefly touched upon the black ribbon that hid her scar. The Sidhe trembled as memories of her younger sisters' tragic sacrifice and a Roman blade being drawn across her throat overwhelmed the peace she had achieved since the death of Primus Pilus, Spurius Sulpicia Longus. As she laid her gray cloak over Morna, blood-tears stained her pure white dress. Her arms rose as she prayed to the Goddess for journeying mercies to Tir inna n-Óc.

The wrath in the Sidhe's face was clear to all as she stepped back from the stone altar. While the child's sacrifice bore the hallmark of Mongfhionn's previous sacrifices, Conall was less certain about the Sidhe's involvement and more troubled at the implications for Mórrígan.

As they struggled - with little success, to understand the savage scene, harried voices signaled a second group approaching from the direction of the broch. A woman broke from the advancing band and ran to the stone. For the second time, a soul-piercing shriek echoed over the land. This time it was not the cry of the bean-sidhe, but of a distraught mother.

Her cries were joined by the wailing and tears of the rest of the group. Their leader – the girl's father, stood apart from his people. Grim-faced, he stared at Conall with a deep hatred, "Bastards. Murderers. Rapists. The depths of the Otherworld are too good for you. The Hag take your souls for this obscenity."

Conall stepped forward to protest their innocence, but spear heads were quickly lowered. In response, came the soft whisper of swords and axes clearing leather scabbards and bow-staffs straining as strings were pulled to rest against tear-stained cheeks. Conall shook his head to those with him. "In honor of the child put the weapons away. We will withdraw."

He turned back to the distraught father and held up his hands, palms forward, "This was none of our doing. We mourn your loss. We will depart," he said. Conall knew in his heart that the father did not believe him.

Pytheas was urged to make the galleys ready for sailing at sunrise the following day. The Greek sailor knew the situation was fraught with danger and organized his men plus the additional help assigned to him into work teams. Fearghal walked with Conall along new defenses hastily erected on the lip of land bordering the beach. Small, half-arm's length stakes, for there was little wood to be had, were driven into the sandy ground and thorn bushes placed around them.

"It's a bad business, Fearghal," Conall said as he stared into the distance.

"Even worse when the two most likely suspects appear to be within our camp," Fearghal replied. "Who can say, but the child's family may have right on their side?" Fearghal had disclosed Nikandros' misgivings about Mórrígan's darker nature and the bloody incident at Taobh Builleach where she had, with relish, slowly dragged a blade across a prisoner's throat. At first angry at what he heard and of what his queen was being accused, Conall conceded that Mórrígan had become a disturbing conundrum. A devoted mother to their son and daughters, Mórrígan had never really cleansed the rage and bitterness of her parent's death from her heart. This darkness blighted her spirit.

"There has to be another explanation, Fearghal, but I'm at a loss to know what it is. It will be a sad and sorry day if we have to move against Mórrígan or Mongfhionn."

Fearghal breathed in slowly and then sighed in agreement. He observed the huge frame of Urard standing guard over the queen, and then at the Sidhe silhouetted against the horizon, her hands clenched and railing against unknown forces. "There will be a lot of blood. That is the one certainty," he said.

Under flickering torchlight a mournful camp listened to the rasp of saws and dull thumping of hammers on wood as the galleys were repaired. The warm glow from the fires and a clear night sky filled with stars failed to dispel the sense of dread that many felt. Few stomachs could face food or drink. They all just wanted to be off the cursed island.

Conall's caomhnóirí stood along the makeshift stockade, alert, javelins stabbed into the earth, swords and shields at the ready. The remaining men were kept in reserve. None feared a fight. Most enjoyed the heat of battle, but few wanted what was coming. In their hearts they prayed that the islanders would stay away. They also knew if they were the child's family, even the gods would not prevent them taking vengeance on those held responsible.

Torches glimmered yellow along the defenses, their smoky trails just visible in the fading light of dusk. A subdued Torcán made his way to where his king was standing and bowed. In a voice husky with emotion he said, "They're coming." Mórrígan's archers had taken up position a hundred paces out, although the queen remained within the camp. Now, as ordered, they withdrew behind the caomhnóirí.

Conall nodded, "Remind the men that we'll not engage unless attacked."

Fearghal snorted as Torcán moved away, "You can't tie the men's hands behind their backs, Conall. It will cause more problems than help." Settling his helmet on red hair sprinkled with silver, he strode to his assigned place. Conall grimaced and resignedly tightened the leather ties on his own helmet. The black plumes rising from the gold raven on the helmet's crest hung strangely limp.

Shouts and cries for vengeance broke the twilight air as men and women at first pale-gray and wraith-like in the failing light took on corporeal form. About seventy attackers – men and women of all ages, naked except for their blue paint and imprinted designs, threw themselves in a frenzy at the defenses without caution for their safety.

"The Goddess have mercy on us," a shocked Torcán gestured at the attackers. Short wooden pickets snapped as women threw themselves across the stakes and thorns. Moans of pain rose up as sharp, ragged wood punched through soft flesh. The warrior's distress deepened further as he recognized the young woman who had favored him the previous day. Across the barrier, he pleaded with her, but her eyes were wild and unfocused and her ears deaf to his exhortations. She was soon entangled in the thorns.

"Good tactics - if pitiless, Conall," Fearghal roared in consternation over the shouts of the islanders. "They're using their women's bodies to bridge our defenses." The tall warrior, a king in his own right, turned to beseech Mongfhionn, "Can you not do something?"

The Sidhe shook her head, "Their minds are closed. They have no fear of death." Eyes black as night held Conall's stare. "Attack. Take as many prisoners as possible. You'll demonstrate more compassion by showing no mercy."

Torn, but unwilling to see his men put at risk, Conall bellowed a command that soured his stomach, "Archers, a single volley into the attackers. Caomhnóirí, form the wall on the outside of the defenses." The bowmen wavered, spurring Conall to fury. "Shoot!" he thundered. "There will be lashes for all, if one hesitates."

Heavy sighs preceded the creak of bows and the thrum of arrows. Shrieks of pain mingled with cries for revenge as arrowheads pierced unprotected flesh. The previously united assault faltered briefly in expectation of another volley. It gave Conall's men enough time to cross the defenses to counter the attack. Thorns tore at their leggings, but did not stop their response.

As Conall's caomhnóirí pushed the attackers back with shields and javelins, Deaglán and Torcán's men ran wide and marched in on the left and right flanks. The pinchers closed. Furiously and relentlessly, men and women threw themselves at the shield wall pounding it in frustration and anger with spears, axes, clubs, daggers and bloody hands. The lucky were bludgeoned to the ground by the raven-emblazoned shields and then kicked senseless to ensure they remained prone. The persistent were impaled on iron spikes and blades.

At the end, his people dead, injured or unconscious, only the child's father continued to rail against the shields. It was plain the man, although late in summers and carrying an excess of weight, had once been a fierce warrior. In frustration he swung again and again at the shields with his axe, but the wall slowly retreated, refusing to fight. As the exhausted man paused, Conall stepped forward. The father with tears rolling down painted cheeks immediately gathered his depleted strength and rushed forward. "Child-murderer," he roared.

He was intercepted and his head separated from his neck by Fearghal's keen-edged longsword. Gouts of blood spurted skywards before the headless body pitched forward to lie twitching on the ground. The head rolled several paces before finally resting. To those present it appeared to be still mouthing curses. Conall looked questioningly at his battle commander and friend.

Fearghal shook his head wearily, "For him, it was a mercy. I hope he has peace in Mag Mell. If his woman is alive we'd be doing her a favor if we gave her a sharp blade. Now I'm going to get drunk." Then he walked back to the camp.

Fall's waning strength allowed a foretaste of winter's rising power in the cold, damp morning. Men shivered around the blazing fires as they forced down food and beer. Although nourishing, the meal was cheerless and swallowed mechanically. Knotted stomachs resisted, but the men knew they needed fuel for the day's work.

They glanced frequently at the small circle of prisoners who stared back with brooding eyes. The group remained defiant, their anger unabated. Of the attackers, less than half had survived the assault. Several had died during the night, refusing to accept help from the healers. Others weakened from their injuries were unlikely to survive the coming winter.

Sensing Conall's thoughts Mongfhionn spoke, "They have the broch, Conall. They have a strong place to build from and herds of cattle and sheep. And there are enough women of child-bearing age to revive their community."

"The child has had no justice, My Lady, and those who committed the atrocity may well be within my camp."

The Sidhe rounded angrily on Conall, "Enough of your complaining, Conall Mac Gabhann. Be a king. Find out who sacrificed the girl. Administer justice – no matter who it may be."

"And what if the guilt lies at the feet of the mother of my children?" he asked fixing his steel-gray eyes on Mongfhionn. "Or the guardian of my children?"

"You're a king. Deal with it." Mongfhionn's words hung in the air as she swirled her cloak and turned to stride away.

Pytheas appeared at Conall's side. "The galleys are ready. Let's leave this cursed island. New challenges will take the men's minds off the horrors the gods have visited upon us."

Conall heaved a great sigh and called Mórrígan, Fearghal, Deaglán and Torcán. "Get the men on the galleys, and then release the prisoners. Leave them enough weapons to defend themselves." To Mórrígan he added, "The archers will board first. Guard the men as they embark." The queen's face was haggard and pale in the gray dawn, yet she was grateful to be assigned a task. She bowed and trotted over to her band.

To Torcán's astonishment and relief, the girl he had mounted, although covered in cuts and wounds from the vicious thorns, had survived. He had spent most of the night trying to convince her to come with them, but with no apparent success. As his men boarded, Torcán once more appealed to the young woman of no more than fifteen summers, only to see her curse him and spit in his face. Deaglán, saddened to see the anguish of his friend, went to his side and put his hand on his shoulder. "You've tried your best. Leave her. It's time to go."

Salty tears left translucent tracks on Torcán's smoke-stained face. With slumped shoulders he turned his back and clambered aboard the galley. There was a scream as the vessel slid into the shallow waters. Curious, the men turned around to watch as the young girl stripped off her remaining clothes and dashed into the cold sea. As she reached the galley, scarred and calloused hands grabbed and hauled her aboard.

Standing proud, her breasts heaving, she glowered at the men. Then with sharp, gold-flecked eyes she held Torcán's gaze without flinching. In a barely understandable burr she said, "My name is Gràinne. I have no family. I have no one. You thrust your manhood into me, you can feed me!"

"Seems like a fair trade to me, Torcán," a voice from the rear of the galley called out irreverently. "She's young, but has a good pair of tits and a nice arse. If you don't want her I'll be happy to take your place."

"She'll fit right in with the others," another added. "Apart from the bush between their thighs, they're more often naked than clothed!"

Both Gràinne and Torcán glared at the taunts. "Pass me a cloak," said Torcán. Then he grinned, "Take up your oars, you bastards. I want you rowing with both hands." The men roared with laughter and the boat moved effortlessly out into the middle of the loch.

CHAPTER 8

Brion, Cúscraid and Nikandros walked the perimeter fence, sharing the early morning craic with the men. They smiled at the raven-emblazoned flags and banners flapping in the morning breeze. Conall's army had staked out its territory challenging the watchers in the woods.

Pre-dawn river smoke drifted over the waters. Nature stirred from its slumbers with random splashes of fish, the whisper of tree branches as birds took flight and the snarling of predators as they awakened to an empty belly. Curses and grunts from the intruders added to the confusion of sounds. Men stretched, slapped their limbs and massaged stiff muscles to spur their circulation. They complained of real and imagined aches and pains and then of the weather – pleasant as it was at this time, everyone knew it would get worse. It was sure to rain.

The night-watch had been relieved and was taking the benefit of the warmth radiating from the fire pits. Bubbling hot stews and gruel cooked in great iron cauldrons blackened with soot filled their bellies. After a round of farting and burping many wrapped a brat around themselves and fell asleep around the fires. Others found a corner to shelter. None cared about the increasing noise generated by the camp. It was a comfort.

Two hundred men, in full battle armor, stood alert along each side of the fence. The men knew they were different, an oddity. In a land where warriors fought naked and put their faith in the swirling sigils that covered their bodies, these men from Ériu wore leather inlaid with iron scales. A few of the leaders were attired in sleeveless chain mail. The mail was draped over soft leather or woolen shirts and covered by a light woolen tunic.

All wore helmets. With wealth gained from battle spoils these very functional protectors were quickly becoming ornately decorated with silver, gold and bronze embellishments. The warriors each carried a curved, oblong shield that stretched from chin to knee. Each shield was decorated with a black raven on a field of crimson. The shields were constructed conventionally with wood and iron and were covered in felt. Since tin was much more plentiful in Albu, there were rumors that in the future the shields would be faced with bronze.

Double-edged short swords sharpened to a vicious cutting edge were sheathed in beautifully designed and crafted scabbards. When in formation, each man and woman carried four javelins – three for throwing, one for stabbing. The javelin was a simple yet deadly weapon – an arm's length spike of iron joined to an ash shaft. Most carried a preferred weapon – their favorite axe or longsword, for when they were allowed to fight "old style" with no constraints. Many had several daggers and knives of various shapes and sizes for throwing, stabbing – or just carving food. For the ones who enjoyed closer contact their hands were enclosed in battle-gloves made of leather strips studded with short iron spikes.

It was a time when barbarians - a name used to describe anyone outside of the tribe, fought as a screaming - often drunken horde, throwing themselves at their enemies in a furious rage and hoping to overwhelm with numbers. Conall's fighters favored an alternate tactic. They fought in a shield-wall. In this wall of interlocked shields, every man stood firm, and every man protected his neighbor. Often well outnumbered by their enemies, Conall's men put their faith in the flesh, bone and muscle of their comrades. The discipline of the wall, not stone or wood, was their bulwark.

"Do we have a plan?" Brion asked wryly.

"If we're quiet and keep our heads below the fence maybe Drostan will think we've run off," said Cúscraid.

"Everyone's a smart-arse this morning." Nikandros gave his companions a friendly thump and then his dark eyes sharpened. "Seems to me the question is – do we stay inside the fortifications and defend? Or do we take the attack to Drostan?"

"Is there a choice?" All three turned as Cian joined their circle. "Likely, Drostan's men are already staring at us from the cover of the forests. He has the initiative and the numbers. We can't risk sending scouts - or Áine's archers, into that wildwood. They'd be dead by the time they got a few paces in or away from the banks of the rivers."

Nikandros sighed in resignation, "So we wait."

Across the river, Drostan scratched his stubbled chin and reviewed the situation with Bearach. "Ten thousand men stand awaiting my orders and I can call on three times as many. They have just over two thousand. Why am I hesitant?"

Bearach, while a formidable warrior, had little use for strategic planning. In fact, he was quite happy to throw men or women into battle as long as they weren't his family – or at least the kin he favored. He also had little comprehension about what constituted a rhetorical question and so grunted an answer, "Attack at once on all sides and with our full force. They will break. We'll slaughter them and take their gold. That's the end of it."

Drostan shook his head, "Oh if it were that simple. Why are they here and not marching towards Dùn Na Mèadaidh?" Bearach shrugged, waiting impatiently for the inevitable command.

Finally, Drostan said, "Signal the horns. Send in the first wave."

Building to a crescendo in the dense woods, the sound of long-necked, bronze war horns gave forth with their loud and mournful *barrr-ewww*. The forest became a heaving, howling beast as several thousand naked warriors plunged into the river waters on two sides of the camp, while the same number broke from the tree-line and raced across the open ground west of the camp.

    David H. Millar

"By the Hag," Cúscraid complained, "I think I'm going deaf with the racket they're making." He stood alongside the bronze-armored Spartan and settled his helmet on his head. "Hold fast. Javelins at the ready. Wait until they hit the edge of the ditch. Send the painted bastards to Mag Mell."

Nikandros smiled thinly and brushed the crimson plumes of his bronze helmet. With slow deliberation, he settled it on his head and hefted his javelin in readiness. His beloved doru, a black, ash-shafted spear as long as one and a half men and topped with a vicious spear-head, lay at his feet. He glanced to his right with a sharp pang of apprehension as he beheld his adopted son, Cathán. Orphaned five years ago by the raid that slaughtered his family, the diminutive boy of ten summers had found refuge in the equally solitary Spartan.

It was often remarked how the young man had grown strikingly like his new father. At fifteen summers old, he was a head shorter than the tall warrior. Under Nikandros' strict, sometimes brutal, style of training he was rapidly becoming an accomplished warrior and had earned his right to stand in the wall. Cathán had eschewed the normal armor of his friends in favor of the bronzed cuirass and greaves worn by Nikandros. Nevertheless, his bravery did not extend to wearing the short red tunic favored by his adoptive father. Taking his cue from Nikandros, Cathán raised his javelin.

"Keep your head. Don't do anything stupid. Stay at my side," the Spartan murmured before howling his battle cry at the attackers.

On the north-facing wall, Brion's mien reflected deep concern for the alabaster-skinned woman to his left. Áine's waist-length, lustrous black hair was held tightly back from her face in intricate plaits and pinned with two long slivers of metal. She had assured him they were not just for decoration. Still, Brion was thankful that, like him, the mother of his son had chosen to wear a tunic of chainmail. It had taken her a while to get used the armor, but as her deep blue eyes took in the horde churning through the river, she took comfort in its weight. Confident in her skills with the smooth bow that rested in her hand and the twin daggers that hung from her belt, she breathed deeply and waited.

"Inform the archers that they should choose their targets well.

Kill the chieftains and any who are carrying grappling hooks or ladders." Áine acknowledged her partner and walked away to pass the word along the stockade. Brion's disquiet did not subside. His brother, Brocc, stood further along the stockade, smiling fiercely and raucously assailing the enemy with an amazing repertoire of insults. Brocc appeared to be looking forward to the battle with great relish.

A coltish yet hard-muscled Fionnbharr ó Cuileannáin, his older brother Labhraidh, and Eirnín Mac Gabhann prepared for battle on the east wall. Fionnbharr took several deep calming breaths. Across the camp and to his right Cian commanded the men on the southern wall including Eachdonn's two hundred and fifty spears.

Cian and his eldest son, Sárán Mac Craobhach – a very tall, mousy-haired man with a scraggly beard, were also responsible for ensuring the men at the stockade were kept well supplied. His head glistened with sweat as he paced around – his helmet discarded to the side. Over the rising din, Cian shouted, "Brace the gates." Large wooden posts thumped into place.

Having set the juggernaut of a screaming horde in motion, there was little Drostan could do to influence the immediate outcome. The two commands at his disposal were either retreat or attack and his men were unlikely to obey a command to retreat. Similarly, Nikandros and Cúscraid were focused on one imperative – keeping the naked bastards outside the stockade. Chaos ensued.

At the river, a solid mass of painted warriors waded forward slowed by thigh-high cold waters. Fionnbharr launched three volleys of javelins as they came within range - over six hundred iron-tipped barbs. Rocked by the impact, the assault juddered as bodies were bloodied and maimed, and bones cracked. The gurgling cries of the dying bubbled upwards as they slowly sank below the water. Pushed aside by their former comrades desperate to move forward, and hoping to avoid the same fate, most drowned before they could die from their wounds. The clear water, stained by the blood of the fallen, bloomed a murky crimson.

The river on the northern rampart was over twice the width of the tributary on Fionnbharr's side. Brion's cohort had already sent hundreds of javelins into the attackers. Steadfast, his men waited as the remaining Aos na Coille warriors splashed into the river. Torn bodies were pushed aside as the men moved steadily toward the palisade.

Áine's sharp eyes scanned for individual warband chieftains. She was hoarse from shouting out orders and stabbed the air with her bowstaff to mark targets. Confusion spread among the Aos na Coille as black shafts sprouted from their leaders. The chieftains on the far bank howled in fury revealing their positions. Áine's powerful bows killed many before the group finally retreated deeper into the cover of the forest.

On the forest side, Cathán's youthful arm muscles burned, as he released his final javelin. He was more than a bit relieved that in this, his first battle, his third throw had reached the outer edge of the ditch rampart. Taking his cue from Nikandros, he hurled curses at the attackers and waited for them to regroup and charge.

Three volleys had arched over the ditch finding unprotected flesh. Stunned by the impact, men and women beheld the shafts of wood emerging from their chests and limbs. Those following were shocked at the fist-sized ragged exit wounds. Blood flecked with off-white splinters of bone spurted from the gash. Those too close were spitted by the same arm's length of ugly black iron and were united in death with their comrade.

Cathán waited, his final javelin held at shoulder height was poised to stab. His arm muscles trembled and the javelin's tip jerked. To Cathán, the movement was obvious and betrayed his lack of experience. He cursed his weakness and rebalanced. Those beside the young warrior never noticed. Their focus was on the flood of warriors that flowed towards the west ditch.

Unable to stop, warriors screamed as they tumbled over the raised bank and into the trench to be impaled on the sharpened stakes. Others found their feet punctured by caltrops and thorns. In the frenzy, many of the dead and injured were furiously kicked and rolled into the ditch in an attempt to bridge the stakes.

Inevitably, the baying pack reached the wooden pales. The

multicolored bark quickly became slicked with blood and gore. Axes and spears were thrust over the stakes and countered with shields or met with javelins. Phlegm and spit mingled with blood.

In the flow of battle, Áine walked along the palisade, sighted another victim, smoothly nocked, drew and released, sending the arrow to its target. This time the distance was so close that she could watch the gray barb penetrate her victim's eye, bursting it. The signature black shaft with its red and white feather flight drove through with little resistance, emerging from the skull in a spurt of bone, brain and blood.

Abruptly, her arm was numb and she was on her arse, dazed. Her bow lay beside her. Áine breathed heavily not fully comprehending what had happened. She felt herself roughly dragged aside by an incensed Brocc. He snarled, turned to the wall and split a warrior's skull with his axe. Then he laid his helmet aside and grabbed her by the shoulders, "Look at me. Can you move?"

Áine winced. "What?"

Brocc smiled grimly and lifted the short throwing axe that lay nearby, "Be thankful for your chainmail. This would have embedded itself in your chest and you would now be in Mag Mell." Brocc called two men over, "Take my sister-in-law to the healers."

Suddenly nauseous, she wretched, wiped her sour mouth and smiled weakly, "Thanks." Brocc was already swinging his axe at another attacker. Supported between the men, Áine staggered towards the healers' tent at the center of the camp.

Cathán wailed and dropped his javelin as a spearhead tracked a deep cut along his right forearm. The young warrior was obliged to the comrade beside him who grabbed and jerked the spear to the side. Quickly recovering, Cathán unsheathed his sword and slashed downwards, cleaving his attacker's spear-arm at the elbow. Hot blood spurted over adjacent attackers and defenders alike as the unfortunate fell back. Cathán's body ached from tiredness and stress. His arms screamed for respite from the constant stabbing, slashing and remembering to hold his shield up. Yet the battle showed no sign of slackening. Beside him, Nikandros fought encased in a robe of blood and gore, hacking and slashing foes efficiently and with no remorse.

Attackers braced themselves against the palisade as stepping stones. Painted warriors tumbled over the stockade. Others used their hands to propel their fellow warriors over the man-high fence. Instinctively, Cathán swung around, bent his knees and lunged forward with his sword. His assailant was left grasping at the blade in her belly.

For an instant, Cathán and the girl stared at each other in shock while a single tear tracked through the grime of battle that coated her cheek. A slashing blade ended the moment, carving a path diagonally across the girl's neck and parting her head from her body. A blood-sodden boot kicked her corpse aside as a gore-encrusted hand gripped Cathán's shoulder and spun him around to face the stockade. "The battle is not over or won. Resume your place." Cathán obeyed Nikandros and gripped his sword.

It was mid-morning when Drostan ordered the retreat and once more the forests reverberated with the *barrr-ewww* of his war horns. The painted warriors paused to stare defiantly at those behind the stockade as their battle-heat subsided and they slowly withdrew. They had suffered many casualties, but their bearing as they melted into the forest told they were far from defeated or broken. Cúscraid heaved a sigh of relief and leant against the blood-soaked stockade, "I wonder how long before they attack again."

Nikandros coughed harshly, spitting out a wad of phlegm, blood and saliva. Pointing to the darkening skies he rasped, "Likely not long. There's a storm coming. I think Drostan will avoid fighting in a mud-bath." He dipped his head to Cian as the older warrior approached, "How do we stand?"

Cian smiled through a mask of blood, sweat and dirt. "None dead. About fifty injured - none serious." He paused, a look of fatherly concern crossing his aged face, "We almost lost Áine. Fortunately, her armor saved her. She's nursing a badly bruised chest and shoulder. She should be fine." Cúscraid and Nikandros sighed, glancing over to the healers' area. A gaggle of men that included Brion, Brocc and Fionnbharr were fussing over her. From the expression on Áine's face she was fast losing patience.

"We've no shortage of weapons or supplies. Sárán's overseeing several scavenging parties to look for weapons that can be used again – especially the javelins and arrows. The blacksmiths and arrowsmiths are working on repairing as much as they can." With a nod to Cúscraid, Cian said, "As usual, our master of defense has worked miracles. The perimeter appears to be intact."

Cúscraid smiled as he gazed around, "I think we should reduce the numbers on the riverside walls. The water is a much better barrier than I expected. They haven't brought any scaling ladders or used grappling hooks yet. My guess is that will come next." Then he laughed, "Tossing warriors over the fence was pretty inventive – and in sufficient numbers could cause problems." A frown crossed the sandy-haired warrior's face.

"What is it?" asked Nikandros.

"Probably nothing. I hear an insistent voice from the Goddess that I've overlooked something."

"Well, we made the proper sacrifices. Surely she cannot be upset at us."

"I'm sure you're right, but she'll not be pleased if she's warned us and we took no heed of it. Anyway I'm going for some food and a quick nap."

Nikandros' belly growled and he concurred, "I could do with some food too." The two commanders walked to the nearest cooking pit.

"Aye, they fight well," said Drostan. Bearach grunted in sullen acknowledgment. "How many did we lose?"

"A thousand dead – mostly on the riverside and from their cursed throwing spears. The same number injured, although they'll recover."

Drostan pointed to the camp and observed somewhat coldly, "Their defenses are intact." Then the king's single, amber eye narrowed, "How many of yer clan died in the battle, Bearach?"

The hulking warrior shuffled uncomfortably, "I'm not sure, My Lord."

"Make sure that ye can answer my question for the next battle. I'll not have the people see their tànaiste blatantly holding his kin back." Bearach glowered, but bowed his head in reluctant obedience. The king smiled, "I'm sure yer kin will be delighted to show how bravely they fight. Now having settled that, ye know the next stage."

Bearach smirked crookedly. His mouth was a mélange of missing or rotting, mildew-colored teeth, "The men are waiting for yer orders, My Lord."

"Let's see how our friends cope with a change in tactics."

The sun was barely visible in the overcast midday sky when Brion called out, "They're back." Nikandros and Cúscraid walked briskly around the perimeter pausing occasionally to study the several lines of men who had emerged from the forests. Facing all sides of the camp, the painted stood silently, watching and waiting. The war horns' *barrr-ewwww* sounded out, but under the blare hummed a strange whirring and droning. Cúscraid's eyes widened as he met Nikandros' stare.

Both said, "Shite!"

Cúscraid roared, "Shields!"

An already gray sky darkened further as a cloud of stones, ranging in size from pebbles to fist-sized rocks, rose high and then dropped on the camp. Only the discipline of the men saved them from severe injury or death as hundreds of Aos na Coille slingers maintained a relentless barrage. Within the camp, the sharp crack of stones striking the wooden stockade and shields concealed the soft and painful smack of rock on skin. Men cursed loudly as sling-bullets found and broke exposed flesh. Pack animals screamed, some collapsing as rocks sunk into exposed skulls.

"At least they can't attack while they're bombarding us," Cúscraid thought, "they'd kill their own men." But a roar from the western forest disabused him of this thought as it was followed by a horde of warriors sprinting for the stockade. While the slingers on the western side ceased, those on the riversides continued their unremitting fusillade.

"Form the wall. Three ranks. Move!" Nikandros stood up, and then flinched at the staccato of stones on his bronze armor. "First rank - defend the stockade, second rank – shields high over the first rank, third rank about face – protect the rear." The rush of the painted flowed in a blue wave across a perimeter ditch still populated with the morning's dead. Ladders thumped against the low wall as the Aos na Coille swarmed the stockade.

Defenders stabbed and slashed viciously with javelins, swords and axes at the baying throng. They gouged eyes with iron studded hand-wrappings and cracked skulls with shields. Gouts of blood splashed and gore splattered on attacker and defender alike as deep cuts took limbs from bodies or opened up bloody gashes on faces and chests. The battle raged relentlessly with wave after wave of the Aos na Coille breaking on the steady defenses. Inevitably, numbers won out and the painted were in the camp.

Once the attackers breached the stockade, the slingers ceased their hail. The camp then became a dirt-floored, bloody cage of snarling warriors facing off in a desperate struggle to survive. Shields battered bodies. Swords, spears and axes slashed flesh. Brocc and Labhraidh, their weapons lodged in some unfortunates, fought back-to-back with daggers, head-butts, teeth, and fists wrapped in iron-studded leather straps. In the confined space of the camp the assault was slowly blunted. Determined defenders gradually regained the upper hand. The flow of reinforcements was stemmed. The Aos na Coille who had gained the inside were pushed back over the fence or brutally slaughtered.

Brion secured the riverside walls and quickly organized several rows of men. He stood them five paces back from the western wall. "Loose javelins on my signal," he ordered. The men roared, "Down!" as Brion dropped his hand. Instinctively those at the wall crouched or fell flat, hearing the swish of javelins arc over their heads. The shower of iron stunned the retreating besiegers. Many fell into the ditch clutching at the gore-smeared iron spike protruding from their chests. Those left standing were relieved to hear the war-horns sound out the retreat. The battleground slowly cleared.

Breathing heavily, Nikandros leaned on his round, bronze shield and glanced around. To his relief, Cathán had survived his first battle. The young warrior was leaning over the fence and throwing up just about every meal he had eaten in the last cycle of the moon. Brocc and Labhraidh, their helmets cast aside, sat back-to-back in the dirt, heads bowed in exhaustion. Despite the swelling and a huge bruise on her right breast, Áine insisted she was fine and ordered Brion to see to those worse off. While bloodied and suffering from cuts and bruises, Nikandros took comfort that the army was largely intact.

The Spartan's gaze then rested on a small group near the southern wall. Cúscraid was stooped over a still form and shaking his head, while Fionnbharr knelt with his healer's pouch beside him. Nikandros walked over and Cúscraid turned, his face stricken with grief, "It's Cian. The eejit never did take to wearing a helmet." The small group parted, allowing Nikandros to crouch beside the man. Cian's face had been wiped clean, but purple blood still oozed into the gray cloth upon which his head rested.

Cian gripped the Spartan's arm with failing strength. "I'm old. I've few regrets," the dying man coughed and chuckled, "apart from not wearing my helmet." Pausing for breath, he said, "My eldest, Sárán, will take my place. He's a good man." As his grip loosened on Nikandros' arm, Cian smiled, "Have a drink on me. See you in Mag Mell," he said, then drifted away. After a moment, Sárán reached over and closed his father's eyes.

Nikandros stood up, "Lay him on his shield. He lived and died like a Spartan. We'll see to his funeral pyre once we've cleared the camp of bodies.

"Brion, organize the men into work groups. Pair them off so that while one labors he is protected by his comrade. Behead the painted – dead or alive. Stake their heads along the forest and riverside. Scavenge anything of use. Toss the bodies into the river after they've been stripped." At Brion's raised eyebrow, Nikandros said, "They may be naked, but many are wearing gold and silver jewelry." Brion nodded and strode away to organize his men.

"We'll need better tactics if we are to survive until Íar returns," Nikandros remarked as Cúscraid joined him. "Any ideas? The slings are a major problem. We don't have close to enough archers to make a dent in their numbers – even if they could match the slingers' range."

Cúscraid grimaced, rubbing his arse where a stone had almost penetrated his pants, "Let me think on it for a while."

Drostan watched his enemy systematically and efficiently take the heads of his men and stake them for all to see. Quite a few of the fallen had not made the journey to Mag Mell before their lives were ended with a sharp blade. Then he watched as the battlefield was stripped of anything of value. As the men completed their task and made their way back to the camp, a great flock of ravens descended to feast on the heads and pick them clean. Their *kraa kraa* would be heard late into the evening. As darkness fell the sound was mixed with the howl and barking of wolves, then the crack and rustle of undergrowth as corpses were dragged into the forest.

The king was pensive as he turned to face his tànaiste and Comhairle-Chatha, "They fight well. Maybe as good as or better than anyone we've faced before. They're strong, well-organized and defend well." Vigorous nods and murmurs of agreement greeted his statement. It had been a long time since the armies of the Aos na Coille had fought a pitched battle. Their great numbers tended to dissuade would-be invaders. Thus, they were more used to hit-and-run skirmishes or cattle raids along their borders.

Drostan looked up at the skies, "There will be heavy rainfall this evening and likely tomorrow. There will be no more fighting. We will use the time to consult the gods and revise our strategy. Go.

"And where are their cavalry?" Drostan worried to himself as the council departed.

CHAPTER 9

Pale shafts of light wove between the shadows thrown by the maze of thick tree-trunks. The forest reverberated to the steady, muffled pounding of hooves on the thick, amber-green, forest-floor. No whips were needed to encourage their mounts, just the occasional shout of praise and a friendly slap on a velvet shoulder. Riding flat-out on an open plain, it would take less time than a single sunset to reach A' Chrìon Làraich. Here in the far north of Albu they had intervening forests and mountains to traverse.

Flocks of cam-ghob, disturbed from their bat-like resting position, startled men and horses. The brightly colored birds swarmed into the air with a shrill, piercing sound, and then took up a deep *toop toop* signifying their annoyance. The birds with their red, green and yellow plumage were of a reasonable size and quite chunky. Many found themselves on the mid-day menu.

Íar's men had spare mounts and made good use of them to maintain their pace. The ponies of Ròidh's men were a hardier breed. Although smaller they did not lack for stamina and were more than able to keep up. Many times they tossed their heads with pride as they edged in front of their taller cousins.

By mid-morning as the riders drew closer to the mountains and the edge of the ancient forest, the mix of trees changed. Instead of pine needles, showers of orange-brown leaves floated to the forest floor as the proportion of hardwoods – oaks, birch, rowan, aspen, juniper and alder, increased. Broad streamers of autumn light penetrated the thinning canopy bringing into bold relief, the clusters of tall ferns and moss-covered rocks that studded the undergrowth and shallow soil.

A black cloud arose from the ground and the familiar *kraa kraa* of ravens greeted them as they broke from the forest. Their tone suggested the fowl were not overly impressed with the men's progress. The flock swept upwards, circled and then flew east calling the riders to the barren slopes of Beinn an Laoigh. Cold air rolled from the mountain's snow-capped peak to the foothills and forest. The warmth generated by the hard ride quickly dissipated once horses and men halted in the gusting wind. Men shivered as sweat-sodden garments became cold, clinging and damp; horses stamped, a soft mist flowing from their nostrils.

"Dismount. Get the fires going. We'll rest for a wee while and eat," Íar called out. "Make sure the horses are fed, watered and checked for injuries. Put some extra clothing on. It will get colder in the mountains." Almost eight hundred riders acted as one in the knowledge that their friends were relying on the success of the raid.

It seemed to Íar that he had only closed his eyes for a moment when a shadow crossed his vision. He raised his head. A ruddy-faced Ròidh stood expectantly before him, the reins of his new horse held lightly in his right hand. "The men are ready, Íar."

Bones cracked as Íar clasped scarred hands behind his neck and stood up. He groaned in mock annoyance as he stretched. With a broad grin he said, "Well then, we'd best be going." As an afterthought he added, "Make sure the fires are doused. We don't want to set fire to the forest – at least not yet."

The riders skirted the bleak western slopes of Beinn an Laoigh, moving north-east. The breeze sharpened further and flurries of autumn snow beat against the cavalry as they journeyed upwards. The men were grateful for the additional layers of clothing. They located and followed a pass eastward, a path which led them to an intersection of three rivers. After plunging through the cold, shallow waters, they again swung north-east, following the narrow stream's path. The river-bed was a mix of shingle and sand and much easier on the horses than the banks of slippery lichen and moss-covered rock.

The mountains and valleys over which Beinn an Laoigh cast its shadow were remote and unforgiving. The area was largely uninhabited save for the few hardy Aos na Coille farmers who, judging by their astounded faces, were plainly not used to seeing a mounted warband of such size. One family tending a fertile track of land was pleased to find that Íar's men were simply in need of any grain they could spare. They were also relieved - and delighted, to be rewarded for the supplies with gold instead of cut throats. As the band moved east along the river, the valley widened and the slopes once more became gentler and densely wooded.

Silvery white breath clouded from men and horses as Íar's riders came to a rest. It was dusk and fall skies blushed pink and purple. Before them, a small cluster of round-houses nestled in the crook of the river. From this point, the burn abruptly turned to flow southeast. Íar hoped that it would lead them directly to A' Chrìon Làraich.

Íar squinted in the dimming light and then spoke to Ròidh, "Take your men and approach the dwellings from the north. My men will advance from the south. Stop any who may be foolhardy and attempt to make a run for it." The younger man nodded and was about to turn away when Íar added, "Avoid killing anyone if you can – especially if they're just farmers, but no-one is to escape and warn A' Chrìon Làraich."

"Who speaks for this community?" Íar's gaze scanned the line of frightened men and women. Tear-eyed children gripped their parents' robes for protection. They stood trembling before an intimidating array of mounted warriors who leered at the women and gazed dismissively at their menfolk. Íar had instructed everyone to appear as threatening as possible. He had also informed them that he would personally cut the balls off anyone who touched any of the women.

Glancing at his men, Íar could barely restrain himself from laughing and prayed that their battle-faces were much better than their current act. Nevertheless, in the twilight shadows they were quite effective.

"I will speak for these people." A tall man, cloaked in gray and holding a thick carved staff, took a step forward. The man was as tall as Íar, but his gaunt face suggested a much lighter frame. Dark eyes held Íar's without flinching.

"Druid," Ròidh groaned under his breath.

"Bollocks!" muttered Íar, wishing that Mongfhionn had accompanied him. He bowed his head to the priest, "We mean no harm to this community, but no-one will be allowed to leave before another sunset."

An elder came forward to stand beside the Druid and whispered in his ear. In a tone of assured authority the Druid said, "That is unacceptable. These men and women have fields and flocks to tend." He was obviously used to being obeyed.

Bowing again, Íar smiled pleasantly, but an edge accompanied his next words, "You misunderstand, priest. On my oath as a king and by the Goddess who protects us, I mean your people no harm, but my men's orders are to kill any who, before the next sunset, flee the safety of the stockade that surrounds this community. Flocks and crops can wait." The Druid's countenance swung between displeasure and resignation as his mouth opened to protest further. Before he could speak, Íar said, "We've business to attend to in A' Chrìon Làraich." The shock on the priest's face was enough to assure Íar that he and his men were on the right path.

The scouts confirmed the route to A' Chrìon Làraich, and now, as the dawn light strengthened, Íar's troop was already cantering along the thickly wooded river plain. Fifty men remained at the settlement to ensure that no-one escaped. Curiously, the Druid appeared to be more upset than the farmers.

Their approach went undetected. The forest had deadened the sound of their arrival on the gently sloping hills that protected the village.

A' Chrìon Làraich was certainly a pleasant location. It nestled on the valley floor, surrounded by forests and mountains. A nearby river and several well-trodden and rutted paths testified to its role as a trading hub. Blue-gray smoke curled upwards, the aromatic scent of pinewood and peat wafted on the early morning breezes forming an undulating canopy above the cluster of roundhouses. The unmistakable gritty scraping of quern-stones grinding wheat sounded out. It presaged the welcome smell of newly baked bread.

A variety of smaller stone and wood buildings were scattered around a substantial roundhouse at the heart of the village. None of the structures had windows. Windows offered no protection against wind, rain and snow. Each had a single entrance facing east - positioned to catch whatever daylight was available. Gray stone walls were stained and darkened by the perpetual rain. Faded brown roofs of thatch and turf were a contrast against the vibrant autumn colors of the surrounding countryside.

The land around the community was cleared of trees and scrub. Crops had recently been harvested from the rich soil and now the air was fouled with the smell of recently burnt stubble. Cattle contentedly ate and drank near the river's edge. Small flocks of skittish sheep scattered under imagined threats and then congregated under the watchful eyes of young shepherds.

Two perimeter defenses enclosed the settlement. The outer stockade comprised a close-linked, man-high wooden stakes. A deep outer trench followed the line of the palisade interrupted only by a dirt-bridge to the single, north-west gateway. Apart from a pair of guards on either side of the heavy wooden gate, the fence did not appear to be defended.

A loud snarling and barking got Íar's attention. He cursed. The two wooden cages of dogs were placed on each side of the entrance. Likely the cage doors were connected by ropes that trailed to guards. Íar cursed once more. It was probable that there were more cages in the gap between the outer and inner fences. Kept hungry, the dogs presented a threat that was not to be underestimated.

The settlement's inner defense was more substantial. It too had a wooden palisade that encircled the community, but with a double row of stakes. In front was a continuous rampart, constructed with sods of peat. The structure was three paces wide at its base sloping to two at the top. The only access to the inner yard and roundhouses was a gated entrance, offset from the outer gate and facing east.

Íar tugged thoughtfully at his beard. The scouts estimated that the settlement had a population of five or six hundred including about two hundred warriors. This made sense given the length of the inner perimeter. It likely meant around one hundred and fifty on the stockade and fifty in reserve or as fighting guard for Drostan's children. Tactically Íar had few choices – and even less time. His advantage was the javelins each of his riders carried – and of course the element of surprise. He turned to Ròidh, "Your men will be our reserve. Follow us in once the ramparts are cleared, but leave fifty to watch the entrance and perimeter." Disappointed at not playing a more prominent role in the attack, Ròidh nevertheless dipped his head.

The black-tipped ears of Íar's great bay horse swiveled to flick away several snowflakes, then turned forward alert to his master's words. Dark-brown eyes watched horses and men. Red fox-tails hung motionless from helmet crests, attesting to the alertness and discipline of the warriors. "We've no time to muck about so let's keep this simple," said Íar. "Kill the dogs first, and then the men on the perimeter. Kill anyone who tries to stop you – man or woman. Drostan's children, if they are in the settlement, will likely be in the main roundhouse. Do not injure them."

Wheeling around and with a great roar, Íar led his riders at a gallop out of the tree-line and towards the outer entrance. The men shouted war cries, as well as an assortment of curses and obscenities, to the blare of bronze horns. They rode through the drifting gray-white smoke that hovered above the empty fields. Caught in the path of the horde, those villagers who had the misfortune to be outside the defenses, were knocked aside and trampled underfoot.

The outer entrance guards were swiftly overwhelmed, but not before they had released the slavering dogs. Several took the opportunity to escape to the woods, the others snarled and bit at the horses with vicious canine teeth. Horses squealed, lashing out with bony hooves as their riders stabbed downwards with javelins or slashed with axes and swords. Before long, the dogs lay dead or dying.

A group of Íar's warriors leaped from their mounts and set about demolishing the outer gate with battle axes. The gate eventually splintered under the onslaught. With an admirable sense of timing and patience the commander of the inner defenses waited until Íar's men had swept through the gateway before ordering the remaining dog-pens to be opened. Trapped in the narrow corridor between two packs of dogs, Íar's riders were unable to bring their superior numbers to bear.

Men cursing, horses screaming and dogs howling echoed off the timber stockade. The fight between man and beast was short, bloody and primal. Eventually the ravenous dogs were put down, but not before they had severely injured or killed several horses and their riders. His face infused with anger, Íar regrouped his men. In a rage they directed their javelins at the defenders.

The inner defenses were sound and would have been a formidable barrier had the community been attacked by a local tribe or brigands. But Drostan's men had little reply to the hail of iron that swept them from their positions. Their lack of clothing and armor served to make their predicament worse and their demise swifter.

Axes were once again hefted and the wooden gates spanning the inner entrance groaned, swinging inward on screeching, twisted iron hinges. Several more javelins cleared the gateway of the few defending warriors who held their ground. Once through the gateway, the mounted attackers walked their horses slowly forward herding terrified crofters before them. Ròidh's men dismounted and searched the smaller dwellings forcing the people towards the large roundhouse at the center of the village.

Here the remaining guards stood *en masse*, spears forward and blocking the entrance. The men looked savagely able, their painted, hard muscled bodies covered in many battle scars. As Íar advanced, hand raised, the men snarled and spat curses in his direction. Any glory that Íar might have gained from the battle had been tarnished because of the dogs. It seemed that he could never find an honorable fight these days. He shrugged and dropped his hand.

At his signal, Íar's remaining javelins were hurled. Belatedly grasping their fate, Drostan's men surged forward hoping to salvage some pride. They were no match for the iron-spiked shafts at such close range or the slashes of axes and swords. It was not long before most lay dead or maimed. The villagers watched in horror as the injured were efficiently dispatched to Mag Mell with a sharp blade.

"Bring them out and let's see what bargaining pieces the Goddess has given us."

Ten of Ròidh's men entered the main roundhouse. The air swarmed with yelps, screams, cries and curses. Seven re-emerged, dragging or carrying four squawking children aged from eight to fourteen summers. One warrior spat as he strode past Íar, "Bastards had a couple of female guards with them. We lost one man, the other two are injured. The women are dead – and they're lucky that's all that was done to them."

Another cursed as he was bitten by a girl of no more than thirteen summers. Eachdonn's men had little love for the Aos na Coille and quickly slammed a fist into the girl's face bloodying her nose. Her brother, a boy of fourteen summers, pulled his sister to him and glowered at his captors, "My father is Drostan Ruadh, king of the Aos na Coille. He will kill you all."

Íar smiled and with some measure of satisfaction said, "Well, that stupid outburst and the family resemblance tell me we've got our prize." Crestfallen, the boy fell silent as Íar barked his orders, "Strip the warriors of anything of value and behead them. The villagers and farmers can keep their belongings." With an appraising eye to the sullen and defiant offspring he added, "Bring four horses. Secure the children to them. If they start screaming, stuff a cloth in their mouth. There will be no more punching or slapping. I want them in good condition."

They arrived back at the smaller settlement north of A' Chrìon Làraich as the early evening meal – a thick mutton stew, was being prepared in fire-blackened cauldrons. A furious Druid stormed towards Íar aiming to protest the behavior of Íar's men. Bloodied faces and broken noses on some of the younger farmhands bore witness that the impetuosity of youth had met the butt ends of spears. "They should be thankful they're alive," Íar mused. The priest was brought up short when he spied the captives, his face ashen and shocked.

"What is the meaning of this? Release these children."

"That's not going to happen, Druid." Íar took note of the flurry of glances being traded back and forth between the children and the priest. "Are you going to tell me what is going on here? You obviously know these children. Where do you fit in?" The Druid chose not to answer.

"No matter, see to it that they're provided with warm clothing. We ride west for the mountains at dawn." Turning to his men, Íar said, "Untie the children. I want a double-guard on the settlement until we ride. I don't want any slipping away during the night." The Druid and children, with an air of confusion, were shepherded to one of the larger roundhouses.

The early morning was filled with the clinking of metal bits and harness jewelry. Decorated leather straps were checked for wear then buckled and tightened. Horses impatient to be on their way were led to be watered. They chomped grain with yellow, grass-stained teeth. Their stamping and blowing joined the *kraa kraa* of ravens roused from their night's rest.

Íar said, "Bring the children out and get them mounted." Ròidh nodded and was making for the roundhouse when five figures emerged. All were dressed for the journey.

"I will be accompanying the children," the Druid stated in a tone that left no room for dissent.

"Somehow I don't find that surprising," Íar replied. "You and the children will ride at the center of the formation. You'll not be restrained – unless you give me cause." Looking at the youngest boy and girl, Íar asked, "Can they ride?"

The Druid nodded, "Yes, but I expect not for the distance and pace that you will likely set. The boy will double up on my mount. Perhaps one of your men would permit the girl to ride with him."

"Well, I can see whose life is considered more valuable," Íar muttered. He beckoned to one of his men, "See to the girl. Make sure she is safe." With a final glance around, Íar swung his leg over his blood bay horse, "Mount up. We've a long ride and friends waiting for us."

CHAPTER 10

As he pulled at his oar, Tadhg ó Cuileannáin's emotions ran the gamut from distress, to anger, to fear and worry, and back to just plain pissed off. The youngest of the ó Cuileannáin brothers, Tadhg was the army's unofficial bard and chronicler. In his less modest musings he considered himself a descendant of Ériu's great warrior poets like the legendary Oisín. Just nineteen summers old, he had the build and coloring of his brothers. Of average height, Tadhg was slim but muscular. His head was crowned with a mop of straw colored hair tinged with copper. On a summer's day his face and arms were a mass of reddish-orange freckles.

Tadhg the poet would typically be contemplating the magnificence of the rugged landscape, the peacefulness of the waters upon which the small fleet of galleys sailed or enjoying the sight of bears scooping silver-scaled fish at the lakeside. Instead, he found himself pondering a terrible dilemma. For Tadhg had another quality much admired by Conall. His brain was as keen as the finest edge on a blade and his ability to observe, analyze and remember detail was the envy of many. Unfortunately, these qualities had walked him straight into a pile of shite, a task he would have rather passed on to just about anyone.

In the aftermath of the skirmish with Morna's community, Conall had prevailed upon Tadhg to investigate who might be responsible. Camp gossip suspected either Mórrígan or Mongfhionn, or both. The burning sensation that spread from Tadhg's chest and soured his mouth worsened. He groaned aloud at the enormity of the task. The rower in front turned his head around and looked at him quizzically. Tadhg shrugged well-muscled shoulders and smiled weakly.

In truth, Tadhg had little to go on. In the early light of the dawn, before the men took to the galleys, he had trotted back to the murder site. It seemed to Tadhg there was a terrible sense of satisfied evil surrounding the blood-stained stone. Equally forbidding was his awareness that the evil's appetite remained unsated.

The ground was well tramped, leaving few helpful signs. Thus, it had been a modest good fortune when he discovered several small footprints in a boggy patch twenty or thirty paces from the murder site. From this point Tadhg backtracked to where the child had been picking berries. A momentary zephyr shook a nearby bramble bush drawing Tadhg's attention to several long threads fluttering in the wind. Gathering up the strands he plaited them and tied the cord around his wrist. It became a permanent reminder of Morna's suffering and his task.

It perturbed him that there only appeared to be one set of footprints and cold shivers ran up and down Tadhg's spine at the implication. What demon had led the girl to her death? Thus, he was enormously relieved to discover a single larger footprint. The impression was of someone who had not worn bróga. That fact in itself did not help as both Mongfhionn and Mórrígan were often to be found barefoot around the camp. The two women, at various times, had also been observed leaving the camp that day. As he rowed, Tadhg reflected on the footprint. There was something about the impression in the soft mud that disturbed him. He could not put his finger on what that was. Tadhg groaned again, this time louder.

"If you're in that much pain, son, you should see the healer – or have a good shite! Get yourself a few stalks of rhubarb."

Tadgh sighed, "If only the remedy were that simple."

Pale skins burned reddish-pink under the autumn sun. Hunched backs straightened, knotted shoulders relaxed as the island that had been the source of so much pain slowly receded from sight. The galleys moved smoothly and swiftly through the waters of An Linne Sheileach. Perhaps, thought Conall, the agreeable sunshine, absence of rain and a light wind were hopeful signs that the Goddess did not assign blame for the recent tragedy. They had certainly been diligent in making their sacrifices to the waters.

In the distance the snow-capped peak of Beinn Nèamh-bhathais broke through a cloak of fog upon on its shoulders. Great bluffs rose up from the water's edge. The land formed the northern borders of the Aos na Coille. Sheltered on two sides, the waters of the loch were calmer, yet Pytheas kept a close watch for fluxes that might prove troublesome. Clouds of their ever-present raven guides rose up from the forests. In the distance aurochs sounded out loud warnings of the approach of wolves or perhaps a bear. A lonely elk responded in a harsh burring tone that echoed the native brogue.

Mid-afternoon, the flotilla approached the narrow neck that formed the entrance to An Linne Dhubh. The steady thump of the stroke drums echoed off rocky hillsides as lookouts in each galley watched warily. Archers, arrows nocked and ready, stood tense, ready to defend the ships. One-by-one the vessels crossed the narrows and entered the lake.

A tall broch perched on the crest of a moss-covered outcrop not too distant from the entrance. Pytheas guided the galleys to the opposite side of the lake, outside the range of potential missiles. The Goddess smiled on them and the fleet glided into a sheltered inlet.

Three large wooden buildings – crannogs, stood within the cove. Each stood on a foundation of thick tree trunks driven deep into the muds of the shallower waters. A perimeter walkway wide enough for one man led to where a large logboat strained against its mooring lines and bumped gently against the pier. The crannogs were connected to the land by a single narrow causeway. Conall saw that the bridge was quite sophisticated. A short section could be quickly hoisted away leaving the building isolated from the land.

Three galleys slid quietly alongside the piers. Men quickly clambered out of the boats, padding warily to each of the buildings. Mongfhionn nudged Fearghal, "An interesting spectacle, three-score naked, armed men searching a series of dwellings."

Fearghal chortled, "Even more amusing if there's anyone at home!"

Fortunately, the crannogs were deserted - apart from swarms of angry, biting midges that rose up from the waters before droning off to the nearby forest. As the rest of the men disembarked, Conall examined the largest of the dwellings with a growing admiration for the builder. The location, a sheltered inlet at the mouth of a river was very defensible. And, the surrounding lands and waters would provide a more than adequate living for the residents with livestock, crops and fishing.

Each crannog was similarly constructed. A man's height of upright stakes was set in a circle and crowned by a cone of lighter, but much longer wooden poles. This particular crannog was about fifteen paces in diameter. The others were smaller - no more than ten paces.

Conall passed through the dwelling's single, east-facing entrance and saw that it was a family home. He was somewhat surprised to find that it had a second level, accessible by a wooden ladder. Walking across the floor of tightly laid timbers in the dim light, he swore when his toe stubbed on a square clay and rock fireplace. There was a sudden flare of smoky yellow light as Mórrígan applied a flame to the rushlights positioned in wooden holders around the wall. The bouquet of burning fat and vegetation quickly permeated the room. Conall looked upwards and said, "I guess we get the upper floor."

"Not unless you want to be as well-smoked as the haunches of meat and dried fish that are hanging up there," Mórrígan retorted. "I think we can rest well on this level. It's divided into different stalls anyway." Then impishly she added, "Fearghal and the Lady Mongfhionn can rest above. Surely the Sidhe can protect them from a little smoke."

Conall rolled his eyes and said with mock annoyance, "Yes, but can she prevent Fearghal from snoring?"

The majority of the men electing to brave insects and beasts made camp nearby on a rocky knoll several hundred paces from the crannogs. Pytheas and some of his men took one of the smaller homes. The other was occupied by Deaglán, Tadhg, Craiftine, Torcán and, as might be expected, Gràinne. Nightfall dropped its purple-black cloak.

During the morning meal the round of complaints from those who had slept in the crannogs was met with laughter from their on-shore comrades. Bleary-eyed Deaglán, Tadhg and Craiftine muttered oaths and thinly veiled threats that included castrating Torcán. Their friend's all night, loud, rutting with Gràinne had kept them awake and in a high degree of frustration. That Torcán appeared none the worse for his nocturnal shenanigans only served to increase their annoyance. For her part, Gràinne appeared more than happy with her new circumstances and the pleasant tingling between her legs.

The other grump was Conall who complained loudly that Fearghal snorted and snored like an elk. Fearghal's retort was a respectful bow followed by, "I apologize my king. Still, given the clamor coming from beneath us, the Lady Mongfhionn and I were afraid for our lives. We had thought a wolf and a wild cat had replaced our king and queen! Thus, how you could hear my snoring is a mystery."

Vainly, Conall tried to glower at his friend. "Bastard!" he said, reaching for a hunk of bread and a tankard of honeyed-beer. Inwardly, Conall was very happy. For the first time since Tuathal had been born, the ginger-red bush between Mórrígan's thighs had been welcoming and he had enjoyed her often during the night. The queen was of one mind with Gràinne, and delighted in her throbbing lips. Knowing glances shared between Mongfhionn and Fearghal made clear that the Sidhe had not been neglected.

Golden-yellow rays burst through sheets of low cloud as the galleys cast off from the jetties. Sunlight danced on the dark waters. Conall was thankful for the pleasant, if brief, sojourn, but could not help wondering when and from where the next trial would come.

Spirits rose as the ships glided over the tranquil waters of An

Linne Dhubh. Insults were hurled from vessel to vessel as they competed good-naturedly for lead position. Spray-splashed muscles had been hardened by the time spent at the oars as well as the battles they had fought. The men were not shy in showing off bodies trimmed of any trace of fat. Sadly, their audience was but three women who looked on scornfully.

Mid-morning, oars were lifted from the waters and the galleys drifted towards a narrow river mouth. Sand banks were cautiously navigated. Pytheas pointed south-east and Conall stared into the distance at the ráth that rose above the forested landscape. It was a simple structure with only a single perimeter stockade.

Within the ráth, Conall could see the thatched roofs of a cluster of small buildings. Ribbons of blue-gray smoke drifted upwards. "A good location to guard the river valley," he said. Surprisingly, the chieftain with the fort appeared to have no interest in resisting their continued passage north.

At this point the river was little more than fifty paces wide. Pytheas' galleys were about five paces wide, but when the length of the oars was added, the width almost tripled. It was only the ships' very shallow draft and flat bottoms that allowed navigation in the restricted water depth. Nevertheless, numerous turns and bends, many sandbanks and in a few places, rock falls had created small natural dams across the river. It was evening by the time the men, exhausted through rowing, hauling and carrying their galleys, reached the lower entrance to An Linne Lochaidh.

That night, the camp was quiet. Men ate and then quickly fell asleep beside the crackling fires. The pink-flushed dusk had given warning of a change in weather and in the morning the camp woke to the sound of hissing as the dying embers from the previous night were doused with raindrops. Cloaks that had been dry when the men turned in were now damp and smelled of mold, wool and old sweat. There was little light, just a gray, threatening sky with low scudding clouds. As the sky darkened, the rain became heavier.

An Linne Lochaidh's northern and southern shores climbed to steep mountains. Between them, the narrow loch lay deep and cold. Thick wildwood and pine forests swathed the lower slopes, but only individual trees or small stubborn clusters survived on the heights. A strong wind blowing from the north-east caused the dark waters to roil until waves rose to half the height of a man. Spumes shot skyward against the shore.

The galleys staggered to the north end of the loch with sails furled. Burning arm, thigh and stomach muscles attested to the effort needed to drive the boats forward. At first they passed small groups of crannogs huddled in sheltered coves. On this occasion the crannogs were inhabited. Curious men, women and children watched as the strange fleet traversed the loch. None were seen once the inlets disappeared and the shoreline ascended sharply.

It was mid-day when an exhausted Torcán maneuvered his galley to within shouting distance of Conall's. "A thousand paces ahead there's a narrow channel that leads to a sheltered cove. A good place to rest," he called out over the increasing noise of the wind. Conall and Pytheas both nodded. As the galleys entered the narrows they were relieved to find that the almost circular cove was well protected from the wind and rain by the thick forest surrounding it.

Hair plastered to their heads, bodies beaten by cold rods of rain, exhausted men hauled the boats ashore and secured them. A camp site was quickly cleared of brush. The dense canopy provided a little respite from the persistent rain. Almost naked, shivering violently and chilled to the bone, they fumbled to get fires going with numb fingers. Thankfully, they were soon rewarded with the heat from roaring fires and the fragrance of wood-smoke. Dry clothes and a hot meal raised the spirits of the party, and in a short time the craic and tall tales began.

Conall was thankful for the men's improved morale. "Take a few archers and scout along the river valley," he said to Deaglán and Torcán. It doesn't seem wide enough for the galleys here, but perhaps the river opens up." Both made to walk away when Conall added, "Take the hounds with you. They've been cooped up on the galleys for days and need exercise." At the sound of whistled commands, Fearghal and Conall's massive wolfhounds stormed across the camp keen to go hunting.

Deaglán rolled his eyes, "So much for a leisurely scouting trip.

Those beasts will drag us everywhere – and at speed!"

Torcán laughed and called out for Gràinne to accompany them. "No," Conall said, "Gràinne can help Mórrígan and Mongfhionn." Surprised at his leader's abruptness, Torcán colored, hung his head and strode off to catch up with Deaglán.

Conall watched the group head away and then beckoned to Tadhg. "This would be a good time to talk to Gràinne – without Torcán present." Tadhg nodded, glancing around for her. Conall fully understood the uncomfortable situation into which Tadhg had been dropped. He was also sure that Tadhg was the best one for this task. While Tadhg was unhappy with the burden put on his shoulders, Conall knew it would not stop the young man from being thorough.

Gràinne spotted the slim warrior's approach and wrung her hands nervously. She lowered her eyes in the vain hope that she was not his target. His shadow fell across her as he stepped in front of the fire.

CHAPTER 11

"Miserable, just bloody miserable," Cúscraid grumbled to himself. The broad-shouldered warrior tramped through the quagmire that was the camp's inner yard. His soft leather boots sank ankle-deep into the black mud and his clothes and armor were sodden. Around him, men cursed the cloying mud that trapped boots and bróga.

His disposition improved slightly as he gazed over the stockade. None of Drostan's men would be crossing the rivers. The heavy rain had raised the normally slow-flowing rivers to flood and the higher waters splashed against the wooden fence. Cúscraid pushed and kicked at a few stakes to be sure that their footing remained solid.

On the cleared ground facing the western and southern walls, scattered pools of muddy water reflected the rays of a weak morning sun. Although not a particularly religious man, Cúscraid gave thanks to the Goddess. The lie of the camp was fortunate and the greater part of the deluge had drained into the ditches. Flooded, only the tips of buried stakes broke the water's surface.

A vibrant rainbow swept across the sky – the promise of better weather to come. Nikandros and Brion came to stand alongside Cúscraid. "The weather's clearing," the Spartan observed wryly. "At least this morning I can see the skulls." Cúscraid nodded assent. Until that morning the staked heads bordering their territory had been but vague shapes, barely visible behind the curtain of rain. Picked clean by flocks of ravens, eyeless sockets stared in permanent rictus towards the forests.

"The rain was bad, but at least it washed away most of the blood and guts." Brion crunched through a hunk of hard bread, scattering crumbs down his tunic. The others concurred. So far they had not had to deal with swarms of flies emerging from the bloated maggots that feasted on the dead. More importantly, they had not had to contend with sickness — always a worry in the confined space.

"We don't have an answer to Drostan's slingers," said Cúscraid. The statement hung in the air for a moment without comment or even a pessimistic joke. "I've added some shelters for the animals and had the chariots upended." Brion grunted his resigned disapproval as he looked at his overturned chariots, their double-shafts pointing skywards like the legs of a striapach waiting to be entered. "The only sure way of protecting us would be to build a roof over the camp." Ignoring skeptical glances and raised eyebrows, Cúscraid explained, "It's not impossible - if we were thinking of staying here for a while. But no, it's not practical for us."

"Well, we can't just wait to be stoned over and over," said Nikandros. "Eventually, our shields and morale would break. Then, we'd be helpless. With Íar's cavalry, we could have mounted fast attacks into the ranks of the slingers — but he'll not be back for some time. Brion, is there space for your chariots to harass Drostan's men?"

Brion grimaced as he located and squashed a bothersome tick that had been feasting on his neck. "I think so. Certainly there'll be room to maneuver in the deeper forest where the trees are older and more spread out. The ground should be reasonably firm even with all the rain we've had."

"Good. Get your chariots and men ready. Stay in the forest unless you need to be resupplied. Use your judgment as to where and when you attack — but sound your horns to alert us. Keep them off-balance. Maybe the knowledge that your chariots are on the prowl will dissuade the slingers."

Cúscraid grinned, "Besides that, getting your chariots and horses out of our camp will give us more room — and relieve the stink of horse shite." With a chuckle, Brion dipped his head at Nikandros and strode off to organize his men.

"What's your strategy for the rest of us?" Cúscraid asked, "I assume there is a plan."

"We do what we know best," said Nikandros. "Draw them to the shield wall and slaughter them. Drostan's men fight like barbarians so we're going to pick a fight. I can't see their warriors standing back and letting the slingers pitch stones at us all day long. The warband leaders will not have the patience for that. There's no glory in it for them."

Once he had issued his battle orders Drostan dismissed the Comhairle-Chatha. The Aos na Coille leader, deep in thought, ignored his scowling tànaiste. Reports from the northern border of a sizable warband making its way along the great lochs disturbed the king. He could not care less about the possible threat to the northern tribes. In his view they were violent and unpredictable - a pain in the arse.

He grumbled when he thought of the Na Daoine Tùrsach. They were fanatics, each and every one. Drostan accepted, with some distaste, that Druids required the occasional sacrifice. Mostly they made use of captured prisoners or criminals, but the Na Daoine Tùrsach's thirst for blood sacrifices knew few boundaries. They persisted in sending their zealots into Cùil Daothail and deep into his lands to show his people the error of their ways. Those who had been discovered were returned – less their tongues and eyes.

Drostan did not want the fragile balance of trade and power in Cùil Daothail upset. To prevent this and to support the governor at Cùil Daothail, he ordered a thousand men north.

It continued to nag at Drostan that the location of his opponent's cavalry remained a mystery. Apart from tracks that led east and south, there was no sign of the mounted warriors. He well knew of the ten war chariots that had rumbled out of the camp and into the depths of the ancient pinewoods. They would provide some useful practice for his chariots and warriors. For comfort's sake, Drostan, positioned two thousand of his men on the southern side of the camp with orders to watch the trails and delay the riders should they return.

He looked up at the clearing, mid-morning sky. The heavy rain had moderated, diminishing to a light mizzle which would likely cease by mid-day. To Bearach he said, "Bring the slings to the edges of the forest. Let them soften the bastards up for a while." Bearach hacked up a great glob of phlegm and spat it against a nearby tree. At Drostan's expression of disgust, the tall, bulky warrior smiled crookedly and grunted.

"The ground before the camp is a quagmire. We should hold the assault for the morrow's sunrise, and then send the main force against the western wall."

Numerous Aos an Coille war horns once again roused the Ériu camp and were quickly echoed with shouts of, "Take cover!" Men hugged the stockade with shields raised or found the nearest available shelter. Slings were simple, but effective. Thrown underhanded, the projectiles arched high in the sky before falling on the camp. There was little the besieged could do, but wait and suffer. Those brave or foolish enough to raise heads above the palisade were rewarded with a shower of sharp stones as the experienced slingers quickly switched to an overhand throw for accuracy. Muttered curses, promises of revenge and yelps of pain filled the air.

Eventually, the force of the bombardment slackened, then ceased. Men held their breath hoping that any ready supply of stones was exhausted. Prayers of thanks were offered to the Goddess. Nikandros nodded to Cúscraid and gave the signal. With a great roar of defiance men flowed out of the western and southern gateways.

About to give the command to launch an attack, Bearach was put off-balance as his enemy's ceannairí céad led their men in a swift charge across the dirt causeways. Instead of a wooden fence, his men faced a shield wall bristling with javelins. On the western side, three rows, each of five hundred men, stood beating shields with javelins. On the southern wall, Cúscraid had formed his cohort of five hundred in a double line in front of the ditch. Eachdonn's spearmen remained in the camp as a reserve should any warriors brave the cold, swollen river. The thunderous din of bodhráns reverberated off the wooden stockade.

Bluff, but not stupid, Bearach signaled and several small bands charged forward across the open ground. Their progress was slow as they sloshed their way through mud and water. Áine's quiver of archers stood on the raised ditch rampart with arrows nocked and ready. On her command, a volley flew into the midst of the Aos an Coille, swiftly followed by more flights. Well-trained, her archers could send a rain of arrows every count of ten. The warbands - men and women, died or lay bleeding before they had covered half the distance to the shields.

There was pause. Then, prompted by the ceannairí céad, the shield wall erupted. Shouts, jeers and taunts flew thick and fast at the Aos an Coille. Weapons crashed against shields. Pale, white arses were flaunted. Behind the stockade, the youngest boys once again took up their bodhráns and thumped out a loud rhythm. As the noise reached a crescendo Nikandros strode forward. With his doru's iron butt spike planted in the soft ground, he stood legs apace, bronze armor glinting in the weak sun, the red plumes of his helmet flaring in the gentle breeze. He roared defiance and hurled curses in a mix of languages.

Bearach's lip curled into a broken-toothed sneer. At a slight dip of his head a tall warrior stepped out from the mass. Lank, copper-red hair flopped on broad shoulders. The designs on his barrel-chest were distorted by scarring. To a round of cheers, spear grasped firm in calloused hands, the Aos an Coille champion loped forward to face the Spartan.

Overly confident in his ability, the man drew close before realizing that the dark warrior's black-shafted spear was an arm's length longer than his. The Aos an Coille warrior stepped within the doru's range. It was a poor decision. At the same time Nikandros took a pace forward, rebalanced and swept his bronze shield across his upper body. The doru, held at shoulder height in his right hand, stabbed forward.

The groan and explosion of breath from the blue-painted warrior was amplified a thousand times by his comrades. The Spartan's iron-gray spearhead burst through his opponent's chest and exited the man's back, pushing skin, blood and ragged shards of bone out of the gaping wound. Impaled, he hung suspended between life and death. Then, with a practiced twist of the doru, Nikandros released the man.

The Aos an Coille warrior collapsed face-down in the mud. The weakening rise and fall of his shoulders as he struggled to keep a hold on life was ended by a thrust of the leaf-shaped tip which nearly severed head from neck. With an outward sign of contempt that did not reflect his real view of the man's bravery, Nikandros kicked the corpse aside and left it lying as discarded meat.

Shield and doru raised, Nikandros turned to face his men, their obvious glee heightened with the quick victory. Then he taunted the enemy once more. Their rage was evident and the high chieftains were barely able to restrain their people. At a nod from Bearach three more champions strode forward – two men and a woman. This time their pace was measured. Small, round shields protected their chests. The Spartan acknowledged the warriors and walked forward to meet them. Howls of rage at the unfair odds erupted from the shield wall. Brocc and Labhraidh took a step from the wall, but at a glance from Nikandros they halted.

A grim ballet began between the opposing sides. At its center Nikandros, eyes alert, crouched, pivoted and swept the air with the doru. Like wolves, the Aos an Coille snapped and snarled, probing for weaknesses with their shorter spears. Their prey responded, blocking, bashing, stabbing and thrusting. Spear and shield worked in concert. His other weapons – patience and luck, remained unseen. Ignoring the shouts of advice from his men and the taunts from his enemies, Nikandros continued shifting and turning, his feet well-grounded and his balance sure.

One adversary's foot snagged against a moss-hidden tree stump. He stumbled and fell to one knee. The boss of a heavy bronze shield slammed against his temple. His skull caved in and he slumped senseless to the ground. To the right, hoping to take advantage of the distraction, the second warrior charged forward recklessly. Her spear glanced of the bronze shield. It quivered in her grasp. From a crouch, Nikandros thrust parallel to the ground. The doru's razor-sharp head bit through muscle and soft tissue. The Spartan twisted and the stench of shite filled the air. Grimacing, the warrior dropped to her knees clutching at the doru and a bloody belly as streamers of intestines burst forth.

The third warrior was not so easily diverted. Nikandros sensed movement behind him and tugged at the doru. It was held firm - the corpse's final revenge. Gripping his shield, the Spartan rolled to his left and heard the scrape of a spearhead sliding across the cuirass protecting his back. He rose and turned to face the Aos na Coille chieftain, xiphos in his right hand. The air sang from quick slashes and high and low thrusts of the short, viciously sharp sword. The Spartan moved forward aiming at his enemy's groin and throat. Skillfully parrying with spear and shield, the warrior was driven backwards. Breathing hard, yet alert and sure-footed he growled in frustration as his spear thrusts were deflected by the Spartan's large shield and bronze armor.

The howling from the Aos na Coille became louder and louder as they grasped what was happening. Their remaining champion, to-tally focused on his opponent, had lost his sense of direction and was being driven back onto the shield wall. It was only when he felt the sharp points of javelins prick his back, that the warrior's eyes acknowledged his precarious position. With a roar of defiance he flung himself forward. His spear's blade sliced along Nikandros' thigh leaving a thin bloody trail.

The Spartan grunted, turned a half-pace to his right and reversed his grip on the xiphos. As momentum carried the tattooed warrior forward, Nikandros' xiphos plunged down and between his shoulder blades. The sword's point narrowly missed his heart and emerged from the man's chest in a spurt of blood. The warrior dropped to his hands and knees as the sword was extracted. With teeth clenched in pain, he looked up at Nikandros, and then bared his neck. A swift slash ended his agony.

"A brave warrior. May he rest in Mag Mell," Nikandros said as he turned to face the Aos na Coille.

"I think you may have pissed off our painted friends," an irrever-ent voice from the rear called out. Laughter rippled along the ranks.

Amid the braying reverberations of war horns, the Aos na Coille horde broke from the woods, howling in fury and wanting revenge for the death of their champions. Thousands streamed across the open ground towards the raven-emblazoned shields.

In the front row another wag remarked, "Doesn't anyone find this a wee bit distracting? They're all either flashing cocks or tits at us."

The row laughed and Brocc chipped in, "You're just jealous that they have cocks worth showing."

Nikandros allowed himself a fleeting smile, and then turned to face his men, "Tighten ranks. Stand firm. Protect your neighbor. No retreat. Show them how to fight." He rejoined the wall as the men roared once more, the bodhráns got louder and a blue tide crashed against the red wall.

Observing the battle with the members of his Comhairle-Chatha, Drostan's scar tightened in anger. From his vantage point he watched as wave after wave of the Aos na Coille attack was thrown back by the solid wall of shields. A red mist of blood hovered over the battle line as the men from Ériu efficiently slaughtered hundreds of his warriors. Worse, the raucous shouting from the bastards' wall showed they were clearly enjoying the carnage.

Drostan paced back and forward cursing the incompetence of his battle commander. "That fool, Bearach, walked into their trap. He fights on their terms and on their ground. Our strength is the forest – not on open ground or inside walled forts."

"I agree that Bearach may not be the most strategic or flexible of commanders." The gray-haired leader of the Comhairle-Chatha spoke slowly and with a strength that belied his years, "On the other hand, how else could he pry this tick from our flesh – from our land?"

Failbhe was tall. His skin, wrinkled and slack, draped a once taut and muscled warrior's frame. His spine had stiffened with age and disease causing him to stoop. Aches and pains were constant companions and he no longer had fluidity of movement. It had been a wise if painful decision to pass the throne to his son. While carrying the appearance of being in his prime, Failbhe knew in his heart he would not have been able to keep the throne if challenged. Better to place it in the hands of his chosen heir.

"Maybe the wise decision would have been to let them pass. What allegiance or loyalty do we owe Finnean Mac Sèitheach?"

"Finnean is a conniving bastard, but he has his uses." Failbhe set his jaw. "Ye gave your word to protect his borders. And, whether they intended to or not, these people have invaded our territory. Ye can'nae show weakness or the wolves within yer own people will see an opportunity for power."

Drostan sighed, "Maybe I should have become a druid like my brother."

Failbhe spat in disgust, "More of that talk and I'll kill you myself. Do yer job. Drive this enemy from our forests."

"I will - but not today." Drostan turned to one of his runners, "Tell the horns to sound the withdrawal."

It was a game of cat and mouse for Brion. Not long after his iron-rimmed wheels rumbled into the deeper wildwood Brion discovered that Drostan also had chariots. They were lighter, smaller and, unlike his, were drawn by only one horse. Some had a slinger on board, most were armed with throwing axes.

Hidden in the forest gloom, Brion observed that the vehicles appeared to be little more than a quick means of transport for key chieftains. He was pleased. The more leaders they could remove the better. After their bloody battles with the Connachta and Eochaidh Ruad's chariots, he knew his force was well practiced in long range, hit and run tactics.

Directed by hand signals and short blasts from Brion's bronze horn the chariots hunted in pairs. They prowled the edges of the ongoing battle, their bridles and chains muffled with cloths. Cruel scythes, almost invisible in the half-light of the woods, spun on well-greased wheel-hubs. Apart from when they bumped over exposed roots of trees, the soft surface made the ride less harsh than normal travel. And this time they were accompanied by the pack of wolf-hounds – gray ghosts in the forest.

Rapid sorties harvested a bountiful crop as Aos na Coille chariots were ambushed. Horses, drivers and warriors were maimed by javelins thrown from the shadows. The ragged, trailing edges of the Aos na Coille horde were bled by the blades of the chariots as Brion led his teams in and out of the fray. Screams of terror rose in the forest as the injured were located and finished off by the sharp teeth of the hounds. Broken and bloodied men, shattered chariots and screaming horses lay scattered over the forest floor. It was not long before those at the rear were fully occupied watching over their shoulders in fear of what might appear in the timber.

Focused on directing his attacks, Brion was startled to hear the battle horns of the Aos na Coille take up their loud, harsh wailing. Caught short, he realized the retreating army was flowing in his direction. Shaking his head in disbelief, he took up his horn, blasted out a warning for his chariots to flee, then wheeled around and sped deeper into the forest.

Bearach howled in anger when he heard the war horns take up their refrain. Although he acknowledged Drostan as both king and commander-in-chief, the hulking warrior was dismayed that his command had been abruptly overruled. He had lost face. A brutal, quick-tempered, and oft times vindictive man, Bearach vowed not to forget this slight.

The blue horde withdrew before the blood and gore splattered shield wall. This was no rout. No back was turned to give their enemy an easy kill. Snarling and spitting hoarse curses, weapons held in defense, the proud Aos na Coille retraced their steps to the forest edge before turning and disappearing into its embrace. The wall advanced slowly in concert with the retreat, tramping over the dead with blood-soaked boots and bróga, stilling the injured with a blade. A new harvest of heads would join their comrades later. In the skies the ravens gathered, eager to feast on the carrion. Dusk would bring the wolves.

The wall halted midway between the camp and the forest. Throats parched from the heat of battle and thick with its bloody debris coughed and hacked up great globs of red-streaked phlegm. Teeth ground down on the grit of battle. Men leaned on their shields, breathing heavily. Some discarded the sodden cloth and leather wrappings from around their wrists. Many a warrior's had already fallen away - a piece of cloth could only take so many cuts and slashes. Wrist and arm muscles so worn and numb that they seemed not to belong to their bodies were massaged wearily. Front and middle row men sounded off with grumblings over shield-bruised backs a gift from those who had braced the wall.

An uneasy stalemate settled as dusk fell. Mists smoked from the surface of the rivers in the chill evening air. Cúscraid studied the waters which were approaching their normal level. "We'll be open to attack from the river sides," he thought. He made his way across the camp passing the welcoming fires that dotted the camp. The men, exhausted from the battle, sat drinking beer, gulping food and sharing stories about their latest scars. Ever vigilant, their weapons lay within reach and the rasp of whetstones on metal travelled far on the still air.

Nikandros looked up and answered Cúscraid's unspoken question as his friend approached the crackling pinewood fire. "A handful dead. Quite a few injured. Given time, the healers can bring most back to full strength."

Cúscraid grunted in reply, "Do we have time? Anyway, we'll be able to rotate the injured with the reserves and put the lightly wounded in the rear row of the shield wall." He squatted by the fire, "What's your guess for Drostan's tactics tomorrow?"

"Bombard us with the slingers. Attack in force. Basically more of the same. What else can he do? The difference is that he won't be baited into attacking foolishly this time." Nikandros rubbed his hands enjoying the warmth from the flames. "Drostan can't be too pleased with his commander, so likely he'll take a more active interest." He tore a strip of meat from the spit, blowing on the roasted rabbit thigh before sinking his sharp, white teeth into its flesh. "With the rivers back to normal, he'll be able to attack on all sides – if he wants."

"I think he'll test the southern wall tomorrow," said Brion. Áine and he had joined them. Áine breathed in sharply, wincing as she leant over to grab a filet of the pink-fleshed fish roasting over the fire. Following the exertions of the battle, her chest and injured shoulder were in perpetual agony. Under her tunic, her breast was a mass of multi-colored bruises. Brion interceded, picking up the fish and handing it across to her. His reward was an appreciative smile. "The smaller force that Drostan set to watch our southern flank never withdrew. My chariot teams saw many of the Aos na Coille swing to the south-west after the battle rather than returning to their main camps."

"That could cause problems for Íar." said Cúscraid. "He may not be expecting to ride smack into Drostan's army."

Nikandros brow furrowed as Cúscraid spoke, but he stood up and stretched, "Nothing we can do about that. Íar's not stupid. He'll have scouts out."

Brocc and Labhraidh, enticed by the smell of roast food appeared beside Áine. Flicking a glance at his brother, Brion, and then to Nikandros and Cúscraid, Brocc said, "We should strike first." Ignoring the doubting looks he added, "A thousand men and the chariots could do real damage – especially if they weren't expected."

"No," Nikandros shook his head at the suggestion. "I won't risk losing men that we'll need for the attack on Dùn Na Mèadaidh." Brion and Cúscraid nodded.

"Old men." The words had slipped from Brocc's mouth before he could recall them and were followed with an "Ooooph!" as the pommel of Cúscraid's sword connected solidly below his ribs. The blow, while not hard enough to cause serious damage was more than enough to make Cúscraid's point.

"Respect your elders – and your leaders."

Nikandros chuckled, "Brion, can your over-enthusiastic brother and his equally keen friend work a chariot?" Brion smiled his lopsided grin and winked. "Good. At first light, Brocc and Labhraidh will lead three chariots along the east path." Pinioning the two speechless young men with a look he said, "You will make contact with Íar and inform him of our situation." The Spartan's smile broadened, "You'll only have about ten thousand of Drostan's men to get through, but that shouldn't be a problem for such brave and experienced warriors."

Trapped by their impetuosity, Brocc and Labhraidh could do little save smile weakly at each other and excuse themselves. Cúscraid watched them march towards the chariots and said, "Bit rough that, don't you think?"

"They're smart," said Nikandros. "They'll figure it out. If they do, they'll be better men and warriors, and they'll learn to keep their feet out of their mouths in future."

Brion nodded and asked, "What about tomorrow?"

"Eachdonn's spears will remain inside the camp and ward off any attacks from the rivers. I'm reluctant to use them outside the camp. They simply don't know our battle tactics. They'll be joined by those too injured to stand in the wall and Áine's archers. The remainder of our force will be divided into three sections – one facing west, one facing south. The third will stand in reserve and support whichever flank is the main attack point for Drostan. We'll take up positions before dawn."

CHAPTER 12

Bodies glistened with sweat and an ever-present mizzle as the galleys were dragged, carried and pushed through the dense wildwood. They followed a narrow stream to the next loch - Loch Omhaich, and were thankful for the cool, fresh water it provided. Work progressed in relative silence. Axes and swords parted the undergrowth, but failed to stop thorns and thistles from taking a final revenge on exposed skin. Velvet nettle leaves brushed against legs and arms — their touch a deception, replaced by burning, red weals that demanded to be scratched. Men swore, grabbing bunches of dock leaves to rub on inflamed skin.

According to Deaglán and Torcán, the loch narrowed at a wooded peninsula and would barely allow the passage of a single galley. A sentinel broch stood guard over the headland. As he stood in the stern of the lead boat, Conall looked back with unease as the fourth galley glided towards the tip of the promontory. A cloud of ravens suddenly rose from the forest, their beating wings and raucous cries were a strident - if belated, warning.

Huge warriors appeared at the point, hefting and then hurling great rocks at the ships. The water churned as an avalanche of tree trunks crashed through the forest and tumbled into the loch. Small bands of slingers opened up on the vessels. The sharp crack of stones on wood echoed off the rocky bluffs across the waters.

Rowers struck by missiles slumped over their oars, releasing them to snag on those of their neighbors. Shouts of "Shields!" rose up from each galley. Every other man rose and swung his shield around to protect the remaining rowers. Archers on the vessels swiftly sent a stream of arrows into the wooded hillside. Slowly the torrent of rocks and stones subsided.

Tadhg's galley was at the center of the maelstrom. He grimaced with each thud as heavy logs propelled by momentum and the current battered the light cedarwood hull. The young man thanked the Goddess as heavy rocks narrowly missed his boat, drenching those within, and cursed as more were tossed. For a time the quick maneuvering of his oarsmen forestalled disaster, but then the Goddess' attention was briefly diverted to more weighty matters. The moment was enough.

An Ériu warrior wailed in agony as a massive rock struck his oar, then his thighs before crashing through the vessel's flat wooden bottom. His legs shattered, he slipped into unconsciousness. Ragged edges of thigh-bones punched through the bloody pulp of muscle and skin. The man's broken oar splintered. Its blade was dragged downward into the water and the ragged shard upward, punching a hole in the man's bare chest before exiting his back. Streamers of skin and muscle hung from its jagged point.

The shallow-drafted galley became quickly swamped with its gaping hull gushing water. "Into the water. Grab whatever you can," shouted Tadhg as another log slammed against the ship rupturing the slender hull. The galley groaned. Cables sheared, lashing the men. Its mast snapped and fell over, shrouding the crew with its black sail as the ship died.

Men tumbled into the cold, dark waters, gripping weapons and shields. The fortunate on the starboard side swam for the shoreline of a small island, which was a short distance away. Those on the port side had to contend with floating timbers pommeling bruised and tired bodies. Treading water, Tadhg scanned anxiously around to locate his men before making for the island. He did not see the green-brown bark of the tree trunk rising from below before it struck. There was an explosion of pain before the black waters reached out to take him.

Conall's simmering anger over the unresolved murder of Morna and the confrontation with her people was a festering wound. Now, as he watched with smoldering gray eyes the struggle in the water, and the galley sink, his wrath overflowed. He reached for his axes and bellowed, "Beach the ships. Kill the bastards."

The cry of, "Kill the bastards!" was taken up by those in the remaining seven ships as they maneuvered into the long, narrow inlet that almost split the peninsula in two. Before the boats ran aground, Conall's warriors grabbed shields and weapons, and foregoing their armor, leapt into the shallow waters. Seeking release from the previous horrors, over two hundred warriors and archers with bows held high, swarmed the beach. Once ashore, the band broke left and right. Conall led his caomhnóirí towards the gray stone broch, while Fearghal swung north to engage the attackers raining havoc on the galleys.

Swords and axes swinging, Fearghal's men cleaved a bloody path through the lightly armed slingers and a cohort of surprised spearmen. Under the fierce onslaught cries for mercy were ignored. Flesh was cut to the bone and corpses kicked aside. They rushed up the long wooded slope towards the point in search of the rock-throwers.

"Heads!" Deaglán's warning cry was followed by the sound of boulders and tree stumps crashing through the forest undergrowth. Men flung themselves to the side attempting to avoid the falling mass, but few escaped the lacerations inflicted by sharp-edged stones and wooden splinters.

"Bastards!" exclaimed Fearghal as he raised his head to observe the source of the barrage. On the crest of the hill stood a dozen of the biggest men he had ever seen. Each was at least a head taller than himself. The men were colossal in all respects with barrel sized bellies and thigh and arm muscles as thick as some trees. Long, shaggy red hair crowned their heads. It was matched by the thick beards that rested on their chests. Their wild appearance was enhanced by the coarse, thick red hair that covered their blue-painted and tattooed bodies. Great axes and clubs were hoisted above their heads as they roared defiance.

"That's just disgusting," said Deaglán, huffing his way up the slope. "They could at least put on some pants."

"The Hag help the mothers that birthed those bastards," said Fearghal. He looked around at his men, scanning to see if any had thought to pick up the thrown javelins. There were only a few. His rage slowly subsiding, Fearghal cursed himself at the rashness of the assault. They were unprepared. "Those with javelins and the archers to the front," he shouted. "Let loose when you're within range. The rest split into groups – one for each of those brutes."

It was a short march through the forest to the broch. Conall's band covered the distance quickly, quietly and without much of a sweat. When they arrived at the clearing, about one hundred warriors had formed a loose band before the tower's eastern facing entrance. Conall guessed another thirty or forty of the tribe remained within the walls of the broch.

The Aos a' Chùirn – The People of the Stone, were plainly not used to eliciting such a fierce reaction from their favorite pastime of "stones and stumps." They milled around in confusion as several warband leaders attempted to establish some level of defensive order. It was a hopeless task. They knew about fighting, but little about standing resolute before an enemy. With a great cry they charged Conall's men.

"Ionsaí!" Conall stabbed one of his axes in their direction and led his men forward.

The clash of bodies, blades and shields in the middle of the clearing rang deep into the wildwood. Several pairs of eagles circled in a brooding sky made opaque with rain. They watched with golden eyes. Both sides wore no armor and were largely naked. The woad-painted, weather-beaten Aos a' Chùirn contrasted sharply with their opponents. Apart from the tracks of previous battle scars, Conall's men were a pale canvas.

Bloody and brutal, the skirmish ebbed and flowed. Conall's arms ached from wielding his axes in countless strikes on stubborn flesh.

Bone and gristle resisted every attempt to be cleaved apart. The twist of the blades to remove iron from body was a hard pull. Without his helmet, his ears rang and bled from the slap of wood and metal. He tasted blood that oozed from the many cuts on his face.

Lack of caution – he was later to reflect that he had got too used to wearing chainmail, had added many slashes, some deep, to his exposed chest and back. Blood streamed down his arms making the axe handles slick. His hands cramped with the increasing force needed to maintain his grip. Unprotected, Conall's knuckles were beaten raw from the countless hits by spear shafts and wooden staffs.

To Conall's right, Torcán had lost shield, axe and sword and now fought with fists wrapped in studded leather. His battle-roar was a challenge to all. His head became a weapon, smashing against hard skulls as he butted, bit and gouged opponents. The old scar on Torcán's forehead opened up and blood masked his face. He turned to Conall baring bloody teeth in a ghoulish smile. "A nightmare," Conall thought. Torcán winced as a spear-point dragged across his shoulders and turned back to vent his rage on the unfortunate.

In the end, the battle turned on the fitness of the warriors. Conall's men were in peak condition and their endurance was greater. They countered, outlasted and then slaughtered the Aos a' Chùirn. The last opponent on the field stabbed his spear forward in desperation and was rewarded with a slashing blow that almost severed his head. Blood pumping from torn arteries, he slumped to the ground beside his comrades.

Conall rested a knee in the dirt, leaned on his axes and gazed around at the blood-soaked field. He coughed up a wad of phlegm and then sneezed loudly blowing out a lump of bloody snot. Cleared, his nostrils flinched at the smell of piss and shite. The ringing in his ears subsided although never quite disappeared. It was gradually replaced by the moaning of the injured and nearly dead. His eyes took in the broch with its high stone walls, likely at least three or four paces thick. The narrow entrance and absence of windows left little room for an attack, but the design also gave no advantage to the defenders. To Conall, brochs were great for storage and shelter, but not for war.

His eye settled on the thick cone of the thatched roof. Standing up, he called to Mórrígan, "Set the roof alight." Intent on his objective, Conall took no note of his queen. She stood naked save for her painted designs and a film of muck. Her nipples were hard and blood-red, her eyes glowed a deep jade from the ecstasy of battle. She acknowledged his command and, walking with a grace at odds with the blood and gore that surrounded her, made her way to her archers.

The thatch was damp and frustratingly hard to set alight, but eventually the flames took hold. Smoky fingers rose to smudge the gray-blue afternoon sky. Before long, smoke filled the building. Muffled coughs and choked cries with oaths and curses came from the broch. Finally, a group of older men, women and children fled the structure, falling about in the dirt as they escaped. All were blackened from soot and ash. A few were burned – their skin a patchwork of blisters and angry red weals.

One elderly warrior attempted to get to his feet, but several black-shafted arrows ensured that he never would rise again. Conall swung round and glared at Mórrígan, "Did I give an order to shoot? Do you still thirst for blood?" Startled at this reaction, Mórrígan hissed in anger and frustration. Chest heaving as she struggled to control herself, she turned and stormed back to the galleys.

The rage of battle had waned and, as Conall looked at each of his men, he saw little taste for more slaughter in their eyes. "We'll return to the galleys. Let the survivors rebuild."

With a sigh of relief, the men quickly searched the nearest bodies for anything of value. Taking up their injured, Conall's caomhnóirí made its way back to the inlet and their ships.

Tadhg floated into consciousness. He was lying on a grassy bank, his face stiff with blood and his head throbbing. His vision was blurred, but for a moment he saw a painted spirit above him. She smiled and continued wiping his face with a cool, wet cloth. He drifted back into the blackness with a huge and somewhat silly grin on his face. "I'm dreaming," he murmured, "or I'm in Mag Mell. Nice tits for a spirit."

Tadhg's brother Craiftine observed from a few paces behind Gràinne. A year older than Tadhg, Craiftine was a skilled harpist. Indeed, as the galley sank, he had first rescued his harp, securing it on his back, before weapons or shield. He was grateful for, though slightly distrusting of the motive behind Grainne's surprising rescue of his brother. Her intervention, diving into the cold waters and pulling Tadhg ashore, had certainly prevented him from drowning.

Craiftine coughed and said, "You've my thanks and that of my brothers for saving Tadhg." Gràinne twisted around to look at him. "The men will make camp a short distance away, but I doubt it wise to move Tadhg. We'll send food to you." He smiled a little, "I expect our friends will rescue us from this island when the sun rises."

The archers and those warriors with javelins had dropped five of the giant rock-throwers. This still left seven behemoths. Feeling secure on their ridge, the remaining Aos a' Chùirn waved clubs and axes in oversized fists and hurled insults at Fearghal and his men. The space between the two groups had become too close for the archers to draw and shoot safely. Those with javelins preferred to hold off throwing wishing to stay outside the colossuses' reach.

Fearghal took a deep breath, jumped up, raised his longsword in a two handed grip and strode forward. He swung the blade across the belly of the giant before him. The blade's point sliced through fat and muscle drawing a thin gush of blood. The man grunted, but ignored the slashing blade, just as he had ignored the four arrows whose barbs were sunk deep into his torso. He continued to swing both club and axe.

To Fearghal's left, Deaglán attempted to maneuver around the warrior. However, while Fearghal had quickly stepped a pace back following his strike, Deaglán's timing was poor. The young man's jaw met an ash club, its roughly hewn knob banded with several iron rings. Luckily Deaglán was already moving backwards, yet the impact was more than sufficient to send him flat unconscious.

The Aos a' Chùirn's position on the cliff edge was virtually un-assailable, but had one weakness. There was no escape path. Behind them was the cliff edge. The cliff foot was a short, but steep descent to the frothing waters below. Quickly regrouping, Fearghal gave orders to those that remained standing. "Ionsaí!" he roared. As one, the men charged the hill crest, shouting and screaming like mná-sidhe. While the Aos a' Chùirn warriors had immense strength, they lacked nimble thought. Startled, they retreated a few paces without considering their precarious position. Immediately beyond the hill's crest the ground was a loose mix of rock and dirt. With the additional weight the cliff edge began to crumble.

The hulking warriors' previously firm stance was gone and Fearghal's men pushed forward again. The Aos a' Chùirn were off-balance and being driven steadily backwards when the edge collapsed. With a bellow of rage and scrambling for any foot or handhold, the giants toppled over the side. "I hope the bastards drown," Fearghal snorted as he glanced over the brink.

The galleys had been dragged ashore and secured. It was late afternoon, as the two bands of warriors sighted the camp set up by Pytheas and his crew. They were met by a livid Mongfhionn. She trembled with fury eyeing the men as they helped support limping comrades. In some cases they carried unconscious friends across their shoulders.

"Eejits! Idiots!" she thundered. "You would jeopardize the mission for what? Petty anger? Revenge? Your foolish bloodlust will have its consequences." The Sidhe fixed Conall and Fearghal with a withering stare. "If you want my help then you, Conall Mac Gabhann, will start acting like a king and you, Fearghal Ruad, like the experienced and wise battle commander that is your reputation." With a sweep of her gray cloak, the Sidhe swung around and strode towards the forest.

"That's telling us," Fearghal said quietly.

Conall sighed. "Problem is that she's right," he said. "We'll rest tonight and see what the damage is in the morning."

It was dusk when Tadhg awoke to conflicting sensations. The right side of his face was tight. His head throbbed and even the slightest movement brought sharp spikes of pain. This, however, was countered by the slow rhythmic stroking between his legs which provided both pleasure and confusion. Gingerly, he raised his head.

"I wondered what might help you recover," an impish smile broke on Gràinne's young face as she continued her attentions to his stiffening manhood. She straddled him. Nipples hard from the chilling air, rubbed across his hairless chest, and her long auburn tresses brushed over his face. "And remember, you did say I had nice breasts – so you made the first move."

"Noise," Tadhg muttered hoarsely as he felt her soft bush rubbing his hardness. "The men will hear."

"Then you'd better be quiet," she responded as she first raised then lowered herself. Warm and very wet, Gràinne cooed a satisfied sigh as she felt Tadhg slide inside. Tadhg groaned, he knew this was unwise on many levels. Then, ignoring his pains, he grabbed her soft round ass and squeezed it roughly as he thrust hard up into her.

Sunrise brought an unhappy chorus of groans and curses as aching warriors stretched and discovered new cuts and fresh bruises or awakened old wounds. Soon the shore waters ran to a weak red as blood was washed from battle injuries. Added to this were the streams of piss that arched and splashed into the loch. Childish competitions as to who could piss the farthest brought smiles and laughter.

Tadhg watched as the galley pulled closer to the island and turned once more to observe Gràinne as she lay, still asleep, beside him. He was unable to stop the stirring between his legs as he recalled the previous night and the slap of his thighs on her arse as he took her. Tadhg savored her young body as she lay glistening in the morning sun and mizzle. Yet there was something about the designs that veiled her skin and shielded her spirit that made him uneasy. Some recollection agitated his memory, but he could not bring it forward.

His musings were brought to a close as Gràinne's eyes opened. She rolled onto her right side and watched him, her head held up as she rested on an elbow. Slowly her left hand traced along her belly, and her leg rose and parted to expose her auburn-red bush, "Enter me again," she spoke huskily. Tadhg was torn between the stupidity of what she was asking and his desire for her body.

Fortunately the decision was taken from him as he heard a twig crack and the overloud voice of his brother, "Galley's arrived." Craiftine sighed and his eyebrow lifted as he saw the startled couple stand up. "No good, no good will come of this," he said to himself. Then he joined them and walked to the waiting craft.

Conall was angry at himself. He knew the Sidhe was right. Their foray on the peninsula was foolish. The skirmish on the island had cost them twenty men. While none were dead, their injuries were severe and would not heal quickly. They would be of no use and likely a hindrance in the campaign. They had lost one galley and with it nine men – almost a quarter of its crew.

"There's no profit in regret," Fearghal said, voicing Conall's thoughts. "If the Goddess allows, we'll probably do more foolish things in the future, but in the meantime we deal with it and move on."

Conall nodded and called Mongfhionn to his side, "Perhaps you would lead our sacrifices to the Goddess before we continue our journey?"

Her countenance softened, acknowledging Conall's attempt to make amends, "Of course."

The seven galleys slid into the flat waters to continue their voyage north and Pytheas prayed once more to Poseidon. According to his calculations and limited knowledge of the area, there was one more body of water, one more loch to navigate - Loch Nis. This mysterious stretch of water, known by reputation and rumor, was by far the largest and the deepest of all the lochs.

Tadhg sat across from Deaglán. Both were sporting new scars.

Tadhg's was a long gash from his right cheek to his jawline — the result of the log that had slammed into him. Deaglán rubbed the ragged, raised reddish-white line that ran horizontally along his jaw and which currently sat in a field of angry blues and purples. For both men, meals in the immediate future were likely to consist of thin soups and gruel.

Deaglán settled quickly, his pains dulled by the monotone thump of the stroke drum and the rhythm of oars striking the water. Tadhg could find no such relief. His mind was disturbed and his eyes were irresistibly drawn to the galley where Gràinne sat alongside Torcán. He recalled lifting Gràinne from the muddy waters' edge into the rescue vessel. He also recalled the imprint of her foot left in the mud before the waves smoothed it.

The footprint was smaller than, though similar to, the one he had seen near the location of Morna's murder. Both were noticeably angled inwards. It was an explanation of the strange, although not unattractive gait that marked Gràinne's walk. "What, if anything, did it mean?" He felt his head start to throb.

CHAPTER 13

Drostan Ruadh sat with his father in the flickering rushlight and tugged his short red beard. He was considering committing another ten thousand warriors to the army already in place. "Well, what's yer counsel? If ten thousand men haven't been enough to claw the rats from their nest, will another ten make a difference?"

"Ten thousand trees are like nothing in our forests," said Failbhe. "Ten thousand men – that's just ten rows of a thousand - twenty of five hundred. A good charioteer could drive through that with little difficulty. The number sounds more impressive than it is. More important is the quality of the men." Failbhe rose stiffly, scratched his arse and paced the tent to loosen his bones. "We have numbers. They have quality."

"Ye'r of little help, old man. Do I need a new leader of the Comhairle-Chatha?"

"Do I care? Slit my throat and let me rest in Mag Mell," the elder snapped back. "The question ye should be asking is how many men do ye want to lose to defeat those bastards? Throw another ten… twenty… thirty thousand at them and aye, there is no doubt ye will be triumphant - but at what cost? So far there have been a few hard and bloody skirmishes. Put their backs to the wall and believe me, they will slaughter our warriors by the thousand before they are finally slain. Have ye enough power and loyal men to survive that?"

The Aos na Coille leader grunted in response. He had reached the same conclusion as his father. He could better manage an unsatisfactory outcome with his current force. A potential defeat of a bigger army or even victory with a heavy body count might cause him problems. Rebellious chieftains would need to be executed. "Maybe, I should join them and fight Finnean Mac Sèitheach at Dún Na Mèadaidh. If that white-haired bastard were dead, who'd care about me breaking an oath to him?"

"That was a choice ye could have made – maybe should have made, earlier," Failbhe said. "Ye need to encourage the Ériu to move on. In a sense they're only here because ye forced them to make a stand. Find the right lever and they'll go away."

A cough at the tent entrance broke the conversation. Drostan looked up and beckoned the messenger forward, "Well?"

"We've reports that several chariots are preparing to move out – likely from the southern gateway."

Drostan smiled and considered, "The cavalry. It has to be the cavalry. The chariots are aiming to break through and warn their mounted friends." He thought for a moment and then issued his orders, "Tell the army on the southern side to let at least one chariot escape – don't make it easy or they'll suspect something." As the messenger made to exit, Drostan added, "Ask Bearach to come in." The man nodded and left.

A morose Bearach squeezed his large frame through the tent's narrow opening. His mood was ignored by both Drostan and Failbhe. "They'll be expecting us to attack heavily on the southern side. We won't oblige. Two thousand will attack the southern wall. The main force will attack the western wall. Soften them up with the slings again." Dismissed and in a slightly better humor at the thought of battle, Bearach bent his head and withdrew.

A raspy chuckle came from the far edge of the tent, "Weaken the south to provide a way for the bastards to retreat. Always assuming they don't believe it's a trick."

"We'll soon see what humor the gods are in." Drostan smiled at his father and left.

"You're an eejit. Next time keep your bloody mouth shut!" Labhraidh berated Brocc yet again as he checked and re-checked their chariot's reins, the wheels, cret, and the horses for any sign of wear or damage. He had already sent one horse away for a minor cut and had new sets of leather and iron reins installed. Brocc gritted his teeth resisting the urge to punch his friend and remind him that he had been equally as enthusiastic about having some action. That said, he too was examining the chariot's weaponry closely. After some quick lessons from his sister-in-law, Áine, he had added a bow and quiver of arrows as well as extra javelins and two spare axes.

Brion and Cúscraid watched with considerable amusement. "Form the men up as planned when they have left," said Nikandros, wiping the last traces of gruel from his tightly curled, black beard before it set like a rock. Recklessly fast in the early dawn light, the three chariots careered out of the gateway and along the eastern path. Almost simultaneously, a war horn broke the morning silence and another hail of stones descended on the camp.

"There are enough bloody stones to pave the yard," said Cúscraid puffing a little as he took shelter against the stockade wall beside Brion.

Brion raised an eyebrow, shifted his shield and continued to gnaw on a meaty rib. "I wonder if Fionnbharr has any peppermint left in his pouch. All these interruptions to my meals makes my belly and throat burn," he muttered loudly enough to be heard above the clatter of stones. Cúscraid rolled his eyes and laughed loudly. The infectious laughter rippled and echoed around the fence.

A hard ride interspersed with frequent stops to rest the horses brought Íar's men to the foothills. To his back stood the white peaks of Beinn an Laoigh. Before him stretched the forests and wildwoods that led to the camp — and their friends. There had been few problems with their captives and a noticeable change in the Druid's demeanor as he recognized the direction they were moving and the familiar landscape of the Aos na Coille forests. Íar smiled to himself,

"The fool thinks we're riding into the hands of the Drostan."

Impatient to be united with their comrades, most would have ridden through the night. Íar, however, knew that the horses needed to be fed and rested if they were to be fresh for the final leg of the journey. He ordered the camp set up and an early night for the men.

Thus, they rose at the first hint of the yellow-gray hues of dawn and rode west to meet the river that flowed past the camp. If the Goddess allowed, they would be re-united before mid-day.

Stray stones rattled off his chariot's cret as Brocc led the small party away from the camp. The likelihood of threading a cautious or unobserved path through the ranks of the waiting Aos na Coille was slender. Hence, their wild dash across the cleared ground and into the ancient forest. As Brion had commented to Nikandros, while young and overly confident of his immortality, Brocc had chosen the teams of the other two chariots well – they were the most experienced. Thus, the seemingly foolish risk was tempered with drivers who could negotiate a chariot through the tightest of spaces.

Aos na Coille horns blared out, announcing the chariots' presence. Warriors, concealed in the forest, took up their war cry and quickly converged on the vehicles. They hurled axes, spears, rocks and heavy branches trying to halt the chariots' flight. The brave – or the foolish, whose approach put them within the reach of the arms-length, spinning scythes were rewarded with severed limbs. Torn, painted flesh splattered the cret and its occupants. A well-placed javelin pinned a few to the trees they loved and worshiped.

They thundered on deeper into the pines, but fewer warriors appeared to harry their progress. "Strange," said Brocc scanning the terrain carefully. Then he shouted, "Shite!" as he was flung to the side and slammed against the wicker cret. Gripping the length of leather rope attached to the cret he shouted, "By the Hag, Labhraidh! I'd prefer to die by a blade than break my neck falling from this chariot."

"Felled trees block our path. Hold on." The chariot swerved to avoid yet another log, then another and another. "The bastards are herding us," Labhraidh said grimly. Brocc watched as all three chariots converged. The trap was sprung as they burst from the forest cover into a large clearing. Before them, on the far side of the open space, were arrayed many Aos na Coille chariots. Behind the chariots rows of warriors formed a thorny fence with their spears.

"Bollocks!" Brocc exhaled. His only advantages were speed and the much heavier chariots. The young warrior, his face tight and teeth bared in a fierce mask, bellowed at the others, "Faster! Hit them hard and fast!" All three drivers cracked whips above their horses' heads. Powerful muscles drove the sweating horses forward.

It was a reasonable expectation that their enemy's chariots would slow and swerve to escape. Instead the trio, screaming like mná-sidhe, axes and javelins held high, stormed onward. Startled into action, the Aos na Coille whipped up their horses urging them to advance. From a standing start the lighter chariots could not match their enemies' momentum. A wedge of three heavy chariots cleaved their formation before they made any headway.

The air filled with the shrieks of men, the screaming of horses, and the tortured sound of twisting and shattered wood. In a ballet of destruction, chariots were pitched into the air scattering their occupants. Wooden splinters, shards of metal and lashing hooves maimed and killed. Brocc landed with a grunt on his right shoulder. In disbelief, both sides paused to take in the scene. The smashed chariots lay ringed with a halo of blood and torn flesh.

Brocc lay where he had been flung for the span of a few stunned breaths before scrambling for his axe. He turned to face the enemy. At the sound of a soft moan he glanced to his left. In pain, Labhraidh had crawled to the overturned chariot and sat with his back to it. A javelin, butt end in the dirt, wavered in his right hand. His left arm hung limp at his side. Blood welled from a ragged-edged wound in his left thigh from which a large splinter erupted. They were joined by a second chariot team – bloodied, but still able to fight. Twenty paces distant, the third team lay misshapen and still.

The leader of the Aos na Coille force was speechless at the damage and the madness of Brocc. He had expected the chariots to swerve away from his barrier. His force would have given chase and pushed them towards the river on the north. After a skirmish that would have satisfied both sides' honor, the Ériu charioteers would have been allowed to escape. Instead, he stared at the wreckage of six of his chariots and the broken bodies of his charioteers and spearmen strewn over the dirt like twigs. "Stupid, bloody eejits," he spat.

Now he had a problem. Drostan had clearly commanded that the chariots should be allowed to escape, but these twisted and broken shells were going nowhere. Added to his worries was his kinship to Bearach. There were well-founded rumors that Drostan's battle commander had lost favor with the king. While the king might hesitate at making an example of Bearach, his kin might serve as a suitable proxy. "Shite!" he hissed through clenched jaws before turning to issue his orders. The best he could do was to pull his men back and hope that no one questioned how the escape went.

Brocc shook his head in disbelief as the forest swallowed the Aos na Coille warriors. "I didn't think we were that good," he spoke aloud, causing a ripple of laughter. The relief was short-lived as Labhraidh moaned and then slumped over. Brocc gently laid him on his back and propped his head up, but Labhraidh's face was a waxy, yellow-gray. His breathing was labored. The thigh wound bled rhythmically.

Frantically, Brocc pulled his belt off and tied it around Labhraidh's thigh. He had watched Fionnbharr and Mongfhionn do this for others to stem the flow of blood. A clammy hand rested on his arm, "Too late, friend. I'll wait for you in Mag Mell."

"No!" Brocc howled in anguish and guilt as his friend began a new journey without him.

The sun rose in the sky and the forest came alive with bird song, the drone of insects and the rustlings of small animals. Two warriors stood silently, taking up guard positions over Brocc who cradled Labhraidh's head in his arms. He rocked to and fro. Tears flowed from Brocc's red-rimmed eyes and dropped onto Labhraidh's face.

Íar surveyed the scene before him as he led his cavalry from the cover of the pines. "By the Hag, I hope that's not all that remains of our army." To Ròidh he said, "Secure the clearing while I find out what took place here." Dismounting, he removed his helmet, shook his braids free and walked towards the small group.

The warriors standing over Brocc sighed with relief as they recognized Íar. He drew them aside and listened to their tale, pausing only to say a short prayer for Labhraidh. When they had finished he laid a hand on Brocc's shoulder, "We should go, Brocc. Pick up Labhraidh. We'll take him back with us. His brothers will want to say their farewells."

Brocc didn't move. His eyes were hollow and unseeing. "It's my fault."

"Maybe it was," Íar spoke gruffly. "But this is not the time for self-pity. Get up, take a horse and ride. We've a camp to relieve and a battle to stop." Brocc continued to berate himself. "I've no time for this," Íar said to the other two as his great fist took Brocc under the chin snapping his head backwards. Brocc sprawled unconscious in the dirt as Íar said, "Tie him to a horse. If he continues to speak of his guilt - gag him."

The slingers' supply of stones diminished and Nikandros said, "It's time, before they charge the walls." Brion and Cúscraid called to the ceannairí céad and three columns of men streamed from the western and southern gates. Each cohort stood five hundred strong, two rows of shields and javelins positioned beyond the perimeter ditches to the west and south. The remaining spears, archers and injured guarded the camp.

Bearach's battle cry was echoed by thousands of Aos na Coille voices and many war-horns. He pointed his axe forward and again the painted wave crashed against the shield walls. Frenzied attackers threw themselves against a wall of spikes that quickly dripped blood. A sticky haze of drool, spit and blood soon coated everything. When it was apparent there was to be no attack on the southern wall, Brion closed ranks with Nikandros forming a line of shields, five hundred men wide and two deep. Cúscraid's men stood in reserve behind them.

The Aos na Coille tànaiste and his captains shouted, cajoled and screamed curses at their men and women urging them on, watching for any sign of weakness. It was not long before the red shield wall was buttressed by the mound of bodies oozing blood, shite and piss piling up before it. The Aos na Coille slipped in blood and excrement. Feet sank to the ankles in a bog of gore-soaked mud. The greater reach of the Ériu javelins helped keep the blue warriors at bay, but gradually the stronger numbers began to tell and push the wall back to the perimeter ditch. Cúscraid called forward an increasing number of reserves to replace the injured and the exhausted.

Nikandros knew his men were in need of a respite. He could only think of one, but it would lose their advantage of reach. Nevertheless, if the shields held, it would be worth the risk. He bellowed, "Front row hold. Rear row throw javelins." Along the shield wall, the order was relayed. Five hundred javelins arced over their comrades and into the morning air. The enemy's ranks shuddered, but kept coming. Nikandros shouted once more, "Front row, pass javelins to the rear. Unsheathe swords. Rear row throw." The second volley of missiles slammed once more into naked flesh. The line faltered. It was enough to allow swords to clear leather and wood sheaths.

Swords glinted briefly in the morning sunshine, and then became dull with blood. The gouging of iron spikes was replaced with the vicious stabbing and slashing of razor-edged blades. As Aos na Coille spears and axes were deflected by the curved, chin-to-knee shields, the short swords lopped off fingers, hands and arms. They sank into bellies. Efforts to spear Ériu shins and legs were foiled by thick leg wrappings, and then rewarded with a slashing downward blow to the head. Skulls opened up, spilling pinkish-tan brain-matter. Both sides began to tire. Frustration and anger made the Aos na Coille more reckless. They lost more men, but kept pushing the wall backwards.

The usual light rain began toward mid-day and Nikandros considered that he had two options - retreat to the camp stockade or attack the Aos na Coille. He quickly discarded the first since the narrow causeways to the camp would expose his men to attack as they retreated. Resigning himself to charging the overwhelming numbers of Aos na Coille, the Spartan tightened his chin strap.

As he opened his mouth to give the order to charge, a loud blast from a familiar horn resounded from the southern edge of the battlefield. To roars of delight and defiance from the shield wall, Íar's cavalry launched their attack on the flank of the Aos na Coille. Three volleys of javelins from Íar's five hundred horsemen disrupted the painted's onslaught. They faltered and began to withdraw as the riders switched to axes and long swords, hacking and slashing at all before them.

On the northern side of the river, Drostan turned to Failbhe, "It seems that the cavalry have returned. What good timing!"

Placing his cavalry before the weary shield wall, Íar trotted over to Nikandros and with a huge smile beamed, "Need some help?"

"Bastard. You cut that a bit fine." Nikandros grasped Íar's arm. "It's good to see you friend, but we're still well-outnumbered. I'm not sure we could have survived my next tactic. My guess is that Drostan has been holding back from sending even more against us."

"Well, I've brought a few fidchell pieces to the game." Íar faced the camp where Ròidh's men had entered by the southern gate and sent several blasts of his horn into the air. The signal was answered with cries, screams and scuffling. Shortly after, a wagon was pushed and pulled out of the camp's west gate coming to a stop on the causeway.

"Clever bastards. Now we know where the cavalry went - to A' Chrìon Làraich." Failbhe shook his head. "I must be getting old not to have considered this."

The king grunted, "They shouldn't have known about A' Chrìon Làraich. Young Ròidh Mac Eachdonn rides with them. He must have told them."

"We should pay Eachdonn Breac a visit when this is over," Failbhe retorted.

Drostan sighed, and then called one of his captains, "Send a signal to halt the fighting. Bring my chariot. Signal the other men to be ready." The man bowed and rushed off. Not long after, the war horns resounded with the message.

Bearach was stunned. In his bones he knew that the tide of battle had been flowing in his favor. At least until the horsemen arrived. Even then he still thought his numbers an advantage and that he would eventually prevail. That was before Drostan's children had been displayed and the great battle horns commanded the fighting cease.

The embittered tànaiste did a quick calculation as to how many men remained under his control and who were their chieftains. By his reckoning he had over five thousand warriors and most of their captains were his kin. He also saw that Drostan's children were vulnerable. Ambition to usurp Drostan over-rode common sense. He ignored the king's call for a halt and re-launched the battle.

Confusion reigned as Aos na Coille battle horns sounded out contradictory messages. Not all the warriors on the battlefield had loyalty to Bearach or his kin and only around half followed the brutish commander as they charged. This time towards Drostan's family.

Íar and Nikandros both uttered curses. Íar's riders moved forward to intercept and deflect the horde while Nikandros signaled a bemused Cúscraid and Brion to protect the hostages.

Meanwhile, a furious Drostan Ruadh crossed the river downstream of the camp. He was accompanied by the leading edge of a second force of ten thousand men. Spotting the unmistakable figure of Drostan enter the field, Íar said, "Let them fight among themselves," and led his men back to support Nikandros.

Although not a very clear or strategic thinker, Bearach became all too aware of his predicament. He considered who he could blame for continuing the battle. In the end he decided to brazen it out. He made his way to Drostan after signaling his men to stop. "It is good to see you, My King. My men were about to rescue your sons and daughters. Let us join forces and drive these invaders from our lands."

Axe in hand, Drostan descended from his chariot. There was an ominous and cruel aspect to the king's face. "The signal for the battle to stop was given. Clearly these bastard foreigners want to negotiate. Why did you put my heirs in danger?"

Mouth dry, Bearach's tongue flicked across his cracked lips. Nervously, he scanned for possible escape routes, "I never heard… misunderstood the signal, My King."

"Which is it? Did you not hear or did you misunderstand the signal? Or perhaps you saw a chance to murder my family and take my place?"

Bearach blanched and setting aside his axe raised his hands to protest his innocence. Drostan's axe took the man diagonally from left shoulder to groin. The huge warrior's eyes teared with pain as the curved blade ripped through soft flesh and broke ribs. He bent reflexively, his hands twitching, trying to prevent guts from spilling onto the dirt. His legs failed and he stumbled to his knees.

Drostan's new commander took a pace forward. A downward sweep of his axe broke Bearach's neck. The head dropped and hung suspended by a thin flap of skin. Drostan raised a quizzical eyebrow as blood gushed from the wound splashing both king and commander. Grumbling, the chieftain took a knife and cut the flap of skin holding head to neck. He kicked both head and corpse aside.

"Hang every chieftain or noble who disobeyed me," Drostan growled. "Execute all of Bearach's kin – men, women and children." A quick dip of the warrior's head showed he understood. As an afterthought, Drostan added, "Hang one in ten of the rest of these men. Perhaps those remaining will understand what a signal means in the future."

Having taken care of his own housekeeping, finally, the king walked across to Íar and Nikandros who had plainly overheard his conversation. "Every king needs a scapegoat. Yer king will learn this." Taking a deep breath Drostan continued, "We'll tend to our fallen. I'll return this evening to hear yer terms." Looking to his plainly frightened children, a father's concern briefly flitted across the king's face before he called out, "Behave yourselves. Ye'r in no danger. I'll return for ye."

The fires roared high in the camp. Courtesy of Drostan, boar, sheep and cattle roasted on makeshift spits and large barrels of beer were cracked open. Sitting on logs on one side of a makeshift table, Failbhe and several members of the Comhairle-Chatha glared at those on the other side. Drostan merely smiled wryly at Nikandros, Cúscraid, Íar, Ròidh, Brion and Áine. A hundred Aos na Coille warriors stood glowering nearby.

"Seems ye'r always eating or stealing my food," Drostan broke the silence. "When do I get to see my children?" Íar smiled, turned and waved. The Druid led the four children to stand before their father. Instantly Drostan's men stood alert, reaching for their weapons.

"Let's not be foolish," said Íar, his deep green eyes glinting in the light of the flames. "The children are scared as it is. I doubt you would make it to the gate and beyond that, my cavalry await. I've no wish to see more bloodshed, but will not shrink from it."

"There will be no fighting," Drostan said to Íar, but his voice carried to his men as a command. In a lighter tone he added, "I suppose I should thank ye since I haven't seen my children in quite a while. That ye also brought my brother, who I haven't seen in an even longer time, is a mixed blessing."

"Your brother? The Druid!" Íar slapped his forehead and roared with laughter, "I'm so bad with family resemblances."

At this Failbhe spat into the fire, "I wanted a warrior to watch his brother's back. I got a bloody priest."

The Druid looked with equal disdain on his father, "It is good to see you too, Father," he said. "I think we're here to come to an accommodation that safeguards the heirs to the Aos na Coille throne." Then smiling at his brother he added, "They have been well cared for. No harm, save a belt across the arse for being ill-mannered, has come to them."

"What do ye want?" said Drostan.

Nikandros said, "You will guarantee safe passage for our people and the army through your lands." Íar nodded at this. "We never had cause to fight the Aos na Coille and will only fight to protect ourselves. For that, we will hand over two of your children immediately. The other two will be sent back once we cross the borders of your lands. The Druid will remain as guardian to those who stay. After that he may travel wherever he wishes."

Drostan cut short a rumble of discontent and angry words at the demand, "There is no choice. The deal is as fair as I would have offered."

Íar held up his hand, "There is one more small condition." Nikandros, Brion and Cúscraid exchanged puzzled looks.

Drostan muttered, "It's never simple." Then to Íar, "Well?"

"The snows are already drifting down the mountains. We need a winter refuge." A sigh escaped Drostan as Íar continued, "We wish to winter at A' Chrìon Làraich."

Sprays of meat and beer exploded from the mouths of Drostan's Comhairle-Chatha, accompanied by the shaking of heads and vehement assertions of, "No." and "Impossible."

"And what compensation do we get for permitting ye to winter in our lands? And for the inevitable complaints I will get from that white-haired bastard, Finnean Mac Sèitheach?"

"I think we can make you a fair offer. A' Chrìon Làraich has the potential to become a major trading center and is strategically located. Cúscraid will rebuild its fortifications. You'll never have a better ráth. We'll defend the village from thieves, brigands and anyone else. Our people will tend the fields and plant crops, so your people will not suffer hardship. Any of the Aos na Coille remaining at the village will be treated well – as long as we have no trouble. And, I'll throw in a chest of gold to sweeten the offer."

Failbhe laughed, "Likely, that would be our gold from the bodies ye stripped." To his son, he said, "The Comhairle-Chatha will support whatever decision ye make."

With a deeper sigh, Drostan rose up, stretched out his hand and said, "Agreed." Íar rose and grasped the king's hand and forearm. "So, who chooses which of my children is to stay or go?"

"You," said Brion. "Your choice will settle a wager among us."

Drostan laughed, "The two youngest will come with me. The

eldest will remain as yer hostages." Cries of protest from the older children were stilled by a sharp, "Ye'll do as ye'r told. Ye will observe these people and learn their ways. Ye might meet them as an ally or an enemy in the future."

Áine smiled at her brother and held out her hand, "Pay up boys."

In a far corner of the camp, Fionnbharr kept guard over his brother's body. Occasionally he glared at Brocc who sat, head in his hands. Labhraidh's corpse had been washed and dressed in his best clothes and armor. Once the Aos na Coille departed, Fionnbharr would take Labhraidh's body and lay it on the funeral pyre. In Mongfhionn's absence, the Druid had volunteered to say words over the body and Fionnbharr had gratefully accepted.

Brocc mourned the loss of his friend. He knew Fionnbharr held him accountable and could see the anger that burned in Fionnbharr's eyes. Indeed, Brocc held himself accountable. He had been foolish and it had cost him dearly. Since his return, however, his constant melancholy and self-pity had worn thin the patience and sympathy of family and friends.

"We don't forget and rarely forgive," Brion thought as he looked with concern at Fionnbharr and Brocc. Sadly, the red hair of the natives of Ériu went with short tempers. They were quick to take offense, quick to take up arms, and resolute in keeping score. The last thing that the army needed was a smoldering feud between the ó Cuileannáins and the ó Cathasaighs. As head of the ó Cathasaighs, Brion would have little choice but to stand with his brother. He shook his head, "No sense in worrying about something that hasn't happened." Brion got up and went to stand before Brocc.

"The situation is shite. Get over it. Get over yourself. Get yourself some food and sleep."

Brocc exhaled slowly and stood up. He glanced self-consciously at Fionnbharr and walked with head down over to the nearest cooking fire. "No sense in starving, I suppose."

CHAPTER 14

Cassius Fabius Scaeva's tongue unconsciously, but persistently worried the ragged edge of the broken tooth. It raised a long blister, adding to his misery. A vain man, Cassius was thankful that it was not a prominently positioned tooth. Once back in Rome he would have it pulled and a gold replacement fitted. He rubbed his swollen and bruised jaw and cursed the man whose fist had caused his latest misery.

Normally cunning and calculating, Cassius' impatience with his captivity had reached the breaking point. His inquisitiveness at the stranger visiting the Na Daoine Smeurta settlement got the better of him and, hoping to glean some useful tidbits of information, he edged closer to the campfire.

In one sense his gambit succeeded. The visitor had informed his hosts, for the price of a meal and supplies, of a small, but well-armed warband making its way north and of a much larger force moving south. Ceallach was a slight man of average height, with well-defined muscles and watchful eyes. Scarred hands hovered over the well-worn, bone hilts of a pair of long daggers.

Hope stirred in Cassius' breast before a kick in the stomach and a calloused fist to his chin laid him out. Laughter from the campfire rang in his ears. His last impression was of the piercing eyes of the stranger taking measure of him as if to determine his value.

Finnean Mac Sèitheach sat deep in thought. His elbow rested on his knee; his angular chin cupped in the slender fingers of his left hand. The fingernails of his right drummed a rhythmic beat on the arm of the elaborately carved wooden throne. A screen of long, white hair hung forward, obscuring most of his face from those in the room. Finnean's mind was disturbed, not from his usual madness, but from the feeling that events were moving beyond his control.

He seethed at the thought of Drostan Ruadh's duplicity. Despite his alliance with Finnean, Drostan had reached an accommodation with the Ériu invaders. And for what? A few tearful children? Surely Drostan could have replaced them from a host of willing women.

An attack on Dún Na Mèadaidh was inevitable, although probably not before the feast of Imbolg, at winter's end. That gave him time to prepare. He would negotiate with the An t-Aos-Sìthiche and Aos nan Con-Seilge for warriors to defend his lands. The bastards would likely want gold and even more access to his mines. He might be forced to buy mercenaries from some of the tribes farther south. Housing and feeding the additional forces would cost him more gold.

Unhappy, Finnean groaned as he lifted his head. In the light his eyes appeared red-violet and glowered at the chosen envoys before him. "Visit with each of the tribes. Come to an agreement that I will approve of. If I do not like what you have negotiated, then you will hang from the walls of Dún Na Mèadaidh. Go!" With a sharp flourish of his bony hand he dismissed the quailing emissaries.

The journey from Loch Omhaich to Loch Nis was arduous. Yet, it served to keep the men occupied as they hauled the galleys along the narrow river linking the two waters. Pytheas reassured Conall that the body of water known as Loch Nis was the last before they reached the settlement of Cùil Daothail. There they would part company. Conall's force would trek north. Pytheas would gather his remaining galleys and sail south for the warmer waters and climes of the Great Sea.

Soothed by the waters' gentle lapping against the ships, the band rested on the loch's southern shoreline. Dusk lowered her mauve cloak upon the land as a honey-colored sun sank through the clouds. Brisk winds flowed down the mountain slopes that skirted the loch refreshing the evening air with the fragrance of pine woods.

Conall spoke to Fearghal, Mongfhionn, Mórrígan and Pytheas. "We'll rest here until the men with minor injuries heal," he said. "The more seriously injured we can do little about, save bring them with us." Resigned agreement and sighs greeted his words. "On the morrow, Deaglán will take his galley and reconnoiter the loch. His orders will be to remain unseen and not engage. The rest of the men who are fit can get in some weapons practice. In the meantime, Pytheas will make sure the ships are ready for this last stretch."

After the group split up, Mongfhionn walked a few paces into the loch's cold waters. She shivered at the chill and her toes curled digging reflexively into the silt bottom. "Taking in the view?" Fearghal asked, as he sat on the sand and pebble beach. He skimmed a few flat stones across the water.

The Sidhe smiled, "There's a strange resonance to this loch, Fearghal."

"Is that good or bad?"

"I'm not sure. My spirit feels comfort from the waters, but there's a warning tone of danger in the depths. Of something ancient that should not be disturbed."

Fearghal chuckled and held out his hand, "Come out of the waters woman. Your toes will be bluer than that design above your eye. Next you'll be telling me there's a monster in the loch."

"Unbeliever," snorted Mongfhionn as she returned to the shore. "You're getting as bad as Cúscraid. Take your penance." Fearghal exhaled sharply as a cold foot was placed squarely on his crotch. "That will also teach you not to go about half-naked. All this rowing has given you men bad habits. Now, warm my feet, slave."

"Slave indeed. You're getting close to a good spanking, Sidhe or not," Fearghal chortled and pulled Mongfhionn onto him, enveloping her in his brat.

"Oh, such promises," laughed the Sidhe.

Hidden by a small copse of alder and birch, Mórrígan gazed across the loch. She wept. The sinister, sometimes mocking, voices in her head had become increasingly louder – painfully louder. She looked first at her knife and then at the new lines of blood on her arm and choked back more tears. The relief she got from the slashes on her wrists and lower arm had become more and more fleeting. With her gaze fixed on a distant mountain peak, she stood up and took a step.

The cracking of twigs in the undergrowth startled her. Thinking that her ever-present bodyguard – the hulking Urard, had found her, she quickly slipped arm-guards over the cuts and turned.

"The water is very seductive, don't you think?" Pytheas deliberately avoided matching stares with Mórrígan and spoke as if he was alone and thinking aloud. "When my life is over I certainly will want to join with it – but, Poseidon willing, not before that time. I think it would be a shame to sacrifice one's youth to this dark, cold water when there is a world to explore, battles to fight, children to raise and loved ones to care for."

"You are a wise and thoughtful man, Pytheas. We have not always seen eye-to-eye, but I will miss you. Take care."

Mórrígan walked away, her spirit lighter; the voices in her head snarled in frustration.

"Remember Uiscí na Fathach in the Ulaid lands? Well, this loch is about a quarter the width, but a good way longer. The waters are reasonably calm, but very deep I think. You can't see a thing further than a spear's length and beyond that it's black as the Otherworld." Deaglán paused to carve a slice of pinkish-red meat from the deer that hung on the spit. Conall, Fearghal, Mongfhionn, and Pytheas sat around the fire. Conall signaled the young warrior to continue.

"To the left of our position and not too far away, is a massive crannog. It's almost the size of a small island, but it seems to be occupied by farming folk and only a few warriors. I don't think they will be a problem – and besides, our galleys can keep well away from it.

"That's the good news. The bad is that two thirds of the way along the loch - to the right, there is a massive ráth. It sits on a mountain with steep cliffs on three sides and is surrounded by thick stone and timber walls. There appears to be only one way into it – from the south-east. The inner citadel is about thirty to forty paces by about twenty paces. There's a lot of activity around the ráth. Likely there are at least one or two thousand warriors."

"The position of their entrance will place them at a disadvantage," Fearghal said. "Surely we can simply sail along the opposite bank. We'll be well past the ráth before they can do anything." With the back of his hand he attempted to wipe off the grease dribbling down his chin, but only succeeded in smearing it.

Mongfhionn shook her head in mock disgust, "A fine example of a king." Deaglán laughed and continued his report.

"Unfortunately, on the left bank there is another ráth on a small, rocky outcrop. They aren't very close, but both are well within signaling range. They would certainly know of our presence. The ráth isn't big, but could cause problems."

Conall considered Deaglán's summary. "We should assume both rátha will have boats," he said. "Can we outrun them, Pytheas?"

The Greek tugged at his thick plait of black hair and thought for a moment, "Most certainly they will have logboats. They are carved from a single tree like the ones we saw at the crannogs and can carry up to twenty warriors. The logboats are light if not the most stable, but then this lake appears to be pretty calm. If they ram us then they could cause enough damage to swamp our galleys, which are also light and low to the water. Our advantage is speed and maneuverability. But that depends on how many boats they can put in the water. We might not be able to outrun or outmaneuver them all."

"So much for a nice cruise up the lakes, to grab that bastard Cassius," Fearghal snorted. "Íar and the rest of our friends are probably sitting with their feet up, feasting and drinking."

Early morning, a light rain fell and there was the beginning of a winter's chill in the air as the chevron of seven galleys slipped past the island crannog. In contrast to previous sailings, each warrior had donned leather armor inlaid with overlapping cycloid iron scales. Shields were strapped to the ship's hull. Helmets and weapons were stowed within arms' reach. The archers in each ship stood with arrows nocked and prayed for calm waters. Oars dropped into the dark water in time to the steady beat of the stroke drum. The pace was slow and even, and breaks were frequent to conserve energy.

On the third sunrise Deaglán signaled that the first ráth was close. Sails unfurled and flapping in the loch breeze, the galleys tacked towards the northern shoreline and away from the impressive structure. "Bollocks," muttered Conall as he saw a wisp of dark, gray smoke rise up from the mountain crag. In a short time, it was followed by the yellow-red flames of a signal pyre. Black flecks of ash and thick gray smoke ascended lazily into the mid-morning sky.

"Boats in the water," Pytheas called out. "Look to the shoreline." Conall watched the long, brown-black shapes cut into the water. There was little chance of the logboats intercepting them, but then their job was probably to cut off his fleet's ability to retreat. His gaze marked the splashes of other logboats ahead, to the fleet's left and right.

"Shite!" Annoyed and helpless, Conall berated himself for not considering the possibility of more logboats further up on the loch's shores. In hindsight, it was a sensible strategy. The signal fire had alerted warriors on both sides of the loch. Frustratingly, there was little he could do or order until the enemy vessels came within arrow range. Their fate was in the hands of Pytheas and a handful of Greek sailors. Conall prayed to the Goddess, gritted his teeth, and kept pulling on his oar.

Perfectly balanced, Mongfhionn stood at the stern. The Sidhe stared at the flotilla that followed and chanted. Her oak staff, held in her right hand, pointed alternately at the sky and the logboats. There was not much the Sidhe could do to disrupt the path of the boats that converged on them from the front, but she could make the lives of those behind miserable. A shrill wail increasing to a loud, ear piercing screech startled the crew.

"By the Hag, could you give us some warning," Fearghal remonstrated, but was ignored. The Sidhe, intent on her task did not hear him.

Unnerved by the wailing, which intensified as it echoed off the surrounding mountains, the trailing logboats lost their rhythm. White fog rolled down the mountainside overtaking them. Boats wallowed and banged into each other. With a final flourish, the Sidhe held her staff aloft and the thick mist enveloping the boats flashed and flickered brighter than daylight. Haunting screams escaped from the fog as the steersmen of each boat found their eyes blinded – some never to see again. Mongfhionn sat on her bench with a satisfied smile.

Even as the hairs on the back of his neck and arms stood on end, the chieftain in the leading logboat urged his men on. The boats were normally used for trading goods or transporting men and supplies along the long, narrow loch - not for battle. In fact, he could not recall them ever being used in a pitched fight on water. For a start, no one wanted to risk falling into the deep, black water that many believed to be the maw of the Otherworld. Then there were the repeated tales of a great creature that lived in the depths. He shivered at this thought as his boats churned up the surface of the lake. If ever the creature were to raise its head, surely it would be at this moment.

While the chieftain had double the number of boats than Conall's flotilla that was a doubtful advantage given the width of the lake. His orders were to engage the enemy and force them to the shore. This was all very well coming from a battle commander with his feet firmly planted on solid ground, but how was he to contest with the enemy? The likelihood was that once his men seized their weapons and stood up their boat would roll over and capsize. It was his hope, that the opposing fleets would simply pass each other or that his boats would be outmaneuvered by the sleeker, faster galleys. Nevertheless, the chieftain was a brave and obedient warrior and inspired his men to greater effort. The fleets drew closer.

Mórrígan raised her bow, drawing the string back until fingers touched cheek. She held the stance – feet bare, muscles taut and eyes closed, as she rocked in harmony with the movement of the boat. The vessel rose on the swell. In the instant before it dipped, her eyes opened, she selected her target and released the arrow. She knew she had hit her target without looking and nocked another arrow.

The brave chieftain had not considered the possibility of archers. After all, bows were for hunting, not for battle. He would have dismissed their usefulness as the boats bounced up and down on the swell. Thus, he went to his death swiftly, but in ignorance as a black-ash shaft punched through his neck, its iron barb severing his spinal cord. The corpse tipped over the side and sank into the black waters.

A hail of arrows sped towards the oncoming logboats, but their aim was haphazard. Many of the missiles did nothing more than make a minor splash in the loch. They did, however, serve to unnerve the Aos na Coille warriors, making them flinch instinctively and break their rhythm. Mórrígan with deadly accuracy calmly, continued to choose her victims. Soon, half of the logboats were missing their steersman and rowed aimlessly ahead.

There was little doubt whose vessels were better equipped for this skirmish and, like the chieftain, it was Conall's wish that they could avoid a major clash and slip through a gap. He was relieved when Pytheas spotted a break in the line as several logboats drifted apart, directionless without their steersmen. Arms in the air, the Greek pointed to the space. Shouts alerted the other galleys and, still holding formation, the chevron moved to break free.

It almost worked.

By the time the two trailing ships of Conall's fleet entered the gap, the Aos na Coille had recovered and replaced their steersmen. Cajoled by their captains, they were exhorted to quickly close on the galleys. One by one, the solid logboat bows rammed galley hulls with a terrific thud and cracking of wood and oars.

"Not again," Tadhg groaned, for he was in the starboard galley.

As his ship began to take on water from a breach in its cedar wood hull, he roared for his archers to aim into the logboat. With the distance between the boats closed, their aim was deadly. At the same time, he shouted for the hole to be plugged and water bailed. Although riding low in the water, his galley gained enough propulsion to pull away from the melee.

The remaining galley was less favored by the Goddess. Its hull was split and the vessel was taking on water at an alarming rate. Its archers kept up a steady stream of arrows until their quivers were exhausted. Soon, it was swarmed by an Aos na Coille fleet eager to salvage some pride from the engagement. As the ship slowly sank, the Ériu crew slashed and hacked at their foes with axes and swords, turning the waters into a bloody red froth. A few leaped over the galley's side crashing into the logboats in an effort to sink them. The tactic worked and several logboats rolled over, tossing crews into the water.

Eventually, the water regained its calm, gentle swell as the galley's mast slipped below the surface. There were no survivors. The black heart of the loch had claimed its toll.

Powerless to intervene, a red rage settled on Conall as he watched his warriors fight their last battle. Instinctively, scarred hands reached for axe handles. He looked across to the ráth on the rocky peninsula. It would be lightly defended. They would not expect an attack. His men waited for the order to seek revenge. Conall gritted his teeth and loosened his white-knuckle grip on the axes. Shaking his head and with a voice full of sorrow he said, "Pytheas, get us out of this cursed loch." The Greek dipped his head and signaled the remaining ships to follow.

"A bitter choice," said Fearghal.

"A king's choice," Mongfhionn replied.

It was evening when the remaining galleys sailed through the narrow channel at the northern end of Loch Nis and into a much smaller, sheltered loch. As they beached the galleys and made camp, Conall knew that his men would not set sail again.

It was a bittersweet meal that marked the eve of Pytheas' departure. Of the original Ériu warband, just over two hundred warriors remained. Mórrígan had lost three of her archers. Two of Pytheas' men had met their death as had two galleys.

At first light, Conall assigned men to help the Greek sailor haul the galleys along the river to the coast. It was a short distance and so the men would be back before sunset. In any event, Conall had decided that all his men should rest for several sunsets before tramping through the forest to the settlement at Cùil Daothail.

"Be safe, friend," Pytheas said as he firmly clasped Conall's hand and arm. "You know where to leave a message whenever you need me in the future."

Conall smiled and nodded, "We'll meet again. Of that I'm sure. Safe journey to the Great Sea, my friend." To rousing cheers, Pytheas waved to the warriors and turned to follow his galleys.

Cùil Daothail was a large, thriving settlement that sat back a short distance from the coast. It nestled on a hill that commanded clear views over the surrounding terrain. There was little doubt that it was the biggest community in the northern lands, although its exact population was hard to determine. A jewel in Drostan Ruadh's rule, its ability to generate wealth had ensured a level of autonomy that few of his subjects enjoyed.

The area's climate was wetter, but being close to the sea was more temperate. The community lay within a glen rich in natural resources: good land for crops, lush pastures for cattle and an abundance of iron deposits. It was a major trading center for livestock and crops as well as for iron goods, leather, gold and silver crafts. Since it sat on the far north-eastern border of Aos na Coille lands, it was often visited by the northern tribes wishing to trade. Proximity to a large, sheltered sea bay made Cùil Daothail popular with merchant seamen from Albu and as far as the Great Sea.

At the village's heart a huge roundhouse stood on a raised circle of stone, dirt and timber. Scattered around it were twenty or so smaller, windowless dwellings, all with the familiar entrance facing east. Workshops, including several forges and iron-smelting furnaces added to the blue-gray haze hanging above dark wood and thatched roofs. The sound of hammers striking anvils was heard, even from a great distance.

Women sat at the entrances to their homes grinding grain on circular quern stones. The harsh sound of stone against stone was softened by the scrape and swish of women and men weaving intricate and highly colored plaids. Bread was baking on iron griddles and the great iron cooking cauldrons would shortly be replenished with simmering hot stews, oatmeal and broths.

Slate gray skies spoke of imminent winter snows as Conall and his men tramped over deeply rutted muddy paths. Conall surveyed the tents and temporary shelters that had been erected outside of the settlement's perimeter defenses. An oval-shaped stockade and ditch, the latter giving off a nose-curling scent of piss, shite and decomposing food, encircled the community. The fence was not a particularly useful defense. It would take thousands to fully man. A more significant threat was the substantial force of men standing watchful at the forest edge.

"Best behavior. Cause no trouble. We keep our heads down and buy the supplies we need. In two sunrises we'll set out for Na Daoine Smeurta territory in the far north-east."

Fearghal's eyebrow rose at Conall's words and he snorted, "I'm sure no-one will notice over two hundred heavily armed strangers. Perhaps if we take our clothes off we'll blend in and they'll just think we're taking the hounds for a walk."

"Póg ma thoin, old man," Conall said, smiling. "Torcán and Deaglán, find a good camp site – away from those warriors. Mongfhionn, Mórrígan, and Tadhg will accompany you and me into the settlement. We'll take the hounds with us."

The tall, red-haired warrior dipped his head, "Sounds good to me. Perhaps there'll be some good beer to buy – and with a bit of luck they'll have some good local special brews."

Conall took a contemplative pace forward then raised his voice to carry to the milling band, "Gràinne will accompany us to Cùil Daothail. We may need an interpreter."

Fearghal looked quizzically at Conall. "You're up to something."

Conall simply smiled and strode ahead. For her part, Gràinne's countenance fell and she took on a greenish pallor. Visibly distressed, she trudged over to the small group and attached herself, leech-like, to Tadhg, a fact noted by Torcán before he and Deaglán led the men away to establish their camp.

The chanting put everyone's teeth on edge. It was a song of despair, melancholy and hopelessness. Dressed in uniform, black hooded cloaks, the small group of acolytes from the Na Daoine Tùrsach chanted their Tuireadh as they tramped along the pathway that lead to the gateway. It was a dirge of death entreating the unfaithful and the heretics to repent. The feeble-minded and vulnerable in the settlement, heads nodding in acceptance of the incantations, were drawn to the hypnotic darkness of the Na Daoine Tùrsach god.

As the priests skirted the entrance of the large roundhouse, Carmag Mac an t-Sionnaich scowled and signaled to a guard of twenty spearmen. He pointed to the chanting priests, but before a single spearman moved, the dour missionaries were brought up short by the imposing figure of the gray-cloaked Sidhe.

Mórrígan, dressed in a cloak of autumn colors, stood wavering and slightly behind. The insistent voices, voices that had driven her to the edge of madness, rose to a crescendo with the chanting. "Stand firm, girl," Mongfhionn snapped as she anchored her oak staff in the sodden black dirt. "Today, you choose a path."

"Abomination!" screeched the shaven-headed leader of the Na Daoine Tùrsach party pointing to the Sidhe. Then, fixing his stare on Mórrígan, he said, "Join us. You belong with us."

Mórrígan's designs glowed, swirling patterns of dark and light. Hands that seemed to move with a mind of their own slipped her bow from her shoulder. The feeling of the weapon calmed the young queen as if the Goddess of battle had touched the bowstaff. Her tattooed hands placed a black arrow on the bowstring. Its red and white fletching fluttered in the soft breeze. She waited.

"There may yet be hope," thought Mongfhionn. Flipping her hood back, the Sidhe's hair formed a red-gold corona. Coal-black eyes peered menacingly deep into the soul of the Na Daoine Tùrsach priest. Seemingly incapable of movement, his feet sank into the cloying mud. His eyes, fearful and wild, watched as the Sidhe glided forward to stand before him.

"I was before your people and its corruption existed. The Ancients have passed judgment on your tribe. There shall be no mercy."

Alongside Fearghal, with ears pricked and hackles raised, the hounds' throats vibrated in two-pitched growls and whines. "Shite!" Fearghal muttered and nudged Conall. Fearghal's longsword slid smoothly and silently from the sheath on his back. "The oak staff is still in the mud. Look to Mongfhionn's hands."

Conall quickly took in the tableau, unsheathed his axes and held them ready at waist height. The Sidhe's hands held two curved sacrificial daggers. He had not seen those particular blades since the Sidhe had removed the heart of Spurius, the Roman Centurion. Spurius had been alive while being eviscerated. Conall started to move forward, but was held back by Fearghal's firm hand, "No. This is not our affair - yet."

The crowd stood still to gawk. A disturbing wailing from Gràinne heightened the spectral atmosphere. Hidden behind Tadhg, she sat cross-legged in the dirt rocking back and forth, her eyes distant and unfocused. The hounds continued to growl and bare sharp teeth.

Mongfhionn slashed the throat of the Na Daoine Tùrsach priest with a swift movement. With equal precision and ease, the second blade slashed upward from balls to chest cutting cut though the priest's cloak and flesh. Blood spurted from torn arteries. Foam-flecked blood flowed from his mouth. In shock, the priest remained upright as if suspended by unseen ropes. His cloak slid to the ground and he stood bloody and naked - apart from his tattoos.

"Fear me," snarled the Sidhe, plunging her blades into the priest's chest. Those nearby winced as they heard bones crack and watched slender, crimson hands reach into the man's chest, twisting and pulling.

The remaining Na Daoine Tùrsach screeched as their leader's

heart was ripped from his body and his corpse finally fell limp into the gore-soaked mud. They rushed forward as one. "Now!" shouted Fearghal, placing himself and his sword in front of Mongfhionn. Conall and Tadhg moved to shield Mórrígan. Gràinne continued her trance-like rocking accompanied by a thin, low moan.

Mórrígan unerringly placed an arrow in each of the leading two priests' eyes and the Na Daoine Tùrsach's rush forward was abruptly halted. The two fell to their knees clawing at the shafts and the queen placed two more black shafts in their remaining eyes. Mórrígan's emerald gaze reflected satisfaction. The small measure of revenge taken against her tormentor's voices was a comfort.

Fearghal's sword took the head of a fourth priest while Conall slashed diagonally with his axes leaving the fifth's head attached by a thin sliver of gristle. Tadhg made to chase the final member of the band, who had turned tail, but was restrained by the Sidhe. "Let him return to his tribe. He will serve us by spreading fear among them." Mongfhionn looked pointedly first at Tadhg and then at Gràinne. "Shut up that girl's moaning."

Shouts of "Clear the way" broke the tension and the silence of the crowd was replaced with restless murmuring.

"Whose bright idea was it to leave the men outside?" Conall growled. "Form a circle. The fighting may not be over."

The crowd was unceremoniously pushed aside by Carmag's guards. Cùil Daothail's governor faced the crowd and bellowed, "Return to your work. There will be no more entertainment this day." To his second-in-command, in a lower, but urgent tone Carmag said, "Make sure the crowd disperses. Watch for Na Daoine Tùrsach sympathizers. Ye know what to do with any ye find."

"Aye, sir." The man smiled broadly through a mouth of broken and yellowed teeth.

Carmag turned slowly to face Conall. "Ye have a unique way of dealing with the Na Daoine Tùrsach. We usually just blind them, rip their tongues out and send them home." Conall smiled warily, assessing their position. Carmag laughed, "Stand easy. There'll be no more bloodshed today. Perhaps ye would take those impressive helmets off. Someone might take a liking to all that gold and silver – must be worth a year's earnings. I'd like to see the face of who I'm talking to."

Conall unstrapped the ornately decorated helmet with its black plumes falling from the small, gold raven at its crest. Mórrígan, Fearghal and Tadhg quickly followed suit. Stretching out his hand, he said, "I'm Conall Mac Gabhann. We're on a quest to find and punish the man who slaughtered our families. No harm is meant to you – or to any of the settlement of Cùil Daothail."

The warrior lifted his chin slightly in acknowledgment, "My name is Carmag Mac an t-Sionnaich. I'm the governor of Cùil Daothail. So ye'r the reason for Drostan Ruadh sending that army to camp outside of the settlement."

Conall nodded. "Likely so."

"Well, and I mean no offense, the quicker ye get whatever supplies ye need and are gone, the better ye and I will get on."

"That's a fair request."

"Good. Well, whenever you've cleaned up the mess ye've made and arranged for whatever ye need, come and see me. Good company is not common in these parts. I'm sure ye'll not refuse some food and beer. By the way, don't dump the bodies in the ditch. We're civilized here."

Tadhg had finally calmed Gràinne and in doing so escaped more black looks from Mongfhionn. Mórrígan volunteered to keep watch over the girl while he helped Conall and Fearghal behead the Na Daoine Tùrsach and strip their bodies of anything of value. The ritual beheading of their enemies made sense. Who wanted unfriendly spirits hanging around?

Tadhg pulled the arms taut and hauled one of the tattooed bodies an acceptable distance from the community. In doing so, he had occasion to examine in detail and with some curiosity the designs painted and etched into the man's skin. The intricate, swirling designs filled him with admiration for the patience of the Cinn Péinteáilte. It must have taken a painfully long time to complete their artwork. Tadhg's explosive, "The Hag, no!" brought inquiring glances from Conall and Fearghal.

"I think I know who was responsible for Morna's death."

"Keep it to yourself for the moment, Tadhg," said Conall.

Two men observed Conall's warband's arrival at Cùil Daothail. Their interest was roused further by the men's shields and the banners emblazoned with black ravens on a crimson sky. They followed at a distance and watched, with some measure of pleasure as the leader of the warband and his companions slaughtered the Na Daoine Tùrsach priests. The two had no love for this tribe.

While nervous at the presence and power of the Sidhe who accompanied the group, they were comforted to see the ravens on the helmets of the leader and his mate. "You should go back to the tribe and alert Artair," the older of the two said. "I will follow this warband and observe." His will was accepted without question and the younger warrior loped off towards the northern forest. A single raven feather fluttered as the thin braid of his dark, red hair lifted in the breeze.

Torcán was troubled. It wasn't just the rumors, winks and grins from the men. He knew there was something going on between Gràinne and Tadhg and it was not related to the murder of the child. To be honest, while he enjoyed having the girl, she had been getting a bit clingy. Besides, he tended to favor women with a bit more meat on their bones. Gràinne was skinny, although she had reasonable breasts and a firm, if smallish, arse.

But how to resolve the dilemma of his bruised ego? Everyone knew Tadhg was greatly favored by Conall. Torcán, on the other hand, had not recovered his standing. The purple mark on his throat still throbbed, reminding him that he would be unlikely to count on any support from Mongfhionn. That also ruled out Fearghal. Aside from all that, he genuinely liked Tadhg and his brothers. They had been friends a lot longer than the short time he had known Gràinne.

Perplexed, the bluff warrior scratched his head and then went off to find Deaglán. The young, red-headed Ulaid warrior, besides being a good friend, was much more of a thinker than Torcán. Perhaps, Deaglán could suggest a way out of his quandary.

CHAPTER 15

It was a full cycle of the moon before the army was re-united with family and followers. Ròidh took his father's spearmen and cavalry back to Dùn Athad, yet shortly thereafter returned with the same force as an escort. He also requested that his men remain with the army for the assault on Dùn Na Mèadaidh. The offer raised some eyebrows and suspicions within the Ériu leadership, but in the end, his request was granted. "Better to keep them where I can see them," thought Íar.

The time was one of healing for the army's injured. It was also a time of judgment. The open sore between Brocc and Fionnbharr over the death of Labhraidh continued to fester and threatened to spread as factions took sides. Fights had broken out, although blades had not been drawn - yet.

One evening, as they met for the usual beer and planning session, Íar, Nikandros, Cúscraid and Brion decided that the boil had to be lanced. Yet, they were at a loss as to how. No one wanted the two warriors to battle it out. They were much too valuable. Still, the resolution could not wait until Conall returned with the remaining ó Cuileannáin brothers and the Sidhe.

On this particular evening, the Druid caught their conversation. Unwilling to interrupt directly, he paused and coughed as he passed the group. "I sense you have something to say, Druid," said Nikandros. "Go ahead. None of us underestimate your powers of observation. You are likely well aware of the topic of our discussion."

The Druid smiled and removed his hood. Dark – almost black, shoulder-length lank hair framed a sallow face that bore the bluish tattoos of the Aos na Coille. "The resolution you seek is straightforward."

"Calling your hosts eejits is not exactly going to get you fed around here," Cúscraid grumbled from the other side of the fire.

The wrinkles on the Druid's face rearranged into a thin-lipped smile, "Your concern is touching," he said. "Shall we get back to the problem? You see it from an understandable, though incorrect perspective."

"My mind is clouded by beer. Speak plainly, man," Íar said with a tone of impatience.

The Druid sighed, "So brief a time and the Fénechas are forgotten."

Gasps of realization burst from Íar, Brion and Cúscraid. "Am I missing something?" Nikandros asked.

"Yes," Íar said, "although you can be forgiven. The Druid speaks of the Fénechas – the Law. The Law governs all that we do, but more importantly it calls for restitution and compensation – not blood." To the Druid he said, "Join us, priest. Are you able – and willing, to be the arbiter in this process?"

Scooping up his long cloak, the Druid stepped over the log that served as a bench. He sat and spoke, "I am well trained in the Fénechas. My duty is to ensure that the Law is preserved and adhered to. When do you wish to convene the assembly so that arguments can be heard and justice meted out?"

"As soon as possible," said Brion. "The wound is festering and needs healing, but…"

"But what?" asked Cúscraid.

"Will the men accept the Druid? He's not from Ériu, not one of us."

"They will accept his office. After all, the Sidhe is not from our lands either and they freely submit to her pronouncements."

"Yes, but she frightens the shite out of everyone," said Íar.

Brion said, "I hope you're right, Cúscraid." Then looking to Íar and the Druid he added, "We should call the assembly at the next full moon. It's not that far away and it will give us time to let the men get used to the Druid and what we're proposing."

"A wise course of action," the Druid said. "With your permission, I will take the opportunity to resolve any minor issues the people may have, but which do not require a full assembly. It may help build their trust in my judgments."

Íar snorted. "I, for one, have no objection to that. Although I suspect you may end up with a great deal on your plate."

Smiling thinly, the Druid bowed his head, "With your permission, I will take my leave and prepare myself."

As the priest departed, Brion scratched at the old scar on his left cheek. "He's an odd one. Will it work?"

Íar stretched and rubbed the nape of his neck with a calloused hand. The others winced as they heard the bones in his neck crack as his head moved in a slow circular motion. Unmindful of his friends' reaction, he said, "Can't do any harm. May do a lot of good. Let's call the ceannairí céad together. They can spread the word among the men."

Dusk had given way to the soft night and the army stood assembled under the yellow glow of fluttering brands and torchlights. Cúscraid had organized the erection of a raised platform. On it stood the Druid, Fionnbharr and Brocc. Cúscraid, Brion and Nikandros stood to the side behind Íar who stepped forward and addressed the gathering in his usual booming voice. "We meet this evening to hear from Fionnbharr ó Cuileannáin and Brocc ó Cathasaigh and to listen to the advice and arbitration from the Druid. Does anyone present not accept the Druid as the arbiter of the Fénechas? Let the ceannairí céad speak for their men."

A low rumbling worked its way through the men. Eirnín Mac Gabhann, Conall's younger brother, halted it, "It is acceptable to me and my hundred." An audible sigh of relief escaped from the leaders on the platform. Eirnín was not noted for being overly agreeable. He lived and sometimes sulked, in the shadow of his brother, resenting the frequent comparisons made between the two. However, on this evening, one after another, the ceannairí céad followed Eirnín's lead. Íar nodded to the Druid, who stepped forward.

In a surprisingly commanding voice that carried to the farthest man in the assembly, the Druid asked, "Who is the accuser and what is the complaint?"

"I am Fionnbharr ó Cuileannáin, head of the ó Cuileannáin family. I speak on behalf of my brothers who are not present. I accuse Brocc ó Cathasaigh of leading my brother, Labhraidh ó Cuileannáin to his death."

"An interesting choice of words, Fionnbharr ó Cuileannáin," the Druid commented before asking, "Brocc ó Cathasaigh, do you accept the accusation?"

By this time Brocc had regained some of his confidence, although his closest friends detected a dimming of the arrogance that he once showed. The slim warrior nodded and spoke in a subdued tone, "Yes, I accept the charge."

The priest observed both men, paused and then said, "That would appear to make a judgment simple, but in truth, it is easier to judge when both parties are at odds with each other." He looked first at Fionnbharr, "Had your brother died beside you in battle, whom would you accuse of his death?"

Startled, Fionnbharr said, "No one."

"Had Labhraidh died in battle on another wall, whom would you accuse?"

Perturbed, Fionnbharr replied, "No one."

"Did Brocc ó Cathasaigh murder your brother, Labhraidh?"

At this, an angry Fionnbharr answered, "Of course not."

The Druid smiled and then turned to Brocc, "Did you murder Labhraidh ó Cuileannáin?

An astounded Brocc quickly retorted, "No." Then he added, "But it was my fault he died."

"So you agree with Fionnbharr that you led Labhraidh to his death."

Disconsolately the young warrior dipped his head, "Yes."

"Did Labhraidh object to your leadership on this raid? Was he forced to go with you?" the Druid probed.

"No. We both wanted the mission. We practically pleaded for it."

"How many battles have you fought, Brocc ó Cathasaigh?"

"Not as many as some."

The Druid swept his hand past Íar, Cúscraid and Nikandros. "Are you as experienced a warrior or leader of men, as these?"

"Of course not, Druid. They've fought many more battles than I."

"Then what is this arrogance that presumes you cannot make a mistake – even a foolish one? You led, you chose a path and you were mistaken. You will live with that decision until you get to Mag Mell, but as to whether it deserves punishment…"

The Druid let his train of thought hang in the air and turned to Fionnbharr. "You lost a brother. Do you also wish to lose a comrade? A childhood friend? Your anger is understandable. Your friend made a foolish mistake and your brother died. Thank the Goddess if you can live to your winter years without making a single foolish choice."

The Druid then turned to the assembled army, "My judgment is that Brocc ó Cathasaigh has nothing to answer for - apart from the foolishness of youth. For that foolishness he will pay restitution in remembrance of a lost friend for the rest of his life." The priest then said, "Even so, I will leave earthly compensation, if merited, to be decided by the brother of the departed." The Druid paused.

"What say you, Fionnbharr ó Cuileannáin?"

Caught by surprise, Fionnbharr searched the faces around him for hints of what he should do. The expressions were either blank or held traces of insufferable knowing smiles. In desperation he blurted out, "Healing! Brocc ó Cathasaigh will learn healing. In doing so, perhaps he will better understand pain and prevent other deaths."

On the platform, Brocc nodded his agreement with the judgment and tentatively reached out a hand to Fionnbharr. It was grasped readily. A deep tremor of approval among the army reached a crescendo as the men cheered and beat on their shields with swords and javelins.

"A good result, Druid," Íar nodded appreciatively and savored the refreshed atmosphere in the camp. "Perhaps your stay with us may be longer than you think."

"This was a simple case, with two who wanted only to do right. Other arbitrations are unlikely to be similar. As to my time with you, I go where I am led. In this, like your Sidhe, I have little choice." The Druid bowed and left the stage.

As he watched the Druid walk away, Íar considered the evening's theater. "Yes, a good result," he thought again. "Maybe Brocc should not be the only one to learn basic healing. Perhaps each of the cean-nairí céad should – or at the least their seconds."

CHAPTER 16

"The way I see it ye've two disagreeable choices," Carmag said to Conall and his friends. Smoke from the wood and peat fire stung already reddened and weary eyes before drifting upwards to the roundhouse's thatched roof. It was late in the evening. The group had eaten and drunk well. Carmag proved to be both a good host and a mine of advice on the far northern tribes and their territories. He rubbed his tired eyes and took another swallow of beer. In the expectation his guests would depart more readily if they had the information they needed, he spoke freely.

"Once ye cross the bay north of Cùil Daothail, ye will be in Na Daoine Tùrsach lands. It's not a large territory. In reasonable weather ye could cross it on foot in three or four sunsets. Ye will have a choice of either a tramp directly north and over the mountains or north-east along the coastline. The mountains are not as high as some, but this time of the year the weather is miserable." Seeing the raised eyebrows of Conall and Fearghal he laughed. "Yes more miserable than what ye've already tasted. It's also unpredictable. Thus, the difficulty of a journey across them should not be underestimated."

"And the coastal route?" Mongfhionn asked in a tone that suggested she already knew the answer.

"Between the bay and the next major river is all Na Daoine Tùrsach territory. The coastal land is relatively flat and lightly forested. Ye would make good time, but that tribe is not friendly - and their queen will not be happy that you killed her priests. They'll fight ye every step of the way."

"How many men can they field?" Conall asked.

"Immediately? Probably one to two thousand. Given longer to prepare, they could gather in about five thousand. Maybe more. If ye take the coastal route, be prepared for many skirmishes followed by a huge brawl once they get organized."

Fearghal laughed. "Good job that all that exercise on the galleys has got us in top condition, eh?"

"If ye succeed in getting through the Na Daoine Tùrsach defenses then ye will face the Aos an Fhithich. They're a strange people and stay mostly in the old forests that cover the low mountains. Their territory is about the same size as the Na Daoine Tùrsach. Their main defensive position is Carn Liath, on the coast, a short journey from the border with the Na Daoine Tùrsach." Carmag filled his cup again and offered the jug around. "The tribes have been enemies since the dawn of time. Càrn Liath is a solid broch on the east shore and is surrounded by other buildings – likely shelters for their warriors. They've a reputation for being good fighters, but I've never seen them in a pitched battle – they tend to stay within their lands and don't bother anyone."

"And the Na Daoine Smeurta?" Conall asked.

"Bastards to a man - or woman," Carmag replied with a twinkle in his eye, "the closest we have to barbarians in the north – apart from ye, of course. There's not that many of them – maybe a few thousand. They live in a narrow strip of land between the Fhithich and Aos nan Caorach – The Sheep People. Why the surrounding tribes haven't wiped them out is beyond me. Filthy, depraved. It's rumored they eat human flesh. Ye'll find it hard to come across anyone with a good word for them."

The Na Daoine Tùrsach's seat of power was a substantial, wooden crannog that jutted out from the shore of a small loch near the center of the tribe's territory. Surrounded on three sides by mountains, the loch was approachable only from a thickly wooded valley to the east. The majority of the tribe dwelled in this fertile glen and the adjacent coastal plain.

The imperial crannog was an impressive structure providing accommodation for the Na Daoine Tùrsach royal family and their guards. It was connected to the shore by a wooden walkway that continued around the building's perimeter. At the rear of the building, the walkway divided into two broad wooden jetties that curved to form a small lagoon for logboats.

A pair of tall, thick, hardwood stakes stood at the end of each jetty. The wooden boards beneath them were stained purple-black where the blood of countless innocents had pooled. Many thought that the small loch contained as much blood as water, a conviction made believable by the poisonous red sheen veiling its deceptively placid surface. On occasion, the bloated bodies of the sacrificed broke free of their stone-weights. Hands thrusting out of water pointed accusingly and dead eyes stared malevolently.

The Na Daoine Tùrsach king sat in the quiet gloom. He was a very tall man and in his youth had been a striking figure. Now, lank and grease-darkened, silver-gray hair lay on his shoulders. Ulcerated, aged skin, broken with crusty sores, draped loosely over his frame. Eyes once a deep, piercing blue gazed vacantly into the distance - one of the consequences of the blend of herbs inserted into his diet for many, many years. He occasionally mumbled platitudes and advice to an audience that did not care. His name, often forgotten and rarely spoken, did not matter since he was of no consequence.

Diadhaidh was a short, stocky woman. Shoulder length, blue-black hair, once vibrant and lustrous, hung thinning and lifeless - the result of the constant application of noxious dyes. Lips and high cheeks that in her youth naturally flushed pink and full were colored a brash red from the repeated used of belladonna. Her eyes glowed with an unusual brightness. Permanently dilated pupils lent a false intensity to her manner and these days she preferred the darkness of dusk and night to daylight.

The true power of the Na Daoine Tùrsach, Diadhaidh was a woman of conflicted temperament. As a child, she had been sickly and quite plain. Her parents, although of a noble clan, were themselves weak-willed. A victim of merciless bullying, Diadhaidh grew up anxious, depressed – and severely disturbed in her mind. The visions of dark powers that commenced in her adolescence first brought mockery and laughter, then fear as those who slighted her disappeared.

In her mind, Diadhaidh had come to believe she was divine and took this as encouragement to be an ill-tempered bully with a lust for blood. She looked upon the king with ill-concealed disdain and on her son, Caol with the frustration of a mother's disappointment.

Her gaze drifted to Caol. Thirty seasons old, of average height and build, the best that could be said of Caol was that he rarely challenged his mother. The worst, that he was addicted to certain herbs, had a weakness for depravity and shared his mother's obsession with blood. As she railed at him, spraying flecks of spit into the air, he stood with shoulders slouched, eyes dull and focused on the floor.

"It was a simple task. Travel east to the Aos a' Chùirn and bring her back. But no, you needed a diversion and now there is a warband in our territory."

"There are only two hundred of them. Our warriors can take care of that."

The queen raised a wrinkled, blemished hand as if to strike and her son cowered. "A ghlaoic! Fool! And what of the two thousand warriors and thousand horsemen crossing Drostan Ruadh's mountains? What if the Aos an Fhithich seize this chance to attack? But worse than all of this – what of the Ancient One who accompanies the warband?" Caol paced the floor uselessly until the exasperated priestess-queen screeched, "Get out of my sight. Send in the commander of my warriors. Perhaps Cesan can snatch the girl in a raid on their camp." Thankful for the excuse to leave his mother's presence, Caol bowed and slunk away.

Conall tramped out of Cùil Daothail through sodden grass and cloying mud. The morning sky was shaded in tones of gray save for a butter-gold band of light rimming the horizon. It held an iridescent tone that enhanced the colors beneath it. The grass appeared greener, the purple mountains vibrant and hardwood leaves glowed in bright oranges, reds and yellows.

Earlier, Conall had recounted Carmag's information to his gathered leaders. "We journey north across the lowland forests and then the mountains. With a hard march we should reach the mountains by sunset if we don't meet much resistance. Once across the mountain range we'll be in a large river valley. On the north side is an Aos an Fhithich settlement called Drochaid a' Bhanna. We follow the valley north and that will lead us further into Fhithich lands. After that, it's northeast across more mountains to the Na Daoine Smeurta."

Once beyond the boundaries of Cùil Daothail, the band advanced resolutely balancing speed and caution. Mórrígan's archers took up the lead. Behind them were two skirmish lines, each with one hundred men. Conall's caomhnóirí formed the front row. To the rear, three wagons creaked and rocked side-to-side as drivers encouraged teams of sturdy horses across the uneven terrain. With every lurch, their precarious loads of supplies, arms and the injured threatened to topple.

The carts and supplies had used up much of his remaining gold, yet Conall allowed himself a brief, congratulatory smile for having persuaded Carmag to part with the wagons. It was also a good deal for Carmag. The wagons would return to him once it became impossible to take them any further. "At least," thought Conall, "the injured will not slow us down."

He re-balanced the oblong, curved shield on his back and adjusted his weapons for comfort. On his right, Fearghal and Mongfhionn matched each other's pace stride for stride, while on his immediate left marched Tadhg. Beyond Tadhg, Deaglán and Torcán appeared to be in deep conversation. Gràinne, still not fully recovered from her experience at Cùil Daothail had persuaded one of the wagon drivers to let her sit alongside.

A wan mid-day sun made a brief appearance, scattering shafts of light across deeply shadowed forest paths. The rain was less of an annoyance in the forest, although it was getting noticeably colder and sometimes mixed with fine snow. As they tramped over the pine-cushioned forest floor, the men snacked on cold strips of meat, cheese and bread. They left a trail of food morsels that were immediately snatched up by the ever-present ravens or the amusing, brightly colored cam-ghobs. Red squirrels, plump from winter foraging, raised their heads from their work and scampered over to steal this auxiliary source of food.

The sound of distant, mournful chants broke the silence of the forest, sending birds and animals for cover, a first warning of imminent trouble. An archer arrived at a run, speaking in gasps as he reported to Conall, "Several warbands are closing in. Each has about a hundred men. They're mostly armed with spears and axes, some carry shields." The man grinned, "They had a few slingers, but the queen took care of that. We'll continue to harass them until you sound the recall." Conall nodded and the archer ran back to rejoin his comrades.

"What do you think, Fearghal? Keep going or stand and fight?"

"Will they fight if we halt?"

"They're barbarians — of course they will," Conall said and laughed aloud. "The scouts say that there's a small clearing not too far away. Let's give them a target and see if they'll take the bait." Then he shouted, "Form a square in the clearing up ahead. Bring the wagons into the center."

Shadows deepened and the forest rang eerily from the increasingly louder chanting of the Na Daoine Tùrsach. In formation, Conall's men checked helmet straps, tightened belts, rammed javelins into the dirt, and slid weapons from sheaths and replaced them. The edges of shields knocked against each other as the wall tightened up, leaving little room between each man. At the center of the formation, the black raven of the army's banner flew on a red sky in the light breeze. Men began to cheer and slapped weapons against shields. Wagon drivers held the reins of their teams of horses mouthing soothing words and stroking velvet necks. They prayed that the men from Ériu's fighting skills matched their form.

A single bronze horn blasted out the recall for the bowmen. Scattered flocks of ravens took to the skies, their familiar *kraa kraa* always taken as a good omen. Close-by, twigs cracked. The men tensed and each balanced a javelin. This time it was the archers who, led by Mórrígan, burst from cover and ran to be enclosed by the square. "They seem to be grouping together," Mórrígan said, panting.

"From which direction will they attack?" asked Conall.

"I'm not sure. They're moving swiftly and keep changing direction. They're good and know the land well, but it's almost as if they are looking for something - or someone." As she spoke, the sinister voices in Mórrígan's head took up their angry refrain calling to her to join them. She took her helmet – a smaller version of Conall's, from Urard, gritted her teeth and wished for battle to commence. For Mórrígan, each arrow that left her bow eased her torment. The spilling of blood quelled the voices, providing a transient relief.

Mongfhionn stood unmoving, like a statue at the center of the square, her face implacable. The Sidhe's spirit moved through the deep forest. It watched and listened, it searched for the few isolated, ancient oaks from which she could garner strength. The spirit felt the evil that was surrounding Conall's band. She was repulsed by its dark taint, but the evil was wise enough not to challenge the Sidhe directly, seeking only to blemish her spirit with smudges of malevolence. Mongfhionn grasped the agonies suffered by Mórrígan and berated herself for her lack of understanding. She was Ancient and brushed aside the crude attempt to corrupt her; Mórrígan was young in the art – and susceptible to both good and evil.

Suddenly, the Sidhe's eyes flashed open and she cried out, "The east!"

Barely had the Sidhe called out the warning than hundreds of warriors broke from the trees surrounding the clearing - less than fifty paces from Conall's men. "By the Hag, where did they come from?" Fearghal shouted orders, "Every other man from the north and south walls form behind and support the east wall. Throw javelins when you have a target."

Eyes wild with religious fervor, the semi-naked Na Daoine Tùrsach threw themselves at the shield wall with a zealousness that Conall had never before experienced. Under the onslaught, the wall released a communal grunt and momentarily trembled before the rear row slammed shields against backs to steady it.

In the background, black-cloaked priests chanted the Tuireadh with mindless monotony and increased pitch. The first few Na Daoine Tùrsach ranks were scythed quickly. Iron thrown with muscles hardened from constant rowing filled the air with dull thuds as flesh was mutilated and muffled cracks as bones were broken. Shrieks of pain rose from the impaled, driven to the ground by those coming behind them. As they fell before the shield wall, the Na Daoine Tùrsach became a barrier of bloody spikes that sought to skewer more warriors.

Behind the barrier of broken bodies, javelins stabbed constantly, biting soft flesh. There was little death doled out - unless a spike found an eye socket or an attacker attempted to scramble over the gore only to find himself impaled and incorporated into the bloody defenses. The air rang with frustrated shrieks and yelps from the Na Daoine Tùrsach, and obscenities and taunts from the Ériu men.

Black ash shafts from Mórrígan's archers disappeared into the folds of the equally black cloaks of the tribe's priests. Pale hands clutched at the red and white fletching. Mórrígan nocked another arrow, scanning for a target. The priests became more cautious, seeking the cover of bushes and trees. Their song was less insistent as numbers dwindled. She breathed, chanting over her arrows and let fly. With an eerie and unerring accuracy her missiles found their targets. She felt each priest's pain as the iron barb broke flesh and bone, felt his spirit wrenched from its sanctuary. She rejoiced in the burst of anguish when the spirit realized it had been deceived.

A lone war horn sounded out *barrr-ewww barrr-ewww* and the Na Daoine Tùrsach disengaged, disappearing like ghosts into the forest. "Tough bastards," said Fearghal taking a gulp of water from a leather pouch, and then splashing more over his blood-splattered face. Turning, he pointed to the bodies, "Check the bodies. Put the injured out of their misery. Retrieve any javelins. And do it quick. We'll take their heads later."

Conall said, "Fearghal, move the reserve to the center of the square. I can't see them hitting the same flank twice in a row." Just then a low keening sound became a loud wail broken by racking sobs. Fearghal glanced around and saw Gràinne sitting cross-legged on the forest floor. She was rocking back and forward. Furious, Fearghal yelled at Torcán, "You brought her. Keep her quiet." Embarrassed, Torcán turned and made to leave the north shield wall that was his command. He was forestalled by a loud smack and a yelp of pain.

"By the Hag, someone stop her." This time, the cry came from Deaglán and was aimed not at Gràinne, but at a hard-faced Mórrígan, who having already cuffed the girl several times, appeared to be intent on strangling her.

"At least she's no longer wailing that awful dirge," Fearghal quipped as he and Conall quickly crossed the square. Conall was just in time to prevent Mórrígan from laying into the girl with her bowstaff. "That's enough. We've more important matters to deal with," Conall said grasping Mórrígan's wrist tightly as he pulled her away.

Mórrígan glared at him, "Don't I have enough to deal with in my head without this idiot girl chanting those laments? The same ones that have plagued me since my parents were slaughtered."

Conall was caught momentarily off-balance, but their exchange was interrupted by a cry, "They're attacking again - from the north and south."

"Shite! We'll discuss this later — if we're alive," growled Conall as he strapped his helmet back on. "Reserve, support the north shields. Deaglán, take half of your men and support the south. Archers, support the south wall."

The Na Daoine Tùrsach warriors threw themselves at the shield walls as more black-cloaked priests arrived to support their comrades and increase the volume of their chanting. The front rows had little time to throw their final javelins, choosing to pass them back to the rear rows. The whisper of short, wickedly sharp swords being drawn from leather scabbards hung from sheaths and baldrics rippled along the square. The sound of wolfhounds howling overlaid the cries of battle and the resounding crash of Na Daoine Tùrsach bodies against the wall.

On the north shield wall, Torcán was happy. At last he had something to take his mind off that wearisome girl - his skill at killing. Thrusting and slashing at the painted warriors, he fought until exhausted and then overcame that weakness to fight more. On more than one occasion as the bodies mounted before him, he was grabbed by the shoulders and hauled back into the wall with a sharp rebuke of, "We're supposed to fight together," from the veterans around him.

Tadhg too felt relief from the constant worries and responsibility that Conall had laid on his young shoulders. Behind him, while the supply of javelins was exhausted, archers continued to send volley after volley into the Na Daoine Tùrsach ranks. Before him rose the nauseating yet addictive stench of warm blood and shite. He roared insults and spat at slavering warriors. An artist with the sword as well as the word, Tadhg's blade severed arms, hands and fingers with graceful flourishes and brutal slashes. He protested loudly as he was roughly dragged from the front row by Deaglán, who said, "Take a look at yourself, man." Tadhg stared at the blood streaming from countless cuts and gashes. The adrenalin of battle subsiding, he succumbed to shock and collapsed.

Again the war horn of the Na Daoine Tùrsach reverberated, *barrr-ewww barrr-ewww* and again, the painted warriors broke off their attack and melded with the forest. They left the maimed and dying to the mercy of their enemy. The Ériu showed none.

Four of the injured were lugged to stakes, set facing north, south, east and west. With swift and practiced movements, Mongfhionn eviscerated and then drew her blade across the throats of the unfortunate. Their cries were short, but rose loud sending a clear message to the forces in the forest. Conall's veterans watched Mongfhionn's sacrifices with a mix of pragmatism edged with well-founded fear.

A perimeter of their enemy's staked heads was erected around the camp in the clearing. Sightless eyes stared reproachfully into the forest. Before the light failed, small groups stripped the headless corpses before dragging them beyond the boundary of the glade. A few paces back from the skull-fence, the men spread caltrops and pushed sharpened stakes into the loose forest debris and dirt - a nasty surprise for any unwelcome visitor whether human or beast.

Pine-scented fires crackled, throwing flickering shades of light and dark against the backdrop of trees. The wolf glanced up from the body it had selected. Accentuated by the flames, its cruel, amber eyes glowed intensely. The predator snarled at the shadows and then hauled its feast deeper into the forest. The pack howled. Another beast padded forward, mouth salivating in anticipation.

Those not on guard duties took the opportunity to rest and take stock of the condition of weapons and armor. All owned a multiplicity of weapons – axes, swords, daggers, studded gloves, and javelins. The wonder was how they were able to carry them all.

Around the fires, warriors debated the merits of bronze-coated, versus traditional shields of wood and leather strengthened with an iron frame. Most thought that bronze would allow them a much more ornate and personalized design. This was always a consideration for a people who appreciated the intricate designs on carved leather and jewelry.

Black jokes were told and ghoulish wagers placed as to how many of the painted they would kill. Occasionally, one would nod his head in the direction of the small group huddled around the central fire and mutter, "Thank the Goddess I'm not a leader," provoking the usual litany of, "Ye'r right there," and a short period of silent contemplation.

The somber group was comprised of Conall, Mórrígan, Mongfhionn, Fearghal, Deaglán, Tadhg, Torcán and Gràinne. Conall spoke first, "As you are aware, I tasked Tadhg with finding out about the child, Morna's murder." He shifted, "Tadhg, it's time to tell us what you know – or what you believe."

Concern etched the face of the young warrior. Barely recovered from the last assault, Tadhg had deep cuts on his forearms and thighs that would turn into impressive scars when healed. He also bore hidden scars from the tongue-lashing he had received from Conall and Fearghal for the reckless rage he had exhibited earlier in the battle. He found it mildly amusing that one of the insults leveled at him was that his behavior "had been as brave and brainless as of that eejit, Torcán."

Tadhg gathered his thoughts and uncharacteristically downed

another horn of beer before beginning. "First, I don't have perfect information and likely never will. That said, I'm convinced that we can rule out any guilt from the Lady Mongfhionn and Queen Mórrígan."

Fearghal exhaled, "Thank the Goddess for that." A quick, curt look from Conall cut off any follow up quip that his friend might offer.

"Go on."

"There was a thread from Morna's léine caught in a bramble bush where she'd been picking berries. Beside that was a footprint. It was a strange print and the person who made it had a unique gait." Tadhg paused and looked at Gràinne. His next point was sure to cause trouble. "It was the same type of print that Gràinne leaves."

"No! It wasn't me," the girl cried under the severe gaze of Mongfhionn and Mórrígan. Feverishly, she scrambled to her feet preparing to flee.

"She's right," Tadhg interjected quickly. "I don't think Gràinne murdered the child, but she may know who did."

Conall's eyes narrowed, glinting harshly in the firelight. His jaw tightened. "Continue, Tadhg," he said. Beside him, Fearghal quietly placed his longsword across his knees.

"In Cùil Daothail, I noticed that at least one of the Na Daoine Tùrsach priests had the same type of track." This drew gasps of disbelief from those around the fire and another exclamation from Gràinne which was followed by sobbing. "Also, when we were getting rid of the bodies after the fight in the settlement, I saw that the paint and tattoos on the priests' bodies were of the same design as Gràinne's." Tadhg let his words sink in.

"She's part of the Na Daoine Tùrsach." Deaglán voiced aloud the conclusion that all had deduced.

Torcán groaned, "I brought her to us. I'm sorry."

"Your only fault is mounting any female who'll spread her legs for you," Fearghal said, cutting off a much sharper retort from Mongfhionn.

"Yes, I believe Gràinne belongs to the Na Daoine Tùrsach," Tadhg said with a note of sadness, "but I don't think she murdered the child. Her foot is too small to have made the print I found."

Gràinne breathed a grateful, "Thank you." She glanced around, her eyes pleading for mercy and understanding from those around the fire.

"Well child," Mongfhionn spoke grimly, ice in her voice. "Your choice is plain. Tell us who killed the child or be sacrificed in her murderer's place."

Tadhg made to object, but Conall placed a restraining hand on his arm. "You've done well Tadhg, but justice will be done. The child must be avenged and since she is dead, recompense cannot be made to her. Or to her family, who are dead by our hands." Conall regarded Gràinne and said, "If there is an explanation, now would be a good time to offer it. Better still to offer up the murderer of the child, for I see in your eyes you know who it is."

Gràinne's hands clutched her breasts. For a brief moment she glowered defiantly and stood proud. Then her shoulders slumped and silent tears streamed down painted cheeks as she spoke, "Morna was my friend. I loved her like a sister. I would never... I could never hurt her. Yes, I'm Na Daoine Tùrsach and likely perceived as your enemy – although I'm not. Yes, the one you seek is from that tribe." She looked at Tadhg and smiled wearily, "Perhaps it would have been better for me to let the waters take you. You're very clever." Unable to meet her eyes, Tadhg stared at the ground.

Twisting her long auburn hair with nervous fingers, she continued, "I ran away from my tribe. I was to be sacrificed – although that was when they thought me pure. I used Torcán to end that value." To Torcán she said quietly, "Sorry." Then she turned to the Sidhe, "Should I end up as your sacrifice, it will not change much for my circumstance, just who wields the knife – and it will not avenge Morna."

"Then who, Gràinne?" Mongfhionn asked, her voice carrying a tone of sympathy. "Who murdered the girl in such a brutal manner?"

"Who sacrifices in such a manner, my Lady Sidhe?" Gràinne held Mongfhionn's gaze, "Who but a Druid... or a Sidhe?"

"Shite, this is hitting close to the mark," said a perturbed Fearghal.

"The one you're looking for is a priest. He is Caol, son of Diadhaidh – the Priestess and Queen of the Na Daoine Tùrsach. Caol is also my father. My mother is dead, sacrificed after she birthed me."

"By the Hag, are there to be any more revelations this evening? I'll need a bath to wash away the stench of what I've heard." Fearghal shook his head in disbelief. Gràinne was heartened to see that he had sheathed his longsword.

"The attacks on this warband. It is likely the Na Daoine Tùrsach warriors have been instructed to rescue me." She sighed, "Hand me over and they will probably overlook the killing of their priests in Cùil Daothail." Gràinne sat and waited.

"No!" an angry Tadhg stood up. "She is innocent. We cannot hand her over."

"Sit yourself down, Tadhg," Conall said patiently. "There is no question of handing her over to the Na Daoine Tùrsach. Yet…" He paused to smile ironically at Mongfhionn. "I sense, like pieces on a fidchell board, we are maneuvered to be the weapon of the Sidhe."

Mongfhionn stood and looked at everyone in turn. "My presence, my protection always has a price – as you surely know, Conall. Morna will be avenged, but that is secondary to the diminishing of the Na Daoine Tùrsach. They are to be broken, vanquished – destroyed if possible. They sow dark corruption and cannot be allowed to thrive."

"That's a tall order with just two hundred warriors," Deaglán blurted out, and then flushed the color of his hair when he realized he had questioned the Sidhe.

"It would seem so," said Mongfhionn, a glimmer of a smile curving up the edges of her lips, "but help can come from surprising places."

"As usual," Fearghal huffed, "we'll be at the entrance to Mag Mell before the help arrives." The bluff warrior's unexpected words relieved the tension and chuckles spread around the fire.

Conall stood up. "This is the plan. Our target and priority remains the capture of Cassius Fabius Scaeva. We'll travel hard and fast over the mountains to the Na Daoine Smeurta and relieve them of their prize. The mountain passes will more than likely be blocked for the return journey, though, and that leaves us to travel the coastal plain route, placing us directly in the land of the Na Daoine Tùrsach. Gràinne will tell us all she knows so that we may be well prepared. We will avenge Morna – and with the Sidhe's help give the Ancient Ones what they desire.

"Let's sleep, we'll have an early start tomorrow."

As the group split up, Torcán approached his friends, Deaglán and Tadhg cautiously. "There are few secrets in this camp, Tadhg," Torcán began and Tadhg tensed for whatever was to come. "We all know what has been going on between you and Gràinne." Torcán held his hand up as Tadhg's hand slipped to his dagger.

"No, let me finish. We've been friends since we were wee uns. We've seen our families slaughtered and have a closer bond than many families. I won't let some slip of a girl break that relationship. If you want Gràinne, that's fine with me." Then Torcán laughed. "Personally, I think she's more trouble than she's worth and I'm supposed to be the reckless one!"

A relieved Tadhg simply said, "Thanks." There was a pause as the trio looked at each other. "Guess the drinks are on me."

"Damn right they are," chorused Deaglán and Torcán.

Morning broke all too early for some. Armor was donned in the half-light, a hot meal taken, and the fires doused. There was a cry, "The girl is missing." Tadhg raced to the wagon under which Gràinne had slept. On the ground lay a crumpled, rust-colored brat, but no girl.

Hoping that she had simply slept elsewhere, Tadhg looked around with growing concern. "Maybe she just took off, Tadhg," Fearghal said with uncharacteristic sympathy. "Couldn't really blame her if she did." Tadhg shook his head in disbelief.

"If what she said about the Na Daoine Tùrsach wanting her back is true then I don't think so, Fearghal," said Conall. "The foolish girl probably needed a piss and was carried off." He put his hand on Tadhg's shoulder. "We'll settle with that tribe when we have the Roman," he said.

In a less certain tone he added, "I'm sure we'll get Gràinne back."

CHAPTER 17

Drostan Ruadh was glad to see the Ériu camp deserted. Flocks of birds circled, swooping to snatch scattered morsels of food and nesting materials. To his chagrin, the Aos na Coille leader was sorely tempted to keep the dùn. It was a strong defensive structure and well-located.

Failbhe stood beside him. "It's not our way, son," he said. The older man's bones grated against each other as he attempted to straighten his back in the morning chill.

The king nodded and replied with regret, "It may be the way of the future. The forests may not remain with us forever."

"Ye'r talking shite!" said Failbhe. "Forests are ageless – and so are the Aos na Coille."

Drostan grunted, "Open yer eyes, old man. The population grows. The farmers are already taking small bites."

"Then slaughter the farmers and let their blood feed the forest," retorted Failbhe.

"Sometimes, there's no talking to ye," said Drostan with affection. He summoned a warrior, "Burn the camp, level it and plow the ashes into the dirt." Turning away he added, "And take those dammed skulls down and bury them."

Íar noted the black smudge above the forest canopy. He grinned at Cúscraid, "Seems Drostan didn't appreciate your work."

"Póg ma thoin, you overgrown, red-haired eejit," said Cúscraid. "The next one will be built of rock and dirt. Let them try burning that!"

Íar looked along the meandering column of warriors, camp followers and tradesmen. Brightly colored garments of reds, oranges, yellows and greens stood out against the dark forest. He shook his head, "How did we get so many, in what seems a very short time? The families of those slain by Eochaidh Ruad and the Roman form only a small part of us."

"A more important question is: why are they so loyal? Most could have stayed in Ériu, yet chose to risk everything to follow Conall."

"It's a puzzle Cúscraid, but my worry is whether we will make it to A' Chrìon Làraich before the harsh weather sets in. Look at the sky. These days it's almost always overcast," Íar said, and then pointed to the dark horizon. "And those are snow clouds. Once we leave the forest, it's a hard trek across mountain terrain with little shelter to protect from the wind and snow."

Cúscraid's hazel-green eyes twinkled, bringing a rare flash of levity to his normally taciturn demeanor, "Speaking for the Ulaid, Íar, we're a tough and proud people – and quick to battle…" the tall, solid-muscled warrior paused, "…maybe too quick."

Íar grunted, "I don't think that's confined to the Ulaid. Maybe, you just don't hide it as well as the rest of us."

"Anyway, our pig-headedness will likely get us through the journey," Cúscraid said, and then returned to practicalities. "Seanán tells me that everyone is in good spirits." Cúscraid cited the civic leader's recent report, "He assures they are well-prepared with good clothing and pelts for the weather."

The big warrior cleared his throat loudly and the eyes of the huge bay-colored beast standing alongside Íar widened in response. "That's all very well, but even the best of cloth and leather rots in this constant damp and rain. Feet don't do so well either – there's many I choose to avoid. Their feet stink even more than usual."

"No remedy for that. Anyway, Sárán Mac Craobhach tells me

that the army and their followers are as well supplied as he could hope for." At the mention of Sárán, Íar raised an eyebrow. Sárán was a thorough planner, but he often drove others to their wits' end over small details. Like stacking shields just so in the wagons to take up less room, or pointing out that the wagon wheels were harder to turn when covered in mud - or shite from Íar's horses.

"In fact," Cúscraid continued, ignoring the quizzical look on his friend's face, "the only complaint we're hearing at the moment is that the people have to tramp through piles of shite dropped by your horses. In the name of the Goddess, what are you feeding those beasts?" Íar laughed roundly, and then mounted his horse to join his men.

The main column made steady progress if at a snail's pace. Nikandros cantered at the center of the skirmish line alongside Cathán, Ròidh, and a century of riders. Their job was to clear the way of opportunistic thieves and outlaws and the more rebellious contingents of Drostan's army. A few warbands still smarted from the bloody nose they had been given. So far, the task had not been onerous. In fact it was as boring as the Underworld thought the Spartan. He sighed and almost wished that someone would be foolish enough to challenge them.

Nikandros paused at a patch of grass that had pushed through the forest debris. Toirneach nickered, tearing at the leaves with strong teeth. Conall's black stallion was happy at being taken for a long ride, even though it was not his master on his back. The Spartan smiled at the horse's mannerisms. He pulled his heavy black cloak, now trimmed with a luxurious silver-gray wolf pelt – a gift from Eachdonn Breac, around his shoulders and refastened it with an ornately designed and bejeweled gold brooch.

Possibly he was getting soft, Nikandros mused as he let his thoughts wander back to his days in the much warmer climates of the Great Sea. Yes, there could be times of severe cold that made the wearing of the short, red, Spartan tunic a challenge, but nothing like this constant rain that soaked into garments. Nothing was ever completely dry. Or the bone-chilling sleet that sucked the warmth from bodies and stuck louse-tight to clothes.

He laughed aloud, startling Ròidh and Cathán who rode on either side of him. It was no wonder, he thought, that these islands never witnessed the massive land and sea battles of the Greeks, the Persians, the Romans or the Spartans. It was too bloody wet and miserable. Nikandros nudged the black stallion forward, gently guiding the animal with his knees. In truth, the horse was as well behaved as his – not surprising since both he and Íar had a hand in the beast's training. The horse picked up its pace with Nikandros' thoughts occupied with warm, turquoise waters, clear blue skies and an unending supply of wine.

A sharp clang ended Nikandros' reverie. Quickly he bent low against Toirneach's shoulders. The stone had flown from the right, leaving a small dent in his bronze helmet. He instinctively reached for his shield, withdrew his xiphos from its leather sheath and shouted a warning. "Slings on the right!" Swing to the right and keep your heads low." Along the skirmish line men scrambled to ensure their helmets were on and tight.

The range of a sling was around five hundred paces. Nikandros knew their attackers probably escaped deep into the forest. Following them was a futile gesture, but provided a diversion for the men. Perhaps the Goddess would favor them with some luck.

Ahead, two singular, flesh-muffled cracks were followed by a high-pitched scream of pain, then silence. The men cringed, the hairs on their necks standing on end. Each had a fair idea of what had caused the distinctive sounds. A few moments later, the silence of the forest was again shattered by a heart-quickening shriek. Weapons ready, the cavalry band warily approached the scene.

The bodies of about twenty warriors were spread across the forest floor. The tattoos told the men and women were Aos na Coille, one of the rebel warbands. All had spear or axe wounds. All were dead. Many had had their throats cut. Nikandros' men gasped as they drew closer. Not at the scattered bodies. They had surveyed such bloody scenes many times, but at the figure posed at the center of the slaughter.

"The Hag preserve me," Cathán exhaled on realizing that the warrior was held upright by a wooden stake. The stake had penetrated her arse and its tip jutted out between her breasts.

The female warrior had been posed on the blood sodden dirt between two trees. Her arms were stretched and held firmly in place with leather cords as if in prayer. Her broken legs could give her no means of support or relief.

"In some ways that could be considered stimulating," one wag opined. "I mean, the stake between those pendulous tits."

"You're a sick and sorry man," said his neighbor.

The conversation abruptly halted as the corpse's head jerked upwards. From the bloody froth flowing from her mouth came a few strangled words. Their meaning was clear. Nikandros dismounted and approached the warrior. Her tattooed neck was exposed; her face lowered until her chin rested on her chest. Fortunately, Nikandros' blade was ever oiled and sharp. A swift merciful slash of the xiphos removed her head. The Spartan scowled and wiped the blade clean on a nearby body. It seemed inappropriate to use that of the warrior's.

A guttural roar followed by harsh laughing came from deep within the forest. "Seems our guardians take their sport seriously," said Ròidh as he surveyed the corpses.

"That's the second time Drostan's warriors have intervened on our behalf," Cathán said. He spoke of the band of about one hundred Aos na Coille warriors who had shadowed the Ériu since the riverside camp had been vacated.

"The king takes his promise of safe passage seriously. And of course, he doesn't want any harm to come to his heirs," said Nikandros.

"Barbarians!" responded Cathán indignantly, his budding sense of honor having been offended.

Nikandros smiled grimly, "I've seen much worse from supposedly civilized men, Cathán. If you live long enough, so will you. Just pray to your Goddess that it is not you who commits such savagery."

The view of snow-capped mountains from the forest edge was both beautiful and daunting. Jagged summits pushed through silver-gray snow-clouds. Soaring high on the wind, wings wide and feathers spread, several pairs of eagles circled the peaks each protecting their territory. The blue-black sheen of ravens rippled over branches at the forest edge, the only sound an occasional *kraa kraa.*

Brats, cloaks and furs were held closer as a cold wind swept across the barren slopes. Flurries of snow skipped and danced over the land, giving all a foretaste of what they could expect. The younger children, ignoring the cold, rushed forward, excited. Many carried makeshift cages made of twigs. They contained the gaily colored cam-ghobs that had been trapped in the forest. The birds' deep tooping noise expressed dissatisfaction with their lot. Silence would have served them better. Many, despite the tears and pleadings of their captors, would end up in the cooking cauldrons or roasted on spits.

Íar called the army and civic leaders together. "It will be dusk soon. Have the people move back into the forest and set up camp. At least we can have some shelter this night." There was vigorous agreement all around. "There are two possible routes to A' Chrìon Làraich – across the mountains or around them following the river valley. The mountain path is much shorter, but more open and dangerous. The weather could turn nasty."

"The weather could turn nasty for either route, Íar," said Cúscraid. "Winter is very close. We'll face snow and high winds no matter the path. I vote we go across the mountains. The Goddess willing, if we're to celebrate the advent of spring at Imbolg, then we'll need to be well settled in A' Chrìon Làraich before the feast of Samhain." Cúscraid found himself a bit perturbed at how much respect for the Goddess was slipping into his daily speech.

"I'm in agreement with Cúscraid," Brion said. "Íar, you also spoke of a river valley through the mountains. Will it allow the passage of wagons and chariots?"

Íar tilted his head back, thinking. "There is a river that flows to the east across the mountain. It's not a straight route to A' Chrìon Làraich, but would be quicker than the forest route around the mountains. The river would provide fresh water and possibly fresh food." Then he snorted, "I think it would be passable, though taxing for the wagons and chariots."

Nikandros slapped Íar on the back, "You're sounding more and more like that horse of yours. He must be having a good influence on you. I agree with Cúscraid and Brion. Let's get the pain out of the way as fast as possible." With a wide grin he added, "If we're finished, I'm off to find a soft piece of forest floor and a woman to keep me warm."

"I'm amazed any woman would let that thing between your legs anywhere near her," Brion commented.

"Curiosity, Brion," the Spartan said with a shrug, "curiosity."

A mere trickle of water, the burn followed the line of the northern mountain slopes. The valley was narrow at barely five hundred paces and exposed to biting winds gusting from the south and northwest. Steep bluffs covered in white morning frost and the beginning of a thin layer of wet snow rose up, challenging all who ascended the heights.

To the south, Beinn an Laoigh, surrounded by its sibling cliffs at almost twice the elevation of the northern heights, soared even higher into the clouds. The constantly wet rock of Beinn an Laoigh's precipitous slopes were covered in mosses and lichens, lending a deceptively pleasing mix of purple, pink and green tones.

Stubborn, hard, stiff-necked… bloody eejits! All could be applied to the caravan of warriors and followers that fought an unceasing battle against the weather during the trek. The cold, harsh environment winnowed the weak — the elderly, the sick and the young. Packs of wolves were a constant companion, waiting to carry off the dead, the foolish and the feeble-minded. The people came to curse and loathe the howling of the wind and the wolves. They also came to love and respect the wolfhounds who steadfastly roamed the fringes of the assembly, driving off the bolder predators.

Exposed faces flared red and raw from the constant battering of wind, rain and sleet. The unforgiving valley of rock and stone stretched seemingly without end. Kindling and wood to support even the smallest of fires was scant. At night they found what shelter they could and ate a cold meal in silence. Only the fire from the special brew the warriors had bartered from the Aos na Coille gave chilled bellies some comfort.

As darkness fell, they slept as one great heaving mass of men, women, children and animals. The children - the heart of the beast, slept in the center surrounded by a bulwark of flesh and bone. As always the warriors protected the perimeter – they were the hide of the beast. There was no room for privacy. The foolish who wandered off into the night to piss or shite rarely returned.

In the mornings, they arose as one, shaking off frost and snow. The ground trembled under the stamping feet of thousands. The air cracked with the clapping of hands. Steam rose, forming a transient haze above the beast. Even in the cold, the mingled smell of sweat, piss and the musky scent of rutting assaulted nostrils. The dawn's activities were promptly replaced by shouts of encouragement and threats from the civic and army leaders as they roused the people for the day's march. Children cried and hid in the folds of their mother's brats. Faces numbed by the penetrating cold streamed tears from red-rimmed eyes. But they moved. Slowly at first, but one step at a time they advanced, eating up the distance.

Mid-way, the river valley turned northwards. The land, barren at first, began to show signs of growth. Beneath the frost there persisted a green hue to the land. Scattered bushes, shrubs, mosses and heathers became clusters of trees. The valley sides were gentler, the river wider, and on the northern side, the forest had re-established its presence. The people rejoiced and praised the Goddess with gifts tossed into the river. They had wood and they had fire. They would survive.

Íar heaved a great sigh of relief as the settlement of A' Chrìon Làraich came into view. There was no friendly blue smoke haze floating above the dark, thatched roofs and no laborers in the surrounding fields. The residents of A' Chrìon Làraich, uncertain of their new masters, had fled.

"How many of this settlement will die while your people shelter in their homes for the winter?" the Druid spat angrily.

"Their fate is their choice," said Íar. "My duty is to this people and its army. If you want, send out word that any seeking shelter will be welcome."

Cúscraid stood on the hillside and surveyed the settlement. As a peaceful farming and trading community its location was perfect. As a defensive position it was a nightmare. After all, Íar had been able to overrun the settlement with little resistance.

The main community lay on almost flat land on the valley floor. The surrounding mountains descended to the valley in heavily forested, long gentle slopes. An army could be hidden a short distance away and the inhabitants would never know until it was too late. At least a river flowed past, providing a barrier of sorts. It also was the main source of water via a small tributary that ran through the center of the settlement.

"What do you think?" Íar asked, interrupting Cúscraid's train of thought. They were joined by Nikandros, Brion and Áine. The latter two struggled valiantly to prevent Cassán, who having recently discovered his legs and mobility was making a determined attempt to escape to the forest.

Cúscraid looked to the sky, "There's little time before the heavy snowfalls arrive. Likely this is a paradise in spring, summer and fall – but winter will be nasty. The valley is perfect for gusting winds." He pointed to the area between the settlement and the river. "We'll build about twenty wooden long-halls there, each big enough to house two hundred. It will be a tight fit, but warm and close to the river. We'll add a thorn and stake fence between the river and the halls to discourage visitors."

Brion scowled, "The Hag, Cúscraid. That's a lot of work."

"Yes, and it's only the beginning. There are no fortifications –

and no shelter for the warriors. We'll need to reconfigure all the settlement defenses – upgrade the perimeter walls with rock and stone, deepen the ditches and then populate them with stakes and thorn bushes. The main roundhouse needs to be transformed into a broch. The other buildings can be improved for the blacksmiths', fletchers' and armorers' purposes."

"What about the men?" Íar asked.

"I reckon there'll be enough space inside the main defenses for about a thousand. The rest will be lodged in more long-halls – likely on that rise to the northeast. We'll also need corrals and pens for the horses and animals."

"Shite Cúscraid," Brion interjected. "We're building Drostan a ready-made ráth and village, not too far from several other tribes – including the Na Mèadaidh."

"Can't be helped. We need the shelter and we need it before the feast of Samhain. We have to assume someone is going to attack us before we leave or while the main army is away trying to take Dùn Na Mèadaidh."

"Well, not including the children you have about five thousand workers," Íar said. "Anyone who can lift an axe or hammer is yours."

The thunder of felled trees rolled through the valley. Wagons grated and creaked under loads of rocks from a nearby quarry. The steady thump of heavy hammers on wood was accompanied by explosive grunts from semi-naked men coated in a film of sweat and dirt.

Peals of laughter arose from the women. Many were barely clothed themselves. More than a few had muscles that put the men to shame and set out to prove the value of their labor. Curses rose up into the air as male thumbs and fingers were caught between wood and iron – mostly from the distraction provided by a neighbor's breasts.

A comforting blur of black-feathered ravens flew back and forth across the valley. Seeking scraps, they eyed the steady line of hunters returning from the forests bearing their prizes – carcasses of red deer, wild boar, along with elks and aurochs. Younger boys and girls had been tasked with rounding up the scattered herds of cattle and marking the location of flocks of sheep. Along the riverbank, men and women used poles, nets and hands to hook or scoop up plentiful silver-scaled fish.

It was a mild and for once a dry day, a deceptive preamble to the coming storms, as Nikandros, Fionnbharr and Cathán tramped across land churned up and rutted from the construction. Nikandros was keeping a watch out for recruits for the army.

There was always a steady harvest of young males and females who could work or fight. Life was often short and brutal. Men and women took their pleasure when they could and their offspring, those who had withstood a harsh youth and entered adulthood, were tough survivors.

Nikandros proposed they should commence training the children, especially the boys, when they reached their seventh summer. This was how it was done in Sparta, he said. Responses varied considerably. The Druid appeared to have fewer issues with the Spartan's philosophy than most, but a glowering Áine said, "You touch Cassán at age seven and I'll stick an arrow up your arse."

Though dissatisfied, the Spartan compromised and it was agreed that anyone twelve summers or older – male and female - was to be trained for battle. Those fifteen or over were expected to fight, if not in the front lines, then certainly in the reserves. It was up to Nikandros to decide the young recruits' aptitude for riding, archery, or sword and axe play.

As they traversed the settlement, Fionnbharr had a vital task – to look out for signs of disease or sicknesses that might ravage the camp. So far, they had avoided a major outbreak, but he knew it was only a matter of time before they might face a silent enemy greater than any of the tribes they had fought. He thanked the Goddess for the cold since it appeared to keep the worst of sickness at bay.

The bonfires roared in celebration of Samhain. The defenses of A' Chrìon Làraich were complete and adequate accommodations for man and beast had been erected. Within and around what was now a credible stronghold, happy revelers feasted, drank and danced themselves stupid. Mock screams of protest were heard as men carried women – or some women carried men, to whatever dark sanctuary they could find. Later, filled with beer and intent on taking pleasure, their amorous activities would forgo even that small amount of privacy. More often than not, their efforts would end in drunken sleep rather than a successful coupling.

Íar noted that even the Druid looked happy, although he sometimes believed the man's face would crack if he really smiled. The Goddess forbid that he might even laugh. The jovial warrior smacked his horn of beer against countless others as he passed through the camp and settlement, "More beer is in the dirt than in my belly," he grumbled, then smiled over-broadly as one of the women filled his horn again.

He surveyed Cúscraid's handiwork and was once again amazed, proud and glad of his friend's ability to plan what needed to be done and then marshal the resources to compete it. Íar was even thankful that Cúscraid had the aid of Sárán who had proven to be as good a master of logistics as his late and deeply missed father, Cian.

While the settlement had long been a significant trading presence in the valley, the stronghold of A' Chrìon Làraich towered over and dominated the surrounding lands. At its heart, rose a solid walled broch, its walls the width of two men laid head-to-toe. The base of the broch was fully twenty paces wide inside and fifty paces tall. An east-facing entrance was lined in cut, gray stone and sealed by a solid oak door with a heavy wood bar that slid into slots carved in the lintel to secure it. A few paces outside of the door, a small cell – big enough for a man - had been cut into the rock.

Inside the broch, and at its center, lay a fire banked with bricks of peat. Now it slumbered, but when stoked, the fire roared casting both heat and light across the room. Red glowing embers lay beneath its dark crust and a steady, lazy stream of blue-gray smoke ascended to the conical, thatched roof. Without the rushlights stuttering in their wooden holders, the fragrant, smoky fire only added to the gloom of the room. An iron spit and griddle waited.

The broch was deceptively spacious. Steps cut into the inner wall led to a second floor. It was constructed with cut planks and mainly purposed for storage. The lower, stone floor was divided into stalls for sleeping and with room for several horses. Meadowsweet had been liberally mixed into the layers of rushes spread in the sleeping stalls - a small attempt to reduce the odors of men and beasts.

As a defense, the broch was as much protection in a siege as a blunt sword. It was a home, a place to eat, to meet and share the craic after a few horns of beer. It was useless as a ráth, but its presence signaled that those who had built it were not to be trifled with.

Íar stubbed his toe and cursed explosively to the amusement of those close by. Head befuddled with too much beer, he had fallen victim to the latest innovation from the mind of Cúscraid. At each of the two perimeter entrances, Cúscraid had sown fields of carefully placed oblong stones. Their function was to disrupt a cavalry assault. Small, shallow pits had also been dug and populated with wooden stakes. With grim satisfaction, Íar reflected that had he faced the upgraded ráth, A' Chrìon Làraich would have been a much tougher challenge. In his estimate, it would have taken too long and Nikandros' camp would have been overrun.

"An impressive work." A startled Íar placed his hand on his dagger as the cloaked shape of the Druid appeared from the shadows.

"You may be a Druid, but you're also an arsehole. Creeping up on someone like that will get you killed. Shite!"

"I apologize. Like you, I was taking in the superb construction. A' Chrìon Làraich will never be the same. Whether that is for good or bad, who can say?" The Druid's breath created a thin white puff in the chill, night air. "Some of the previous occupants would like to return. They are farmers, skilled artisans and tradespeople. I foresee no issues."

Íar nodded, "It's their settlement. We've only got temporary possession. Tell them they're welcome. Ask them to meet with Sárán and Seanán. They'll sort out where they can stay — and see what work they might be able to do."

In the darkness of the mid-night, Íar sensed relief from the Druid, and then a lift of unease. The Druid coughed, a quick clearing of the throat. Íar smiled and waited. "The Aos na Coille warriors who have accompanied us have, as you may have surmised, two responsibilities: to ensure that you reached A' Chrìon Làraich without mishap or diversion and to watch over Drostan's son and daughter. All are pledged to protect the heirs with their lives if needed." The Druid paused.

"And?"

"They have asked permission to stay at A' Chrìon Làraich over the winter." Reacting to Íar's grimace the Druid said, "I will be the guarantor of their behavior. I doubt that they will be perfectly behaved – they are warriors after all. But I will judge fairly any complaints and set out restitution, if required."

"Alright, Druid. Inform their leader that they should come to the settlement in a few days – when the headaches from the feasting and drinking have receded. Cúscraid and Brion can get them settled in one of the long-halls."

The Druid bowed in the darkness, "My thanks."

"Well, I'm going to take advantage of that great broch Cúscraid has built and get some sleep." The Druid nodded and smiled at the receding hulk. Before Íar had gone beyond earshot, the big warrior chuckled and turned, "See Fionnbharr about that cough, Druid. It wouldn't be good for us to lose our arbiter."

CHAPTER 18

The band followed the wooded valley north into the mountains. Slopes rose gently upwards to meet barren, moss covered rock. Jagged peaks glistened in the rain. After consulting with Fearghal, Conall decided that although they could push and haul the wagons over the rocky terrain, they would make better pace without the carts.

On hearing that they were to return to Cùil Daothail, the wagon drivers were most helpful in unloading their cargoes and providing advice on balancing packs. They also volunteered information on various minor lochs and landmarks that would signpost the journey.

Conall's hundred caomhnóirí and the other warriors protested loudly, if half-heartedly, about taking on the work of pack animals. Each, in addition to his or her weapons and armor, carried several layers of clothing or pelts and as much food as possible. "I'm remembering the packs of rocks we lugged up and down the slopes of Taobh Builleach before the assault on Ráth na Lairig Éadain," one warrior mused. "At least this time, our packs are loaded with something useful." The others laughed in agreement.

Several mornings later, the party descended into a forested river valley. All were rain-sodden and shivering in the falling temperatures. As expected, the tributary led to a bridge of old timbers. The soundness of the bridge was suspect, but it held. Crossing meant that they had left Na Daoine Tùrsach lands. The border of the Aos an Fhithich territory was marked by a group of three upright standing stones. The smallest was the height of two men and all were inscribed with tribal symbols.

They entered the small settlement of Drochaid a' Bhanna not long after. It was little more than a cluster of various sized round-houses and wooden buildings. Men, women and children direct-ed wary glances their way. All but the youngest bore distinctive designs and paint on exposed faces and limbs. Many had a black feather hanging from a thin braid of their hair. Conall flicked a look to Mongfhionn. The Sidhe just nodded and smiled.

There was a stir from the main building as they approached the center of the settlement. Three tall, well-muscled, red-haired men dressed only in pants exited the roundhouse and stood with arms crossed.

"You recognize them?" Fearghal asked quietly as they drew closer.

Conall frowned. "The two on the right have been following us since we left Cùil Daothail."

"Guess they've been expecting us then!" Fearghal said. Conall recognized the warning note in the offhand remark.

Conall halted a respectful distance from the trio, removed his helmet and turned to face his men, "Mórrígan, Mongfhionn, Fearghal and I will go forward. Stay alert, but do not threaten – a wee smile or two might help." Given such license, Torcán and Deaglán immediately removed their helmets, releasing long, braided red hair and were flashing broad smiles at the nearest group of girls. A sharp frown from Mongfhionn elicited a tinge of regret at his choice of words.

Making a show of laying his shield on the ground, Conall then deliberately unbuckled his leather belt, dropping sword and sheath onto the shield, followed by his axes. He kept his helmet under his arm. Fearghal and Mórrígan followed suit. The Sidhe slipped the hood of her cloak back from her face, releasing her golden cloud of hair. She simply waited with her oak staff in hand. An audible gasp made its way through the crowd and they edged closer.

"I hate to bring this up," Fearghal said, only half in jest, "but without Gràinne, we have no one who might speak their language – and I don't think Torcán or Tadhg were focused on learning the dialects of the Cinn Péinteáilte when they were between her thighs."

Conall grimaced. "Let's just see how it goes." He strode, arms held out and palms upward, towards the small group. As he approached, the warrior in the middle took steps forward to meet him and called out a greeting in a voice with a rumbling burr.

"Fàilte - welcome."

"Well, the accent is a bit thick, but that sounds friendly to me," said Fearghal.

Conall smiled. "Go raibh maith agat – thank-you."

"My name is Brandubh Mac Artair. I am the son of Artair, the leader of the Aos an Fhithich – the Raven People." Pointing to the younger man behind him, Brandubh introduced him as his brother, Blàr. Then, he bowed to the older man, "This is Ailde, he is the leader of this settlement at Drochaid a' Bhanna. You may have some problems with Ailde's stronger accent. Rather than cause you embarrassment, he has asked that I welcome you and your men on his behalf. The night is drawing near and Ailde has arranged for food and shelter with his people. He requests that you, the ladies, and your captains should eat with him and lodge in his roundhouse."

Conall bowed to the elderly Ailde, held out his hand and clasped the older man's arm "Once more, thanks."

Predictably, Tadhg and his brother Craiftine took up Ailde's offer, but Torcán, hoping for some female diversion, decided to take his chances with the residents of Drochaid a' Bhanna and dragged Deaglán along with him. Sadly, Torcán's plans were thwarted. A quick word in Brandubh's ear by Mongfhionn and the amorous duo found themselves quartered in a house with two pairs of twin girls aged two and four summers.

The Aos an Fhithich hosts were delighted to hear that Craiftine was a harpist and his brother, Tadhg, a seanachaí - teller of ballads, myths and legends, and entreated them to entertain. A hoarse throat eventually removed Tadhg as a diversion, but Craiftine who truly loved his harp happily played into the wee hours of the morning. Even Blàr, who at first appeared somewhat dour and withdrawn, had slowly migrated to where Craiftine sat and gave instruction on some new melodies.

"It strikes me that we were expected," Conall said as he reached across the table – a solid block of smooth, red stone, to carve a pink slice of roasted wild boar.

"I followed your trail from Cùil Daothail," responded Brandubh.

"I know," Conall laughed, and wiped warm blood and grease from his chin. "My sense is that even had we not met in Cùil Daothail, our arrival wouldn't have caused a large amount of concern." It was then that Conall caught the glances traded between Mongfhionn and Brandubh, and the short nod from the Sidhe.

"There is a geis upon the Raven People," said Brandubh.

Fearghal guffawed, spraying drink on those nearest. "She suckered a whole tribe this time!" Fortified by beer and undaunted by the furious looks he was getting from Mongfhionn, he said, "I am both amazed and impressed, my love."

In the convivial atmosphere within the roundhouse, even the normally stern Sidhe was unable to maintain a veil of anger or disapproval, however thin. "Bah, you haven't experienced a tenth of my powers, you drunken eejit," she said.

Ailde's naturally thick accent was further blunted with many beers. "We've heard tales of the Ulaid warrior and ruiri called Fearghal Ruad," he said. "I just hadn't considered that the man might live up to his reputation." Then the Elder nodded to Brandubh to resume his tale.

"It is told that in the earliest times, when the tribes of the north were but fledgling bands of roaming hunters my ancestor was visited by the Aes Sidhe. In return for their blessing on the Aos an Fhithich and our loyalty to the Goddess, we were granted, in this land of barren mountains, a home that was fertile and forested." Brandubh paused to wet his throat, using the back of his hand to catch a dribble of beer that escaped his lips.

An irreverent Fearghal cut in, "And the price?"

The tall Aos an Fhithich warrior smiled and nodded, "Yes, there was a price, but then that is the way of things. A balance must be maintained. Passed from generation to generation the geis goes –

'An làthair fhitheach, dubh air balla fuilteach, seasaidh Làmh na Bain-dé.
Éirichidh ciad-ghin an rìgh leis gus an aingidheachd àrsaidh a sgiùradh.
Ma dhìobras sinn, cha mhair Aos an Fhithich tuilleadh.
Afore ravens, black on a bloody wall, the Hand of the Goddess will stand.
The firstborn of the king will join with him to purge an ancient evil.
Fail us and the Raven People will be no more.'"

Brandubh grinned at Conall, "It would be hard for us to ignore such an omen as you and your men at Cùil Daothail. The red shields emblazoned with black ravens and your banners are as plain a sign as anyone could hope for."

Conall sighed and waited for the inevitable. It came with a loud and heavy slap on his back. "Hand of the Goddess, eh!" Fearghal roared. "That has a certain ring to it – Conall Mac Gabhann, ruiri of Ráth na Conall, conqueror of Eochaidh Ruad, thorn in the side of Ailill Mac Máta and Medb of the Connachta, tamer of Macha Mong Ruad, High Queen of Ériu, and Hand of the Goddess!" Fearghal laughed again reveling in his ruiri's discomfort. In a more serious aside he said to Mongfhionn, "That's a heavy burden to put on a young king's shoulders."

The Sidhe nodded, "Only if he cannot bear the load – or has no one with whom to share it."

With a grave look on his beer-flushed face, Conall rose unsteadily and faced Mongfhionn. "With all respect to the Lady Sidhe and our hosts, I've but one mission to see through to its end – the capture of the Roman responsible for the slaughter of my friends and my family. I'll not be diverted from this quest. I believe this man is a slave of the Na Daoine Smeurta and so it is to their lands my men and I travel." A ripple of disquiet moved around the room as the Aos an Fhithich sought to reconcile their geis with Conall's pronouncement. As the rumble diminished he said, "Once the Roman is secured, a friend needs be rescued from the Na Daoine Tùrsach."

The Aos an Fhithich present excused themselves and drew aside. There then ensued a semi-private and at times heated discussion that was all but unintelligible to Conall's group. "Do you think we're as hard to understand when we talk?" asked Fearghal attempting to add some levity into an evening that had become quite sober despite the volume of beer consumed.

"Probably," said Conall.

Presently, their hosts retook their places around the stone table. "It would seem that in order to fulfill the geis that has been laid upon us, we must ensure your mission is successful – and accomplished with all speed. Winter skies are already with us and with them come much stronger winds and storms of sleet and snow," Brandubh said. "If your Roman is considered valuable, then he'll be held in the settlement protected by a dùn on the northern coast.

"In any event, once the Na Daoine Smeurta know we're on their land, they'll move him to the dùn. It's at the furthest end of the tribe's land and just short of Aos nan Cat territory. I'll be your guide across the mountains – perhaps I can at least save you from falling into one of the many crevices. Our lands are beautiful, but dangerous.

"Blàr will journey to our father's broch at Càrn Liath on the northeastern coast. He'll ask for my guard to meet us in a valley mid-way between here and the Na Daoine Smeurta dùn." Brandubh paused as if considering how his next remark would be received. "Blàr will also escort your badly wounded to be cared for at my father's home. They cannot travel with us, the mountains are cruel, the injured will be too great a burden."

"How long will the journey take?" asked Conall, accepting the offer with what he mused later was a high degree of trust. "We have friends, family and an army from which we have been away for too long."

"It's a tough hike, especially at this time of the year – and with your men's armor and carrying packs. If we push hard we can make the dùn of Na Daoine Smeurta in five or six sunsets. We'll return by way of my father's dwelling and talk further about the Na Daoine Tùrsach." Then, in a waggish tone Brandubh asked, "Out of curiosity – how many people follow you? We've only seen this warband, which in itself is impressive."

Fearghal answered with a glint in his hazel eyes. He scratched the back of his head as if needing time to consider, "Oh, the army with cavalry and warriors was about two thousand five hundred strong when we left. The Goddess knows how big – or small, it has grown to under Íar's command. Our civilian people: families, tradesmen, artisans and whores, number at least that many." The Aos an Fhithich present gasped, although in respect rather than fear.

"Bigger than some of our tribes," Brandubh said.

Conall rose and stretched his hand out to Brandubh, "Then we should be friends." Both men smiled and clasped arms.

In her half-awake, half-dreamlike condition, Gràinne's hand glided over the smoothness of her belly and between her legs. Her thick bush had been scraped smooth – a sure sign that Diadhaidh had marked her for sacrifice. There was a brief sensation of unfamiliarity, but this passed and her fingers slipped into the warm wetness. It was not orgasmic pleasure, however, that interrupted Gràinne's pleasurable trance, but the fetid, putrescent smell of blood and decay that assaulted her nostrils.

She woke choking on the odor. Her head was confused from the mix of herbs she had been forced to swallow since her capture. Gràinne cursed the moment of modesty that had led her to piss away from the camp. As her eyes focused, she recoiled from the sight of the decrepit king of the Na Daoine Tùrsach. Drool dribbled from quivering lips leaving a milky-white trail on the weakened left side of his face. But it was the sight of the leer on her father's face which made Gràinne's stomach sour. It was obvious that both had been watching for some time.

It was not, however, her disgust that caused her to spew the contents of her stomach over the straw on which she lay. Rather it was the booted foot of her grandmother. She cried out in pain, then coughed and gagged as the bile burned her throat. She scrabbled away, trying to get out of reach, but was prevented by the rough iron manacle that wrapped around her ankle. It held securely to the wall of the wooden stall. Again she cried out as the shackle tore her skin.

"Your whore daughter is awake, Caol. Since she's been taken, she's useless as a sacrifice of purity." Diadhaidh wore a general air of disappointment and disgust, a not unusual state for her. "I suppose we can bundle her with four or five others for the Blood Moon offerings." In her darker musings, she considered offering up Caol as a blood sacrifice along with this daughter. She had not totally discarded this idea. Power, ancient power, was what she coveted and she would do anything to gain it.

A perceptible change had come over Gràinne since her kidnapping. It was as if she had plumbed the depths of despair, had found nowhere else to go, but instead of crumpling, her mind had sharpened and her spine stiffened. Defiantly she pulled herself up to stand on unsteady feet, her gold-flecked eyes burning with rage, "I've brought your death with me, old woman." Diadhaidh feigned ignorance and turned away in a show of indifference. "You can't ignore me, old woman. You know the ancient prophesy as well as any."

"The Sidhe?" Diadhaidh glanced over her shoulder at Gràinne without fully turning to her. "She cannot touch me. I am protected."

"The Sidhe comes and she is more powerful than you, but she is not the instrument of prophesy – as well you know. I have brought the Sidhe, yes. But I have also brought the Dark Huntress." Gràinne watched with pleasure as what little color remaining in the queen's face drained away leaving a greenish pallor.

"Tales told to frighten children. Myths and legends spread by old men and women drunk on beer."

Tha an tìr seo 'ga toirt dhan chinneadh.
Dèanaibh sealgaireachd, buaineabh am bàrr agus théid gu math leibh.
Seachainibh an Tuireadh agus an fheadhainn a leanas e gu h-aineolach.
Glanaidh Làmh na Bain-dé an corp.
Gaorraidh a' bhan-sealgair a cheann.'
This land is given to the tribe.
Hunt, gather in crops and prosper.
Shun the Deathsong and those who blindly follow it.
The Hand of the Goddess will cleanse the body.
The Dark Huntress will pierce its head.'"

Gràinne repeated the geis given to the tribe's ancestors, watching the conflict in Diadhaidh's face - a visage that normally was a mask of control. The queen turned to her guard, "Take her to the stake in the center of the community. Whip her without mercy. Break her." A gasp escaped from Gràinne, but she held her body proudly. Too proudly for the queen whose staff was brought down on the girl's head. She crumpled to the floor.

Dragged to the whipping post, the semi-conscious young woman was brutally lashed until her flesh was torn and bloody. Yet those who heard her screams knew that while her body was flayed she was not broken.

Cassius Fabius Scaeva picked at the grime embedded under his cracked, patrician nails. "Like reading a book," he thought as he observed Ceallach. The Na Mèadaidh spy was ever on his guard and always seeking an advantage. A piece of information he could trade. Since his arrival in the camp, Ceallach had bit by bit persistently interrogated Cassius about his background, his benefactor-employer, Marcus Fabius Ambustus, about Rome and particularly his enemy, Conall Mac Gabhann. Answers that were considered useful were rewarded with food and short walks. That the Na Daoine Smeurta tolerated Ceallach was a mystery to the Roman and raised his suspicions. Was he to be traded?

In his prey, for that was how he considered the Roman, Ceallach recognized Cassius' innate cleverness and guile. Likely he would kill without a qualm. In many ways the two men were mirror images of each other. It showed in the slave's cruel, wine-colored eyes. Like a hawk tracking its prey or a snake waiting to strike, the Roman watched with a patience born of necessity. Flecks of white in his normally dark brown, almost black hair bore witness to his more recent trials. His body and threadbare clothes were filthy and the worse for wear, but his eyes, alert and calculating, told a different story.

Ceallach had two questions that needed answered. What was the Roman's worth? And who would pay to see him safe or to have him silenced? The answer appeared to lie with Cassius' benefactor, Marcus

Fabius Ambustus. Yet Marcus was a long journey away. Even travelling by sea it would take several cycles of the moon to reach Rome. Ceallach had deduced that Cassius would not receive an overly friendly reception by Marcus upon his return. Anyone accompanying him might be as unwelcome and suffer the consequences.

That left the Ériu warrior-king, Conall Mac Gabhann. Perhaps there would be a reward for the person who delivered the Roman to Conall. The forests spoke of a heavily armed warband making its way north under the command of a young warrior. Likely, it was Conall. In this, time was not on Ceallach's side. The territories of the Cinn Péinteáilte were comprised of dense forests, tall mountains and moorlands with few good pathways, but it was a small land and could be crossed swiftly. Ceallach smiled through yellowed teeth. It was an opportunity – a small one that needed to be acted upon immediately.

He rose and strode to the cooking fire around which several of the tribe's elders sat warming their bones in the mid-day chill. The grease that covered their torsos glistened. Ceallach looked to the Roman's owner and then nodded in Cassius' direction.

"What will you take in trade for him?"

The Na Daoine Smeurta chieftain grinned and spat a wad of gristle into the burning embers. Whatever he had been about to say was lost in the screams and cacophony as several men ran into the small settlement shouting, "Barbarians!"

Cassius glanced up and sneered. Ceallach's face briefly contorted in frustration before he regained control. "Too late friend, too late," said the Roman. "My rescuer comes."

The elder rose with deliberate slowness from the fire and reached for his axe. He had come to two conclusions. First, his people should flee to the dùn on the coast. They could make safety before nightfall. Second, it was not coincidence that Ceallach happened to be in their community at this time. He must be working for the barbarians.

Ceallach's eyes opened wide as he comprehended the thoughts in the elder's dark eyes. He reached for his knives, but this once, Ceallach's instincts had failed him. As he tensed to spring, knives in hand, the elder's blade came down on his skull. The fire hissed as blood and brain gore splattered on its embers. Sparks and burning logs scattered as Ceallach's body fell forward onto the fire.

The elder wiped his bloody axe on Ceallach's body then bellowed, "To the dùn. Leave everything. Run or die."

CHAPTER 19

Conall's warband scrambled down the mountain slopes to the edge of the clearing. Alert and weapons unsheathed, they moved with measured steps in a loose skirmish-line, slowly encircling the cluster of Na Daoine Smeurta dwellings. Conall knew that he was being overly cautious. His scouts had reported that the inhabitants were gone – although blue-gray smoke still drifted lazily upwards from smoldering fires.

An aroma of charred meat and burnt hair carried on the light breeze as Conall walked towards the center of the settlement. He approached the main cooking fire and using a javelin prodded what appeared at first glance to be a pile of smoking clothes. The bundle rolled over and the clothes parted to reveal a body.

"Can't say I recognize him," Fearghal said with an adolescent grin. The combined leadership of the Ériu and Aos an Fhithich rolled their eyes and groaned.

The head was bald, the flames having first licked off the hair. High cheekbones were burnt to the bone. Blistered red eyelids sealed and protected sightless eyes. Smoke wisped from a blackened, flesh-less ear. The man's woolen clothes burned slowly, releasing a dank smoke and fouling the air with the acrid smell of burnt feathers. Patches of the cloth had melted into black beads, which scattered as the body was turned.

A suddenly angry Conall snapped, "Take this away and bury it. Search the buildings." The stench of burnt flesh had brought to mind the painful memory of the death of his father, Bréanainn. It was not long before one of his men brought to Conall a large square of cloth. The cloak was both fashionable and functional having a purple silk outer layer and a black wool lining. Grease and oil stained it and the garment smelt of rancid fat.

At one corner there was a small tear from which both purple and gold threads had unraveled. Grim-faced and with tears in his eyes, Conall fingered the circlet of threads that he always carried with him. The threads his mother had torn from her killer in her dying moments. They matched the cloak. "The time is close, Conall." Mórrígan spoke softly, but with an anxious tremble in her voice as she grasped his hand. "We will have our revenge."

Conall nodded, "Close, Mórrígan, but this Roman's death will neither end the journey nor give us peace."

Mid-afternoon had just passed, but already the darkness was drawing in, signaling the cusp between autumn and winter. Conall had decided that they should rest for the night. The Na Daoine Smeurta settlement provided dry shelter and was a welcome change from the open forest and mountain camps of late. A quick scavenge of the rock and wood roundhouses had uncovered a trove of food left behind by the fleeing community. The break would also give his men some respite from the bruises, grazed legs and arms and thorn-torn flesh that they had suffered in the hike across the mountains.

As he ate and drank, Conall observed Brandubh and his interaction with the others of his tribe. There was no doubting the respect with which the Aos an Fhithich held their leader. Conall judged him to be around the same age as he – possibly a little younger. The Aos an Fhithich had suffered much less than the Ériu during the journey, seeming to glide over the terrain. Sure-footed and silent, Brandubh had led Conall's warband to a small gorge in Na Daoine Smeurta territory. The valley with its quiet lush pastures and crashing waterfalls reminded Conall of the gleannta in the Ulaid lands.

There, they had been joined by Brandubh's guard, a group of fifty warriors – men and women, a mix of youth and experience, and mostly armed with spears and axes. A few had small shields. Most were lightly clothed – although not naked. They wore woolen, plaid pants of forest greens and black. Wolf-pelts and plaid brats covered their upper bodies. When they moved there were glimpses of their tribal paint - the intricate designs etched permanently onto their skin. All had bright copper hair. Indeed, Conall mused there seemed to be more red-haired people in this land than in Ériu. All were taller than average and well-muscled. They could not be described as skinny, but neither were they burly. Most had fair skin and a strange mix of blue-green colored eyes. As with Brandubh, all had a raven's feather dangling from a single, thin braid of hair.

Around the fires that evening, the camp was one of contrasts. The heavily armored Ériu with their multiple layers of clothing constantly moaned about the weather. The Aos an Fhithich, lightly clothed and lightly armed sat at separate fires and were plainly unsure about their new allies. Neither party had much of a clue what the other was saying, so broad were their accents and quick their speech. It was not long, however, before one wit from Ériu commented in a loud voice and with a wink to his friends, "I'm a bit disappointed. I thought the Cinn Péinteáilte all ran about naked."

The Aos an Fhithich men and women appeared mystified as the Ériu warrior spoke, but after a quick comment from Brandubh, they erupted into an infectious round of laughing. In the still night, it echoed off the steep mountain slopes. A statuesque female of about twenty summers stood up, pointed to the Ériu and in a loud, broad and almost unintelligible brogue said, "Ye'r just disappointed that ye can'nae see my tits." Then, to more uproarious laughter as she sat, she added, "As for our men, they just didn't want to embarrass ye by showing the size of their cocks."

And so, while the ice in the air remained, the ice that separated the two bands quickly thawed. Around roaring fires that scattered bright sparks high into the air, tales of battles were shared, scars proudly compared, weapons and armor displayed, and the meanings behind the Aos an Fhithich tattoos were explained.

The change in scenery was remarkable. A short trek along a narrow valley lined with steep rock faces and a multitude of small waterfalls had brought the band to the northern coast, where waves crashed against ancient cliffs. In the distance they could see the wavering outlines of craggy islands. Beyond that was more sea. "End of the world, that's where we're at," murmured one of the men to nodding agreement.

Conall was astounded as he looked eastward. Equally magnificent as the sea and towering mountains, the landscape from this vantage point was rolling heather moorland. The land showed a reddish hue. "Bogs, moors and red-stone," Brandubh observed, seemingly reading Conall's thoughts. "The land of the Aos nan Caorach – The Sheep People. They mostly live quietly in scattered settlements behind the doors of very solid red and gray stone brochs. They trade sheep and woolen garments with us once or twice a year – otherwise you'd hardly know they existed."

Again seeming to know Conall's mind, Brandubh glanced at the overcast sky and pointed to the northeast, "We'll catch first sight of the Na Daoine Smeurta dùn around mid-day. It's on the edge of their border with the Aos nan Caorach and sits on a promontory. There are steep cliffs on three sides and the south facing approach is guarded by a massive rock wall, maybe the height of two men and seven paces wide. The wall runs from cliff-edge to cliff-edge; about two hundred paces in length with a single entrance cut into it just forward from the inner face. Rumor has it that there is an escape route to caves below the dùn.

"Inside the fortress there's not much to see – a fairly big blockhouse for the warriors and some roundhouses for the trades, women and children. Food's not a problem. They can catch whatever they need from the sea. They draw water from a spring." Brandubh smiled archly, "There's little use trying to be stealthy. They'll see us well before we can see them. There's no cover apart from the gorse bushes and heather."

Conall nodded briefly in acknowledgment and turned to his men, "Eat up, pack up and move out. There's a storm coming and I want to be within sight of the ráth before it hits."

Flashes of lightning on the horizon mercilessly spiked deep, slate-gray clouds before striking the roiling sea. Long rumbling peals of thunder signaled the Goddess' approval of the sport. Conall flinched, compelled to shield from the brilliant flashes even as he sought refuge against the slippery cliff face. All were soaked by driving rain and lashed by the salt spray.

In contrast, Mongfhionn stood high above them at the cliff's edge, reveling in the display and drawing power from it. The entire band observed this act of courage – or foolishness. Blustering northern winds howled around her awakening furious waves that dashed themselves against the rock. Fingers of spray fell back into the sea frustrated at being unable to dislodge her. Her gray cloak, clasped by an ornately designed gold brooch decorated with blood-red rubies, whipped in the wind. Her drenched white gown was fused to her body like a second skin.

The band had intended to erect shelters in the small, protected cove on the east side of the promontory. The Goddess had other ideas. Instead, they huddled against dark gray plates of rock layered with bright rust and orange sandstone. Rivulets cascading down the broken cliff face poured over them. Only their feet remained anchored as they stood calf deep in the sand and shingle, while the surging waves threatened to dislodge and toss them into the stormy waters.

Natural oils in their woolen garments offered limited protection. The material became sopping wet and twice as heavy, plastered to their bodies. Even the shields of wood and hide began to swell and warp in the torrential cloudburst. Conall considered that perhaps Nikandros' bronze-faced shield might indeed be a better option for the future. He wiped a stinging mix of salt water and rain from his eyes for what seemed to be the hundredth time.

The storm raged throughout the night then moved off as the morning sun broke over the horizon leaving a steaming, sodden mass of warriors. The strident, husky shrieking of hundreds of large white seabirds unhappy at having their nesting place disturbed was deafening. In many ways the noise was welcomed. It heralded a morning shaded from a burnt-orange hue at the horizon to a glorious deep pink. Save for a few ribbons of gray-black cloud the sky was clear. Even better, the wind and rain had abated. The amorphous mass of men and women disentangled and went in search of wood to start the drying fires.

Fallen boulders of gray and red-orange stone littered the beaches. The moss and seaweed covered cliffs, constantly battered by wind and sea were a mass of cracks and crevices. Long, narrow tidal inlets notched the rock and in some instances had created small isolated crags in the sea. The entire landscape was riddled with irregular caves above and below the tidelines.

Fearghal chewed on the roasted leg of one of the seabirds and thought that, apart from a slight fishy taste, it was quite good. Raw egg yolk stained his chin and he absentmindedly crushed chalky blue eggshells beneath his leather boots. In between bites, he pointed with the leg to the ráth, "Cúscraid would say that was a pretty good defensive position. It's a bit like Eochaidh Ruad's ráth at Caher Conri, but the buildings are mostly stone. We won't have the advantage of setting them alight. There are likely women and children in there as well – not a demented ruiri and his gold-crazed followers."

"We could scale the cliffs. Plenty of grips. We've done it before at Ráth na Lairig Éadain. There can't be more than five hundred warriors in the ráth. Good odds against our two hundred." said Conall.

Fearghal grunted, "Yeah, but you didn't have to contend with thousands of seabirds screaming and shiting on you. There'd be no element of surprise. If we're lucky, the Na Daoine Smeurta would throw us back into the sea. More likely we'd end up on the rocks." The sound of murmuring prompted Conall and Fearghal to turn.

"The ground the ráth is built on is not very stable," Deaglán ventured. He pointed to the eastern end of the perimeter wall. A short stretch of the wall had collapsed.

"I don't think we have the time to wait for more to collapse," said Fearghal dryly.

"No, but we have the Lady Sidhe," said Torcán, nervously kicking several smaller rocks over the cliff edge and studiously avoiding

Mongfhionn's gaze.

The Sidhe uttered a husky laugh as she viewed the small group, most of whom seemed preoccupied with their feet. "I can provide some diversion when the time comes – although carving a piece off the promontory and sending it crashing into the sea may be beyond my powers and likely not what you would want anyway. What if the Roman went into the sea with the cliff?" Conall and Fearghal smirked at Mongfhionn, but their boyish exuberance was diminished when the Sidhe added, "You know my price – no innocent in the ráth is to be killed. For each killed, you will lose a warrior in the battle."

Conall called Brandubh to the group and then described his plan. It was to be a combination of terror and negotiation. As he outlined the role of the archers, Brandubh turned to Mórrígan and asked, "How far can your archers shoot?"

"Most can hit a target five hundred paces distant. Why?" Mórrígan answered.

The Aos an Fhithich chieftain smiled, "I think I may be able to add to your impact." He signaled five of his men and pointed at the defensive wall. They grinned and moved to within about five hundred paces. Then from around their waists they each unwound a length of braided, woolen cord. Each length had a small leather centerpiece. The warriors stood two paces apart and the air was filled with a whirring hum.

"Not a belt, then," muttered Fearghal. There was a soft snap as the stones left the sling and a much louder crack as each of the stones smacked against the ráth's wall.

Mórrígan acknowledged the marksmanship in a somewhat defensive tone, for she was extremely proud of her archers. "A good show, but you can't hurl fire – can you?"

Brandubh cocked his head to the side, "No – not yet. Nor can we pierce armor, but we can crack skulls, break bones and bruise flesh." He pointed to the beach below, "We have an endless supply of missiles. My warriors can clear the wall of spears – and keep them clear."

Mórrígan scowled. Conall smiled.

The Na Daoine Smeurta Elder stood on the inner rampart alongside his spearmen. He was confident in his fortifications and in many ways that belief was justified. Who in their right mind would attack? He observed the force organizing before the dùn with a mixture of curiosity and admiration. Five hundred paces from his defenses two lines of warriors were arrayed, each man an arm's length from his neighbor. Their shields rested an edge on the dirt making a crimson slash across the winter rusts and oranges of the landscape. Each man held a strangely-shaped spear with three more stabbed into the hard ground. Their alien helmets and armor were uniform and impressive.

In front of the shield wall stood two women and three men. One of the women was taller than most of the warband. She was hooded and held a great staff in her right hand. The second was not as tall and gave the Elder the impression of being younger. Flame-colored hair escaped the confines of an ornate gold and silver helmet. A strangely curved bow was held in her hand. The sharp eyes of the Elder saw that the parts of her body not concealed by armor were covered in swirling designs. Both women exuded an aura of power and darkness that sent a shiver down his spine.

The men seemed normal. The one at the center was slightly above average height. An elaborate helmet with trailing black plumes from a raven crest added half a head to his stature. He stood easy and was clearly confident in his commanders and men. To his right stood a tall, muscular warrior, who from his demeanor was definitely the battle commander. He barked periodic orders to the men behind. The warrior's bearing was regal, yet he appeared content to stand in the shadow of the younger man. The Elder was wary of this. He could not underestimate the leader. The Elder grunted and swore as he recognized the tall, slender warrior on the far right. Brandubh Mac Artair of the Aos an Fhithich was well-known — and respected for his bravery and battle prowess. Behind the shield wall stood another rank of warriors, apparently waiting for a command.

The Elder spoke to the burly warrior beside him, "When this is over – cut the slave's throat and toss him over the cliff. The gold was welcome, but he's brought more than enough trouble. He's pathetic for useful work." The warrior dipped his head in agreement.

"What's their plan?" The Elder puzzled as he drew his sheepskin wrap closer around him. Out of habit he still covered his body in grease, but no longer felt the need to stand naked as his warriors. He had proven his worth a long time ago. Besides, the northern winds rushing off the seas behind them tested the metal of the bravest of warriors.

Shortly, Conall's rear rank moved forward to take up position in front of the wall. Several small fires were lit. The wood, still damp from the storm caused streamers of white smoke to rise into the air as the flames struggled to catch. The Elder watched as arrows already nocked on bows were dipped into the fires. He heard the grunts as bowstrings were pulled until the flames licked hands and then heard the twang as the arrows were released. Smoky trails scraped the sky as the missiles peaked then dropped. Arrows thudded into the thatched roofs and timbers of the barracks and dwellings. The men on the wall flinched, but then realized that they were not the target. The barrage continued until the dùn was shrouded in choking smoke.

"Bastards!" exclaimed the Elder as he coughed and rubbed away salty tears from bloodshot eyes. He held back the water carriers sensing that it would only prompt further clouds of fire-arrows. His people were used to living in the moors and forests, many times with little cover. They could put up with this discomfort. The archers stepped back closer to the shields and were replaced by about fifty semi-naked warriors. "Aos an Fhithich bastards," the Elder spat.

The air was filled with thrumming as fifty slings whirled rapidly before being released with the whip-snap of cord. The Elder had barely time to shout a warning when the first volley thudded into the spears on the wall. A score of men fell, their skulls laid open to the bone. Crimson-purple blood pooled on the gray stone. Curses and grunts from others along the wall testified to the accuracy of the slingers. "Hug the wall," the Elder shouted. Few had shields and since they could not give up the wall there was little else to do but suffer and wait as the slingers kept up their steady bombardment.

At mid-morning the barrage finally ceased. The skies remained mostly cloudless. The mild breeze that blew from the north carried the smell of smoke from the fortress. It also bore the taint of rancid animal fat. "With that stench, it'd be hard for that lot to take anyone by surprise," offered one Ériu warrior causing a ripple of laughter along the row.

"Let's negotiate," Conall said. Slamming javelin shafts against the shields with each step, the men of the shield wall marched to within a hundred paces of the structure. As they came to a halt, Conall, accompanied by Mórrígan, Mongfhionn, Fearghal and Brandubh moved even closer, stopping at fifty paces from the defenses. Conall removed his helmet, ran long fingers through shoulder length, dark-brown hair and called out, "Send out the Roman and we'll depart your lands without further injury."

The Elder's quandary was simple. Could he swallow his pride? He had no interest in keeping a useless slave, but arrogance won over prudence and set his mind against giving up the Roman. That he had rivals for the throne of the Na Daoine Smeurta also dictated he should put on a show of strength. Convinced of the unassailability of the dùn and feigning ignorance of the language of the foreigners, the Elder did nothing.

Anyone could see by Conall's body language that it was perhaps the worst path the Elder could have chosen. With a curt bow he addressed the Sidhe, "Your turn."

The Sidhe nodded and shed her cloak. Her white gown flared, caught by the breeze as she raised her oak staff. A gasp came from the Na Daoine Smeurta as they beheld Mongfhionn. Waist length, almost white, hair was highlighted with streaks of red-gold. The milk-white face accented with fiery red cheeks and full, blood-red lips. Eyes black as the night sky seemed to bore into each man who gazed upon her.

Fearghal braced himself to expect the full-throated shriek of the bean-sidhe. Instead there came a melodic song, a chant that stole into his head bringing pleasant reminiscences of days long past. He, as did the rest of the warband, stood rooted to the spot enjoying the warmth of memories as the temperature around them dropped.

Within the Na Daoine Smeurta fortress, the Sidhe's song brought with it the chill of death and corruption. No fond memories kept them warm. They were fully aware of a nightmare slowly descending. Translucent tendrils of sea smoke on the horizon coalesced and moved slowly, but purposefully towards the land. The mist rolled over the cliff's edge transforming into a dense, glowing fog leaving a layer of frost on each surface it touched whether man, beast or rock.

The undulating, bone-chilling fog smothered the fortress. Everything wore a crust of ice from the freezing drizzle. The screams of the terrified were muted to those who stood outside the dùn. As she held the nightmare in place, the Sidhe's cry spiraled to a crescendo and a tone as cold as the icy conditions within the fort. Stone and rock cracked reverberating with a sound of hundreds of lashing whips.

The fog lifted, dispersing as it drifted across the moorlands. The weak winter sun cast its pale golden light on the ráth. The ráth stood covered in a blanket of ice, a thing of wondrous beauty as it sparkled in hues of gold, red and orange. Something out of the age of myths, Fearghal thought as he surveyed the fort. "I never cease to be impressed – and terrified, by your imagination and power," he said. "Tadhg will have a field day putting this into one of his tales."

Smiling wanly, the Sidhe, exhausted, gripped the oak staff tightly to steady herself. "Water and cold can be very useful. Enough water remained from the storm. Transformed into ice, it will undermine foundations and force small fissures. I suspect their wall is not quite as perfect as it was."

By mid-afternoon, the dùn had lost its icy cloak and once again stood drab and gray against the skyline. Conall was beginning to think the Sidhe's efforts had been wasted and a more bloody assault would be needed when the great oak door slammed open against the rock. Three men, seasoned, but not beyond their prime, strode from the fortress. At the apex of the formation, the Elder walked slowly, his head held high with the conceit of leadership. The two flanking him were decidedly nervous. Behind them a guard of ten matched their pace. The small group came to a halt before Conall.

"Barbarian thieves. Murderers of women and children. Leave

our lands." Still confident in his defenses, the Elder had decided to forego a path of humble submission, even though the other elders had urged this pragmatic tactic.

"You know what we want," Conall said through clenched teeth. "Send out the Roman and we will be gone. Ignore my offer and I will level your fortress and slaughter all inside. It will be as if you or it had never existed."

Before the Elder could reply, the Sidhe growled, "Foolish, stubborn man." She fixed him with her dark gaze. "It is only by my will and wishes that your people – men, women and children, live. Do not waste this chance to retreat with honor." The Elder's eyes flickered from the Sidhe to Conall and there was a slight diminishment in his bearing as he listened. His colleagues had taken a step backward. Fearghal reflected that Mongfhionn, even in anger, always chose her words carefully. She was well aware that the word "retreat" would rankle with this Elder.

"This man you speak of is a valuable slave. How will you compensate us?"

"By letting you live, you miserable creature. You and your people." Conall stood quaking, barely able to restrain himself from reaching for his axes. The Elder opened his mouth, seemingly unmoved and oblivious to Conall's stance. It was to be his last voluntary action. With unnatural speed and grace, Mórrígan swept her bow around, nocked and set loose three black-shafted arrows. The first entered the Elder's mouth, effectively ending his further participation in the negotiations. The second and third thudded into his chest and pierced his heart.

"The slave is yours," blurted the two remaining elders. They dropped to the ground, keeping their eyes firmly focused on the heather.

A furious Conall rounded on Mórrígan, pulled the bow from her hands and tossed it away. "Defy my authority again and you'll lose your head," Conall snapped. Out of the corner of his eye he saw Mórrígan's guard, the giant Urard, move without hesitation to shield the queen. Conall's eyes flashed a warning to the huge warrior, "Your loyalty is commendable. You would do well to remember that

I am ruiri. Your oath is sworn to me."

Urard was a simple, uncomplicated man. Simple - but not stupid. At the sound of feet crunching on stone behind him he glanced over his shoulder. A small group of warriors, led by Torcán stood with javelins ready. There was no enmity towards his comrades in Urard's smile as he turned to them and then back to his king. He bowed and his axe-head was lowered to the ground.

"The man was an arsehole," snarled a hostile Mórrígan, her cheeks flushed red in anger and embarrassment and her swirling designs prominent. "Now we'll get what we came for."

Taking a breath, Conall looked at Mórrígan and said in a low voice, "Don't think my love for you will save your neck if you challenge me." The quiet surety in Conall's words caused Mórrígan to pause. She knew her king, partner and childhood friend would not flinch from taking action. For the first time, however, she considered the possibility that her arrows might prevail over his axe.

Whirling around to face the confused duo of Na Daoine Smeurta elders, Conall said, "I've had enough. Bring the slave."

A tall, female Aos an Fhithich warrior sidled up next to Brandubh and spoke quietly. There was a smile in her voice, "Not exactly a trouble-free relationship."

"Be careful sister. Your head could be removed just as easily as hers." He glanced sideways at her. "And, I think that Mórrígan would make a very bad enemy."

CHAPTER 20

Calloused, greasy hands dragged Cassius Fabius Scaeva out of the dùn and a few final, well-placed kicks left him sprawling at Conall's feet. The reek of the Roman was an offense to all. Attempting to regain some dignity, Cassius pushed against the dirt, propped himself up and peered upwards. Hard, steel-blue eyes locked onto bloodshot eyes rimmed with bruise-colored circles. It was the first time the men had met. They stared at each other. One man's demeanor reflected vengeance, the other uncertainty tinged with deceit and cunning.

The Roman flinched under the stare and glanced away. His eyes were drawn to Mórrígan. The sigils etched into her face glowed brightly making her eyes more black than green. The two smoky emeralds bored into Cassius for only a few moments yet his mind became confused with awful visions.

At that moment, Cassius tasted the bile of fear. While Conall would likely take his life, the witch Mórrígan would take his soul. Despite the cold air, beads of sweat rolled down his dirt-streaked face. He tore his eyes from Mórrígan only to face the Sidhe. Full, blood-red lips curled into a cruel smile. "Retribution," she hissed before turning away. Cassius almost wished he was still a slave of the Na Daoine Smeurta.

"His smell disgusts me," said Conall. "Throw him into the sea. Find him some clothes, feed him and bind him." Cassius had expected something more along the lines of barbarian rage accompanied by the loss of a minor appendage or at least a good beating.

To be dismissed so offhandedly by this young leader offended him much more than had he been tortured. He was after all a Roman. His superior breeding deserved respect. However, Conall appeared to be preoccupied with other matters. The Roman was left to sulk and observe.

In the fading light of dusk Cassius studied his new captors. He was surprised that there were only a few hundred warriors with their so-called king. He had heard of the battles with Ailill Mac Mata and Medb, the Connachta king and queen, and the humiliation of Macha Mong Ruad, the Ulaid Ard-Righan, at Ráth na Lairig Éadain. Perhaps, he thought, all that was left was a well-armed warband feeding off Conall's thirst for revenge.

Whatever the circumstance, Cassius was well-aware that the current lack of attention to him could and probably would come to an abrupt end. He needed to consider how to escape. Perhaps if the group kept to the coastline, he could elude his captors and seek passage on a vessel sailing south.

Cassius settled near one of the campfires. He had eaten a decent meal, his first in a long time, and was wearing serviceable clothing that did not stink of rancid fat. In the flickering light of the wood fire, the Roman regarded those around him.

His guards were ten hard-looking men led by a young warrior who appeared to be recovering from earlier wounds. The men lay around the fire exhibiting a fine display of weariness. Cassius snorted - an action still painful due to his broken nose. He suspected that the guards were enticing him to escape. Indeed the Roman was right. The guards were hoping that he would try. Then they would serve up their own version of justice. This alone salvaged some of the Roman's pride. He had value after all.

The following morning after breaking their fast, the warband loaded up packs and set off along the coastline towards Aos nan Caorach territory. The Aos an Fhithich and the Aos nan Caorach had a friendly co-existence and Brandubh foresaw no major difficulties. The land was so desolate that Brandubh thought it unlikely they would come across any of the Aos nan Caorach's settlements. Besides, given the almost level terrain, it was relatively easy to spot and give a wide berth to the tribe's gray and red stone brochs. As a precaution, Brandubh sent scouts ahead to smooth the way. Mórrígan's archers took up their usual role as skirmishers ahead of the main band.

While the most direct route to the main Aos an Fhithich community at Càrn Liath was south over the mountains, Conall had decided instead to tramp east to the edge of the Sheep People's land, then southeast until they reached the coastline. Once there, they would trek southwest skirting the coastal forests, wildwoods and plains until they arrived at Càrn Liath. The distance was longer, but the land easier to cross.

Unable to resist testing his captors, Cassius whined constantly about his poor health, his inability to walk quickly due to his recent confinement, and even his lack of bladder control due to a chill in his kidneys. Conall and Mórrígan offered disinterested glances followed by a nod to Urard. The hulking warrior calmly strode over to Cassius, smacked him in the face and slung him over his shoulder as if he were an empty sack. The Roman regained consciousness around mid-day with a bruised and dislocated jaw. As Urard dropped him to the ground, he smiled at Cassius and patted the flat side of his great axe. The message was clear and understood.

Evening was drawing in as the group again tasted salt in the moist air. It had been a hard if uneventful hike, but they had made good time across the rolling moors, avoiding the worst of the bog and marsh-land. Camp was set up in a sheltered cove on the eastern coast. It was a clear night and the indigo sky was bespeckled with thousands of flickering pinpoint lights. Having eaten and seen to their weapons and armor, the band made their beds adjacent to fires fueled with driftwood and pine.

A discordant voice intruded on the fragrant and calm night, "What do you intend to do to me, Barbarian?"

"We intend to kill you Roman," said Mórrígan in a chillingly conversational tone. Then she scowled. "We haven't decided on how yet."

Conall spoke in a somber monotone imbued with contempt. "Your life is forfeit, Cassius Fabius Scaeva." He tasted bitterness in his mouth as he addressed the Roman by his full name. "How you die – quickly or slowly - is partially in your hands."

Cassius smiled crookedly. "The path of vengeance does not end with me, Barbarian. The ones you seek are too powerful, too well-guarded and too wealthy. The might of Rome is their bulwark. You will never get close enough for what you want. You will die and be forgotten. They will live and be remembered."

"We all die, Roman. It is how we die that makes the difference." Conall nodded to the waiting guards and in a voice that was as cold as the night air said, "Search him well. If he has a blade then take his eye, he only needs one to see. If he resists or tries to escape, break a leg. He can use a staff."

Conall awoke with a start and immediately grasped the axe that lay by his side. He came into a crouched stance, uncertain as to what had broken his slumbers. As a child he had been a good sleeper. More often than not he needed encouragement from his mother or father to waken. Since their murder, his sleep was light and fitful and he was prone to waking at the slightest noise or premonition. He fought to marshal his senses, but all he could discern were grunts and snores from sleeping warriors interspersed with sporadic, muffled cries of pleasure. These he chose to ignore – for the moment.

"Open your eyes, Conall Mac Gabhann. See the Goddess at play." The voice of Mongfhionn came clearly from the shadows. Conall saw that everything was bathed in an eerie green light. Unsure of whether he should be fearful, Conall looked upwards to witness a sky that pulsated with every imaginable shade of green. As he stared, enthralled by the beauty, the colored arcs changed to columns and waves of green, purple and magenta. Each painted the nightscape with magnificent color.

As Conall watched, the sky was transformed into a huge green eye interwoven with shades of violet. He felt the intense berry-red center of the eye peer deep into his soul. Although rooted to the spot, Conall felt neither threatened nor any urgency to move. A voice spoke from the flux. There were no words to describe the voice save that it spoke with the omniscience that accompanies great power.

"Dèan seirbheis mhath, mo Làmh. Agus caochlaidh tu ann a' sìth.
Cuir mi gu dùbhlan, Agus sgriosaidh mi thu, do theaghlach agus do charaidean a-mach ás an tìr.
Serve well, my Hand. And you shall die in peace.
Defy me. And I will erase you, your family and friends from the land."

Conall shivered at the promise and the warning. Released from the Goddess' stare, he watched as the multicolored tones that swept across the sky slowly became subdued and then submitted to the Goddess of the dawn. He looked to Mongfhionn, who smiled enigmatically. "Sometimes the Lady can be infuriatingly smug," he thought.

At the rustling to his left, Conall turned to see Mórrígan return to the brat that served as her bed. Her face was paler than usual in the pre-dawn light, her eyes were troubled and her movement unsure. He wondered what the Goddess had said to his queen. By her expression, whatever was spoken was not altogether comforting.

Mórrígan pulled her woolen brat tightly around her, attempting to snatch a few moments of sleep before the camp stirred. Of all the words that the Goddess had spoken to her, one phrase reverberated over and over in her head, "An Fiagaí Dorcha – The Dark Huntress." Was she never to break free of the darkness?

Shivering, Mórrígan reached out to Conall. She needed his warmth and pulled him on top of her with a strength that told him that resistance was not an option. She gasped as he entered her. In the euphoria of passion the darkness was pushed to the far corners of her mind.

Before reaching Brandubh's kingdom, the group once more crossed a strip of Na Daoine Smeurta territory. The narrow neck of land was sandwiched between the Aos nan Caorach and Aos an Fhithich. As usual, the borders were marked by tall, standing stones with swirling tribal designs. Those of the Aos nan Caorach, however, were striking, being made of rust-red stone.

Apart from the odd scowl, there was a subdued, almost disinterested reaction from the few small bands of Na Daoine Smeurta that strayed across their path. The younger warriors who chose to challenge the group were quickly chased off with a flurry of arrows if they got too close.

More upright stones marked the group's arrival in Aos an Fhithich territory. They crossed the border mid-morning. Staying close to the coastline, they avoided the dense tangle of undergrowth, thistles and thorns from the wildwoods. The persistent mizzle had re-established itself, although it was not as deeply cold since they were closer to the sea. In fine spirits, the band remained alert. Good-natured insults were traded between the warriors. Also, the fact that male and female warriors on both sides had got to know each other intimately colored the conversation with sexual innuendo and outright bragging.

Hidden behind the veil of gray, its presence marked only by the occasional shaft of pale golden light piercing a gap in the clouds, the sun reached its zenith as the coastal settlement of Càrn Liath came into sight. The community lay about twenty paces back from a narrow sandy beach. Thus, the crash and roar of waves was both constant and comforting to its residents.

Càrn Liath broch sat on a grassy nub overlooking a flat landscape. Smaller stone and wood buildings with thatched roofs were clustered around the broch. It offered long sightlines, in part due the tribe's king encouraging the forest cleared around the settlement and crops planted, but little in the way of natural defenses.

As they crossed the outer ditch and perimeter fence of man-high wooden stakes, the rumble and burr of excited chatter swelled into loud cheering as the people caught sight of Brandubh. "Popular, isn't he?" said Fearghal.

Conall nodded and called his ceannairí céad to him. "Be friendly but alert. Keep your weapons close – don't make it too obvious.

I don't expect trouble, but you never can tell." Deaglán, Torcán, Craiftine, and Tadhg nodded and trotted off to inform their men.

"I doubt you'll get the same reception in Rome, Barbarian — if you make it that far," sniped Cassius.

A fist, covered in leather strips studded with iron, thudded into the Roman's belly. He doubled up in pain and fell to his knees.

"Been looking for an excuse to do that," chortled Torcán. Conall smiled thinly.

Just short of the broch, Brandubh broke from the group and strode to bow to, and then embrace, the tall man who stood next to his brother, Blàr. The older man's bearing was regal and even haughty, but then what leader does not need a measure of arrogance? His long hair, gray with the occasional streak of flame-red, was braided. The man's posture was erect, showing none of the stoop that often accompanied age. His frame was perhaps slimmer than the rest of his people, making his appearance more gaunt and angular. In contrast to his sons, his eyes were dark brown. His nose was thick, slightly curved and hooked. By Conall's judgment, the leader of the Raven People had taken on many of the characteristics of the flock of ravens that circled the settlement.

At a signal from Brandubh, Conall, accompanied by Mórrígan, Mongfhionn, and Fearghal approached. All but the Sidhe bowed. The king acknowledged his guests with a smile. Then with a look that signaled distrust and fear mixed with resigned reverence, the king bowed deeply to Mongfhionn. "Welcome to Càrn Liath and my home. Your stay with us will be short, but I hope pleasant." The king added, "It is not often that the Aes Sidhe calls upon us, especially to fulfill a geis long forgotten by many of my people."

The Sidhe remained silent, but her expression said, "We will talk of this later."

While not as high as some, Càrn Liath was a much sturdier broch than most seen on their travels and well able to weather assaults by man or nature. The broch's wall was particularly thick with an outer face that was thirty paces in diameter and an inner around fifteen paces. The entrance cut into the stone faced east and was over six paces wide. Access to the interior was through two sets of solid oak doors secured by sliding drawbars. On the right-hand side of the entrance passageway there was a small cell. Considering the average height of the Aos an Fhithich it was hard to see how it could be a guard nook and so its use remained a mystery.

Within the perimeter, the settlement hummed with activity. The steady scraping of quern stones combined with the heavy metal on metal clamor of the blacksmiths and the lighter tapping of artisans producing fine gold, silver, bone jewelry and decorations. Samhain had passed, the crops had been harvested and fields prepared for the next season. Thus, there was little activity outside the community, apart from a steady stream of hunters moving to and fro from the forests. Young boys and girls continued their watch on scattered herds of cattle and flocks of sheep.

Mead and honey-sweetened beer flowed as Artair and his guests ripped pieces of meat dripping with blood and fat from the carcasses roasting over the broch's central fire. Hot grease was sopped up from glistening hands and chins with bread broken from freshly baked rounds. The ruddy-faced nobility of the Ériu and Aos an Fhithich sat around the great table and shared the craic.

The evening was proceeding well until Artair stood, took a deep breath, and with a smoke-roughened voice said, "So we're here to celebrate the unholy aligning of an Aos an Fhithich geis and a Na Daoine Tùrsach prophecy." He held Mórrígan's gaze. "Our warriors will die, and I will lose my firstborn as the price of our presumed victory." The bitterness in the king's voice was plain to all.

"Be careful, Artair." Mongfhionn smiled, but her tone was sharp. "Too much beer may cause a tongue to speak that which cannot be taken back."

"Do not patronize me, Lady Sidhe," Artair said. Amid the dim aura of guttering of rushlights, he held Mongfhionn's gaze until it was she who broke the stare.

"Not often, you'll see that," a partially drunk Fearghal slurred. He shook his head as if to clear his mind and looked around the table with deepening concern.

Artair was in no mind to be subdued and spoke bluntly, "You're not the only Ancient One who has visited us since the geis bound us. It is the Goddess we serve, not the Aes Sidhe and she knows we have been faithful." Vivid fury leapt in Mongfhionn's eyes and her cheeks flamed red, but not with the heat of the fire. Gripping the edge of the oak table she opened her mouth to bring Artair to heel, but Artair had not finished. "Be sure you know the ground you stand on is solid, Mongfhionn. And that your motives are pure. That sigil over your eyebrow was given by the Ancients as a reminder that obedience doesn't only apply to the people who worship and revere you. Take heed of their warning."

Dumbfounded and ashen-faced, the Sidhe grabbed her oak staff and stormed from the broch, scattering any unfortunate in her path. "Shite," said Fearghal rubbing agitated fingers through his tangled mop of red hair, "Have you any comprehension of the destruction Mongfhionn's rage can wreak?"

"She is Aes Sidhe, she is not the Goddess. Better that I should bring this message than others who would not be as sympathetic," replied Artair.

"That was you being sympathetic! Remind me not to cross you," said Fearghal.

"Enough of this," Artair gestured as if to clear his thoughts. "There is a campaign to plan and a tribe to destroy." The king smiled at a skeptical Conall, "It is not a fight you wanted, is it? Yet you are the Hand of the Goddess and will lead her chosen army."

"What army, Artair? My two hundred and fifty warriors? Albeit, they are the best fighters in the land. Brandubh's guard is brave, but numbers only fifty. I can and I will mount a raid to rescue our friend, Gràinne, from the Na Daoine Tùrsach. Maybe we can kill some of their leaders during the raid. That's hardly the scattering of a tribe or the fulfilling of a geis."

The king smiled. "Just because I took the Sidhe to task, does not mean that we are unprepared or will not fulfill our appointed role. Brandubh's guard is akin to your caomhnóirí, but he also leads one thousand chosen warriors. They wait in a camp in the forest." The king paused, reading in Conall's eyes the seed of hope that the task might not be altogether impossible. Having already demonstrated a flair for the dramatic, Artair added, "Blàr, along with my trusted chieftains, will take command of the main Aos an Fhithich army. Five thousand men and women are resting around fires in the woods to the south. They are ready to march at dawn if you so order."

"What of the loss of your firstborn? You surely can't be embracing a battle that leads to such a result." Conall eyed the king, while watching Brandubh from the corner of his vision. Both seemed too accepting of the prophecy.

Lines crinkled upwards from the corners of both men's lips almost touching the dimples that father and son shared. "It is for Brandubh to enlighten you on that particular prophecy, when he deems it fitting."

"Don't challenge him to a game of fidchell, Conall. That sly bastard would win hands-down." Fearghal laughed and lifted his beer, "Slántu. Here's to a good battle." Loud shouts and cheers resounded around the stone walls of the broch, as those present once more filled their horns and tankards and attacked platters of roasted meat.

Conall reflected wryly that he cared little for being the Hand of the Goddess. A good battle - yes. He hoped for Tadhg's sake that they could rescue Gràinne. As he watched a quiet and troubled Mórrígan, he pondered the words she had spoken in her dreams. The stirring between his legs also had him wondering if she was going to be quite as demanding on this night.

Gràinne wept as she lay in her stall. Another day of scourging with the leather lash had left her body burning. She was a mass of angry, long red and white weals on a multi-colored canvas of bruises. Fragile skin had broken where the whip-ends had torn her flesh. Only the remaining fragments of her blue-paint stemmed the flow of blood. Scabs formed only to be re-opened at the next beating. The young woman was miserable, but she was defiant. With each new day, her rage burned hotter and her thirst for vengeance grew stronger.

Ashamed of her treatment, but fearful of helping, the people of the settlement avoided her eyes as they passed. She did not blame them. The few who had offered her water or small pieces of bread were never seen again. She hoped that they had been simply exiled to another part of the Na Daoine Tùrsach demesne, though it was more likely that they had been selected for sacrifice on the orders of Diadhaidh.

The king avoided her. Even his vacant eyes were not immune to the fury that seethed in Gràinne's jade ones. Caol, her father, continued to leer occasionally at her nakedness, but from a distance. He had come too close one evening and she had bitten off his left ear. She smiled at the memory of the taste of iron from his blood as it flowed over her teeth and lips, and the visceral pleasure as she spat the ear at his feet. It was worth the additional beating and withholding of food.

Diadhaidh stormed into the crannog, ignoring the king and sweeping aside her son. Her impatience with them and disgust at their weaknesses had spiked recently. Both slunk into the shadows of the wooden building to escape her tirades. She was followed by her battle commander Cesan, Spear of the Na Daoine Tùrsach, and the high nobles and warband chieftains. Most averted their eyes from Gràinne or tried to ignore her presence.

The young girl did not allow them that comfort and before Diadhaidh could club her with the oak staff, Gràinne uttered a single sentence that chilled their hearts.

"Tha Làmh na Bain-dé agus A' bhan-sealgair Chiar a' tighinn."
"The Hand of the Goddess and the Dark Huntress come."

The men's eyes constantly looked to the queen and each other's faces for assurances as to how they should act. Or what would be the best response to her words. Spies had reported the massing of Artair's forces at Càrn Liath. The army, and the Ériu warband, was expected to march anon. It was known to them, as prophesy had foretold, that command of the Aos an Fhithich army had been given to the young Ériu king, Conall Mac Gabhann. His acknowledgment as the Hand of the Goddess made them anxious.

"How strong are we?" the queen snapped.

Cesan spoke plainly, "We can match their numbers, but no more. Many of our tribe who could have been forced into the front ranks has already fled to the hills and forests. It was impossible to keep the rumors of prophesy from them. The people fear judgment. Only the loyal will stand with you."

"They should fear me. They *will* fear me when this is over," said the queen. Her spray of saliva doused Cesan and the nearest chieftains. "You will hold the valley. Mountains and a lake protect three of our flanks. Surely, a competent commander can hold the fourth. It is mostly forest land." The Na Daoine Tùrsach commander bit back any retort and refrained from obviously wiping his wet cheeks. Instead, he bowed to the queen and signaled his chieftains to follow as he exited.

Diadhaidh paced the crannog's wooden floor. Her staff click-clacked as she muttered to herself, "The Blood Moon will give me the power I need. I will sacrifice all for the promise of power."

In her stall, still in the twilight of unconsciousness, Gràinne smiled.

CHAPTER 21

Dawn started with a heavy drizzle. Undulating layers of fog drifted among ancient trees. Deep in the forest the canopy was dense, but the trees with their tall, thick trunks were spaced well apart and the army made good progress. There were few paths or tracks, yet the Aos an Fhithich warriors led on, effortlessly and unerringly. The beat and rustling of feathers from flocks of ravens followed the army's muffled tread.

Little resistance was offered as they trekked south through forest and bog, climbed gentler hills and negotiated fast running rivers. They encountered small clusters of deserted wood and stone houses where scattered livestock had stubbornly resisted a hasty round-up. It was a gift well-received by Conall's band and the errant beasts were soon roasting over the cooking pits. Each settlement was left in rubble. Anything that could burn was torched. On this third sunrise since departing Càrn Liath, the combined army of Ériu and Aos an Fhithich warriors camped at the neck of the valley leading to the dark heart of the Na Daoine Tùrsach.

The valley sloped downwards from west to east. It was bordered on its northern side by a river no more than forty paces wide. Swollen by late fall rains and early mountain snow, frothing waters flowed over the river's many gravel banks. Behind it, the pine forest rose to meet the mountains on a long sweeping incline.

The southern side of the valley was less forgiving. With a glowering beauty, mountain bluffs rose sharply from the valley to snow-capped peaks shrouded in cloud. The narrow valley floor was dense-ly wooded with a thick undergrowth of ferns, mosses and thistles. A man could walk from one end to the other in less than a morning.

From his vantage point on an outcrop midway up the southern mountain slope, Conall surveyed the valley and loch before him. A huge red-brown crannog stood in the water like a malevolent beetle. It towered over the smaller, nondescript buildings scattered around. The sloping land before the crannog had been cleared of trees for several thousand paces. Crops had been planted and harvested. Now it was the perfect killing field – if only they could force, trick or en-tice the Na Daoine Tùrsach army to fight there.

"Our position is shite," said Fearghal, in a grumpy mood as he considered the potential disaster waiting if they fought in the forest. "They'll have traps set and their warriors will be well hidden. If we fight from the river, it's all uphill."

"My people know how to fight in the forest. We've fought on the mountains and in the ancient woods for generations," said Brandubh. He bristled that anyone should doubt his warriors' bat-tle skills or courage.

"I'm counting on that," said Conall. He turned to Mórrígan. "How will your archers fare in this rain?"

"The rain's not heavy. Eventually the strings will be soaked and useless, but all of the archers carry several spare bowstrings greased to resist the damp. It's more likely that we'll run out of arrows before the bows become unusable. Each archer can only carry a few quiv-ers, after all."

"What about your slings?"

"They will last longer than bowstrings, but eventually will be of little use," said Brandubh. "My men each carry at least four or five slings."

"Any news of Mongfhionn, Fearghal?" asked Conall.

The Ulaid warrior grunted. "No. The woman hasn't been seen since she stormed out of Artair's broch. But you know her, she'll likely show up and scare the shite out of everyone – us included."

Since leaving Càrn Liath, they had argued over, debated and ruled out a range of strategies. Given the terrain, the advantage lay with the Na Daoine Tùrsach. If their leaders were wise, they would use hit-and-run tactics and slowly shred the combined army. Conall finally brought the discussion to a close and outlined his chosen plan. Like a hunted beast, their enemy was to be driven from the forest and into the open ground before their queen's crannog.

Five hundred from Blàr's force would remain at the camp at the neck of the valley. They would cut off any organized retreat. The main body would form two lines, ten paces apart, across the valley. Creating as much noise as possible, they would march steadily towards the loch driving man and beast before them. Another five hundred would serve as a reserve force. It was hoped that the packs of deerhounds accompanying Blàr, perfectly camouflaged in the woods with their fawn shaggy coats, would give some warning of traps and men.

Meanwhile, the smaller force of Conall's Ériu and Brandubh's men would cross the river at night. They would make their way along its northern bank until they came to where the river entered the loch. Conall hoped that their surprise appearance would be seen as a major threat to the royal crannog and force the Na Daoine Tùrsach battle commander to pull his forces back to protect the queen. The challenge was the lack of daylight. At this time of the year the time between sunrise and sunset was very short, leaving little time for Conall to hold until Blàr had traversed the forest.

Land and loch were bathed in spectral moonlight. At the edges of the forest shadows moved silently, circling the Na Daoine Tùrsach encampment. Cesan cursed what he considered to be an ill-omen and prayed that the shadows were wolves.

As morning approached, Cesan contemplated the sky. Like skittish overgrown sheep the few clouds were being herded off the pale gray-blue canvas by the wind. Cesan knew in his gut that the battle would be today even were it not for the scouts concealed in their hides or the sounds of many hounds baying deep in the forest. He studied his nobles and warband chieftains. Many were young, never having fought in anything bigger than a cattle raid. They joked and told unbelievable tales of how many of their enemies they would kill. Fools! Most would be dead by nightfall.

The older chieftains were wiser. They were quiet, fingering weapons, eyes constantly scanning the land, receiving reports from their spies and scouts. They were unafraid, but knew that the field upon which they stood would soon become a bloody graveyard. Ten thousand men did not take to the battlefield to exchange pleasantries.

A screeching voice behind him interrupted Cesan's thoughts. "The Hag take that woman," he murmured beneath his breath. Removing the queen's head and going to Artair to work out an accommodation had occurred to him more than once. He was convinced that he would make a much better ruler. The older chieftains could be relied upon for support. The younger would be killed to ensure more sympathetic successors. A sigh escaped his dry mouth. Too late, he had left it too late. The prophesies were in motion.

Another stronger and louder shriek rent the air echoing off the cliff faces bordering the loch. Hand raised and at the end of his tether, Cesan rounded on Diadhaidh intent on delivering a swift backhand. After all, he would probably be dead by the end of the day. What harm could the witch do to him? And besides, who else would lead the army? She detested him, but needed him now more than ever.

It was the open-mouthed expression on the queen's face as she stared to the east that stayed his hand. On a mountain crag stood the tall, gray-cloaked figure of Mongfhionn. Flurries of snow gusted about her feet giving the impression that the Sidhe floated above the rock. The wind lifted her golden mane of hair and carried her wailing chants across the natural auditorium of valley and loch. The air grew colder.

"I'd like to say that you get used to her, but I'd be lying," said Fearghal.

Tadhg laughed and said, "Two or three thousand warriors stand before the crannog. The rest must be in the forest." Conall nodded once in acknowledgement.

"We'll hold here until Blàr has had time to get about half way through the woods," said Conall. "Here" was the southern side of the river where the Ériu and two hundred of Brandubh's warriors lay on a sloping shale and dirt bank. The warriors had made good use of the moonlit night to cross the cold, chest-high waters. Now they lay shivering, praying that battle would commence before they froze solid. The rest of Brandubh's guard remained out of sight on the opposite bank.

"Hold here. Is that the plan?" the wit of the Ériu band said. "My toes are freezing, dangling in this water – and someone owes me for a new pair of boots."

"If you don't shut up," growled Fearghal, "it will be your balls dangling in the water."

"I'd like to see you find them," was the quick riposte.

"It would seem that the Lady Sidhe has given us permission to attack," Brandubh said, rubbing the crown of his head. Although a young man, Brandubh's hair was thinning, much to his annoyance.

Resistance was light as Blàr led his men through the trees. Muscles strained within the confines of gold, silver and copper arm bands. Many sported thick torcs of gold and silver around their necks. The jewelry showed status and wealth, but many had also fended off a slashing blade. Imbued with good omens, those pieces had become as much a part of their battle armor as their tattoos.

Thick plaits of copper-red hair swung to and fro as the warriors – men and women, novices and experienced - took up a half-jog. Most wore plaid pants, a concession to the cold weather. The calloused soles of thousands of imprinted feet flattened debris on the forest floor. Faces and taut torsos freshly painted blue to match the swirling designs etched into their skin glistened in the light mizzle.

Any advantage might save them from Mag Mell and so the

chosen weapon was the spear. Its longer reach was valued when the enemy was unseen. Small round, wooden shields complemented the spears and the fighters carried a wide range of additional weapons. Knives and daggers for stabbing, small axes for throwing, and larger axes, clubs - even hammers, for delivering trauma were strapped to bodies or sheathed, hanging from belts. Unlike the Ériu, few carried swords.

Blàr grimaced at the cries of his men who had stumbled into concealed traps. He mouthed a silent prayer of thanks to the Goddess that, so far, he had avoided the pits, the tumbling logs, the snares and sharpened stakes. The number of injured was not huge and quickly replaced from the reserve. In his head he knew, despite the shouts and roars from his men, the howling dogs, the slapping of spears against shields, and the blasts of bronze hunting horns, that they had forced more animals to run before them than Diadhaidh's warriors.

They had almost reached the western half of the valley where the Na Daoine Tùrsach were holding their main strength. In this he took some relief, as surely they would not lay many traps where they expected to fight in close combat. The harsh, reverberating blast of a war horn startled Blàr. It was followed by the swelling chant of the Tuireadh. Ominous as it was echoing out of the morning forest mist, Blàr considered the priest's chanting infinitely less unnerving than the periodic shrieks from the nearby mountain peak.

Just as the Na Daoine Tùrsach broke from cover to charge Blàr's front row, the Sidhe ripped the air with a wailing scream that all but silenced priests and warriors. Blàr seized the brief moment. "Stand firm!" he shouted to his commanders. An axe tumbled towards him and Blàr took a defensive quarter swerve to his right. Unfortunately the warrior behind Blàr had no time to do likewise. She gasped and stumbled backwards, the axe head buried in her chest. The forest floor swallowed the crimson blood as she lay dying.

They absorbed and then threw back the first assault. Leafshaped iron spearheads stabbed high and low. Blàr's command to move forward was relayed along the line. Instinctively, the rear rank closed to within a few paces of their comrades. Their task was to ensure that any of the enemy breaking through the front rank went no further. The orders were no prisoners. The pleadings of the Na Daoine Tùrsach fallen were ignored. Their lives ended with a downward spear thrust.

Progress was painfully slow for Blàr, a consequence of him being the main target of the Na Daoine Tùrsach warriors. His personal guard of a hundred warriors had, once battle was enjoined, moved to support the heir to the Aos an Fhithich throne. Their support was not to prevent him from fighting, but rather to ensure that he faced no more than two or three warriors at a time. The blood and gore-spattered Blàr smiled grimly, acknowledging this sign of their respect for his fighting prowess. A pulsing stream of hot, red liquid washed those nearby as his spearhead sliced the throat of another fighter.

Conall judged it time to enter the fray and signaled his commanders. Another blood-chilling wail from the mountainside transfixed the enemy momentarily. With a great shout, those hidden by the river bank rose up and sprinted towards the nearest Na Daoine Tùrsach. Leading the charge were Mórrígan's archers and Brandubh's warriors. The remaining Ériu formed two rows behind and prepared to launch javelins. Meanwhile, on the far side of the river, the rest of Brandubh's guard had already plunged into the freezing waters. They struggled against the river current as well as a river bottom of mud and gravel.

Flights of arrows from recurved bows and stones from whirring slings competed for first blood. Much to Brandubh's delight, a few of his men edged the archers. Rocks thudded against flesh amid yelps of pain; cries rang out as barbed arrows sank deep. The injured fell and pleaded with friends to be dragged to safety. The dead fell and lay in the dirt. They were kicked aside having become an obstacle to be cursed.

Cesan swore at being taken by surprise. The Spear wondered whether there were more warriors hidden beyond the river as he watched the Aos an Fhithich make the crossing. Was the battle in the forest a feint and the main attack to be from the river? His head pounded from the continuous ranting of the queen and the depressing and increasingly shrill chants of her many priests. Worse, the Hag on the hillside hurled furious words of ancient power at every moment of advantage for the attackers.

Of two minds, Cesan hesitated. Not long, but enough to allow more volleys of stones and arrows to shred the ranks of his men. More seriously, the crossing of the river went unchallenged. "Sound the war horns. Recall the men from the forest," he bellowed, shaking his head in annoyance. He snapped at his chieftains, "Are you going to do nothing and let them flay your men until it is only their bones that stand? Attack those bastards!"

Conall watched with satisfaction as his force came together. The archers and slingers had winnowed out the front ranks of the Na Daoine Tùrsach. He noticed that Mórrígan, while directing the archers, curiously had not nocked a single arrow to her bow. His shield wall stood ready to throw their javelins. Brandubh's remaining force had crossed the river and fanned out on either side of the shield wall. The raven formation was in place, with Conall's men as the head and Brandubh's as the wings.

The warriors of the wall roared defiance, slapping javelins against their shields. Brandubh's fighters quickly joined in, increasing the ram of noise. From the mountainside the Sidhe shrieked her approval. The Na Daoine Tùrsach warriors briefly milled about uncertainly, seeking direction from their chieftains. It was not long before the taunting of the enemy enraged the mass sufficiently and, despite their dread of the apparition on the mountain and the constant hail of missiles, they surged forward.

Two rows of men hefted and hurled the first of three volleys of javelins as the seething horde closed on Conall's shields. Clouds of iron-hail broke the flesh of the brave and the foolish. A sticky mist of blood and gore sprayed upward.

Encouraged by threats and swearing from their chieftains, men and women stumbled over the slippery bodies of the fallen trying to maintain momentum. Behind the Na Daoine Tùrsach ranks, hundreds of priests chanted with increasing volume and shrillness.

Their supply of throwing javelins exhausted, Conall's men waited expectedly. Each held a remaining javelin firmly in hand and the shield wall instinctively tightened up. The archers stepped behind the wall and let loose their final flurry of black arrows. The slingers, also behind the wall, provided a steady barrage.

Conall raised his javelin and uttered a blood-curdling roar, "Forward, no prisoners. The Goddess has spoken."

The wall moved as one.

CHAPTER 22

At nineteen summers Blàr's experience of battles was limited. As he surveyed the growing slaughter of the Na Daoine Tùrsach - a people for whom he previously had little regard, he wished the fight over and for the enemy to slink away into the dark forest. His desire was not granted and once more he wielded his bloody spear. The shaft was covered in a thick film of gore. Even were he able to release his grip, the spear felt as if it would remain glued to his hand. Countless blows to his shield had left his shoulder bruised and arm aching. This was his third shield. Two others had disintegrated.

Along the line, Blàr's men followed his lead and had formed a series of wedges, each with the more experienced warriors at the apex. The second rank moved steadily behind. The formation resembled the teeth of a saw, cutting and ripping the flesh of anything that still breathed.

In the distance, war horns sounded the recall. While the Na Daoine Tùrsach warriors attempted an orderly retreat, the priests accompanying them gathered up their black cloaks and ran. More than a few were tripped up, stamped on or received a friendly spear in the back. They were left to wait on the mercy of the Aos an Fhithich.

Withdrawal was a mistake. A fairly even fight between the two opposing forces quickly turned in Blàr's favor. His offensive saw pressed forward, slashing along the line of retreating fighters, penetrating deeper into their ranks. It became a challenge for Blàr to hold his formation tight and his men under control. They sensed that the tide of battle had turned and wanted to quickly pursue, kill and strip their enemy. The result was an increasing number of personal duels and with it a rising number of casualties. Blàr's men followed the Na Daoine Tùrsach to the western edge of the forest. By his reckoning he had lost one-in-ten – over five hundred men, dead or injured.

The position of the sun told Blàr that it was only mid-morning. Had the Goddess suspended time to ensure her will was accomplished? The young leader snarled his disgust yet knew his duty. He would see that his father, Artair's will, if not the Goddess', was done.

The impact of the shield wall, even one as small in numbers as Conall's, was immense. Normally a formidable defensive tactic, the wall was difficult to break and presented a merciless hedge of spikes and blades. Today, Conall aggressively marched the wall forward and up the long incline. Their foe faced a solid line of black ravens glaring at them from a blood-red background. Behind the wall the slingers kept up a steady stream of stones arching high into the sky before falling to crack skulls and bruise exposed flesh.

To the Na Daoine Tùrsach, the omens were dire. On the far horizon, waves of violet and indigo hues splashed the skies above a landscape of ambers and greens. Flashes of lightning from an awakening, dark power were answered by the rolling snarl of the Goddess.

Flocks of ravens circled above, adding their raucous *kraa kraa* to the clamor of battle. Animals disturbed from their burrows and caves turned against Diadhaidh's people. A great brown bear forced from its den and driven onto the battlefield, tossed bodies aside with great raking claws before bellowing defiance and shambling back to the forest.

Cesan stood before the royal crannog. He watched the Na Daoine Tùrsach break from the forest and allowed himself a momentary smile. Reinforcements would allow him to drive the Aos an Fhithich and their heathen allies back down the sloping valley floor and into the river. There they would be slaughtered. He called war horns and messengers to him, readying them with orders for the arrivals, but his hopes diminished as he counted how few were emerging from the tree line. He watched with trepidation as they were closely pursued by Blàr's force.

The Ériu shield wall ground its way slowly forward, its blades leaving a path of torn and broken bodies. At its edges the wall of shields deflected and bounced some of the Na Daoine Tùrsach onto the wings where they fell to the spears of Brandubh's force. Cesan's newer arrivals scrambled to link up with their comrades, but were constantly harried by Blàr. The Na Daoine Tùrsach battle commander's only consolation was that the wailing and chanting of the priests was waning significantly. The Huntress had found an outcrop of rock and with deadly accuracy was sending arrow after arrow into the priests, easy targets in their black cloaks.

As the battle surged, Diadhaidh alternated between cursing the invaders and chanting and praying to the darkness, to the power to which she had sold her soul. The king and her son cowered in the shadows. She edged across the wooden boards and peered outside. Her army was being pushed relentlessly towards the crannog and the loch. She glanced hopefully at the sky, but mid-day had just passed. It would be some time before dusk and the ascending of the Blood Moon.

The queen stomped back inside and glared at the crumpled and bruised Gràinne. The girl had continued her defiance and in a fit of rage, Diadhaidh had personally vented her anger and frustration on the young woman, dispensing a vicious beating with staff, feet and fists.

"The Dark Huntress," her granddaughter repeated over and over through bleeding lips. Diadhaidh slammed the base of her staff against Grainne's temple. The girl was silent, but the cacophony of battle continued to pound against the crannog's walls.

Cassius could not help but observe that apart from the occasional animal sound, the woods were strangely quiet. His guard, led by the monster of a barbarian, Urard, was harsher in its treatment of him than usual. This was not surprising. They blamed him for being left out of the battle. Now they moved with alacrity, half-pulling, half-dragging him, hoping to reach the fight.

The vista was grim. Broken bodies, severed limbs, and slashed and frayed flesh lay everywhere. None lived, no breath rose up to form a mist in the cool air. Apart from the occasional splash of crimson-purple on moss-covered rocks or broad-leafed ferns, the ebbing lifeblood of the dead flowed into the forest floor and was gratefully received as a sacrifice.

The small group broke from the trees. To the east, the battlefield sloped downwards to the river. To their northwest lay the small loch, its waters placid and still - a stark contrast to the fury of the battle around its shores. Occasionally, there was a flurry of activity at the entrance to the crannog as a short, dark-haired figure screamed at those fighting to preserve her life. "A highly ungrateful woman," Cassius thought.

It was a scene of noise, chaos and death. Even to Cassius' untutored eyes, the Na Daoine Tùrsach army was in retreat - albeit slowly. They fought for each pace of land, but each step was backwards and each paid for in blood. They were assailed on several flanks, losing warriors faster than their enemies and they were being pushed towards the crannog and the loch.

A glint caught the Roman's attention. The leaders of the Ériu were easily recognizable in their ornate helmets. The witch, Mórrígan, had found high ground. She nocked an unending supply of arrows to her bow and her shots were frighteningly accurate. The contrast between the three sets of warriors compelled Cassius to reexamine his opinion of his captors.

The Aos an Fhithich and Na Daoine Tùrsach in their battle frenzy had reverted to the traditional individual barbarian fighting tactic of scream, charge and kill anyone in the way. Led by Conall, the Ériu kept a disciplined formation. Sword blades flashed as the shield wall, a bloody purple in battle gore, plowed a wide furrow of death through the center of the Na Daoine Tùrsach. There was no pity, no mercy.

It was a terrifying sight. Cassius shivered as the premonition of a greater slaughter on the banks of a slow flowing river rose in his mind. He shrugged. "A land of visions and dreams," he thought, shaking his head. The battle ebbed suddenly and his attention was drawn to a tall, shaggy-haired warrior with a great red beard striding from the Na Daoine Tùrsach lines.

Cesan knew he was being selfish, but better the glory of a warrior's death immortalized in song and an honored place in Mag Mell than watch the butchery before him. His veteran eyes told him the battle was lost. The fight was far from over, but the tide was flowing steadily in favor of the implacable enemy. Cesan rationalized that the action he was about to take would give his chieftains time to reorganize their warbands. The men would have a short respite from the battle.

The Spear of the Na Daoine Tùrsach strode forward and roared his challenge. "Fight me, Conall of the Ériu, called Hand of the Goddess. Let the Goddess judge whose cause is just."

A scrape of shrieks from behind Cesan showed that his invocation of the Goddess was neither appreciated by Diadhaidh nor the priests surrounding her. They took up dark incantations for the destruction and torture of their general's body and spirit. Cesan turned and took a deep breath. He held the queen's gaze and snarled, "The Huntress take you, striapach." Then the grizzled, red-haired commander hesitated.

"Perhaps he's changed his mind," said Conall in a low tone.

As if he had heard, Cesan tossed Conall a look and grinned. With a nonchalant twist and thrust, Cesan's spear opened up a deep gash in the throat of the priest immediately next to Diadhaidh. There was a gurgle of blood and froth as the blade passed through the priest's neck, emerging with ribbons of flesh dangling from its dark iron tip. The adjacent priests quickly stepped back. Diadhaidh stood stunned, splashed with the priest's blood. The Spear had sent a clear message to his army. The eyes of many reflected the message had been understood.

"Perhaps, he wants to join us?" Conall remarked to Fearghal.

"I doubt it. That's a very dangerous man, Conall. He's made peace with death. Kill him quickly," an anxious Fearghal advised. Conall handed his shield and sword to his friend, mentor and battle commander. Then he slid the pair of axes from their sheaths on his back.

"Why do the useful ones have to die?" he muttered before striding to within a few paces of the Na Daoine Tùrsach warrior.

Cesan flexed his grip on the spear shaft, feeling the ash's slightly coarse grain and settling his hand comfortably against the familiar wood. The round shield that rested on his left arm was brought around to protect his tattooed, barrel-chested torso. A great ginger-red beard hid half his chest as he took measure of the warrior before him.

Apart from his arms, the young man's body was almost fully covered. Thick and intricately designed circlets of gold and silver gripped upper arm muscles. Plaid pants of autumn colors were tucked into calf-high soft leather boots wrapped with leather thongs. A light, red woolen tunic covered his torso from the red and yellow gold torc on his neck to his thigh. His tunic was a patchwork of blood and slashed in numerous places, showing the warrior had no fear of battle.

Underneath the tunic, Cesan could make out grey rings of mail. He smiled grimly. He had heard of such armor from the traders of the Great Sea. The warrior's head was shielded with an ornate helmet crested with a golden raven and trailing black plumes. Cesan saw that his options to strike were limited. The areas where Cesan could deliver a killing blow were few.

In his twenty-fourth summer, a blood-spattered Conall reflected, somewhat sadly, that he was no stranger to duels – or death. He had travelled a long and bloody path from his beginnings as an apprentice blacksmith in his father's shop. The hammers and tongs that he had used to create had been replaced by blades of destruction. The axes he held in scarred hands rotated and scythed the air as Conall loosened tired and sore muscles. He preferred his weapons. That they felt so comfortable frequently caused him concern.

Conall's opponent was big. The Na Daoine Tùrsach warrior was heavy-set and solidly-muscled and he was at least a head taller than Conall. The many scars on the man's upper body and face spoke to his experience. The spear gave him the advantage of reach. He was also fresher, having mostly directed the battle, not fought in it.

"A gold piece says the big one wins," Cassius' words leapt from his mouth before his brain could intervene.

"You have no gold, Roman," said Urard. Then he pointed to the duel, "But I will take your wager." Surprised, Cassius began to take a greater interest in the contest. His interest grew more urgent when the huge Ériu warrior, to the laughter of his comrades added, "For my part, I will remove one of your fingers or toes each time our ruiri draws his opponent's blood. Pray to your gods that the fight is over quickly."

The two warriors circled each other, making a series of feints and faux attacks. An early thrust by Cesan was deflected downwards and to the side by crossed axes. Conall quickly stepped inside to deliver a knee in the groin, but Cesan had already brought his shield around slamming the edge into his opponent's side. Conall winced and stepped outside of the range of Cesan's spear to resume his circling motion. A series of spear thrusts and shield slams drove Conall backwards. It also convinced him that Fearghal was right. He had to end the contest speedily. In an extended fight, this champion had too many advantages.

Conall rolled to his right several times in a semicircle and came to a crouching position. Cesan was fractionally slower in turning. It was enough for Conall's right axe to slash high on his enemy's calf. The cut did not threaten Cesan's ability to fight save that it made him more cautious – and slower to move. Conall moved inside a spear thrust aimed at his head and rammed his shoulder into Cesan's chest before the man could bring his shield around. The man grunted in surprise and staggered backwards. Not allowing his opponent to bring his spear to bear again, Conall reversed the grip on his axe and slammed the butt against Cesan's nose.

The Na Daoine Tùrsach Spear howled in pain as he tasted blood and snot from his broken nose. Blinking tears from his eyes, Cesan swung his spear recklessly in a wide arc. To his amazement he heard a loud gasp from Conall. As his vision cleared, Cesan saw that Conall was on one knee. The spear had ripped his left pant leg revealing a deep gouge through skin and muscle from thigh to calf. The Ériu king had also let go of the axe in his right hand. Both warriors locked eyes. Cesan, sensing victory, moved in for the kill.

The spear thrust should have been fatal. Conall anticipating was already moving. As it was, the blade carved a ragged track along the right side of his neck. Fortunately, the Goddess protected her Hand. The cut was bloody, but not deep enough to tear the artery. Conall dropped under Cesan's thrust, then twisted and rolled against his opponent's feet. In his right hand was no axe, but a long-bladed dagger which he stabbed upwards. The blade carved its way through the soft flesh of Cesan's balls, sliced through the tailbone and erupted from his arse.

Cesan roared like a bear, tossing his head in disbelief as he saw the dagger's bone hilt protruding in place of his cock. He felt the flow of warm blood. Conall rolled to the side and stood up, his back to Cesan. Swinging his remaining axe two-handed in a backward arc he caught Cesan on the chest, almost cleaving the warrior's heart. The axe remained embedded, trapped in Cesan's flesh and muscle. A glint of metal flashed. Fearghal's longsword was tossed and caught by Conall. In the same movement he severed Cesan's head.

There was a pause. The rabid priests fell silent. With Cesan's death, there was little doubt that the battle was lost. Diadhaidh had barely trusted Cesan's influence and hence there was no strong candidate for a battlefield promotion.

Chaos ensued as the Na Daoine Tùrsach army fragmented. Many fled to the hills and mountains to escape the inevitable slaughter. They fought their way through former comrades and friends, and killed any priest that crossed their path.

The foolishly led prepared to stand and fight. These were the fanatics, the young chieftains who dreamed of a glorious death and those simply resigned to their fate. Numbering about a thousand, they formed up before the queen's crannog, cursing and screaming at their enemy.

They were engulfed by the Aos an Fhithich.

Conall's shield wall finally bludgeoned its way through the melee until it stood before the royal crannog. The building's wooden bridge had been withdrawn and it now squatted in the water, isolated from the land.

At the entrance, and clearly losing her tenuous grip on reality, the queen alternated between laughing hysterically and screaming and cursing all before her. Unable to accept defeat, Diadhaidh's madness continued in the hope that the approaching dusk would be followed by the rising of the Blood Moon and her power.

"It appears we have a stand-off," said Fearghal. "We've won the battle. The Na Daoine Tùrsach are dead or scattered to the mountains with little prospect of surviving a harsh winter. Yet that woman continues to defy us."

"Burn the crannog. Make it her funeral pyre." All turned as Mongfhionn joined the small group of Ériu leaders.

"No!" countered Tadhg, glaring at the Sidhe, "Gràinne is in there."

"No, Gràinne *may* be in there or she may be dead," Mongfhionn said fixing Tadhg with a stern glance. Surprisingly the young man did not flinch, "I must be losing my touch," she thought, suppressing an urge to smile at Tadhg's defiance.

Ignoring the Sidhe, Conall barked orders, "Deaglán, Torcán and Tadhg, take twenty men who can swim. Bring me the girl – alive or not." Shields, armor and clothes dropped to the dirt as the group prepared for the short swim.

The Goddess, however, had other ideas which were apparently more in line with Mongfhionn's thinking. A flash brighter than daylight split the sky. From the clouds, a fork of lightning struck the apex of the crannog. Wood exploded, showering those nearby with smoking splinters. The fragrance of smoke and burning thatch permeated the dusk as fire took hold.

A scream of rage came from within the burning building. Soon Diadhaidh reappeared. Alongside her, she dragged Gràinne by her long hair. A glint of metal flashed in the queen's left hand. It was clear what the queen intended as the pale neck of the girl was exposed. "No!" roared Tadhg in desperation. Sword in hand, he flung himself into the cold waters of the loch. Deaglán and Torcán quickly followed.

Invisible in the mantle of dusk, the black-shaft flew from the bow. Mórrígan stood in the shadows, helmet at her feet, her presence betrayed only by the glowing, fire-red sigils on her face and hands. For an instant, Diadhaidh's eyes were drawn to where Mórrígan stood. The Na Daoine Tùrsach queen was speechless at the sight of the apparition that was the Dark Huntress. She was still in shock as the first iron barb thudded into her right shoulder through flesh and bone, driving her backwards. The second arrow took her under her left breast, narrowly missing her heart.

Gràinne's final vision before she slipped from Diadhaidh's grasp and into the embrace of the dark water was of the queen still alive, but whimpering and grotesquely pinned to the entrance post.

"Good aim," Conall said moving to stand beside his queen.

"Her head was the target," Mórrígan said with displeasure.

Conall pointed to the fingers of fire eating their way down the crannog, "The Goddess is not as merciful as her Huntress."

Loss of blood rendered Diadhaidh helpless and she slumped against the entrance post. Unable to escape the creeping fire, she began to scream. It was her hair that first flared bright in the darkness. Soon the flames engulfed her, consuming her flesh until the arrow shaft burned through. She crumpled, now merely cinder, onto the disintegrating wooden jetty.

The Na Daoine Tùrsach king sat placidly awaiting his fate. Gradually overcome by smoke, the king offered no resistance and died as he had lived.

Within the growing inferno, Caol lay on the wooden floor. He had listened in horror to his mother's final moments and now wept in self-pity. Ever-thickening smoke swirled above him. He coughed raggedly as the noxious air filled his lungs. His eyes streamed with smoke-filled tears.

In a fit of bravado, the Na Daoine Tùrsach prince took a final gulp of air, rose up and lunged towards the entrance. He had thought to fall into the waters of the loch and slip away in the darkness.

In the confusion, it was a somewhat successful strategy. Caol splashed into the water. He flailed awkwardly towards the shore, swallowing water and almost drowning in his panic. Then Caol's toes touched the rocky bottom of the loch and here the Goddess turned her back.

Caol staggered ashore gagging and coughing. He straightened up and looked into the merciless faces of the Sidhe and Conall. Caol shrieked as the vice-like talons of Mongfhionn reached out and tore his heart from his chest. He was still standing, his mind registering excruciating pain, when Conall's axe split his skull in two.

Gentle waves lapped against the charred piers that once formed the foundation of the royal crannog. The aroma of smoke and burning flesh more filled the dawn air, but this time from the cooking fires of the victors. A pale sun rose over the mountains to cast a yellow-gold shimmer across the loch.

They had camped overnight at the far end of the Na Daoine Tùrsach settlement, mercifully out of sight of the main battlefield. It had been a night filled with the growls, snuffles and yowling of predators as they ate their fill or dragged the corpses off to dens where the young waited. The bounty would be a brief respite from the cold maw of winter. Clouds of ravens swooped in waves to pick skulls clean and claw at meaty bones.

Once the morning meal was eaten, the Aos an Fhithich retrieved what remained of their dead and built their funeral pyres. Of the five thousand men Blàr commanded, one in five had been killed or so badly injured that a sharp blade from a friend was seen as a mercy. Brandubh's force had not suffered as badly, with only a hundred dead or unable to carry on. After some discussion with his brother, the shortfall was replenished with volunteers from the main force.

The Ériu sported an even larger selection of scars of which to boast and an agreement had been reached between the men that formed Conall's caomhnóirí. His personal guard would now include all who fought in this battle and who had endured the waters, mountains and weather since leaving Eachdonn Breac's lands. The few dead were honored with gifts made on their behalf to the Goddess and were sent to Mag Mell with a celebration that lasted well into the night.

"Are we leaving?" asked Fearghal. He sucked noisily and picked at a piece of gristle stuck in his teeth. Having finally wrested it from its place, he spat it into the loch.

Conall nodded, "I miss my children and the others - Íar, Brion, Cúscraid, Nikandros. Our path back takes us through Cùil Daothail. I'm hoping that Carmag Mac an t-Sionnaich will have some news of our people."

"It seems not all prophesies are fulfilled," said Fearghal, somewhat gleefully, as Mongfhionn joined their group. "Brandubh is still with us. Not that I'm complaining. I like the lad."

"Have you informed Brandubh that you are leaving as soon as the camp fires are doused?" Mongfhionn asked. Conall dipped his head, fingering the new wound on his neck. He looked quizzically at the Sidhe. She turned to Fearghal shaking her head in admonition, "Will you never learn?" As she spoke, the tall, red-headed figure of Brandubh approached from his brother's camp.

"I'm ready to leave when you are," the Aos an Fhithich prince said.

There was a startled pause before Conall asked, "Why?"

Brandubh smiled. "The Goddess has made it plain that my future rests with yours. My father and brother know this — they don't like it, but they have always respected the geis."

Mongfhionn allowed herself a smile at the look on Fearghal's face. "Close your mouth, man. You'll swallow a cloud of midges."

Recovering from the surprise announcement, Conall stepped forward and grasped Brandubh's forearm, "Welcome. Better get your pack and say your goodbyes. We're leaving."

The young commander laughed and whispered to the towering female warrior beside him. She shook her long thick plaits of copper hair and gave three short blasts on a bronze hunting horn. The ground trembled as a thousand Aos an Fhithich warriors rose up and jogged to stand behind their leader. "We're ready. I'll be bringing a few friends!" said Brandubh taking great delight in the expressions on Conall and Fearghal's faces. "Their families already wait beyond the camp."

"Shite!" said Fearghal. "By the Hag, Cúscraid and Seanán will kill us when they see they have to provide shelter for this lot."

Cassius had regained his composure from seeing the work of Conall firsthand. The young king's pragmatic and efficiently executed battle plan sent a shiver up his stiff Patrician spine. Enemies were dispatched without mercy. Tripped up by his loose tongue, he now found himself in more immediate peril.

In a far corner of the Ériu camp the small group of men gathered before joining the rest of the army. Urard looked at Cassius, who was sprawled face in the dirt. His right hand was bound tightly by cords to a tree stump while the rest of his body was weighted down by several Ériu warriors. "Time to pay on the wager you made, Roman," the huge warrior said as he hefted his axe. "I make it three fingers that you owe."

The Roman begged for mercy. The axe rose, glinting as a ray of sunlight struck the blade, and swiftly descended. Cassius screamed. He also pissed his pants and shit himself. The sharp pain that stabbed through his right hand halted his shrieking. Blinking tears away he sighed in relief. His fingers were still in place – well almost. The blade had neatly trimmed his middle finger by a single joint and blood streamed from it.

"Next time my blade will not be as forgiving, Roman," Urard

said as he wiped the blade on Cassius' tunic. "You should mind your mouth."

As they walked briskly through the woods, Fearghal caught up and matched Mongfhionn's long pace. After a few moments' silence he said, "Forgiveness is not usually among your many qualities."

The Sidhe smiled, knowing to what her lover referred, "Blàr will make a good king, respectful to the Goddess and the Aes Sidhe."

"He's a boy. Artair has a good few years left in him," Fearghal said, his brow furrowing with a premonition of what was coming.

"Blàr will be king – when he arrives back at Càrn Liath. And we will talk no more of this."

 David H. Millar

CHAPTER 23

A thin sprinkling of snow gave the green pasture around Cùil Daothail a crisp appearance. As the sun rose, Brocc and Fionnbharr took up their watch. They sat on a fallen tree trunk. The position offered a good view of the trail that led north. Plus the soft crunch of footfalls on the underlying frost made their task less onerous. It was hard not to hear any who approached. Thick furs and the small fire that crackled before them were also very welcome. It had taken the two men and a small band of warriors almost half a cycle of the moon to travel from their temporary home at A' Chrìon Làraich to the thriving coastal settlement.

Íar had proposed their task in his growing concern over Conall's absence. The die was set when Brion, Cúscraid and Nikandros decided that Brocc and Fionnbharr should spend some time together. All wanted to be sure there were no lingering problems from the death of Labhraidh. The Druid prepared them with his knowledge of the terrain and prevailed upon the leader of the Aos na Coille observers to let one of his men guide the group. The warband chieftain agreed on the basis that it was prudent to know the location of his enemy.

The trek across the highlands was brutal in mid-winter. Deep snow drifts, biting winds and icy rainstorms accompanied the pair for most of the journey. Neither was enthusiastic about the return hike to A' Chrìon Làraich. Thankfully, the location of Cùil Daothail meant that it had a friendlier climate. It also helped that the duo were greeted with a warm welcome from Carmag Mac an t-Sionnaich. Their mood brightened further on hearing that the Ériu raiding party had been in good form - at least when it departed Cùil Daothail.

Of the two, Brocc was the more nervous and uncharacteristically subdued. He remained uncertain as to how Craiftine and Tadhg ó Cuileannáin would react to the circumstances of their brother's death. While Fionnbharr appeared to have resolved his issues, blood was blood. Brocc was in no doubt as to whose side the tall, fairheaded healer would take.

The toe in Brocc's ribs, meant to be a gentle prod, was delivered by a warrior who was as broad as he was tall. Hence, the impact carried quite a bit of force. "Carmag says that your friends have arrived," the man said gruffly before leaving the shelter. It took around the same time for Brocc's eyes to get used to the gloom of the dawn as it did for the pain in his side to recede. He resisted the temptation to waken Fionnbharr in like manner. Reluctantly awake, they grabbed some food and made their way at a fast clip to the main gate.

Squinting at the stark, white landscape before them, Brocc scanned the open ground between Cùil Daothail and the forest. Fionnbharr was slow to wake and grumbled something about Carmag having an overactive imagination. There was a tap on his arm and Brocc pointed to what appeared to be flickering torches emerging from the forest edge. The possibility that there might be substance to Carmag's claim brought Fionnbharr's senses into focus. The shadows abruptly faded as the torches were smothered. Brocc swore under his breath and strained his eyes again.

"You better have hot food on that fire and good beer." Fearghal's distant voice was instantly recognizable bringing huge smiles of relief to the watchers. Brocc and Fionnbharr strode quickly forward to meet their friends, but pulled up short at the sight of the Aos an Fhithich warriors. Hands went instinctively to swords and axes. The pair was nonplussed by loud peals of laughter from their Ériu comrades.

"Sheath your weapons," a smiling Conall said, "they're with us." Unsure of what was going on, the two young men relaxed. Then the ranks of the Ériu rippled and broke as Craiftine and Tadhg ran to embrace their brother. Observing as Fionnbharr dipped his head and led his brothers to the side, Conall said, "Perhaps you should explain what is going on, Brocc."

With his usual forthrightness, Brocc told of his foolishness, Labhraidh's death and the subsequent intervention of the Druid. "Well, everything appears sorted," said Fearghal. The involvement of the Druid was of great interest to Mongfhionn. She appeared to be satisfied with his judgment, yet ambivalent to his continued presence.

Conall was less sympathetic to a potential confrontation. "We all do stupid things. We'll continue to do things we regret. Brocc was foolish, but Labhraidh died as a warrior and is in Mag Mell where, if the Goddess wills it, we'll all end up. I hope good sense will prevail as I've no time for squabbles. Heads will be knocked together if needed."

In a short time, Fionnbharr and his brothers returned and gestured for Brocc to join them. Craiftine was later to reflect that had it not been for Tadhg and his experiences on the raid north, things would have turned out much differently. As it was, they asked for Brocc's side of the story, accepted his remorse as genuine and once more confirmed their friendship.

"Perhaps I should join your army too, Conall. It seems like everyone you meet either joins you or is dead," Carmag said. He drained a horn of beer while supervising the supplies being purchased or traded. The combined Ériu and Aos an Fhithich force and its followers would only be staying until the next morning. Conall was impatient to re-unite with his people and in Carmag's estimation was weary of the recent fighting and bloodshed.

Conall inspected the fresh lines of scars on his hands, and thought Carmag was not too far from the truth. He smiled, "I've always room for a good man, but I think you're too comfortable here,

Carmag. Besides, Drostan might object." Carmag nodded, though Conall noted the doubt in the chieftain's eyes.

Drostan Ruadh, king of the Aos na Coille, clasped calloused hands behind his shock of red hair and deliberately placed his soft leather boots on the oak table. The table was laden with platters of cold meat, cheese, bread and berries, and jugs of drink – mostly leftovers from the earlier feasting to celebrate Samhain. He noted with pleasure the look of annoyance that fleetingly crossed the face of Finnean Mac Sèitheach before the white-haired leader of the Na Mèadaidh pursed his lips into a thin smile.

After days listening to the constant bleating and pleading of Finnean, Drostan was bored, his patience as thin as the ice that covered the smaller lochs. If Finnean gave him the right excuse, he might just take his father's advice and open the arsehole's scrawny throat. Added to this, the Aos na Coille leader was not enthused about the other company around the table.

He looked condescendingly on the An t-Aos-Sìthiche and Aos nan Con-Seilge whose leaders bowed and scraped before him. Drostan's instincts told him to beware of the always smiling, ever watchful leader of the southern mercenaries that Finnean had bought. He had no love for the southern tribes and their expansionist ambitions.

He chortled to himself, once more receiving raised eyebrows from the others. He apologized, pointing to the beer before him and wondered if Finnean was aware that Eachdonn Breac's son, Ròidh, and five hundred spears travelled with Conall Mac Gabhann. The Aos na Coille leader saw the fair hand of Ceana nic Sèitheach, Finnean's sister and Eachdonn's queen, moving her pieces on the fidchell board. It appeared that the queen had her eyes firmly set on reclaiming her former home at Dùn Na Mèadaidh. Her partner would have little regret at the removal of the pale thorn in his side. Drostan mused that perhaps Eachdonn would make a more reliable and stronger buffer between his forest people and the southern tribes. Yes, he could do business with the king of the Aos an Eich.

Drostan abruptly stood up, stretching his muscled limbs. "I'm leaving," he said.

A confused Finnean managed to stammer, "What? What about our discussions of warriors to defend Dùn Na Mèadaidh?" Then with more composure he asserted, "There is an understanding... an agreement. You gave your sworn oath to provide warriors to defend Dùn Na Mèadaidh, if necessary."

"I must have been drunk at the time," Drostan mumbled to himself. Then addressing the group he said, "My warriors will arrive in the spring. It's unlikely Conall Mac Gabhann will attack before then, unless you give him cause." With his one eye, Drostan winked at the chieftains who had accompanied him and they quickly acknowledged the signal. "My men are ready to leave."

Around the banqueting table, the leaders of the An t-Aos-Sìthiche and Aos nan Con-Seilge intently studied their horns of beer, not wanting to look at Drostan or Finnean for fear of offending either. At the far end of the table, the mercenary leader smiled at the obvious insult and noted who held real power in the north.

Once beyond the perimeter of Dùn Na Mèadaidh, Drostan turned to his second-in-command with a broad grin. "I'm feeling fatherly, he said. "I think I should visit my children at A' Chrion Laraich."

CHAPTER 24

Fionnbharr remained with the main body because Conall thought it prudent to have an additional healer on the trek across the mountains. Torcán and Brocc were therefore tasked to return to A' Chrìon Làraich as speedily as possible. They were to give advance warning of their imminent arrival, and more importantly, of their numbers. Presently, the two stood before Brion, Cúscraid, Íar and Nikandros, attempting - with little success, to project an air of sobriety.

"He's bringing how many with him?" An agitated Cúscraid looked beseechingly at his comrades for support, but only received broad grins. "In the name of the Hag where are we going to put them?" Cúscraid tugged his recently trimmed sandy hair and then fixed his comrades with a stern, disapproving stare. "You eejits can grin all you want. This time I'll need every pair of hands I can call on, so grab an axe or hammer. We'll see if blisters will remove those smirks." After some half-hearted protests, the trio stripped to the waist along with the rest of the camp.

Conall heaved a great sigh of relief as A' Chrìon Làraich came into view. His disappointment at not entering the gates of Dùn Na Mèadaidh before winter was tempered with his admiration of Cúscraid's work and an acknowledgment that the Goddess had her own view of time and priorities. His caomhnóirí and archers tramped in disciplined rows behind him, followed by the Aos an

Fhithich and their people.

The hike across mountains, valleys, and forests covered in deep winter snow had been a trial of perseverance and sheer bloody-mindedness. Conall was thankful for the presence of their guides. Their knowledge of the landscape kept casualties to a minimum. A few hundred had perished on the journey – mostly the sick and elderly. A few eejits ignoring advice stumbled from mountain paths to their deaths. Their final resting place was in the snows of the valley floor as an unexpected winter meal for wolves.

Tired eyes travelled from the dark snow-laden clouds to the blue-gray haze of smoke from the settlement's fires. The wind carried the scent of wood and peat and the promise of hot food and shelter to the weary travelers. Hope was renewed and broad smiles broke out on ruddy, wind and ice scarred faces. Children were loosed to laugh and play in the soft, white snow.

The massed ranks of the Ériu spanned the frosted white valley. Three rows of red and black shields, the heart of Conall's command, stood at ease but alert, javelins ready, raven banners flapping in the wind. In front of the shields, Áine stood with one hundred archers. Alongside her, Brion's ten chariots rocked back and forward with iron bits and buckles chinking. Horses snorted steam into the cold, damp air. To the right of the shields, Íar's cavalry, swollen with newly trained recruits, stomped the frozen ground. Sporadically, heads would dip to snatch at a patch of green. On the far left, Ròidh's horses and spears waited. They were a part of the force, and yet were separate.

Suddenly, a large black shape charged from the ranks, tossing its head in joy as firmly muscled legs made little of the distance. Conall wiped a tear from his cheek with fingers numb with cold as the great black stallion came to a halt a short distance from its master. The horse snorted dismissively at the mass of people, its brown eyes wide and nostrils flaring. Despite entreaties, it refused to take one step further.

"So, Toirneach, this is my punishment. You want me to come to you?"

The beast's great black head nodded several times, it nickered quietly and pawed the ground as if to say, "I deserve it, you left me."

"Oh ho!" Conall crowed with laughter, then handing his shield and weapons to one of the men behind him, walked to the horse and rubbed the warm, velvet neck. He smiled as he spied the small pouch that hung from the horse's neck, reached in and brought out a handful of winter-sweetened parsnips. He would thank Íar later for his thoughtfulness. Both man and beast sighed at being united and Conall swung up onto its back.

Mórrígan thought, "He loves that beast more than me."

Beside her, Mongfhionn, caught the frown, smiled and said, "Toirneach's loyalty is unreserved and uncomplicated."

"What, no horses for the rest of us?" a voice queried. "My feet are aching and sore." Chuckles rippled through the ranks of men.

"Any more cheek and you'll be shoveling horse-shite until the next new moon." rejoined Fearghal.

Íar, Nikandros, and Cúscraid trotted forward. Alongside them the iron-rimmed and spoked wheels of Brion's chariot bounced and crunched over the solid ground. All removed their helmets, dipped their heads and offered their weapons as a sign of respect for their king. Then all cantered forward to embrace him as a friend. "It's good to be united again," boomed Íar. Then peering over Conall's shoulder he said, "Even the sight of that red-haired bastard, Fearghal Ruad is welcome."

"Hah, you're putting the beef on, Íar. Must be all that sitting around eating and drinking while the real men were out fighting," Fearghal said. He clasped his friend's proffered arm.

"I see you've brought us some new friends, Conall," said Íar. When he spied Cassius Fabius Scaeva, an aspect of savage dislike crossed the normally jovial warrior's face. "And some not so welcome."

Nikandros walked his horse forward to inspect the ranks of the Aos an Fhithich. As always, the olive-skinned, black-haired Spartan cut a striking figure sheathed in polished bronze armor, his helmet's red plumes flaring in the breeze. His black cloak, trimmed with silver wolf pelts, flipped over in the wind, revealing its silken cherry-red

lining and the short matching red tunic that he favored. The Aos an
Fhithich nodded their approval of the strange warrior who would
fight almost as naked as they.

The Spartan retraced his steps until he loomed over the bound
figure of the Roman.

"Assassin," spat Cassius.

"I see a dead man." said Nikandros in clipped tones. "Perhaps
Conall will permit me to finish my last assignment, the one purchased by your employer, Marcus Fabius Ambustus. You will die as
you lived, without friends or honor." He wheeled around to rejoin
Conall and Íar.

It was a hard blow to Cassius's ego to have it brutally confirmed that not only was he condemned to die, but that the head of
his Roman clan had deemed him expendable. Worse, that he was
a threat to be disposed of. While in his head he knew his position
was perilous, in his heart he had clung to the apparently foolish no-
tion that he remained a valued member of the Fabius family. That
thread of credulity had been severed.

"It seems that our future will be more interesting than I thought,
Brandubh." The tall female warrior's impressive chest heaved, putting strain on the ornately designed silver and gold clasp that held
her fur in place. As she surveyed the Ériu army with her brother,
deep green eyes sparkled. Her tongue flicked over full red lips.

Brandubh loved Mòrag. Many times he had, with some guilt,
imagined and wished that they were not brother and sister. With
her gaze obviously drawn to the exotic Spartan and the huge warrior with the booming voice and infectious laugh, he was relieved,
apprehensive and a little protective. His relief was that Mòrag's
attention had been diverted from Conall. That would have resulted
in too many complications and perhaps a few deaths. He was apprehensive and a little bit jealous of the Spartan and Íar. Both were
in for a wild ride.

It was Brion who called Conall's attention to the Aos an

Fhithich leader with a sharp cough, a raised eyebrow and a nod in his direction. "May the Goddess forgive my lack of courtesy," called out Conall as he slid from Toirneach's back. "Come greet our new friends. This is Brandubh, Prince of the Aos an Fhithich – he would be king, had he not chosen to join us. We are his family, make him and his people feel at home."

Brandubh smiled. "Thank you," he said. "This is my sister and my second-in-command, Mòrag." He noted the raised eyebrows from Conall and Fearghal at this announcement and reddened a bit at having held back this piece of information.

"Tadhg," Conall called out, "come over here and bring Gràinne with you, if she is able." Despite care from Mongfhionn and Fionnbharr, it was evident the young woman had suffered terribly. The slightest movement caused her deep pain, yet with eyes that flashed defiance, Gràinne stubbornly refused to rely on help from Tadhg – or anyone. Holding onto a staff for support, she carefully picked her steps forward.

"Gràinne is originally Na Daoine Tùrsach," he said and paused to let the wavelet of unease run its course. "She, like many of us, has been through severe trials. You will care for her as if she were my sister." Conall's statement had some foundation. For Gràinne reminded him of his twin sisters who would have been a summer or two younger, had they not been murdered. Turning to Íar, Conall said quietly, "Have you a spare mount? Although she will never admit it, she is in great pain."

Before Íar could answer, Brion interjected, "In that case, she would be better on my chariot than a mount. I'll lay some furs on the cret floor to lessen the impact of the hard ground. Íar can choose a suitable mount for her when she is ready. I'll take her to your new home, Conall." Íar grinned and nodded his agreement.

The momentary solemnity burst when a hoarse, burring voice said, "When do I get mounted?" All turned to stare at Mòrag who managed to adopt a look of both innocence and wantonness. "Did I say the wrong thing? This new language is very hard for me." Íar and Nikandros responded with alacrity. Mòrag had made her wishes perfectly clear.

CHAPTER 25

The valley surrounding A' Chrìon Làraich resounded with the har-monizing of pipes, bodhráns, harps and song. Huge bonfires flared, burning well into the night. Never a people to turn away the oppor-tunity for feasting and drinking, once the settlement had roared their joy at their king's return, they set about stoking up the cooking pits, spitting hundreds of carcasses and opening the great kegs of beer. Special brews made, not for the faint-hearted from winter parsnips and wild sea beets, were passed around with a wink and a nod. The aromatic scents of peat, wood smoke and roasted flesh were later augmented with the earthy muskiness of sweat and rutting.

Conall sat for most of the night with his arms around Danu and Brighid. His daughters perched on his lap as he enjoyed their screams of laughter at the antics of the grown-ups. Mórrígan sat with their son, Tuathal, his head cradled by her breasts. Concern clouded Conall's blue-gray eyes as he studied his son. To his eyes, the boy did not seem to be thriving and, while the people of Ériu were known for their pale complexion, Tuathal's skin had an unhealthy tone. The boy's wet nurse, a heavy-set lady with a bountiful pair of breasts overflowing with milk, feared that she might be blamed for the child's condition. She told Conall and Mórrígan that often Tuathal just did not seem interested in feeding. Conall assured her that no blame was assigned to her and encouraged her to persevere.

Mid-evening, a drunken eejit jumped up on a nearby table and flashed his manhood. It was his vain hope that it would prove a successful lure for the equally drunk women who cheered him on. The act caught Conall's attention and he thanked the Goddess that it was not one of his commanders. Then he smiled. Was he becoming a bit of a yawn?

Nevertheless, adopting a fatherly role, he bent his head to Mórrígan's ear and said, "Perhaps, this would be an appropriate time for the children to go to bed." Their mother nodded her agreement to exaggerated cries of protest from Danu and Brighid. Though, when Mongfhionn stood up and announced, much to Fearghal's surprise, that they were going to take a walk and would love some company, the girls immediately rose to the bait.

Mórrígan was well aware that Conall was only mildly enthusiastic about the boisterous feasting and drinking of his people. Even as a boy, unless one of his friends had plied him with beer beforehand, he preferred being the one who kept watch. On this night, Conall seemed preoccupied and his face more aged. Mórrígan's instinct told her that her partner's thoughts concerned the Roman, Cassius, who at this moment remained well-bound and guarded.

Her head was unsettled about Cassius. It had been over five summers since the slaughter of her parents. Her rage and thirst for vengeance had not subsided, but was tempered with caution and a desire not to awaken the darkness that had ruled her. She wondered if Conall had considered that time may also have dimmed the anger of the others who had suffered from the Roman's actions. Yes, the Roman should and would die. That was a given. Whether and how much mercy might be extended to Cassius was uncertain.

A sigh from Conall interrupted Mórrígan's reflections. She watched his gaze follow their departing son. Naturally, Mórrígan was also worried about Tuathal. Her prayers to the Goddess had brought only silence – the gods were capricious. She had consulted the Sidhe, but found little by way of consolation – or hope. Thus, Mórrígan had determined that there was only one path she could take. Hidden by the shadow cast by the table, she placed her hand on Conall's crotch and gently stroked and squeezed. She was rewarded by the stirring of his manhood under the plaid woolen pants. "Perhaps we should also leave before it becomes obvious why we are departing," she said and smiled, her emerald eyes meeting deep blue, "or maybe you would prefer to take me on the table before all?"

The latter caused a definite increase in Conall's hardness. With her hand firmly grasped in his, she was just able to keep pace with Conall as he charged towards the exit. Jaw firmly set, he guided her towards their broch avoiding the feverish coupling of others in the shadows. The broch was still in sight, its somber gray walls painted in fiery reds and yellows, when she was thrown to the ground in his impatience. She felt herself mounted, penetrated and filled with his seed. The raw passion of the moment made her climax quickly, her muscles spasming with intense pleasure. Ignoring the cold, damp ground, she knelt before him and took his manhood in her mouth savoring its taste, enjoying the growing hardness. "Again," she purred as she lay back and spread her thighs.

Mórrígan awoke in the broch on a bed of meadowsweet-scented rushes covered by soft furs. A single shaft of sunlight found her face. She had little recollection of how they had got there, only remembering the fiery passion they had enjoyed. Beside her, Conall gazed at the sun as it rose in the east, a burning yellow-gold orb. He turned, smiled, gently squeezed her breast and softly ran his hand over her belly. He seemed to know, as did she, that another life had begun.

The surviving members of the community of Ráth na Conall – those who had lost parents, brothers and sisters by the orders of the Roman and Eochaidh Ruad had assembled in the broch. The Chomhairle was also present and much to Mongfhionn's chagrin, the Druid. The discussion about the Roman's fate, while full of passion, was tempered by the fact that they were no longer children. All had taken lives in the heat of battle.

Cassius had been quite forthcoming during the journey from Cùil Daothail to A' Chrìon Làraich. It was beyond him to envisage a scenario where Conall's army would get anywhere close to Marcus Fabius Ambustus and his sons, Quintus, Caeso and Numerius.

To kill Marcus, Conall would first have to fight the might of Rome with its armies of tens of thousands. Thus, the Roman had decided that there was no reason why he should not tell as much as he knew. In doing so, it extended his life while preserving a slim chance of escape. Even after having seen and grudgingly admired the full might of Conall's army, as far as Cassius was concerned, Conall's mission remained hopeless.

"So, what is your intent for the Roman?" asked the Druid, bringing focus to the discussion. His words were few and direct. "It strikes me that you have two choices – execute him or let him go."

There was a rumble of nays to the idea of letting the Roman go and Conall held up his hand to still the voices. "The Druid has a point," he said. "But rather than let him go, maybe we should let him escape. He could be a real nuisance spreading fear among Marcus and his family. And we will know where to find him for his final retribution." Íar shivered at the pragmatism and coldness of Conall's words. Cassius lived only by Conall's decree and until he wanted his life. Palms on the table, Íar made to stand up and object, when there was a commotion from outside the broch.

Deaglán, who was closest to the entrance, ducked quickly outside. He returned almost immediately with a grin on his face. "We've got company."

With his guard, Drostan Ruadh guard strode through the inner gateway of A' Chrìon Làraich, and was greeted by the fully armored men of Conall's caomhnóirí. The tall leader of the Aos na Coille did not slow his pace. Outside the broch, Fearghal grinned and called out an order. The caomhnóirí divided into two rows of locked shields that ushered the small group towards the Ériu leadership. Drostan chuckled at the double-edged honor. Each man held a single javelin at the ready.

Drostan's lone eye took in the line of leaders, many of whom were already known to him. He laughed loudly as he pointed to Fearghal. "An old and grizzled warrior like me," he quipped, "and of noble blood I suspect, but not the leader of this rabble."

At this, Íar stepped forward and with a sweep of his hand said, "My friend – and enemy. Allow me to introduce our king, Conall Mac Gabhann and his queen, Mórrígan." Then with a great laugh Íar added, "Old and grizzled over there is a degenerate character named Fearghal Ruad. Beside him is the Lady Sidhe, Mongfhionn. The rest you likely know."

For a moment, Drostan ignored Conall leveling his stare on Brandubh, "I knew yer father well. He was a good man. In destroying the Na Daoine Tùrsach ye did me a service." Pausing for effect, he continued with a note of gravity behind his smile, "That's the only reason I allowed ye to travel through my lands to this place." Brandubh held the king's gaze. That Drostan had spoken of Brandubh's father as if he were dead had not gone unnoticed.

"Is there a reason for this unexpected visit?" Conall inquired after he and Drostan had embraced.

"Can a father not visit his children?"

Conall raised an eyebrow and looked up at the king. Drostan was a head taller than he and packed muscles as hard as stone. The air of concern on Drostan's scarred face was real, but fleeting. It was not difficult to discern that Drostan had other things on his mind and remained wary.

"Are our young guests in the usual place, Nikandros?"

The Spartan laughed, nodded and led the way to a fenced-off area beyond the ráth's perimeter. Conall chuckled at the perplexed look on Drostan's face and said, "They are being trained along with our other young."

"What's this? Training – I gave no permission for this. Ye'll not make my children yours." To the king's bewilderment, Conall appeared neither offended nor angry. Instead, a broad grin had spread upwards from his mouth and his blue eyes glistened.

"Know your enemy, Drostan."

They walked through the entrance of the square and were greeted by the sounds of wooden swords clacking against wooden shields, bowstrings thrumming and arrows thudding into straw and wood targets. In a far corner, young apprentices sat on ponies for the first time. A scream of recognition was heard and Drostan's son and daughter separated from the mass and ran towards their father. Flushed with the exertion of the training, they came to a halt a pace from their father and bowed. The boy held sword and shield; the girl a bow and quiver.

"It was their choice," said Nikandros, "I think they were bored doing nothing while the other young appeared to be having fun."

For once Drostan was speechless. He was obviously also relieved and pleased. At the pleading faces of his children, his face broke into a wide smile and he nodded, "Go back to yer training. I'll not have ye disgrace me by missing lessons. Show these bastards how we fight and endure." Then in a more serious tone, he said to Conall, "It'll be dark in a while. Stoke the cooking fires and bring out the beer. I'm yer guest of honor and deserve a feast. We have important things to discuss."

The three turned and headed for the entrance to the settlement. As they strode towards the towering broch, Drostan noted the bound figure of Cassius and paused within earshot of the Roman, "Is that who's responsible for yer presence in my land?" Conall nodded. "Perhaps I should kill the bastard myself. Why's he still alive?"

Noticing the uncertainty in Conall's eyes and his clenched jaw, Drostan spoke again, "Allow an older warrior and fellow king to give ye a piece of advice. Always keep things simple. However useful ye think he may be in the future, forget it. It likely won't happen and ye'll have to dig yerself out of the shite ye find yerself in. Kill him in whatever way gives ye the most satisfaction. Then forget the bastard."

Conall inwardly groaned at the friendly rivalry for Mòrag. He could hardly blame Íar and Nikandros or order that they stay away. She was a sumptuous feast for the eyes as well as a formidable warrior, but the last thing he needed was two of his best commanders squabbling over the Aos an Fhithich princess. As he glanced around the table, the look on Brandubh's face told him that he was experiencing the same trepidation.

It was noticeable as well that Mongfhionn and the Druid had yet to come to a workable accommodation. Conflict simmered below the surface of that particular deep and dark pool.

Drostan's voice brought his focus back, "I've no love for Finnean Mac Sèitheach. I'd prefer a sturdier neighbor to keep the bastard southern tribes that he seems so keen to cultivate in their place. Yet, he has my oath to defend his territory. Although I may stretch it, I will not break my word. If ye haven't taken Dùn Na Mèadaidh and left these lands by spring, then I have little choice. I'll send enough men to support Finnean and hold the dùn." There was no animosity in Drostan's voice as he spoke, just an acceptance of reality.

Conall scratched at a scraggly beard. He sat back in the wooden chair, his fingers beating an uneven tattoo on the arms. He had envisaged a spring campaign after a winter's rest, but now everything pointed to a battle in the cold, tear-drawing winds and snows of winter. At least, he reflected, the ground would be firmer in winter. They would not have to contend with the rains of spring and the muddy marshlands that surrounded Dùn Na Mèadaidh. Did he see the hand of the Goddess in revising his plans? He straightened up.

"Imbolg! We attack on the feast of Imbolg," he said.

"Will we be ready?" asked Cúscraid.

"The men are in good condition," said Íar. "Between the work at A' Chrìon Làraich and the fighting, we're in better battle condition than expected. The men just won't have their usual winter hibernation!" To Conall's unspoken question he added, "The horses are in great condition too. If we have to fight in open ground then the frost-hardened dirt will suit us."

In the end there was only mild disagreement with Conall's choice of timing and possible tactics. He was still left with the problem of Cassius. Drostan's counsel burdened his thoughts.

CHAPTER 26

It was a stark, crisp night. Clear skies were sprinkled with glimmering stars. Silvery moonlight reflected off the snow-covered landscape giving it a bluish sheen. The guards positioned around the settlement and outer dwellings stamped their feet and clapped hands. The sound was muffled. Both were swaddled in strips of cloth to keep their circulation flowing. Most had multiple layers of clothing and pelts to keep the cold at bay. Only eyes were visible on faces masked to protect against the bone-chilling gusts of wind.

Thankfully, they would shortly be relieved. A hot meal was always available from the huge iron cauldrons simmering over hot embers. Then it would be time to sleep. The lucky ones had a family they could burrow into or warm body to snuggle against. Others invested in a camp whore. In a cold winter it was well worth the cost.

From the mountains they came. Hundreds moved silently through the forest, hunger gnawing at their bellies. They halted at the forest edge, waiting for the leader to give his commands. His yellow eyes scanned the valley and settled on the dark shapes that rose from the snow-covered ground. He sensed danger, but food was more important – and his strong sense of smell knew food was plentiful in the dwellings of this tribe. The leader barked softly. The call was relayed and the families moved from the cover of the trees into the open ground. Gray shapes trailing long black shadows padded towards the community, their speed increasing with each pace.

In the broch, Conall's wolfhounds growled. Low at first, but with increasing loudness and urgency. Their hackles stood up and they moved towards the entrance. They were joined by hounds belonging to Fearghal, Íar and Brion. Conall rubbed gritty, tired eyes, rolled over and tossing his coverings aside reached for his axes. Curses from the adjacent stalls and above told him that they too were reluctantly arousing from their slumbers.

Soon, in the dim light shed by the glowing central fire and remains of the rushlights, an assortment of naked and semi-naked men and women joined the hounds and listened. Outside the howling and barking from the settlement's many wolfhounds began to crescendo. An occasional sharp, "Shut up!" from a master did little to stem the noise.

It was then that the alpha chose to announce the raiders' presence. Across the valley resounded a long, smooth call to the kill. It was immediately taken up by the family packs alternating between a howl and a rolling high-pitched, two-tone whine. The harmonizing between the packs was as beautiful as the threat was awful. It also gave the impression of thousands rather than hundreds.

On the mountainsides the wailing of the mná-sidhe commenced. "To arms! Let the hounds out," Conall ordered as he ran for the settlement gates. Like the alpha-wolf, Conall's call was quickly taken up by those around him. Battle horns blasted out to rouse those within the solid walls of the perimeter and to alert the surrounding dwellings and barracks. Within the settlement, men and women grabbed weapons, shields, and torches. Some were able to grab an item of clothing; most took to the field in whatever they slept.

The settlement dwellings were a mix of family housing and warrior quarters. Their guards had little warning and no chance to defend themselves as snarling masses of fur, muscle and teeth leapt from the shadows. Yellow teeth bared and lips drawn back, the first wave ripped throats and crushed bones with impunity. Blood splashed wooden buildings and spilled onto the dirt as men fell. They quickly became carcasses to be torn apart. Lumps of meat and streamers of flesh, skin and bone were tossed into the air.

A new shrieking tone rose high above the nightmare of ravenous wolves and the screams of male and female guards being clawed and bitten. Women and children, unprotected and at the mercy of an enemy whose hunger was insatiable cried out for help. Many dwelling entrances were not barred, carelessly left unsecured after someone had taken a midnight piss. The invitation was readily accepted by the packs. Mothers and grandparents threw themselves between their children and the beasts or shielded babies with their bodies to little avail. The pack slaughtered at will in the tight confines of the wooden buildings. Mothers lay torn and bleeding. For some, their last sight was of their offspring being dragged out into the cold.

To Conall, it seemed an agonizingly long time before the warriors from the settlement and the outside barracks reached the carnage. By this time the second and third wave of wolves were deep in the camp. Dark shapes prowled in small groups between the wooden buildings, looking for prey. They were prevented from entering the settlement as the solid, oak gates slammed shut. The few wolves that came close were met with javelins and arrows. Their bodies were dragged off by their companions – after all, flesh was flesh.

The first wave of wolves was the strongest and the fastest. Having taken their prey, they savored a quick feast before dragging the carcasses off toward the forest. Subsequent waves were caught between three formations of warriors moving in from the west, east and south. Cúscraid had chosen to lodge with his men on the western hill camp and brought them to the battle. Likewise, Brandubh had elected to remain with his warriors on the eastern camp by the river. His spears moved steadily towards the struggle.

The wolfhounds made contact first and the air was filled with snarling and the snapping of teeth as beast fought beast. Muzzles and teeth were stained red, bones were crushed with vice-like jaws, and throats were ripped open. The wolf attack faltered, and then came to a standstill as the human warriors finally engaged. The alpha-wolf's bright yellow eyes constantly scanned the field and he howled warnings. Long scars on his face and body witnessed that he had fought men before. He knew of their sharp teeth – their swords, axes and spears. From their diminishing voices he knew his army was losing ground. He knew the wolf could never win and that men were less merciful than the wolf. He growled and whined, took a final bite of soft pale flesh from the small body at his feet and then howled for the pack to retreat.

Grim-faced warriors hacked, sliced and stabbed at the retreating wolves. In contrast to the snarling and howling of the wolves they slaughtered in almost total silence. Brandubh's and Cúscraid's contingents closed off the escape route for the predators and a triangle of death snapped shut. The alpha trotted in the shadows, herding his army, driving them north to escape the trap. He snapped and snarled at the stupid with their muzzles still deep in bodies – some alive, most dead. From the calls of the families, he knew that they had lost over half of their numbers. Yet this was not a bad thing, less mouths to feed. In the spring and summer the bitches would bring forth their crop and the packs would be replenished.

The humans closed in, hacking and stabbing at the dark shapes. Many, being unarmored or even clothed were badly bitten. A few fell to the beasts. The wolfhounds circled the triangle seeking out those wolves who had escaped the trap. Some bounded towards the forest hoping to catch the wolves before they melted into the dense woods. The alpha grew concerned as his numbers dwindled. He drove his packs forward with more urgency. A few sacrificed and a breach in the line of warriors would see the pack escape.

He was almost successful.

Before him a dark presence rose from the shadows. He was confused. The female had no scent, but his keen eyes saw the curling designs on her naked body and the aura that surrounded her. The alpha-wolf whined as he heard the vibration of the bow and sprang towards the archer. The arrow pierced his left eye, penetrating his brain. In the instant before his body struck, the Huntress had dropped her bow and slid two long blades from their sheaths. She did little more than hold the blades steady as his momentum plunged the iron deep into his chest. He whimpered as the life flowed from him.

The Huntress fell under the weight of the beast. As she lay gathering strength she felt the wolf's warm blood soak her body. To her mind it was not an unpleasant feeling.

A light fall of morning snow did little to cover a landscape stained a dull red and clotted with the remains of people and beasts. Younger warriors viewed the butchery inside the dwellings where the wolves had gained entrance and threw up. Floors were covered in frozen pools of crimson-black. Gore was splattered on walls. Mutilated corpses and body fragments of all ages lay strewn about.

Families had died together, their eyes still open in terror. As he stepped inside one home, Conall forced his stomach to hold his food. His eyes glistened with tears as he took in the tragedy. Turning to Cúscraid he said, with a harshness that belied his feelings, "Burn the buildings. It will serve as their funeral pyre." Cúscraid dipped his head. No words were adequate.

A soft cry came from the far end of the building as they turned to leave. Startled, Conall strode through the blood and gore, his eyes searching for a sign of life. Perhaps a spirit remained or his mind was playing tricks. The cry came again, stronger. Conall's eyes fell on the body of a female. What remained of her head slumped against the wall. Her back was carved open to the bone and her neck slashed so deeply that only gristle and shards of bone held her head in place. Gently he nudged a bloody shoulder. The woman fell backwards and her head rolled to the side. Arms locked by death held her baby tight to her breast. Conall gently pried the arms apart and lifted the child from the torso.

Once outside he snapped at the pale-faced warriors, "You will search all the dwellings thoroughly - again. Lay the bodies and parts out so that no-one is missed. I will inspect the homes before we fire them." Then, baby in his arms, he strode towards his broch.

It was the Winter Solstice before the horror of the attack faded. It would never be forgotten. The dead wolves were skinned and their pelts salted and stretched on racks made of alder branches to dry. In the harsh conditions of the north, the need for warmth and survival overcame any distaste in wearing coverings, even from a tainted source.

CHAPTER 27

Gràinne had almost fully recovered. A spider's web of fine scars covered her body – a permanent reminder of Diadhaidh's abuse. The scourgings had uniquely altered her tribal designs. Indeed, not even one of the Na Daoine Tùrsach would have recognized the curling patterns that now graced her body. The Goddess had purged her body of the taint of the tribe.

Nightmares continued to plague Gràinne, although their frequency had lessened. With the help of Mongfhionn, and even Mórrígan, she had come to terms with the trauma. That the king chose to treat her as a younger sister, and widely broadcast this, made it easier for her to overcome the suspicion provoked by her heritage, particularly in the minds of the Aos an Fhithich community. Her gratitude crept into her dreams causing her to blush as she looked on Conall - especially if coincidently he returned her glance.

Although still young - she was only fifteen summers, Gràinne had, with Conall's approval, adopted the rescued baby. Tuathal's wet nurse was more than happy that the milk flowing from her nipples would not be wasted.

A very curious young woman by nature, Gràinne often made her way in her odd rolling gait, child in arms, around the settlement and the outer buildings, simply observing. Thus, she was among the first to recognize the signs of disease.

The odd sneeze had increased greatly and was often accompanied by a wet-sounding cough, usually followed by a disgusting glob of yellow-green spit. Children's noses ran freely at this time of the year until the winter winds froze the snot in a frosted glaze above their lips. This year the number suffering was uncommonly high.

Gràinne was not alone in her concern. Fionnbharr had also noted the growing number of runny noses, flushed cheeks and coughs. His supplies of herbs were already becoming strained so that he limited his cures to only the sickest. His concern intensified as he observed films of blood in the spit of the sick. The last time he had seen similar signs was at Ráth na Chrúachain when he tended Medb, the queen of the Connachta.

"Have we displeased the Goddess?" Conall asked. "Perhaps the aes-sidhe? First the wolf attack and today we are being weakened from within. It seems too much of a coincidence." The others around the table marked the consternation on the Sidhe's face. She too had watched, with rising concern, the sickness take root and spread. Her interventions so far had done little to halt or even hold back its progress.

"No," she said, with more hope than certainty. "You have been faithful to the Goddess and the aes-sidhe. It cannot be their will."

"It's the darkness," said Mórrígan. The members of the Chomhairle greeted this with silence. "I felt its presence when I slew the alpha wolf. I still feel it when I walk around the community. We executed its priestess and slaughtered its people. This weakened the God greatly, but that is not the same as destroying it. So, it seeks revenge upon us." All felt that Mórrígan was right. None wanted to acknowledge it.

"Then we'll fight with our strengths," said Conall. "Ensure whatever sacrifices are due to the Goddess and the aes-sidhe are continued. The surface of the river is frozen but can be broken to drop the gifts into the waters." To the Druid, Conall said, "It is your duty to ensure that we do not anger the Goddess or the aes-sidhe." The Druid bowed his head. As Mongfhionn stood to protest, she was halted by Conall's raised hand. "The Druid can handle the ceremonies. I need your powers focused on healing. As usual, Fionnbharr will assist you." There was no argument to Conall's commands.

"What will we do with the sick – and the dead?" Cúscraid asked.

"The dead? That's a bit pessimistic - even for you," Fearghal said with a grim face.

Nikandros said, "He's right, Fearghal. We need to be prepared for the worst. I've seen whole villages wiped out by pestilence. We should set aside two or three of the furthermost buildings from the river. The very ill can be cared for there."

"And the dead?" Cúscraid persisted.

Conall lifted his hand in a gesture of pragmatism, "The Druid will say words over them and they will be burned. We'll trust that their journey to Tir Tairngire will be swift and their reward great. We'll take care of their families."

The sickness spread unchecked. The short winter days were filled with wracking coughs, aching bodies and fevers. The pungent odor of shit and sour vomit was omnipresent. Babies with arses raw from diarrhea and small children unable to breathe through constantly blocked noses wailed deep into the night. Parents rocked them to a fitful sleep, cried and prayed to the Goddess for mercy.

A troubled Conall watched with pride as his people fought an unseen enemy. The cooks kept the fire pits going and the huge cauldrons filled with stews and soups. Squads of warriors patrolled the community making sure that the people had fires for warmth and something to drink. The healers, under Mongfhionn and Fionnbharr, worked to exhaustion. Brocc's teams of men and women scoured the forests seeking supplies of herbs, grasses and barks. The very sick were encouraged to rest in the buildings set aside for them. Few wanted to, but fewer were strong enough to resist.

Fevers and dehydration killed the young, exhaustion slayed the elderly, and adults drowned, their lungs filled with fluid. More than a few, too weak to fight, died by their own hand or with the help of a friend. Within less than a cycle of the moon, over a thousand had succumbed - men, women and children, young and old, warriors and tradesmen who would never feel the sun on their faces again.

The funeral fires never died. The smell of wood-smoke and

burning human flesh was inescapable. Towards the end of this dark battle a wail arose from the settlement's broch. Hundreds of tired and red-rimmed eyes turned to the building where Conall emerged carrying the limp body of Tuathal. Behind him Mongfhionn stood helpless, her face fighting for control of the rage that burned within her. Conall's children were as son and daughters to her. Beside the Sidhe, Fionnbharr slumped, exhausted and defeated, against the gray stone wall. Danu and Brighid screeched and ran to join their father, but were quickly caught by Fearghal and Brion who returned them to the broch and their grieving mother.

The people quickly lined the path to the funeral pyres. In the short time that it took Conall to tramp the distance men had built a separate pyre for the Ériu prince and draped it in white cloth.

Craiftine stood beside the pyre and as Conall laid the body of his son on the pyre, he played a haunting melody on his harp. In the background, the bodhráns had taken their mournful beat from Craiftine. A gem-encrusted dagger – a present on his birth, was laid on the cloth. It was a fitting tribute to the young prince.

The Druid stepped forward, but on seeing Mongfhionn approach, he bowed and stepped back. She acknowledged the Druid with a nod and took her place beside Conall. Fearghal handed Conall a burning brand, laying a hand on his friend's shoulder in support. Then, as the torch was put to the pyre, Mongfhionn chanted. Her lament was filled with sadness harmonizing perfectly with Craiftine's harp.

The flaring heat scorched the ground, yet Conall stood steadfast and stone-faced beside the pyre until it had become ashes. His friends and commanders stood at his back. To their rear his loyal caomhnóirí lined up. Behind them, all who could remain upright – army and followers, stood with heads bowed. Many wailed and wept openly. Tears left pale tracks on faces darkened by grime and smoke. In this manner, they bade farewell to Tuathal Mac Conall, Prince of Ráth na Conall, son of Conall and Mórrígan. All prayed for his safe journey to Tír inna n-Óc.

On the mountainside, the wailing of the bean-sidhe ushered Tuathal's spirit to Tír inna n-Óc. In its wake arose a disturbing refrain as Mórrígan lifted up her arms and mourned her son. On each arm, blood trickled from shallow, criss-crossed cuts.

Conall turned to the mass before him, uttered a hoarse, "Thanks," and strode off in the direction of Mórrígan's song. A loud cry of anguish came from the king as he disappeared into the dusk.

His people wept.

The halls that had housed the sick and the dying lay smoldering as white, vaporous tendrils curled up into the snow-laden sky. Each building was encircled with a corona of scorched dirt. No-one stepped onto that blackened ground. The price had been paid, the pestilence gone, defeated. Cassius surveyed his surroundings as he took his first piss of the day. The scene was eerie, ethereal, and unnatural. Banks of fog and snow settled over the community. The fog had a gentle swell and from time to time wisps broke away guided through the settlement by ghostly winds.

Time paused.

Men and women walked around and the warriors trained as if in a trance. They did what was necessary to survive, without any sense of joy or pleasure. Eyes stared to nowhere, in need of a spark that would relight the fires in their spirit. Their faces were streaked with gray-black ash in remembrance of the dead. One long diagonal smear for each family member dead. For some, their faces were black. In sympathy, the fortunate marked their foreheads with a smear of ash. Occasionally, the people would pause and look to the mountains. Each time they would heave a melancholy sigh and continue their chores.

Cassius shivered and longed for Rome, for civilization and for civilized gods. These barbarian lands of superstition and blood did not rest easily with him. He had overheard the advice that Drostan Ruadh had given Conall. Worse, Cassius had seen Conall's eyes. The young king's heart might still be wrestling with the decision, but Cassius knew Conall's reasoning agreed with Drostan. The Roman was a loose end to be tied off and buried. To where could he run?

Brion paced to and fro on the ramparts. He scratched the stubble on his uncharacteristically unscraped chin and ran fingers through unkempt hair. In his agitation, the long scar on his cheek appeared as a stark white line. Áine tried to soothe her partner, but gave up. The ruiri and his queen had vanished. Brion had lost both his sister and his childhood friend. Hundreds of patrols had been sent out in search of them, with no result. Risking his passage to Mag Mell or possibly ensuring an imminent journey there, he cursed, shouted and railed against the Goddess, Mongfhionn and the Druid. Exhausted from a lack of sleep, he slumped against the cold stone and simply wished for their return.

He heard the tramp of boots on the ramparts and the creaking of iron hinges as the great oak gates of the settlement were thrown open. Turning around he glared at Íar who was in animated conversation with Nikandros, Cúscraid and Brandubh. His confusion was complete as he watched the two hundred men of Conall's guard exit the settlement in full armor.

"The Hag take you all," Brion barked. "What's going on?"

For a moment, Brion's three friends looked at him as if he were mad. "Someone here will die if I do not get some answers. All I see is white snow on the ground and trees covered in more white snow," growled Brion.

Then they understood, "You're blind as a bat, Brion ó Cathasaigh," said Íar pointing to the north. "Look." But Brion and Áine had been staring for so long at the stark white landscape, that they truly had become blind.

By this time Mongfhionn had joined the group. She grabbed Brion by the shoulders and whirling him around thumped her oak staff against his forehead. Dazed, he sat down hard on the walkway. "What was that for?"

"Look, you stupid man," said Mongfhionn.

As he turned around, the landscape seemed changed and he could make out much more detail. In the far north of the valley, he saw two shimmering shapes. His eyes glistened with hope. "Could be anyone. Could be animals." he said, for once wishing that someone would tell him he was being an eejit. His friends did not hesitate.

By the time Conall and Mórrígan had got to within five hundred paces of A' Chrìon Làraich, the whole community had assembled and a thunderous roar assaulted the heavens. The spark that gave them purpose had returned. Even the ravens, silent for so long, took to the winter sky, filling the air with their song. The pair halted as if uncertain, and then started walking again. It was then Cúscraid groaned, "They're both naked, you know," he said to Íar.

The huge warrior grinned and nodded, "Strange times, Cúscraid. Strange times." Beside them, Brandubh nodded his approval at the lack of clothing and murmured something about Conall and Mórrígan being more Aos an Fhithich than Ériu.

Fittingly, it was Fearghal who strode forward to meet them. Taller than both, he towered over the pair as he stared them up and down. His inspection was so intense that Mórrígan mocked, "Fearghal Ruad, Mongfhionn will not be pleased at your close appreciation of my body."

Surprisingly, Fearghal ignored the banter and walked around the pair. There was a sharp, stinging smack delivered without restraint by a rough calloused hand almost the size of her round cheek. It was accompanied by a yelp of disbelief, followed by anger and embarrassment as Mórrígan rubbed her fast reddening arse. Conall turned to admonish his second-in-command, too slow to avoid the fist that smacked his jaw and landed him on his arse.

"I'm curious as to how this will turn out," said Nikandros to Cúscraid.

"You and me both – and about ten thousand others as well," replied Cúscraid.

"Are you going to explain yourself, Fearghal?" Conall asked rubbing his tender jaw.

Fearghal met Mórrígan's the eyes first, "You may have been spirits sent to deceive us. Apart from that I should have smacked your arse long before this. You're a queen – act like it." Then he looked into Conall's eyes, "As for you, you're a king. Your duty is to your people. You do not go wandering off. If you have issues, you get drunk, you talk to your friends and advisers. The people need their king to be with them – not moping about."

Shamefaced, Conall and Mórrígan, nodded. Then Conall added, "I suppose I'll not have Urard take your head for striking your king - and queen."

Fearghal said, "Hmmmmph," After giving Conall a hard stare he stretched out his hand to help him to his feet. "If you think I'm going to shave my head, get tattoos like yours and run about naked, you've another think coming. Put some clothes on. You'll freeze your balls off." He flipped a hand at Mórrígan, "Her nipples are already dangerous weapons!"

He spun around and took a single pace before he turned back, "We all loved Tuathal and suffer from his loss, but many of your subjects lost mothers, fathers, partners and children. You're not alone. Be with your people." As he stalked back to the settlement he passed Mongfhionn bearing two cloaks.

"Interesting choice of sigils, Conall," Mongfhionn said inspecting his chest and arms, "You will of course tell me about them – when you're ready. I am averse to mysteries." Then the Sidhe noticed two small matching designs on Mórrígan and Conall's face. "Tuathal?" she queried. They both nodded assent.

The Winter Solstice approached as the Chomhairle, expanded to include Brandubh and the Druid, gathered around the solid, oak table in the broch. A few members paced the wooden floor and others lounged against the stone-faced walls. They assumed that they been called to discuss the assault on Dùn Na Mèadaidh. This idea was quickly disabused when Conall said, "I want lookouts placed on the mountains to the south. Three teams of four should be sufficient. Mix the teams with warriors from both tribes."

Nikandros said, "I take it we're expecting company." Long tresses of blue-black hair touched the table and obsidian-black eyes reflected the red, glowing fire. His lips parted in a smile of expectation.

"I think we may be attacked – soon," Conall replied.

"You think – or you know?" Cúscraid asked. "When and by whom?"

"I don't know who. As to when, I hope it is not too late for the lookouts to be useful." Conall paused and added reluctantly, "I had a premonition… a dream." Rolling eyes, raised eyebrows and skeptical sighs greeted his words.

Fearghal immediately turned to Mongfhionn. "Did you have anything to do with this?"

The Sidhe laughed shaking her head. "No, but I sense he is right."

It was the pragmatic Cúscraid who closed the line of thought. "I believe Conall."

Íar slapped him hard on the back. "By the Hag, the Sidhe's finally converted the non-believer."

A smiling Cúscraid bowed to Mongfhionn, "Not quite." He paused to scan the curious eyes trained on him and said, "Things come in threes. We've had wolves and disease. Makes sense that we're due a third trial." The room was silent for a moment and then, led by Íar, it erupted into laughter.

Mórrígan followed Nikandros as the Chomhairle dispersed. Weaving a path between the houses and then out of the perimeter gates, she kept a discrete distance between them. The Spartan turned east towards the buildings at the river and Mórrígan still followed. She increased her pace to approach him, but as she emerged from between two buildings, the Spartan was nowhere in sight. Angry at losing her prey, she let herself stamp her foot and turned to retrace her steps.

The cold, point of steel against her throat brought her to an abrupt halt. "I was an assassin in a former life. I know when I am being followed. I also know there have been differences between us in the past. Why are you stalking me?"

Startled, Mórrígan stammered, "Stalking? No. I need to speak with you - in private."

"I am also not in the habit of bedding my king and friend's lady," Nikandros said. That remark elicited a sharp slap in the face.

"Your ego blinds you Nikandros, although your loyalty does you credit. I have a more basic need that requires your expertise." Nikandros' right eyebrow turned up as Mórrígan said, "I want you to train me to use these." Mórrígan held out the knives she had taken off the charred corpse in the Na Daoine Smeurta village.

Nikandros reached out and held the knives, "Assassins' blades. Good balance, good steel, longer than a dagger, but shorter than a sword, one edge serrated, the other sharpened to a cutting edge. Why? You're good with the bow – likely the best in the camp, excluding me."

"I need to know how to fight in the battle – not from afar. My future is not as an archer. Áine can lead the archers. She's as good as me and a better captain. I have had a glimpse of my future and it is – complicated."

As he handed the blades back, Nikandros bowed, "Meet me on the training ground every morning at dawn." Mórrígan nodded and smiled. The Spartan laughed, "Likely, you'll not be smiling after a few sessions with me."

The face of Finnean Mac Sèitheach, king of the Na Mèadaidh, was suffused with rage. Blue veins, visible through the thin screen of his snow-white hair, throbbed on his neck. He had discovered that Ualraig, the commander of the southern mercenaries, had sent half of his force, almost three thousand warriors, on a raid to A' Chrìon Làraich.

The mercenaries were from the Aos na h-Àirde – the High Peoples. Finnean had seen the tribe as an ideal addition to his plans for confederation. Those plans were rapidly becoming obsolete. Worse, the mercenary leader had not consulted with him.

"You're a fool, Ualraig! Besides dividing your force and weakening the defense of Dùn Na Mèadaidh, do you know who lives at A' Chrìon Làraich? Drostan Ruadh's heir and his eldest daughter. We need Drostan's men or the kingdom of Na Mèadaidh will fall to this barbarian king." It frustrated Finnean beyond words that even as he

fulminated at the man before him, there was little response save a
mocking smile and an occasional sigh of boredom.

Finnean finally started to use his considerable mind and he
slumped back in his throne in shocked realization of what was happening. "That's your real mission – to kill Drostan's heirs."

"I'm disappointed in you, Finnean," said Ualraig. "I had heard
your cunning and intelligence was to be feared. It appears that is not
the case. Dùn Na Mèadaidh will become our base of operations for
our conquest of the north. You, if you behave, may be allowed to
govern your territory – meagre as it is. The Aos na h-Àirde already
outnumber the Aos na Coille. In the name of our Goddess, Brighid,
we will be victorious." Ualraig stood and breezily bowed while in no
sense acknowledging Finnean's authority. It was as if Finnean were
already a puppet.

"Your men will perish in the mountains," said Finnean.

"We come from the mountains. We live in the mountains, the
high places. They hold no fears or surprises for us."

In a final act of defiance, Finnean held the mercenary's gaze with
his violet-red stare and snarled, "My forces in Dùn Na Mèadaidh outnumber yours by three-to-one."

Ualraig smiled cruelly, "True. Even though my men are worth
three or four of yours, you might well prevail, but how will your
rabble fare against the ten or twenty thousand of my people who will
be here in the spring?"

Their orders were clear. If they spotted the attackers they were
to light the bonfires, wait until they saw a flaming arrow in the sky,
then douse the fires and return to A' Chrìon Làraich. The fires were
built below and on the northern slope of the peaks from which they
watched. Hopefully, they were out of sight of the enemy.

It was a hard tramp for the Aos na h-Àirde, if not overly haz-
ardous. They were used to the mountains so their pace was steady.
The mercenaries struck out heading west from Dùn Na Mèadaidh
until they reached a large loch dusted with snow. In mid-winter the

time from sunrise to sunset was short and made worse by the almost permanent cloud cover. So the band also travelled by night, making use of torches and the moonlight when the skies cleared. They held axes or spears. A few had swords. Few carried shields. Multiple layers of clothing and animal pelts would minimize or even stop a blade. Legs were well wrapped and hands were bound with strips of cloth – enough to prevent freezing, but not to interfere with the use of their chosen weapons.

A few were lost testing the thickness of the ice on the southern, wider stretch of the loch. So the raiding party clung to the banks, plunging through deep drifts of snow, until the loch narrowed and the ice became stronger. Once the ice was firm, they picked up the pace, arriving at the mountain range to the south of A' Chrìon Làraich. Keeping the towering crag of A' Bheinn Mhòr in sight they marched along the crest of the smaller peaks. Mountains were home to the Aos na h-Àirde. Even in the thick snow and ice, they made excellent progress.

A' Chrìon Làraich lay bathed in hoary moonlight. There was not much to see from this distance. Snow blanketed the landscape and the settlement. Solid shapes were softened and blurred with no distinction between buildings or mounds of dirt. A faint smell of wood-smoke and old food hung the air.

The slope to the settlement was gentle and heavily forested with pines. It merged with the level wooded valley and its wildwood blend of hardwoods and thick undergrowth. Closer to the village, the trees had been cleared for crops. At the sound of horses snorting and whinnying, the leader of the band cursed. It would be difficult to maintain their advantage of surprise once they reached the corrals and animal pens. He signaled his men to move to the edge of the tree line. There, they waited for the dawn.

Beauty and ugliness are often fellow travelers. The attackers were aroused from their brief sleep to a glorious sunrise. It was one of those rare winter mornings when the sun ascended, a burning orb that hovered over the horizon burnishing the land in fire-gold tones. It had rained during the night, covering the valley and forests in a glaze of crystal that glittered and sparkled under the sun. To the residents of A' Chrìon Làraich it was a beautiful scene; to the raiders a bad dream.

The Aos na h-Àirde chieftain was stunned. He had been expecting a small village. Instead he saw a fortress. The towering broch was surrounded by two circles of glistening stone walls. Numerous wooden halls and animal shelters were grouped around the fortress. Thick grey-blue smoke curling upwards and the mouth-watering aroma of the cooking pits pointed to the inhabitants having been awake for some time. Of more concern to the experienced leader were the areas and channels that had been obviously left clear of obstruction – the killing fields. Yet the chieftain clung to the hope that while it was impressive, it was still a settlement populated by farmers and tradespeople – not warriors. That was his information.

The skirmish – for to call it a battle would imply that there were two reasonably similar opponents, began as the Aos na h-Àirde leader roared, "Attack!" The three thousand poured from the edge of the forest, flowing towards the western entrance of A' Chrìon Làraich. "It's too easy," the breathless chieftain thought as he came within sight of the main gateway. It was then he broke his ankle on one of the many traps laid by Cúscraid.

As the chieftain stumbled, cursing his luck, he saw the red shields appear before the gateway. He smiled, only maybe two hundred. His men would slaughter them. This perception dimmed as a cloud of arrows and stones fell on his men as the bows and slings on the wall went into action. The blood of his warriors began to flow. The sound of horses to the north diverted his attention. He watched as the Ériu cavalry, red fox tails spinning atop their helmets, galloped past and crashed into his force. A huge warrior gleefully roared commands as he chopped right and left with a long-handled axe. The bronze-armored apparition beside him carved a bloody path with an impossibly long black spear.

The Aos na h-Àirde men broke, but were unable to scatter. More accurately, they were not allowed to disperse. On their western flank, a long double row of red shields with black ravens glared at them. On the eastern flank, Aos an Fhithich spears marched steadily forward driving them onto the red wall, a wall as hard as rock, but with iron teeth.

Driven south by the mounted warriors, the Aos na h-Àirde could either face the wall or retreat to the mountain. Their commander snarled and snapped like a wounded animal. Helpless and isolated from the fight he could only watch. The two hundred shields from the entrance marched toward him and his bodyguard. He attempted to stand. His ankle would not support his weight and he fell to one knee. His guard took up position between him and the shields. They lasted no longer than a few ragged breaths before being brought down by a volley of javelins.

He waited behind their bleeding corpses, axe wavering in his hand. A single warrior stepped from the shields. He was of average height, well-muscled and covered in scars. He removed an ornate helmet revealing a shaven head which showed signs of dark stubble. Steel-blue eyes looked upon the mercenary leader with a smoldering anger. The Ériu warrior handed his shield to a tall, red-headed man and, axe in hand, he moved closer. The mercenary scowled. Seeing little point in prolonging their meeting or engaging in conversation, he simply said, "End it," and exposed his neck.

Conall's axe severed skin, flesh, muscle and bone. The sweeping arc jarred his arm as the curved blade met increasing resistance. Blood spurted outwards and upwards from ruptured arteries then ebbed. It took Conall another cut to severe the remaining strings of gristle and tendons before the head rolled free.

Like an animal caught in a trap and forced to bite off limbs to survive, the attackers left a bloody trail of bodies, limbs and guts while retreating to the forests and southern slopes. The Aos na h-Àirde chieftains who survived wondered why their enemy did not follow them into the woods. The same though occurred to Conall's commanders.

"They will not make it home," he said.

A third of the attacking force escaped to the mountains. They heaved great sighs of relief as they approached the ridge. Then a thick line of Aos na Coille appeared along the crest.

"That bastard Conall didn't leave many for us. I want one alive.

Slaughter the rest." Drostan Ruadh's commander smiled crookedly through missing teeth and lifted a scarred chin to the warrior next to him. Battle horns sounded out across the mountain top and the mass of warriors descended on the remnant of the raiding party.

The survivor was bloodied and feverish, but thankful to be alive. He stood before Finnean and Ualraig and waited to be dismissed after recounting the tale of the disastrous raid. "Not one survived?" queried Finnean in a tone that sent shivers up the warrior's already chilled spine.

"None."

There was the barest flicker of Finnean's eyebrow and the warrior standing behind the survivor in a swift motion slid a blade along the poor man's throat. Gargling blood as he slumped to the floor, the man died after a few spasms. "His report is truly accurate. There are no survivors."

Ualraig would likely have done the same, but was enraged at Finnean usurping his authority. He stood up, hands hovering over his blades. "If your fingers touch your blades," said Finnean, "you will suffer a worse fate than this unfortunate messenger." The hackles on the back of Ualraig's neck told him that there was more than one Na Mèadaidh warrior standing behind him. He slumped back into the chair and rubbed his chin as he considered his precarious position.

"Good. Let me summarize. Without my approval, you sent a raiding party – an army, into Drostan Ruadh's territory to attack A' Chrìon Làraich and assassinate his heirs. Your men were slaughtered, many by Conall Mac Gabhann's warriors, the rest apparently by Drostan's men."

"I will remove the rest of my warriors from Dùn Na Mèadaidh and return to Aos na h-Àirde territory."

"No you won't. If you try, I will hang you from a tree and gut you in front of your men." Finnean relished the shock on the face of the Aos na h-Àirde. "The passages south are blocked by snow. There is no retreat for you. You will remain and support the defense of Dùn Na

Mèadaidh. You will take orders from me and my battle commander.

"All you have achieved is to give Conall Mac Gabhann battle practice. I'll be surprised if he waits until spring to attack. And if he waits until the spring then I can assure you that the promised warriors from Drostan will not materialize. In fact, we'll be fortunate if Drostan and Conall have not already joined forces."

Ualraig inwardly seethed. Gathering his thoughts he stood, bowed and left the room. Like a wasp caught in a spider's web he would bide his time until he could strike.

CHAPTER 28

They set out in the pre-dawn light. Boots crunched through the icy crust of freshly laid snow. It was a small party. The surviving members of the families murdered at Ráth na Conall – the Mac Gabhanns, the ó Dubhghaills, the ó Cathasaighs, the ó Cuileannáins and the ó Brics, along with Fearghal, Mongfhionn, Íar, Nikandros and the Druid. The Druid's presence was an enigma, although no objections were voiced. Nikandros was present at the request of Cathán. A normally talkative group, on this morning they were silent, caught up in their own sober reflections and memories.

The sun rose, bathing the pristine white landscape in pale golds and pinks. At the center of a small, natural clearing stood two men - the Roman, Cassius Fabius Scaeva and the colossal Urard. Cassius shivered as he observed the party approach and drew his purple cloak tighter around him. Urard stood like a rock, impermeable to wind or cold.

Inwardly, Cassius remonstrated with himself. He had left it too late to run, to escape. The attack on A' Chrìon Làraich had prompted a revision of Conall Mac Gabhann's thinking. There was a need to clear away some outstanding matters – including Cassius. He smiled, it was a pity that he would not see how Conall fared against the might of Rome or even the other barbarian tribes. While he stubbornly was unable to accept that Conall was equal to any Roman, Cassius recognized the Ériu leader as a clever and ruthless enemy. His eventual death would be a thing of beauty to watch.

Under the snow-burdened canopy of trees, the cathedral atmosphere of the forest lent a solemnity to the occasion. No animal or bird call echoed through the woods. The tall, black-cloaked Druid stepped forward. "The Law is for our tribes, not foreigners," he said. "Yet, it seems to me that natural justice approves what will be done." He addressed Cassius directly, "Do you have anything to say? Any prayers to offer to your gods?"

The Roman straightened himself up, his proud lineage reasserting itself and was about to shake his head. He had after all talked incessantly throughout his confinement, but he changed his mind. "I wish you luck, Barbarian," he said with an oily smile, "and hope you do get justice with the death of Marcus Fabius Ambustus. I fear, however, you will die – likely gloriously, before the might and walls of Rome.

"I leave you with a single piece of advice – beware of family. They deceive and disappoint." Cassius regarded Conall. "And I ask one courtesy," he said. "That it is by your hand I die. Let our eyes meet when you take my life."

The silence deepened. After a moment, a few whispered, "No." Conall raised his left hand to halt the murmuring and walked forward to stand a pace in front of the Roman. Perhaps for the first time, both men looked deep into each other's souls with some measure of understanding. Conall placed his left hand on Cassius' shoulder, as if brother were greeting brother. There was a soft, quick movement followed by a grunt from both men.

The sword was thrust between Cassius' ribs and upwards to impale his heart. Its point exited between the Roman's shoulder blades. Hot blood streamed over the sword's hilt and Conall's hand, splashing his tunic and boots. Cassius's left hand gripped Conall's shoulder, almost drawing a gasp of pain from the Ériu king. Wine-colored eyes held Conall's for a moment. A whispered, "See you in Tartarus, Barbarian," croaked from bloody lips as the Roman's life ebbed and his grasp slackened. The corpse of Cassius Fabius Scaeva, son of Rome, slumped into the snow.

"You could be right, Roman," sighed Conall. "You could be right."

CHAPTER 29

The army said their goodbyes at A' Chrìon Làraich, leaving friends and loved ones under Cúscraid's protection. Two hundred and fifty Ériu men and a handful of archers remained under Cúscraid's command. On the instruction of Drostan Ruadh, the hundred Aos na Coille warriors also submitted to his authority. As a precaution, since many of the inner dwellings were deserted, Cúscraid ordered all remaining to gather within the settlement's stone-walled perimeter.

Only Ròidh Mac Eachdonn and his five hundred Aos an Eich spears choose to lodge outside the ramparts. The official reason for the separation was that they wanted more room. Privately, Cúscraid was aware that Ròidh was pissed off at not being included on the attack on Dùn Na Mèadaidh, and chose to sulk in one of the outer dwellings.

The column was a slash of vibrant colors against a stark background and stretched for almost two thousand paces as it snaked its way southwards. At the army's head, Brandubh's thousand warriors forged a path through the wooded slopes and valleys. Dressed in their usual dark green and black plaids, even they stood out against the white canvas.

Sweeping along the flanks of the main army, Íar's cavalry – over seven hundred horses, wore an assortment of pelts and furs over their reddish-brown, boiled leather armor and plaid pants. Mounts snorting great plumes of steam into the cold mountain air bounced in and out of deeper drifts and the red foxtails hanging from the crests of their helmets slapped against ruddy faces. Each man carried three javelins in the leather sheaths strapped to their horse's flanks; all carried the long-handled axes and the longer swords made for slashing.

The main column, consisting of two thousand five hundred warriors carried the distinctive raven banners which flapped in the occasional gust of wind. Each warrior's red and black shield was slung on his back along with several javelins and an assortment of blades. All wore armor - reddish leather inlaid with plates of iron with their plaid pants, tunics and brats in a splash of reds, yellows, greens and oranges. Many took advantage of warm wolf pelts.

Apart from random curses and oaths as men were snagged on the undergrowth or plunged through thin ice and had to be hauled, wet and shivering, from the water, the column was remarkably noiseless. Most of their weapons were covered by layers of clothing or safely sheathed in wooden scabbards covered in ornately designed leather. Many kept a javelin in their hand, not as a weapon, but to help them find and stay on a solid path.

Sárán Mac Craobhach's wagons followed. Sárán, dressed in his usual striking orange plaid pants and brat, paced constantly alongside the wagons. Most of the solid-wheeled, wooden box wagons were drawn by teams of four horses, but some had teams of oxen as a precaution in case wagons became stuck and more pulling power was needed. The wagons contained neatly stowed supplies javelins and arrows for the Mórrígan and Áine's hundred archers. The Aos an Fhithich slingers laughed at this, since they only required being near a river bed to replenish their stones. Of course, other cargo on the wagons included a band of young boys and girls with their bodhráns.

Brion's chariots brought up the rear of the column. Ten creta on iron-rimmed, spoked wheels bounced and trundled over winter-hardened ground. Their springs and chains had been muffled by cloths, but grumbled as much as Brion and his men as they struggled with the terrain. The chariots were missing one piece of equipment – the long scythes which when attached to the axel hubs would wreak savagery upon the enemy.

They crossed the narrow, frozen ponds that lay at the foot of A' Bheinn Mhòr and stumbled and ploughed their way through snow drifts that lined the river banks and concealed the tangles and thorns of the wildwood brush. Traversing frozen waters, they listened anxiously to the cracking of the ice and wondered if they would disappear into the dark waters. As they reached the shore, individually they offered up prayers to the Goddess and scrambled onto uneven, but solid ground. Camp was made in the shelter of the hills and woods near a place known as Comh-ruith - the coming together of three rivers.

Embers from the night's fires were stoked to life and the camp awakened from its slumbers, encrusted in snow and frost. A cloud of crystals rose into the air as flailing arms pumped blood around sluggish bodies. Grunts of satisfaction echoed with shouts of laughter as men stained the snow yellow and competed for the longest piss or best shape. The women rolled their eyes at such childish antics and squatted, some yelping as cold ice met bare white arses.

Conall surveyed the wide patchwork of moors, bogs, farmland and forest. It was a foreign sight. He had grown accustomed to the mountains and lochs that lay behind them. Before him, gusts of bone-numbing wind swept across a largely level terrain, whipping loose snow upwards and giving the landscape a feeling of constant movement. The snow was constantly replenished by the purple-gray clouds that hovered above.

In the distance lay a long range of rolling hills, dimly visible as a shimmering purple shadow. They were not high mountains. The crests could be readily gained – even by chariots, if they negotiated the gentle foothills that flowed from the peaks down to the northern side of the valley. In the spring, mosses, heathers and gorse covered the hills. Apart from scattered clusters of trees on the slopes, any wood had long since been removed and the ground used for meagre crops.

Dùn Na Mèadaidh lay at the far western end of the range, on

its southern side. The fort had a commanding view of the surrounding vale and hills. It also overlooked the main valley that led to the southern lowlands. Strangely it was located on the lower of two sister peaks. The dùn extended about one hundred and fifty paces in length and seventy across, with two thick stone outer walls built close to each other. The walls were linked by spanning walls at the single western entrance. Within the enclosure, a second smaller but thicker defensive wall, offset from the center, enclosed Finnean's quarters. It too was joined to the western gate and walls by a single, broad wall.

"All this to get us a winter home," Fearghal ventured, rolling his eyes as a grin spread across his face.

"If you believe that, you'll believe anything," retorted Conall. "Ròidh was a wee bit too upset at being left behind on this campaign. I think Eachdonn Breac has designs on reuniting Ceana with her family home."

"Can you blame him?"

"No, and likely the king of the Aos an Eich and his queen will get their wish. But only when we no longer have a need for the ráth and that might be some time away." Conall scratched at his head. He was still unused to its cooler, naked feel and oft wondered at the wisdom of having removed his hair in winter. Smiling at the commander of his forces, he asked "What do you think of the plan?"

"We have a plan?"

"Mongfhionn must be treating you well. You're in an exceptionally good humor," said Conall, a tinge of exasperation creeping into his voice.

Fearghal shrugged off his king's anxiety. "If our information is right then Finnean has about one thousand men inside the fort, not including several hundred of his personal guard within his inner compound, likely his best and most trusted warriors. The rest of his men and those of his mercenaries and allies are on the outside - divided between the western and eastern approaches. In total around seven thousand men. We should thank the Goddess that Finnean's ráth is small and can't hold too many warriors, so the majority has to fight on the open hillsides. Otherwise the battle would be long,

                    David H. Millar

bloody… and hopeless." Conall digested this and signaled Fearghal to continue.

"We put the archers and half of Brandubh's men on the hilltop that overlooks the fort. They kill as many as possible with stones and arrows. A contingent of five hundred shields will accompany them as protection," Fearghal ran his fingers through his long, red hair absently thinking the shaven style might be more practical. "Cúscraid would never have built his defenses on the lower peak. What was Finnean – or his predecessor, thinking?" The tall warrior shook his head.

"The rest of our shields," Fearghal continued, "about two thousand, will form up in two rows and attack and clear the eastern slopes. I'm hoping these bastards will charge down the slope and attack us. That way the shield wall and javelins will take a heavy toll. If they stay on the hilltop it will be a bloody fight for each step. Brandubh's remaining warriors will keep up a barrage of stones and clear small groups of defenders. Íar and Nikandros will bring their cavalry around to face Finnean's northern flank. That way they can fight north-south and on reasonably level ground. I'm not sure what use Brion's chariots will be – he may do better to join the shields this time.

"Once we overcome the outside defenses, then it's a bloody fight on the walls with whoever is left in the fort. This will not be pretty. The Sidhe will, as usual, improvise with her unique form of terror."

Conall sighed. "The feast of Imbolg is tomorrow. We'll rest here today, get our men in position tomorrow and start the battle at dawn after the feast. Perhaps, they'll be too drunk and will just surrender."

"Some hope!" said Fearghal.

In his gut, Ualraig knew they were close. He paced the outer walls looking for a hint, a sign of their position. His eyes were bloodshot and his vision was blurred by the snowfall. The snowfall was light, but steady and swirled under the gusting winds that buffeted the walls of Dùn Na Mèadaidh. The mercenary leader stamped feet and clapped hands to keep the cold at bay, but refused to leave the walls. Scouts had been sent out, none returned. Lost, killed or deserted he suspected.

He turned as the sound of feasting rose like a wave around him. "Shite!" he murmured, as roaring bonfires lit up the sky and the dùn. "Why not just invite them in for the feast and let them cut our throats?"

Many of the men, inside and out were well on their way to drunkenness. Flushed cheeks glowed red from the flames, the beer and the wind. Cold or not, in the small hours of the morning they would be senseless and useless in battle - except as spear fodder. The exceptions were Ualraig's two thousand Aos na h-Àirde warriors. He had warned them that he would personally flog any who were drunk. Ualraig wanted them ready for the battle. Whether or not his men would flee in the melee and let Finnean face his fate alone was unknown.

Finnean sat on the carved, wooden chair in his throne room. He rubbed two, long thin fingers along an almost invisible eyebrow. To anyone watching it was the briefest hint of self-doubt, but was quickly replaced by a sneer of condescension. He had considered the possibilities and concluded that he was safe. In an attack, it could, and likely would, get messy outside of his walls, but no one would breach his defenses.

Unlike the Aos na h-Àirde leader, Finnean's instinct told him that an attack at this time was improbable. Only a madman would fight a major battle during a midwinter storm. In his mind he saw Conall's barbarians getting drunk and carousing around their fires at A' Chrìon Làraich in celebration of Imbolg. He laughed. It was in none of their natures to forego a feast. He frowned as his mind added…or a fight.

Mórrígan's single flaming arrow made a charcoal flourish on the clear dawn sky. It signaled that she was in place on the crag overlooking Dùn Na Mèadaidh. Even with the advantage of height, it would be a stretch for the archers and slingers to reach the fort. But that was not Mórrígan's target – yet. She waited for Conall's response. It soon came, another smoking arrow shot upwards. Arrows were nocked to bowstrings and then dipped in the flames of the many small fires that had been started. Arm muscles strained as the strings were pulled back to touch wind-burned cheeks. Muffled grunts of pain escaped as flaming arrowheads licked unprotected fingertips. At a nod from Mórrígan, Áine smiled and called out, "Loose arrows."

Finnean's dùn was too small to house all the warriors assembled. Hence most lived in makeshift dwellings made of wood, stone and animal hides. For protection from the wind, these buildings were clustered against the outer perimeter walls. Snow did not bother the men. It provided a barrier to prevent warmth escaping during the night and in the morning could be readily swept off to prevent the tent from collapsing.

Wood fires burned continuously providing warmth and food. Random blazes were quite frequent among the temporary homes. Thus, the smell of burning wood and hide at first did not unduly alarm warriors whose senses were dulled from the previous night's feasting. The stink of burning flesh and black arrow shafts sprouting from their comrades' chests and backs, however, did serve to jolt them into action. They grabbed heavy clothing, spears, axes and small shields, and with gritty, bloodshot eyes searched for the enemy. By the time they were organized and moving forward, their camp was in flames and the Aos an Fhithich slings had started to whirr. Yelps accompanied the dull smack of stone on flesh and shrieks of pain from iron arrowheads.

To close on their attackers, Finnean's warriors had to descend a slope, cross a rocky gully and then charge up a snow covered hill. They had to do this in the face of a constant bombardment of arrows and stones. The men from the western camps were breathing hard by the time they came within javelin range of Torcán and Brocc's five hundred-man shield wall. The wall, two rows deep was positioned to protect the archers and slingers. Javelins were readied.

As always, each warrior held one in his hand and stuck three in the dirt. Throwing downhill, their range was longer than usual and the wall made good use of the additional time that this allowed them. At an almost leisurely pace, three volleys of javelins pinned the Na Mèadaidh force to the ground.

The shattered western flank of Finnean's forces was stunned. In an instant, its strength had been cut in half. Around and behind them lay a field of blood and gore. The cries and whimpers from injured comrades confused the wavering and unprepared. Wild-eyed and one step away from panic, they looked to their remaining warband leaders for direction. A series of quick signals from the chieftains settled the question. Those who were Na Mèadaidh gathered up their courage and charged the shield wall. Those who were Finnean's allies turned and fled to the gully and then scrambled north along it to the sloping hillside and valley floor.

Torcán grinned at Brocc as he gutted another opponent and felt the splash of warm blood on his hand and arm. Enough of thinking, this was what he understood and loved - a good fight. He was not a clever man, but he was battle-smart. Further along the line, Brocc, having also lost his last javelin, stabbed and slashed with his sword, maiming and killing. He roared challenges and taunted his enemy. All the while he regretted that Labhraidh was not by his side.

The bows and slings had ceased. Arrows were replenished by the gang of young boys and girls, who had travelled with the supply wagons. Mórrígan's archers left the remaining Na Mèadaidh force to the blades of the shield wall, saving their ammunition for the next stage of the plan. As the attack on the shield wall was brutally repulsed, she called to Brocc. He nodded and shouted, "Forward!" The shield wall steadily advanced, tramping through a slush of blood and ice, and over the torn bodies of the fallen. There would be time later to strip the bodies and give the mercy of a sharp blade to the badly injured.

Finnean was a heavy sleeper and he snored. Indeed, his snoring was so loud that it was said that the walls of the dùn vibrated.

Neither was he was a morning person. Having been encouraged from his bed by Ualraig, who stood with an insufferably smug expression on his face, there were short odds that someone's life would end in torment.

The thick walls of Finnean's sanctuary deadened most noise. It was understandable that he was angry as the king of the Na Mèadaidh was only dimly aware a battle had commenced. He was also hungry, had a foul taste in his mouth, and a sour belly. As the Aos na h-Àirde leader escorted Finnean along the wall to the western gateway, Finnean was roused enough to experience an increasing sense of foreboding. The smell of burnt wood, burnt flesh and the noise of the dying assaulted his senses.

He surveyed the surrounding landscape. It was not the pristine white winter snow broken only by bird and animal prints, to which he habitually awoke. Neither were the redcurrant hues attributable to the prolific heathers and brambles that often covered the hills. This was a scene of carnage painted with the colors of death.

"Impossible," he stammered, trying to collect his thoughts. Then he turned to the captain of the guard at the entrance. "You will hold the gate and the wall – or you will die." The captain bowed. Although comforted that he was behind two very thick stone-faced walls, he noted the strength of the besiegers as they advanced down the slope and crossed the gully. While not a pessimistic man, it struck him that he was likely going to die.

"It's only a small force," Finnean snarled. "They will not breach our walls. We will throw them back and slaughter them for their insolence."

Ualraig nodded affably, which in itself made Finnean suspicious. In a voice laced with sarcasm he said, "The view from the eastern wall is interesting." With a much more urgent step, Finnean pushed past Ualraig and strode quickly to the other end of the ramparts. Finnean's face, a naturally milky white, could not get much paler as he surveyed the vista before him.

The rest of Conall's forces stood about a thousand paces beyond the eastern wall. The ground had a slight incline in favor of the Na Mèadaidh, but as they drew closer to the dùn that advantage would lessen since the land leveled out. The shield wall was divided into three divisions. The larger consisting of two rows of five hundred men was led by Conall. To his right and left, two walls of five hundred men in two ranks were led by Fearghal and Brion. Mòrag stood with Brandubh and five hundred Aos an Fhithich in front of the three shield walls. To their far right, Íar and Nikandros waited with the mounted warriors.

"Impressive. Aren't they?" said the Aos na h-Àirde commander. "They make a great sight against the background with their banners and shields. I've heard they wear armor that can turn a blade." While his intention was to mock Finnean, Ualraig was genuinely impressed by the force arrayed before him.

"Bah! Rumors of old women afraid to fight," snapped Finnean. "Do the job you've been paid for. Perhaps you can save some honor after your recent failure."

The edge of the Ualraig's lips flickered at the insult, "I will do what must be done and for my queen." He bowed, turned his back on Finnean and walked along the eastern wall where two men held a knotted rope. He used it to lower himself to the ground. Finnean's teeth ground in displeasure at Ualraig's behavior and he vowed the Aos na h-Àirde commander would meet his end precipitously – if not in battle then a poisoned dagger would be sufficient.

Ualraig trudged through pools of slush as he wended his way through the camp that rested against the eastern wall. He was grateful that it too was not in flames. Eventually he reached his men. Ualraig was fiercely proud of these warriors and they were equally loyal to him. Calling his chieftains together, he ordered them to gather their men and follow him. Two thousand marched a few hundred paces beyond the wall and halted. Accompanied by his second-in-command, Ualraig walked forward another hundred paces and waited.

"Another one wanting to challenge you, I think," Fearghal called out.

"Maybe," said Conall. Let's see what he has to say."

It was with respect that Conall and Ualraig inspected each other and their men. Ualraig had already assessed his enemy, noting their strength and discipline. Up close, their scars told him that they were not just pretty, and after all, they already had slaughtered several thousand of his men. He watched as Conall slowly removed his helmet, handed it to his companion and took another few paces forward. There was a disturbing confidence in his stance, his blue-gray eyes and the firmly set jaw. Not to be outdone, Ualraig took several steps forward.

Conall studied the warriors behind Ualraig. He saw two groups of men. Those closest to Ualraig, while not as disciplined as the Ériu, stood erect and proud. Their weapons glinted in the early morning sun. Many carried small shields, and they had carefully arranged multiple layers of clothing and leg wrappings. Some had painted faces, but few had the intricate tattoos of the northern tribes. From the south, he surmised. Many carried the scars of previous battles. These were men to respect. The posture of Ualraig told him all he needed to know. The commander had total confidence in his men.

"I take it we're not going to duel," said Conall.

"Nah. Would serve no purpose other than getting one of us killed or injured. You think you can take this dùn?"

"We've overcome harder and my people need a home in which to rest."

"Why here?"

"It's complicated."

"Always is," agreed Ualraig. "There'll be ten, maybe twenty thousand of my tribe here in the spring."

"Then you should wait until the spring and join them. If you stay, then you and your men will die here - today. Go home. Enjoy life for a wee bit longer."

Ualraig held his hand up, palm outward, as if asking Conall to wait and walked back to his men. After a brief discussion, he returned.

"It will be a great battle in the spring. My men and I would hate to miss it," said Ualraig. With a mocking, sideways bow to Finnean, who was pacing the walls with increasing agitation, he signaled his two thousand. The warriors cheered, turned to the hillside and began to scramble and slide down the southern slopes.

Conall retrieved his helmet and Fearghal said, "I take it all back. Maybe you are good at diplomacy."

They walked back to their ranks to the accompaniment of screams of rage from Finnean.

At a signal from Conall, Íar's cavalry swept around the eastern perimeter. The makeshift camp nesting against the solid walls was soon in disarray as the thundering hoofs and broad shoulders of hundreds of horses rampaged throughout. Caught flat-footed by the desertion of the Aos na h-Àirde warriors, any immediate resistance was disorganized and quickly overwhelmed by javelins launched from horseback.

Finnean's ire boiled as he paced the inner wall. He ordered his second-in-command to take control of the battlefield. The dùn had only one entrance which was set in the western wall. Thus, by the time the man and his guard had exited the gate and negotiated their way round to the eastern wall, Conall and Mórrígan's forces had closed in on both flanks.

In calf-deep snow, Conall's force marched to within sling range of the fort and the defenders before it. The air was suddenly filled with the thrumming of cords. A cloud of stones flew upwards, paused briefly at the apex of their arc and dropped. A fair number overshot the Na Mèadaidh forces cracking against the gray stone walls, though even these served to keep the spears on the walls under cover. It also sent Finnean scurrying back to his throne room. The rest brought yowls of pain from the defenders.

Eventually, the Na Mèadaidh commander took control. Initially, his technique of encouraging the warriors to engage their opponents by cursing, shouting, kicking and punching the reluctant warband chiefs was not overly successful. Most chose to mill around in the shadow of the ramparts. However, after he gutted a few leaders, his message became clearly understood. Filled with anger and senses dulled by drink, the Na Mèadaidh force gathered and charged.

The sound of bodhráns swelled as young Ériu drummers thumped out stirring rhythms. Flocks of ravens hidden by the rolling hills took to the air adding their dissonant *kraa kraa* to the battle. Hearts beat faster in muscled chests, breaths were shorter, jaws clenched and eyes squinted. They all waited for the one missing sound.

Their wait was brief as the fear-provoking wail of Mongfhionn slashed the air from the hilltop. This time, it was met with a shriek of equal ferocity from Mórrígan. "The Hag preserve us. Now there's two," thought Fearghal and then yelled encouragement to the men. "They're on our side – I think!"

Brandubh's contingent threw one more volley of stones and then dropped to one knee. Spear butts were stuck in the snow and dirt, iron heads poised at belly-level waited for the oncoming horde. Standing an arm's length forward of the shield wall, they waited. The screaming Na Mèadaidh force was about thirty paces away when, with practiced ease, three volleys of javelins were launched. Thousands of iron-tipped missiles broke the Na Mèadaidh charge. Conall shouted, "Forward!" and the three shield walls tightened up, locked shields, balanced their remaining javelin and moved towards the bloody mass that had been the Na Mèadaidh attack.

The force on the eastern wall was comprised equally of Finnean's men and his Aos nan Con-Seilge and An t-Aos-Sìthiche allies. Faced with an almost certain death and little hope of glory, those who could still run scattered to the north and prayed they could avoid the mounted warriors. The remaining Na Mèadaidh retreated to the dùn.

Finnean returned to his smoke-stained ramparts. He glowered at the camp fires that flickered around his dùn. It was dusk and the Ériu had cleared the battlefield of bodies. They had stripped and beheaded the corpses. To his surprise they burned the bodies rather than let fowl or beasts have their fill of man-flesh. He had some admiration for the ominous practicality of Conall Mac Gabhann. None were taken captive. The injured were served a cut throat or a blade to the heart. Conall's focus was on the siege not guarding prisoners.

The Na Mèadaidh king ruled by whispers and by stratagems. He was not a warlord, although he could certainly hold his own in close combat – especially with weapons enhanced with a variety of poisons. His commander's best advice was to shelter behind the walls of the dùn, repel any assaults and hope that their opponent got bored and left. Finnean was inclined to concur with this plan. He had considered negotiating with the barbarians, but his hand was weak. In the end, they wanted his fort and he had nothing to dissuade them from their chosen path.

Conall met with the Chomhairle around a blazing log fire that fought bravely against the rapidly cooling night air. The silhouette of Dùn Na Mèadaidh stood in the background. "Is there an alternative to throwing bodies at the walls of this ráth?" he asked over the thin rasping of whet stones on metal as his army tended their weapons.

"We've no siege machines and no time for undermining the walls. Our archers and slingers will soften them up, but their ramparts will stand. The double walls are about three paces apart so even when we scale the outer wall, we'll still have to leap across the gap to engage their warriors," said Nikandros.

"Yeah, and in the meantime they'll be tossing everything including the piss pots at us," growled Fearghal.

Conall looked hopefully at Mongfhionn, who shook her head, "I've held the weather at bay and given helpful winds for your arrows. The end of this battle is in your hands."

"How many do we think Finnean has with him?" Mórrígan asked.

"Over a thousand, but probably no more than fifteen hundred," said Fearghal. "Why?"

"Our men scaled a sheer mountain cliff and the walls of Ráth na Lairig Éadain. Surely a rampart that is the height of two men would not be impossible."

"It was during the day, we had the cover of the mists and clouds and a diversion at Dithorba's gates, Mórrígan," Fearghal said, somewhat dismissively. "There's no way a similar strategy would work here. Finnean's men would see us approaching."

Mórrígan's glare at the veteran was plain across the flames. Conall held up his hand before hostilities broke out. "There's merit in what Mórrígan said." Curiosity kept the group quiet as Conall continued. "We'll attack at night with a small force. Perhaps the Lady Sidhe would relax her grip on the weather. A fall of snow would cover our assault and deaden any sound."

"What size of force and who?" asked Íar. "You're not leaving me outside."

"Around five hundred should be enough - Mórrígan and Áine's archers, my two hundred caomhnóirí, and the best of the Ériu and Brandubh's guard. Plenty of fighting and glory for all, Íar."

Íar beamed and slapped two massive hands on the backs of Nikandros and Fearghal, "Praise the Goddess. None of this bloody long range fighting. There's little honor to be had or tales to be sung about killing someone from five hundred paces."

Finnean was anxious. The sun had risen and set without much more than a few minor skirmishes between the two forces. Sporadic showers of stones from slings kept his men from raising their heads. Anger simmered and their frustration increased. The Ériu archers located on higher ground and rocky outcrops closer to the fort were a curse. Fewer arrows arched towards the dùn, but they were much more deadly and had already depleted his leadership.

There had been an earlier spate of assaults. Now, the fights appeared to be aimed at preventing Conall's men from getting bored rather than any real attempt at taking the walls. The Na Mèadaidh king suspected that underlying the clashes there was a worrying level of organization taking place. Certain faces and helmets that had become familiar to him were no longer to be seen. Dusk fell and there came with it a light, but steady, fall of snow. The wind remained uncharacteristically low.

The western walls had a higher number of guards, so the shadows crept towards the eastern wall as the moon slid behind the clouds. Clad only in pants and boots, their upper bodies and faces already camouflaged with their traditional blue paint, the Brandubh's hundred were led to the base of the wall. They had foregone shields as being too cumbersome and carried only spears and a wide range of daggers. Once at the wall, ten stood with their backs to the cold stone, cupped their hands and grinned with teeth that gleamed white in the darkness. Propelled by muscled arms, ghostly shapes floated upwards landing with a muffled crunch on the thin covering of snow. The few startled guards were quickly killed.

The Aos an Fhithich leaped across the gap between the outer and inner wall with ease and spread out east and west. Pebbles tossed by Brandubh alerted Conall that they were in place. One elicited a grunted "Bastard!" from an unfortunate whose nose was bloodied by a heavier stone. Mórrígan's archers were next. Mórrígan and Áine, under orders from Conall and Brion, wore their mail armor; the other archers had left their usual armor in the camp. They approached the wall wearing several layers of light woolen clothing in subdued colors. Their pale faces were muted with a mix of ash and grease.

At the wall, twenty of their more heavily armored friends plus Urard awaited. In pairs and with their backs to the wall, each held a shield between them. The archers quickly jumped on the shields and were boosted up onto the wall. Urard's technique was simpler although no less effective. He grabbed one archer after the other and threw them upwards. As with the Aos an Fhithich, the archers floated across the gap. Mórrígan and Áine with the weight of their mail found this required much more effort.

Conall smiled as he glanced around him. The always faithful and steady Fearghal, Conall's brother Eirnín, and childhood friends, Brion, Brocc, Torcán and the three ó Cuileannáin brothers, as well as new friends, Nikandros, Íar and Deaglán, had insisted on being part of the assault. The youngest, Cathán ó Bric was also with them after a fierce argument with Nikandros.

They were all heavily armored. So much so that Conall wondered if they would be able to scale the wall. The choice of weapons had been left up to each man. Thus, each carried a variety of long and short swords, axes, daggers, and studded hand-wrappings. Only a few brought shields placing their faith in their blades and armor.

"Are we going to sit here until our balls fall off?"

Conall's eyebrow twitched at the always irreverent and irrepressible voice. Then he smiled and turned to the warrior. "Perhaps *you* would like to lead us this night?" The man grinned broadly and took off at a run towards the wall. "Shite!" said Conall.

"I take it you were not expecting that response," said Fearghal before he too sprinted for the wall.

Several things conspired to warn the occupants of Dùn Na Mèadaidh of the attack. The clinking of daggers on stone as men scrambled up the outer wall feeling for grips, the steady thump of heavily armored men on shields, the increasingly loud curses of those holding the shields, and the oaths and gasps of men as they leapt across and narrowly missed the inner wall, scraping knees, knuckles and heads as they fought for a foothold.

It was, however, an explosive, "Shite!" from one who, having fallen between the walls, found himself in a sludge of shite and piss that alerted everyone. The residents of Dùn Na Mèadaidh evidently used the gap between the walls as their waste pit.

Rubbing sleep from their eyes, the Na Mèadaidh grabbed weapons and made for the entrances of their barracks. Horns blasted out raising the alarm and alerting Finnean that his defenses had been breached. His personal guards were ordered to protect the inner compound. Powerless and unwilling to intervene, Finnean watched the battle unfold in the shadows below.

The first of the Na Mèadaidh through the doors of their quarters were met with a storm of arrows. Dead or bleeding they slumped back and were dragged away by their comrades. Fires were quickly extinguished, torches doused. The fort descended into total darkness. The silence was broken only by the sound of boots on frosted dirt as Conall's force dropped into the enclosure and by the muted creaking of door-hinges as Finnean's men cautiously exited their shelters.

Then, from the higher hillside came the shriek of the Sidhe.

It was taken up and echoed by mná-sidhe. Winds shepherded the clouds from the skies. The snowfall waned. The moon, full and glowing white, smiled and dispersed the darkness. In the spectral light, men and women faced each other. Battles are rarely a thing of beauty. What transpired was a brawl within a walled cage.

Only the archers remained on the walls, picking targets to send to Mag Mell. Their usefulness dwindled once the two sides clashed and became indistinguishable. Mórrígan split her force. She and twenty others made their way along the connecting wall that bridged Finnean's inner and the outer enclosures, and then they waited. Áine took the remainder and continued to seek targets that had become separated from the fight.

The night air filled with cries of pain and the ripping of cloth and flesh. In the glowing light of the moon, blood ran black, pooling on snow-frosted dirt. The battle became a series of acts, each like a verse in one of Tadhg's ballads.

By choice, Conall, Fearghal, Brandubh and Urard fought alone. Their weapons – Conall's twin axes, Fearghal's longsword, Urard's great axe and Brandubh's spear – did not encourage cooperation. The ó Cuileannáins fought as a team, they had no wish to see another brother die. Deaglán joined them, not for protection, but because the brothers fought in a style close to his.

For Torcán and Brocc, the battle was fought back-to-back, in the midst of the Na Mèadaidh. Both men roared challenges, insults and battle shouts. What little finesse they had was swamped in a welter of eye-gouging, head-butting, teeth-tearing, clawing and studded fist-fighting.

Nikandros and Cathán fought side-by-side. Armored in bronze, holding round shields and wielding sharp xiphos they slaughtered as father and son.

The strangest team was that of Íar and Mòrag. Both were larger than life. Íar huge and gloriously delighted to finally be in a fight at close quarters swung sword and axe with equal skill. Mòrag fought with daggers and spear and with a zeal that matched Íar's. She was stripped to the waist save for leather cross-straps that secured her more than ample breasts. Their battle dance whirled at a furious pace.

Finnean paced the wooden boards of his throne room feverishly reviewing his diminishing options. His general had informed him that the west entrance was breached and that in the half-light of pre-dawn the main Ériu army with shields and javelins was flowing into the dùn. Only Finnean's inner compound remained. Its single entrance, being a small doorway onto the link-wall, was easily defended.

"Surrender or starve," he muttered. The inner compound had a limited store of food and water. The Ériu bastards could simply wait until he succumbed. If the builder of Dùn Na Mèadaidh was before him, Finnean would with some satisfaction cut his throat. "Time to negotiate terms," he announced and was somewhat annoyed by the signs of relief on his commander and guards' faces. Gathering himself together he strode towards the exit.

The Dark Huntress had learned patience and so she waited - a shadow on the stone. Sharp ears pricked up at the groan of the oak door as it was slowly pushed open. She smiled. The battle commander and several guards were the first to walk out onto the wall. Finnean was not altogether stupid. Finally, the gangly, white-haired king of the Na Mèadaidh stooped to go through the doorway. He hesitated then emerged into the dawn.

The shadow rose up, bow in hand and arrow nocked. Fluidly the bowstring was drawn back and loosed. Another arrow was already in place as its mate flew towards Finnean. The Na Mèadaidh king locked purple eyes with those of his executioner and sighed. He fleetingly appreciated the style of his death before the barb entered his eye. The pain was ephemeral as the arrow continued its path through his brain and exited his skull in a gush of bone, blood and gore.

The commander of Finnean's forces stood in shock. Unthinking he raised his sword. Mórrígan's second arrow emerged from his forehead and he slumped to the ground. Having had a few more moments to consider their actions, the remaining guards dropped weapons and held their hands high.

EPILOGUE

It was spring and the air smelled clean. Across the valley, rivers ran full and fast. Waterfalls splashed over rocky hillsides. Drostan Ruadh's son and daughter after a surprising flow of tears returned to their father. A clearly unhappy Ròidh Mac Eachdonn and his spears had been packed off back to Dùn Athad to face an equally unhappy reunion with his parents, Eachdonn Breac and Ceana.

Conall sat cross-legged on the walls of Dùn Na Mèadaidh and looked across the valley. The view was breathtaking even if the defensive capability of the ráth was ohite. He should get Cúscraid to build more functional defenses, he thought. Conall knew it would not be long before his neighbors got restless and tested him. And there was always the threat from the Aos na h-Àirde.

An immediate priority for Conall was to find or build homes for his people. Each day more arrived from A' Chrìon Làraich. Fearing retribution or slavery, many of the Na Mèadaidh abandoned their homes, farms and communities preferring to take their chances in the mountains or with the neighboring tribes. The dwellings closest to Dùn Na Mèadaidh solved an immediate need for housing. The Ériu would also make use of the outlying mining settlements on the mountainside. Conall, however, wanted his people close for their protection and in the knowledge that they would not be staying.

Mórrígan continued her dawn training with Nikandros and from Conall's observation was becoming more than proficient. Conall smiled. There was little that escaped the ruiri of Ráth na Conall and

Dùn Na Mèadaidh, and the Hand of the Goddess. Only the round-ness of Mórrígan's belly frustrated any immediate plans that the Goddess had for her Huntress.

A tanned Gaius Aurelius Atella watched the galley draw up alongside. A small man with shoulder-length black hair jumped from the vessel onto the wooden jetty. It was a pleasant summer's day, the sky a panorama of cloudless blue. The sun shone brightly and shim-mered off the aquamarine waters of the Great Sea. Fishing boats and trading ships jostled for position at the jetties.

"Hail Pytheas. You appear well. Business must be good," Gaius smiled good-naturedly at the Greek merchant.

"I can't complain, Gaius. The gods are good," Pytheas replied. He liked the young Roman who was commander of ten centuria. Sadly, Gaius was still in the employ of Marcus Fabius Ambustus, Pontifex Maximus of Rome. The young commander knew too many of Marcus' skeletons. Hence there was little chance that he would be released to take up the many offers Pytheas knew had been put di-rectly and indirectly to the soldier. Despite Marcus, Gaius had made a good marriage - one that provided not only additional wealth, but also political flexibility and a measure of protection.

Within Marcus' personal army, Gaius had recruited a body of men loyal to him. Unfortunately, although his sons were not the sharpest, Marcus was neither stupid nor blind. Thus, Gaius and his men were constantly being volunteered for the most dangerous as-signments on the expanding borders between Roman territories and the barbarian tribes. Nonetheless, Gaius had survived. Indeed he had thrived. He and his men continued to grow in battle experience. While a thorn in the side of his master, Gaius had become a valued asset to Rome.

"I doubt you're here to trade pleasantries, Gaius."

In a moment of remembrance Gaius touched the jagged scar on an otherwise unblemished face. He felt the dull ache in his shoulder where an Ériu javelin had pierced flesh and bone. Normally steady, battle-scarred hands twisted unhappily before grasping the ivory hilts of a pair of cavalry swords. "Is he coming, Pytheas?" Both knew of whom Gaius spoke.

"Yes, he is. Maybe not this year or even the next, but Conall Mac Gabhann is relentless. His thirst for revenge has been transformed into a search for justice and that may be more dangerous." Pytheas paused. "Did you know Cassius is dead and by Conall's hand?"

Gaius shook his head, "It is no loss. Marcus will be happy to know this. He should have died long ago. Perhaps if he had, Conall would be a blacksmith today, not a barbarian king."

"Maybe, maybe not. His Goddess favors him," said the Greek merchant. "Conall has become a very able king as well as a warrior. He is shrewd, and has learned from many harsh lessons. He rules with iron and wisdom and has a loyal, almost fanatical following. Conall never considered himself to be a barbarian. Neither do I and neither should you. He is the match or the better of any Roman noble."

"Don't voice that opinion too widely in Rome, Pytheas," Gaius warned, "yet, you confirm my dreams and the words from several oracles."

"Several?" Pytheas laughed.

"Never trust the words of a single oracle, Pytheas. The gold is too much of a temptation and they will tell what they think you want to hear," Gaius said. "What's his strength?"

With a wave of his hand, Pytheas dismissed the question's relevance. "The numbers will likely change before he stands at the gates of Rome." Gaius flinched at the inevitability in the Greek's words. "He has about five thousand battle-hardened warriors. Archers, cavalry, slingers, chariots – even a thousand of the Cinn Péinteáilte kneel before him as their leader. Of course, the Sidhe, Mongfhionn, rides with him – as well as a Druid priest."

Gaius again flinched at the mention of the Sidhe. "And Mórrígan? Does she travel with Conall?"

"It was touch and go for a long time as to whether the dark spirits would take her. I think she came to terms with her challenge rather than got rid of it. The Dark Huntress, as she is known, is fast becoming the most ruthless of Conall's commanders. The blood she spills in battle appears to assuage her demons."

"Will you transport them when the time comes?"

"Of course."

"Then if I may ask a courtesy?"

The Greek smiled. "You can always ask."

"Let me know when his army sails and if possible, choose a port a long way from Rome."

"To the first, I will certainly inform you. As to the location, Conall would say that the Goddess will make that choice."

Gaius bowed. "Trade well, Pytheas," he said and turned to walk to the town.

"Be safe, Roman."

The End

NOTES

At the end of *Conall: The Place of Blood - Rinn-Iru* I left Conall gazing across the narrow waters that separate the Northeastern coast of Northern Ireland from Scotland. In my mind, and as it turns out somewhat naively, I had pictured Conall interacting with the Picts: the mysterious warrior race that kept the might of Rome at bay.

I was soon to discover that the Picts never made an appearance until around 200 A.D. or about six hundred years after Conall's time. In fact the first written reference to the Picts was by the Romans in 297 A.D. and by 1000 A.D. the Picts had disappeared, probably integrating with other tribes. So the question became – who was in Scotland before the Picts? Who were their ancestors?

The quest became one of clues and first principles. Claudius Ptolemy a Greco-Egyptian writer and also a Roman citizen drew a tribal map of Ireland and Great Britain around 150 A.D. Most writers and academics appear to take their lead from his naming of the tribes, although being somewhat contrarian, it struck me that the names are more Greco-Roman than Celtic.

Therefore I took my direction from authors who suggested that the Northern tribes took their names from their environment or a particularly noticeable trait they exhibited. Hence the Aos na Coille (People of the Forest), the Aos na h-Àirde (People of the Heights), and the Aos an Fhithich (Raven People) etc. My intent was to present a logical rationale for the tribal names. Hopefully I achieved that aim. The Na Daoine Smeurta (The Smeared) and Na

Daoine Tùrsach (The People Who Chant) tribes were an imaginative interpretation of Latin first principles that suited the storyline.

Contact between the peoples of Ireland and western Scotland dates to prehistoric times. At the closest point, Ireland and Scotland are separated by 12 to 25 miles of sea. Irish-style pottery and axes were found in western Scotland from the Neolithic period. This contact grew closer with time. Iron-Age Celts first entered Scotland around 500 B.C.

I was, and am, fascinated by the Iron Age architecture of Northern Scotland. The brochs and crannogs are a unique feature of the land and the time. Crannogs were known in Ireland, but not to the same extent as in Scotland. Please read Ian Armit's excellent book, *Towers in the North: The Brochs of Scotland* (The History Press, 2003.) I have tried to be as faithful as possible to authors such as Armit and Cunliffe in my descriptions of dwellings and fortifications.

The buildings and fortifications were amazingly solid constructions using rock and dirt. Walls ranged in thickness from 15 feet to 30 feet or more. Coming from Ériu where most of the buildings and fortifications were constructed of wood, this would have been a daunting obstacle to overcome. However, the choice of building materials is logical. In areas that had little forest cover, what else would be used to build apart from stone and dirt?

As far as possible, I have used places (forts, brochs, crannogs, mountains and communities) that existed and wherever possible I have used the Scots-Gaelic translation of their names. I found it fascinating that I could zoom in and see the ruins of brochs and forts using Google Earth. Try it.

While, Scotland today is a beautiful country, the Scotland of 400 B.C. must have been truly amazing. The land would have been covered with vast swathes of ancient pine forests – the Caledonian Forest. Sadly, today less than one percent of the great forests of Scotland remain. Perhaps Failbhe was correct and Drostan Ruadh should have slaughtered the farmers. The forests did not just contain pine, but also birch, rowan, oak, and juniper. Oak and birch predominated on the west coast. The forest ecosystem would have been rich in ferns, mosses and lichens.

Wildlife flourished in the forests. Wolves, lynxes, deer, aurochs (giant wild cattle), elk, boar and bears hunted or grazed. Many species of birds, including ravens and eagles were present. My favorite was the *cam-ghob* or Scottish Crossbill. I envisage this as Scotland's parrot. It had brightly colored plumage of red, orange, green and yellow and had a habit of hanging upside-down. The other bird mentioned in the story is the *sùlaire* or Northern gannet. These birds dived vertically into the sea at speeds of over 60 mph.

Although Conall did not appreciate it at first, it was time to introduce him to boats and sailing. The character of Pytheas is based on a historical figure, a Greek merchant also named Pytheas. Around 320 B.C. he sailed to the Northern Sea and the Tin Islands (Great Britain). The Tin Islands, also known as Pretannia, Albu (to the Ancient Irish) and Cassiterides (to the Greeks) was an area known for its high quality tin – an essential element of bronze.

There is a long history in Britain of the logboat and of planked boats. Apparently their size was dictated by how big a tree you could find, although I was surprised to learn that logboats were quite light. The Poole Logboat (circa 300 B.C. – 200 B.C.) was made from a single oak tree, was 33 feet long and could accommodate 18 people.

Galleys or sea going boats originated from around 800 B.C. in the Mediterranean. The galley is characterized by its long, slender hull, shallow draft and low clearance between sea and railing. Most galleys had sails that could be used in favorable winds, but human strength was always the primary means of propulsion. This allowed galleys the freedom to move independently of winds and currents, and with great precision. Tension between cables and the hull gave the galley its shape and kept the vessel watertight.

Galleys were highly maneuverable, able to turn on their axis or even to row backwards. They required a skilled and experienced crew. Contrary to that portrayed in popular movies, slaves were not normally used as oarsmen simply because they could not be trusted, especially in battle.

A cruising speed of 7-8 knots could be maintained for an entire day. Sprinting speeds of up to 10 knots were possible, but only for a few minutes and would tire the crew quickly.

Lebanese cedar (*Cedrus libani*) trees were highly sought after as an excellent source of timber for ancient woodworking. The wood's high quality, pleasant scent and resistance to both rot and insects made it a popular building material for seagoing vessels.

A brief word on time and distance. I very much doubt that the Ancient Celts thought in terms of days, minutes and hours - or in feet and inches, which is really quite a boring way to view such concepts. Therefore, as far as possible, I have tried to measure time and distance by referring to natural or physical attributes and to common festivals such as Samhain (November 1), Imbolg (February 1), Bealtaine (May 1) and Lugnasad (August 1).

Thus, in describing time I have tended to use the cycles of the sun and moon, with a heavier emphasis on the moon. Oddly, the ancient Irish counted time by nights rather than by days. In coupling together day and night they always put the night first. Had Moses been a Celt, then he would have spent "forty nights on Mount Sinai without food or water" rather than "forty days and forty nights."

Distance is an easier concept to convey than time. The use of metrics such as a hand, arms-length or pace is readily understood. Where one gets into difficulty is in describing long distances. Sometimes this can be resolved by comparing the distance to how long it would take a person to walk it or to ride it on horseback. I did read that some Ancient Celts measured long distances by how far away they could still hear the clang of a bell. One measurement of area was based on how many cows could graze sustainably on the land. As I said, much less boring than the metric or imperial systems.

SUGGESTED READING

The historical period in which Conall Mac Gabhann lived was around 400 B.C. and is part of the mid- to late-Iron Age. It is a time that is not addressed in great detail by historians or archeologists, possibly due to the lack of artifacts that remain. This is particularly true for Ireland and Northern Britain. However, for those interested in reading more about this slice of history, the following books are recommended.

1.   Ian Armit, *Towers in the North: The Brochs of Scotland* (The History Press, 2003)

2.   Barry Cunliffe, *Iron Age Communities in Britain: An Account of England, Scotland and Wales from the Seventh Century BC until the Roman Conquest*, Fourth Edition (Routledge, 2005)

3.   Laurence Ginnell, *The Brehon Laws: A Legal Handbook* (Forgotten Books, 2012)

4.   D. W. Harding, *The Iron Age in Northern Britain: Celts and Romans, Natives and Invaders* (Routledge, 2004)

5.   Alistair Moffat, *Before Scotland: The Story of Scotland before History* (Thames and Hudson, 2009)

THE CHARACTERS

<u>THE ÉRIU FAMILY</u>
Conall Mac Gabhann
Mórrígan Ni Cathasaigh (joined with Conall)
Brighid Ni Conall (daughter of Conall and Mórrígan, twin of Danu)
Danu Ni Conall (daughter of Conall and Mórrígan, twin of Brighid)
Tuathal Mac Conall (son of Conall and Mórrígan)
Eirnín Mac Gabhann (brother of Conall)
Brion ó Cathasaigh (brother of Mórrígan)
Áine Ni Dedad (joined with Brion, sister of Íar Mac Dedad)
Cassán Mac Brion (son of Áine and Brion)
Brocc ó Cathasaigh (brother of Mórrígan and Brion)
Bricriu ó Cathasaigh (brother of Mórrígan and Brion)
Beacán ó Cathasaigh (brother of Mórrígan and Brion)
Labhraidh ó Cuileannáin
Fionnbharr ó Cuileannáin (a healer)
Craiftine ó Cuileannáin (famed harpist)
Tadhg ó Cuileannáin (famed storyteller)
Fearghal Ruad (sometimes known as Fearghal ó Maoilriain)
Mongfhionn (the Sidhe)
Nikandros (the Spartan and former assassin)
Cathán ó Bric (adopted son of Nikandros)
Torcán ó Dubhghaill

Íar Mac Dedad
(son of Deda Mac Sin, King of Curraghatoor and brother of Áine)
Cúscraid Mac Conchobar
Urard
Deaglán ó Neill
Cian Craobhach
Sárán Mac Craobhach
Seanán (Elder of the Ériu people)
AOS NA H-ÀIRDE
Ualraig (Chieftain)
AOS A' CHÙIRN
Morna

THE AOS NA COILLE
Drostan Ruadh (King of the Aos na Coille)
Bearach (battle commander of Aos na Coille)
Failbhe (former king of the Aos na Coille,
father to Drostan, leader of Drostan's Comhairle-chatha)
The Druid (brother of Drostan)
Carmag Mac an t-Sionnaich (governor of Cùil Daothail)

EMAIN MACHA
Macha Mong Ruad (Ard-Righan – High Queen)

AOS AN EICH
Eachdonn Breac (King)
Ceana nic Sèitheach (Queen, sister of Finnean Mac Sèitheach,
King of the Na Mèadaidh)
Ròidh Mac Eachdonn (son of Eachdonn and Ceana)

THE AOS AN FHITHICH
Artair (King of the Aos an Fhithich)

Brandubh Mac Artair (son of Artair)
Blàr Mac Artair (son of Artair)
Mòrag Ni Artair (sister of Brandubh)
Ailde (leader at Drochaid a' Bhanna)

<u>GREEKS</u>
Pytheas (Merchant and sailor)

<u>THE NA MÈADAIDH</u>
Finnean Mac Sèitheach (King of the Na Mèadaidh)
Ceallach (a spy and assassin)

<u>ROMANS</u>
Cassius Fabius Scaeva
Marcus Fabius Ambustus
Quintus Fabius Ambustus
Numerius Fabius Ambustus
Caeso Fabius Ambustus
Gaius Aurelius Atella (Centurion in Marcus' army)

<u>NA DAOINE TÙRSACH</u>
Diadhaidh (Queen of Na Daoine Tùrsach)
Caol (son of Diadhaidh)
Gràinne (daughter of Caol, granddaughter of Diadhaidh)

ABOUT THE AUTHOR

Born and bred in Belfast, Northern Ireland, David H. Millar is the founder, president, CEO and Keurig operator of a boutique strategy-consulting group and the founder, managing director, and author in residence of a publishing company that promotes Celtic literature and art.

Millar moved to Nova Scotia, Canada, in the 1990s. After ten years shoveling snow, he decided to relocate to warmer climes and settled in Houston, Texas, where he is a member of the board of directors of the Irish Network Houston.

An avid reader, armchair sportsman, and Liverpool Football Club fan, Millar lives with his family and Bailey, a Manx cat of questionable disposition known to his friends as "the small angry one."

Conall II: The Raven's Flight - Eitilt an Fhiaigh Dhuibh is the second book in the Conall series. *Conall: The Place of Blood - Rinn-Iru* was published in May 2014.

CONTACT THE AUTHOR:

www.aweepublishingco.com

Email: davidm@aweepublishingco.com

Twitter: @DavidHMillar

Facebook: https://www.facebook.com
/pages/A-Wee-Publishing-
Company/601748196610367?ref=hl

Blog: http://www.aweepublishingco.com/david-h-millar.html

www.ingramcontent.com/pod-product-compliance
Lightning Source LLC
Chambersburg PA
CBHW031212120726

47905CB00002B/312